RAVEN'S

LIGHT

BOOK 1:
EULOGY
FOR THE LIGHT

RAVEN'S LIGHT
BOOK 1:
EULOGY FOR THE LIGHT

BY
STEFAN DUNCAN

RAVEN'S LIGHT
Book 1 : Eulogy For The Light
Stefan Duncan
Copyright © 2013 Stefan Duncan
All Rights Reserved
Print version ISBN-13: 978-0-9894330-0-6
Publisher: Raven's Light Publishing
Raven's Light Productions, L.L.C
Charlotte, NC
Published 2013
Cover illustration: Stefan Duncan
Editing: Howard Ward
Final editing and digital formatting: Karen Troutman
Available as digital e-book
Find out more about the author and upcoming books online
http://www.stefanduncan.com

Dedication

I dedicate this book to Karen. She has been responsible for 2013 becoming my year of dreams in so many ways. Without her love, her support, and sacrifice of time, RAVEN'S LIGHT would still be sitting as a stack of typing paper on my desk. One question, Karen, *"Will you marry me on Oct. 14th, 2013 under Angel Oak Tree?...well, not under....by?"* To the readers: being she's co-editing this book with my dad, Howard Ward, I thought this would be a sneaky way of doing this and making it official before all. Gosh, I hope I don't see the word "NO" when this is printed…. Thank God for the e-book versions, you can continue edits on them.

PREFACE

According to the Scripture of the El Qui Bible, the Malbolian King, Sastorm El Qui, father to Shabael El Qui, was known as the Eclipser. He sacrificed his life to slay the Sun and Day of Moon from the sky so that the Malbolians may have eternal darkness and Dark Magic with God.

Prior to the atrocity, there had been an equal balance of Light and Dark maintained between the Malbolians and the Ravenites. The Ravenites received the Light of Magic with the Sun and the Eternal Flame in the Tree of Light during the day. However, when evening came, there was a shift of the magic power. Under the blue tint of the moon and the Dark Flame of the Tree of Dark, the Malbolians possessed the Dark Magic.

Under this uneasy detente, there was a balance of power and magic. The two kingdoms of Skyeden prevailed on equal terms. Nevertheless, when the Eclipser slew the Light from the Sun, turning the once shining orb into a black mass, it created the two moons that now orbited Skyeden. The Ravenites lost their magic of the light, while the Malbolians gained total control of the Dark Magic. This access to the unyielding Dark Magic allowed the Malbolians to become the conquerors and controllers of Skyeden. The new rulers were brutal, offering no terms of surrender to their foes and killing the Ravenites wherever they found them. For a thousand years, they had held this control and terrorized the out-numbered and ever-hunted Ravenites.

Owning the Dark Magic was vital to the Malbolians. It meant achieving immortality and Descension. Prior to the slaying of the Light, persons proven worthy through deeds and heart could dedicate their souls to either Light or Dark and, upon Ascension or Descension rites, become immortal, ceasing to age and receiving their spiritual wings. Once the Light had been killed, the Ravenites lost this ability and their rites of passage to immortality and birth of spiritual wings ceased. Those born before the death of the Light continued to be immortal and never aged. However, those born after the slaying, they aged and died. For a thousand years, the Orb of Light had been held by the Malbolians.

Until one day, a raven mysteriously appeared in the royal garden of the Ravenites' Skye Castle carrying the Orb of Light.

For more than a month, the Ravenites' High Council debated and argued about what should be done with the Eternal Flame. As the Ravenites argued among themselves, the Malbolians were massing their forces to search for the vanished light.

And God made two great lights; the greater light to rule the day, and the lesser light to rule the night. — King James Bible, Genesis 1: 16

And out of the ground made the Lord God to grow every tree that is pleasant to the sight, and good for food; the tree of life also in the midst of the garden, and the tree of knowledge of good and evil. — King James Bible, Genesis .2:9

And the Creator Highest out of nothingness did come and spake his name in a blaze of lightning. As the vibrations slowed, they created space, stars, and worlds across the ever-moving filament. And the lightning divided into two and struck the earth, thus connecting the spiritual and physical world so that man may know him and the way of the all. As the ethers cooled from the impacts upon the earth, two trees arose. A tree of Light and tree of Dark. Within the bowels of each ever living were the Orb of Light in the Tree of Light and the Orb of Dark in the Tree of Dark. — King El Qui Bible

RAVEN STEALS THE LIGHT

This is an ancient story told on the Queen Charlotte Islands and includes how Raven helped to bring the Sun, Moon, Stars, Fresh Water, and Fire to the world.

Long ago, near the beginning of the world, Gray Eagle was the guardian of the Sun, Moon and Stars, of fresh water, and of fire. Gray Eagle hated people so much that he kept these things hidden. People lived in darkness, without fire and without fresh water. Gray Eagle had a beautiful daughter, and Raven fell in love with her. In the beginning, Raven was a snow-white bird, and as such, he pleased Gray Eagle's daughter and she invited him to her father's longhouse. When Raven saw the Sun, Moon and stars, and fresh water hanging on the sides of Eagle's lodge, he knew what he should do. He watched for his chance to seize them. When no one was looking, he stole the Sun, Moon and stars, fresh water along with a brand of fire. Then he flew out of the longhouse through the smoke hole. As soon as Raven was outside, he hung the Sun up high in the sky. It made so much light that he was able to fly far out to an island in the middle of the ocean. When the Sun set, he fastened the Moon up in the sky and hung the stars around in different places. By this new light, he kept on flying, carrying with him the fresh water and the brand of fire he had stolen. He flew back over the land. When he had reached the right place, he dropped all the water that he had stolen. It fell to the ground and became the source of all the fresh water streams and lakes in the world. Then Raven flew on, holding the brand of fire in his beak. The smoke from the fire blew back over his white feathers and made them black. When his beak began to burn, he had to drop the firebrand. It struck rocks and hid itself within them. That is why, if you strike two stones together, sparks of fire will ignite.

THE MAGIC OF THE WORLD

What exists as the law of physics in one world is the magic of another. History creates legends and myths based on truths. Bearing this in mind, I will relate to you the story of how the Raven stole light from another world and brought it here. However, I will give you a word of warning before you proceed. Take this opportunity to leave now or accept that your life will never be the same.

Two moons hang over Skyeden: the moon of Day and the Moon of Night. There is white magic during the day and dark magic during the night, creating a precarious balance within the two predominant kingdoms of nine. There is a tree of darkness and a tree of light. It is said that the branches of the two when rubbed together create the small orbs of light of the sun and moon. When the orbs of sun and moon are placed in the crown of their respected trees, a physical and spiritual union forms to produce a media of magic that the perspective kingdom is able to tap into. What has taken centuries to discover is that through the acts of what is known as "Ascension" and "Descension", individuals are endowed with powers of magic and near immortality. Similar to the Kabala in one world, the symbolic trees are branched into vibrational spheres that a person may tap into. Working through the spheres of vibrational states, one seeks to rise in the plane of the Creator.

When a preternatural event occurred that removed the sun from the sky and the Light form the Moon of Day, the Moon of Night was predominant, giving the Malbolians a continuous power that they used to conquer other kingdoms. For a thousand years, the Malbolians have ruled since gaining possession of the small Orb of Light that was once held by the Ravenites. Myth has it that should the Ravenites regain possession of this orb, it could be used to create the Sun and Moon of Day again. Thus, the balance of magic would be restored. This was the miracle that the Ravenites dreamed about. But it was the last thing the Malbolians would allow to happen. There had been no day in a thousand years and the Ravenites' dreams were as dim as a thing that had died a millennium ago. Until the day, a raven appeared in the courtyard of the Ravenites' castle on Skye Castle, clutching the orb of Light in its talons.

Big Spider said *"At the end of the world there shall be seen a white raven as a sign that the world is coming to an end. That will be the last of it."*

—*according to Native American mythology.*

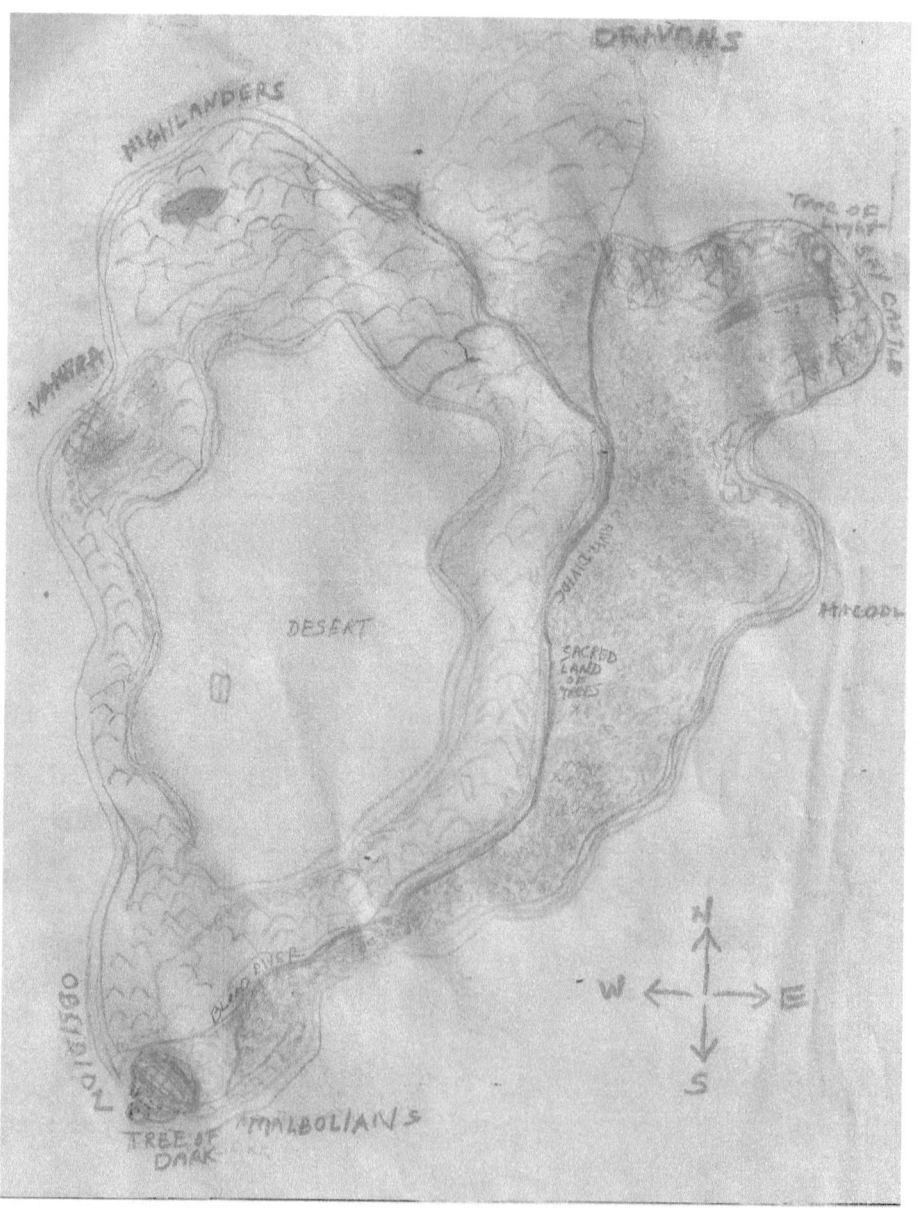

CHAPTER 1

THE RAVEN AND THE LIGHT

"It's too late!" Richard cried. "We'll never make it out," He glanced over his shoulder, flinching at something crashing against the outside of the building. His older sister, Dayanna, disappeared around the next corridor.

"We have to!" Dayanna answered back. "Keep running! It's right around the corner."

The sounds of fighting seemed to come from the walls. Swords clanged. Death cries sounded. The air smelled of blood and fire.

Dayanna burst through the swinging doors of the aviary. "Give me the raven, now!" she demanded. Her long dark hair flew from over her shoulders like a hairy flying banshee, obscuring her face.

"God!" cried Bryan, the keeper of the ravens. His brass goblet clattered upon the stone floor sending the caged ravens into a frenzy of fear.

"You startled me. I thought … I thought it was them!" Bryan stammered. He was dressed in his finest black leathers. Spilled wine flowed from his white beard creating an illusion of the blood to come.

"Give me the raven now!" the dark-haired girl almost screamed. "Hurry!" Dayanna suddenly realized that the old man was dressed in his finery and partaking of the wine in preparation of dying at the hands of the approaching Malbolians.

1

Bryan sputtered, spewing more wine. He staggered backward, kicking the goblet and adding to the cacophony of ravens' wings flapping and frightened caws.

"We're all going to die, aren't we?" Bryan asked.

"I'm sorry,' Dayanna said, as gently as she could, realizing that the old man had thought her rushed entrance to be the first thrust of the attacking Malbolians. "We have no time to talk. They're coming! Give me the raven." Her voice was pleading over the chaos.

Glancing over her shoulder, Dayanna saw Richard in the doorway, his eyes begging her to hurry. Richard was always impeccably groomed, but now his usually smoothed black hair hung across his forehead and partially spilled over his eyes. He held a dagger in his right hand and swiveled his head to scan the hallway in both directions. Shouts and cries could be heard from below. The clash of swords rang through the hall. The very foundation of Skye Castle seemed to tremble from the pounding of battle drums.

Bryan steeled his nerves and began fumbling with the latch on the cage housing the raven. In exasperation, he gripped the fingertips of his left glove with his teeth and ripped it from his hand. With adrenalin-fueled panic, he yanked so hard at the door of the cage that he almost sent it toppling off the table. The startled raven sprang from the cage and wrapped its talons around the wrist of Dayanna, which she had exposed by attempting to cover her face from what she had perceived to be an attack by the bird. She cried out as one of the razor-sharp talons broke the skin of her wrist. Working quickly, she took the free end of a leather strap attached to her wrist and tied it to one of the raven's legs. The bird made no protest and simply gripped the leather with both feet.

"*Dayanna, please!*" Richard was urging her to hurry as the clamor of the battle outside grew louder.

Dayanna put her free arm around the white-haired Bryan and pulled him to her.

"I pray to the Gods for you."

"And I for your family and the king's," Bryan murmured.

Dayanna paused in mid-turn and put her arms around the old man. She felt the grizzled beard on her cheek and blinked away a surge of tears. Pulling free, she stared directly into Bryan's eyes, willing him to know that he would always be with her. Bryan smiled and gave a dismissing wave with his gloveless hand.

2

The frenetic Richard grabbed his sister's hand and pulled her into the hallway. Dayanna was a full head taller than her 15-year-old brother and until that moment had always felt like a protective older sister. However, now he had assumed the role as her protector, her knight.

Richard looked like a rogue in his soft leather pants, black knee-high boots, and white jerkin. There was an air of danger surrounding him as he brandished the dagger he had christened "Dragon Fang". The dagger was a roundel, an experimental weapon presented to him by the king's blacksmith. A decorative red stone cut in the shape of an eye fitted into the hilt, but the design of the blade was the most outstanding feature. The weapon was designed for thrusting with a round blade ending in a needle sharp point. Slipping the tip of the blade between the spaces of an enemy's armor would produce deadly results. Thus far, Richard's use of the dagger had been to pry the meat from the nuts he found under the walnut and hickory trees. But after this day of infamy, the innocence of both the boy and the blade would forever be compromised.

Dayanna's heart went out to her brother as she followed his half-crouched figure down the hallway.

A door at the end of the hallway burst open as a Malbolian soldier shouldered his way through it. The soldier was dressed in full battle regalia, his coat of arms visible with a white raven, talons spread to strike amid a field of blood drops emblazoned across his armored chest. His sword was stained with the blood of the men he had slain on his way into the building. The raised visor revealed eyes burning with malice and bloodlust.

Without breaking stride, Richard veered left into a room, knocking over a shelf filled with clay pots that shattered and sprayed gray shards into the air. Clutching his sister's hand, he led her through another room, then came to an abrupt halt while a group of Malbolian soldiers raced past the doorway.

Dayanna placed a hand on Richard's shoulder and felt his heart pounding and his chest heaving. His body was trembling like a just-plucked guitar string.

"What are we going to do?" she whispered.

"If we can get through across this hall and into the next room, we can enter the courtyard," he answered in a surprisingly calm voice. "There's a drainage tunnel there that leads to the west gate where

Eradrin waits." Richard dared to ease his head through the doorway to see into the hallway.

"Clear," he said. "Come on." He ran into the hall, towing Dayanna and the still attached raven behind him.

The new room was filled with stacked tables and chairs but they were able to work their way through it to the other door. The sounds of battle raged outside. Screams of wounded men rent the air.

"The drain tunnel is only about five feet to the right," Richard whispered. "The vent is heavy, so you'll have to help me lift it. I think I can pry it open with Dragon Fang."

Dayanna was flushed and panting from the exertion and the danger. Her ponytail of jet-black hair had loosened and strands ran at angles across her face. She and Richard stared at each other for a moment, drawing strength from the other's proximity, expressing a wordless encouragement that everything would be all right. She felt a warmth in her heart as memories of quieting him as a frightened baby during the night flashed though her mind. She had always been able to comfort him when everything else had failed.

Richard seemed to sense her thoughts and leaned in so that their foreheads were touching. "I love you, sister. I will protect you now."

"I love you, too, brother," she whispered, fighting the urge to say 'little' brother. "She glanced at the raven perched on her wrist and added, "We'll save you, too."

Richard brushed a strand of hair from Dayanna's face and winked. "You ready?"

"I am." She inhaled a deep breath and whispered to the raven, "Hold on."

Richard slowly pushed the door open, scanning the terrain, squeezed his sister's hand tightly and led her outside. The Moon of Night was full, but in the process of being eclipsed. The shadow moving across the moon was red, casting an eerie burgundy hue over everything. Moving quickly, darting from shadow to shadow, Richard led Dayanna to the wall and quickly found the grate to the tunnel. Warriors from both armies filled the courtyard, but were so occupied with their hand-to-hand scrimmaging that they were unaware of the furtive couple. Smoke hung low over the courtyard like a fog, burning eyes and clogging nostrils with the odor of burning wood and the stench of scorched human flesh. Flames rose from several of the surrounding towers that had been set on fire.

The scene was a living nightmare for Dayanna. "This isn't real," she tried to tell herself. She prayed silently, pleading for the Creator to come to their aid. She felt Richard tugging at her arm. He motioned for her to lift the grate as he pried one side up with his dagger.

"Come on! Come on!" He half screamed. Dayanna gripped the stubborn grate with both hands and put all her strength into lifting it. It seemed hopeless, but just as she thought her strength would fail her, she felt the heavy grate move. There was a screech of metal against concrete and the grate was shoved to one side. It was too heavy to lift, but the opening was large enough for them to squeeze through.

"Hey! You!" The warrior's shout rang above the clamor in the courtyard. One of the Malbolian soldiers had spotted them and he started toward them.

Richard grabbed Dayanna and helped her into the drain. It wasn't deep and her knees were just above the surface. "Run," he shouted, and dropped down beside her just as an axe thrown by the warrior whizzed past his head and clanged off the stonewall, sending a shower of sparks flying.

Dayanna ran with the raven still attached to the strap on her arm while flapping its wings to keep pace with the fleeing girl. Richard ran just behind her, the rancid sewer water spraying them as they raced through it. The stench was almost overpowering.

Ahead of them in the tunnel, an eerie light suddenly cut though the darkness and Dayanna knew someone had just opened another grate. She ran on, but as they passed beneath the opening, a huge hand darted down and grabbed her hair.

Dayanna's feet left the ground as she was jerked backward and upward. Above her, one of the enemy soldiers was leering, straining to lift her by the hair. She cried out in anguish and clawed at the man's arm. However, he was too strong.

The soldier struggled against the girl's weight and reached down with his other hand to get a stronger grip on her hair. Richard saw what was happening and swung his dagger at the man's face. Dragon Fang sliced through the man's cheek and clipped his nose. The man released his grip on Dayanna's hair and clutched his hands to his ruined face while releasing a stream of obscenities.

Richard seemed stunned by his own actions and stood frozen in the tunnel, his eyes wide, picturing the blood gushing from the wounded warrior's face, which had disappeared from the opening.

"Richard!" Dayanna's voice snapped Richard from the trance and he whirled toward her. "Come on!" she half-screamed. "We have to get away from here!"

Richard took the lead this time and they ran on, splashing through the sewage. Behind them they heard other splashes and shouting as the enemy warriors entered the tunnel and came after them.

The water was getting deeper, making it harder for them to run. It was almost to their thighs and Dayanna felt something soft bump into her leg. She did not want to know what it had been.

They reached one of the tunnel junctions and heard voices off to their right. Richard tugged at his sister's arm, veering them to the left, and motioned for her to duck underneath the water. Gasping for air, she didn't close her mouth tightly enough and the fetid water made her retch. Moments later Richard pulled her upright; and, they listened for a moment, but the searchers seemed to have disappeared. The water was less than knee deep as they moved onward and within a few yards found the grate where they planned to exit.

Richard dropped to one knee and patted his shoulder. Dayanna placed a foot on the shoulder and pulled herself upright until she could reach the grate. Peering outside, she had to restrain herself from shouting. It was Eradrin. Prince Donachie. Her betrothed. Her racing heart filled with joy. Eradrin had waited for her! He was standing with two horses as he and a dozen armed guardsmen were scanning the horizon.

Dayanna forced her hand through an opening in the grate and waved, crying "Eradrin!"

The prince turned to the sound, saw what appeared to be a severed hand flopping on the grate, then recognized the voice.

"Dayanna?" He dropped the horse's reins and rushed to the grate, taking her hand in his. "Help me," he called to the soldiers. Two of them rushed forward to lift the heavy grate. Richard lifted his sister and Eradrin pulled her from the tunnel.

As Dayanna's legs cleared the opening, one of the Malbolian pursuers rushed at Richard, slamming into the boy with such force that it tore Richard's hands from his sister. Dayanna almost fell back into the tunnel, but Eradrin pulled her free.

She was safe, but Richard wasn't. She stared down into the tunnel and saw that two other enemy soldiers had joined in the attack on her brother. The men were sloshing around in the water, splashing so

much that she was unable to tell exactly what was happening. She screamed her brother's name and was about to leap back into the tunnel to help him when Eradrin lifted her bodily off her feet.

"We have to help him!" she wailed, but Eradrin had other concerns. A group of Malbolian soldiers had arrived and were surrounding his men. The prince mounted his steed and pulled the sobbing Dayanna up with him. He raised his sword in one hand and commanded, "Ride!"

Dayanna fought to free herself from the steely grip. "We can't leave Richard," she cried. From her perch on the mount, she could see down into the tunnel opening. She saw a hand rising and her brother's prized dagger gripped in it. But the hand was attached to the Malbolian soldier whose face Richard had slashed earlier. And even as she realized this horrible fact and what it meant, the man scowled through his bloody face and hurled the dagger at her.

As the man released the dagger, Eradrin jerked the horse's reins. As the animal turned, the dagger whizzed past Dayanna and struck the prince in the back with the needle point piercing the chainmail armor. Eradrin flinched in pain, but remained upright. Dayanna gripped the dagger hilt and pulled it free as the powerful horse bolted off after the prince's men. They were heading for the West Gate, hoping to reach it before the enemy soldiers were able to block it.

From a distance, the group of riders appeared as a black dot moving over the snow-covered slope. It could have been a young girl's fairytale dream, galloping on a black horse with her beloved; a gentle snow falling; a raven flying alongside, still attached to her wrist by the leather thong; a large moon dimly lighting the scene. No sound pierced the world that the terrified girl had created in the white haze. She felt no physical sensations, oblivious even to the jolt of the horse's gallop. Her once beautiful gown was ruined from the sewer water and she wondered how Eradrin could stomach the stench emanating from it.

Dayanna snapped out of the dream world with a scream. Everything came back to her with a rush. She was barely holding on to the horse; the sound of hooves crunching through snow; the howling, icy wind burned against her cheeks; the raven pulling so hard it had her arm extended. She was wet and deathly cold. And worst of all, she could still see the soldier's face as he had hurled Richard's dagger at her. She screamed.

"Hold tight, Love! A little more!" Eradrin encouraged. He lowered and gave the horse an extra kick.

Richard! Her brother was dead. She was certain of that. The odds had been too great despite the boldness of the fighting young heart. She moaned as a dreadful ache filled her bosom. She took a deep breath of cold air, trying to control her emotions. The side of her face was pressed against Eradrin's back as she studied the surroundings, trying to get a feel for where they were and where they might be heading. The huge Moon of Night was half hidden behind a red aura as if it were being consumed by dark magic. She turned her head and saw the black orb over the western horizon that had once been the Moon of Day.

There was no hope. There was no kindness in this world anymore, only ever-encroaching evil and coldness and death – Richard's death.

The Light ... the light of the world was gone, save for the glow over the next slope that was growing larger and brighter as they neared it.

Her gaze followed up her arm, to her hand, and along the leather strap to the Raven. It seemed to possess the same intent as Richard to push ahead.

It was then that Dayanna understood what she had to do. She must set the Light free and keep it from being regained by the Malbolians.

For all the death, the squelching of the Light, the enslaving of kingdoms for hundreds of years, she would accomplish this one defiant act against the evil Malbolians. Whether it meant weeks or only moments of depriving them of the Orb of Light, this would be her victory in the face of hopeless defeat.

She knew now that all her dreams would be denied. She would never wed Eradrin, whom fate had seemed to pair them together. She and Eradrin were promised to each other since birth. Her father had been Viceroy to the king, Eradrin's father, and the pledge had been made with great pomposity. That dream was over. Even if she and Eradrin were somehow to survive this battle, all they had planned would be denied. There was no free will under Malbolian rule. Those who chose not to serve their new masters were put to death.

However, if she could deny them the Orb of Light she could at least win one battle. That had been the reasoning for going to Bryan and asking for the raven. This was the raven that had brought the

Light to the Ravenites; and, he would be the one to deny it to the Malbolians.

They were racing to the site of the ancient oak tree where the Ravenite priests had placed the Orb of Day in the crown. If they could reach the tree in time, she would attach the orb to the raven and watch him fly away with it. It did not matter where, just away from the Malbolians.

The raven cawed as though seconding that motion.

They were nearing the old oak and she could see the beginning of its branches as they crested the hill. Angel Oak, as it had been christened by the priests, appeared as a giant octopus against the darkening skyline, its branches like tentacles, seemingly frozen in mid-undulation.

Peering over Eradrin's shoulder, Dayanna could see the light glowing from its resting place in the core of the old oak's branches. The Orb of Light was not large, but it would burn forever if not purposely extinguished. Angel Oak had become the Ravenites' Tree of Light, clutching the orb to its bosom. This light was the symbol of hope for the Ravenites in the belief that the once powerful magic could be restored by some miracle of faith and it could once again be used to create a Sun and ignite the Moon of Day.

The raven had brought the orb to them and with it the wrath of the villainous Malbolians. In their quest to retrieve the orb, the Malbolians were slaying everyone in their path as they sought to reach its location and reclaim it. Dayanna had accepted that she and those she loved would be dead soon. The only thing she could do was honor her doomed people and her country by freeing the raven with the Orb of Light.

The raven cawed again.

Dayanna had never seen the Light until the day the raven had flown over the castle wall with it clutched in its talons. It had been in the possession of the Malbolians for all of her life and generations before. She had spent many days during her childhood in the Gallery of Art, marveling at the huge mural depicting a sky clouded with ravens descending with the Light to Lake Waccamola.

When the raven practically placed the orb in her hands, Dayanna at first thought that the gods had favored the Ravenites with an enormous blessing. As she and the others in the courtyard looked on, the area began to brighten. It was a surreal scene with the raven still

9

holding the orb and the growing light illuminating the faces of the astonished onlookers. The orb continued to brighten and the raven perched on the branch of a young maple tree only feet from Dayanna, cocked its head to the right, and stared at the young woman.

"Caw!"

The Raven's cry startled the onlookers, causing many of them to flinch backward, but Dayanna remained still. The Light reflected like a fire in the big bird's eyes.

"Caw!"

Somehow, Dayanna understood that the raven wanted her to take the Light. She slowly rose from her seat and held a hand out, palm up. The raven left the maple branch with a flap of its wings and gently placed the Light in her palm. Strangely, the object seemed to be almost weightless. It was no larger than a hen's egg, but there was no doubt in Dayanna's mind as to its identity. The raven cawed a third time, this one quieter, almost reserved, a caw of approval. No longer demanding. It flapped its wings and returned to its perch in the maple. It watched the girl intently; its head tilted to one side.

"Rozeann," Dayanna said to one of her attendants, a small dark girl with quick movements and large brown eyes. The girl was several inches shorter than Dayanna, but she was lithe and strong. Her black hair hung to her knees in a single braid. She was Dayanna's most trusted aide.

"Go straight to the prince," she whispered, "and tell him to come immediately. Do not speak to anyone else."

"As you will, Milady," the girl said, backing away from her mistress, then turning and dashing from the courtyard.

"Where did you get this? How? Why me?" Dayanna asked aloud. The raven turned its head to the south, then back at her.

"Can you understand me?"

"Caw!"

Dayanna's two other handmaids gasped, then giggled.

She looked at the Light sitting in the palm of her hand, drawing in a deep breath. "This is the Orb of Light," she said more to herself than a question. Light illuminated her face, making her blue eyes almost white, and causing her to blink the pain of brightness away. It was bright enough to cast shadows and reflected brightly in the black-eyed bird. The blue of its wings gleamed almost electric.

The raven nodded its head and stamping its right claw on the tree branch. Then the bird leaned forward turning its head so each eye got a full look at her. Both of the handmaids instinctively moved closer to Dayanna. This bird showed signs of intelligence.

Eradrin appeared suddenly in the courtyard breaking the spell of the moment. The Light took him aback.

"*This can't be,*" he said incredulously. This raven brought you this?"

The girls nodded in unison.

"All of you come with me now," Eradrin ordered. "Take your cloak, Dayanna, hide it. No one must know of this. Come!"

As they turned to leave, the raven flew from the branch toward Dayanna and flapped its wings to perch on her shoulder.

Eradrin grabbed the bird beneath its wings.

"No! He doesn't mean harm," Dayanna said.

Eradrin looked at the large bird for a moment then extended it to Rozeann. "Take it to the aviary. Tell Bryan to know its markings in case we need to see it again."

"Aye, Milord," Rozeann said, gingerly reaching out. The Raven didn't rebel.

The Light was taken to King Aremis. Council members were summoned quickly and quietly. Great vigilance was used to avoid alerting any of the many Malbolian spies who had infiltrated Skyeden.

The arguments were intense. Heated discussions raged as to what to do with the Light. They decided to place the Orb of Light back into the Tree of Light. They prayed this act could ignite the sun and bring day back. The powers of Light and Dark Magic would be balanced again. They could have the rites of Ascension and have their children become immortal.

When the Orb of Light was placed in its old bedding of a thousand years ago, it began to brighten. In the semi-darkness, they could see lines like human veins glow and spread throughout the tree. The people cried out joyously. Then the veins began to darken. The Orb of Light flickered brightly then lowered to a very dull glow. Joy turned into the weeping of tears. It was at that moment that King Aremis was delivered the message: The Malbolians were coming.

Not just a few, but an army.

The report was that the Iron King, Shabael, and his mother, the Queen Highest, were leading the main body of the army north and were already crossing the Great River. They were obviously pursuing the Light and were heading directly for Skye Castle. One of their spies had sent the message concerning the arrival of the raven with the Light.

Days passed and reports from scouts about the progress of the Malbolians increased with urgency. Fear rose across Skyeden like the mist from Waccamola Lake. Many terrified residents fled Skye Castle, some leaving their personal belongings and pets behind. Those loyalists who remained braced themselves as though for an approaching storm. The temples were filled with people praying for protection. There was the smell of fear in the air.

The path to the Tree of Light was a rugged, winding way that could only be reached by passing through Skye Castle. Anyone taking the path had to enter through the fortress and then exit through the Northwest Gate. Advance parties of the Malbolian army had already reached the great bridge that led into the fortress built literally out of the side of the mountain from its jutting platform of rock that extended outward like a flat hand. The north and south gates opened to a three-mile wide ring around the mountain. Its west side over looked the Eternal Sea. The west gate leads to the long narrow bridge across the Waccamola Lake. To the right of the west gate was a narrow flight of steps that led down to the lake's shore. A large lift was built between the west gate and steps. These were closed off now. Ravenite guards and citizens watched the massing army on the distant shore. A Malbolian advanced unit stood in formation on the bridge amassing for an assault with a metal ramrod on wheels rolled only 200 yards from the closed gate.

Meanwhile, the Malbolian guard units stationed within the Ravenite walls made a great show of honing their weapons and holding twice-daily drills. Since the defeat to the Malbolians a millennium ago, these guard units had had permanent residency. The Ravenites were granted permission to maintain a 400-man army. Two hundred stationed at various outposts of the kingdom were inside the walls. A curfew was mandated and King Aremis ordered his army to standby status.

When the Malbolian army appeared on the opposite shore of Lake Waccamola, King Aremis summoned his generals and ordered his elite guard troops to surround the Tree of Light.

"We cannot and will not allow the Malbolians to regain control of the Light," he told his officers. "It must not happen. Better that we all die while defending it! It was by divine act that the raven delivered the Light into our hands and we must not fail to guard it to our last man."

King Aremis then made a bold decision. Refusing to leave Skye Castle without defenses, he ordered the main body of his army to remain within the walls. He gathered his elite guard; and, the one hundred brave men left the West Gate and rode to the Tree of Light.

"We must all perish someday,' he told his council, "and for myself, I had rather die with a sword in my hand defending the Light than to see it return to the Malbolians while our people simply wither away in the darkness."

The Tree of Light stood only a mile from the west gate of Skye Castle and the elite guard made their exit as quietly as possible, hoping to be able to reach the tree before the Malbolians realized what was happening. The winding, narrow path was concealed by jutting mountain rocks and was more than a thousand feet higher than the surface of Waccamola Lake. The rugged path was not easy to travel and was only wide enough for three horses abreast. This was a vital necessity if the elite guard could be expected to hold off the horde of enemy troops. The path ended with the opening into a large plateau of three rising knolls. Only after the third knoll could a person see the Tree of Light.

As Prince Eradrin's mounted party neared the old tree, Dayanna, from her perch on the steed behind the prince, could see the Light shining among the branches. It seemed to be pulsing, like the light from a dying ember. The branches of the tree were vaguely illuminated. Dayanna had always dreamed of seeing the rays of sunlight touching the bark and leaves of the old tree. She loved the old oak, which had been here for her entire life. A shudder passed through her slender body as she recalled the happy moments that had been spent playing under the branches of the tree with Richard. Now Richard lay dead in a sewer drain and the Malbolians were coming to kill her and take back the Orb of Light.

The raven squawked and fell back to her side at eye level.

"Caw Caw Caw!"

Dayanna felt dizzy and grabbed tighter to Eradrin. Her sight blackened.

The Tree of Light was burning so bright that its flames reflected off the bottoms of enclosing clouds. She heard the screams of her people. The Earth trembled. Flames whooshed upward covering root to top of crown. Lightning cracked above. Winds howled.

"*Noooo!*" Dayanna cried.

"*What?* Eradrin glanced around for impending danger. He was almost to the tree now.

"*What if they destroy the Tree? We can't let them.*" Dayanna pleaded.

"That would be madness," Eradrin said over his shoulder. "Destroying the tree would mean destruction of the world. That would be suicide for us all."

"I had a vision," Dayanna said.

Her arm lifted higher as the raven exerted more into its flight.

"That will never happen. God would not allow it," Eradrin said.

And yet, the Malbolians' King Shabael seemed intent on ridding his people of what he considered a threat to their dominance. He was ever intent on crushing the spirit of the Ravenites but not even he dared hint of such an act.

Malbolians had plunged Skyeden into perpetual darkness eons ago with the seizing of the Orb of Light. The fragile balance of light and dark magic had been broken and the Malbolians, controlling the Light, were determined to control the rest of the world. They had defeated the Ravenite army, marched to the Tree of Light, and removed the Orb. If there were any desire to destroy the tree, it would had been then.

The moon hovering in the sky over Prince Eradrin's galloping party cast their shadows before them. The world behind Dayanna was being destroyed and she shuddered at the thought of them setting fire to the Tree of Light. She tightened her grip on Eradrin's waist. Even from their distance, she thought she could make out the reflected light of the orb the priest had placed on the trunk of the tree.

Dayanna knew that the approaching Malbolian soldiers would find them soon. They would see the emerging Light and race toward it. The hundred loyal troops of King Aremis would be massacred and they would all surely die. She felt a surge of panic rush through her body. This was what it was like to face certain death. The knowledge that she was going to die kicked her mind into overdrive and the world around her seemed to go into slow motion.

Eradrin spurred the horse to go faster and gave Dayanna's arm a reassuring squeeze. The pain from the dagger wound in his back was fierce, but he was almost oblivious to it. "Hold on, my love," he said.

"We're almost there. Here," Eradrin retrieved a dark, thin strip of cloth and gave it to Dayanna. He wrapped another around his eyes.

The vision wakened the fighting spirit of Dayanna. Her passions burned like the tree. They killed Richard. Her people have suffered a thousand years. The whole world suffered because of the lack of Light. So evil were the Malbolians that they slew the sun from the sky. There will never be a wedding or experiencing all the phases of motherhood. They even destroyed the ability of immortality for her people, offering droves of Light People to denounced their faith and pass through Descension for the Dark so they may have immortality. She could feel the heat of her tears as the cloth around her eyes absorbed them. She knew in her heart that before this day was done, she and all those she loved would die at the foot of the Angel Oak. The only victory she could achieve would be to set the raven free with the Orb of Light and watch him fly away with the treasure that the evil Malbolians were so determined to own. She hoped she was dead before having the chance to witness the fall of the Tree of Light.

The powerful warhorse heaved its haunches and blew a cloud of frosted breath from its nostrils as it crested the slope and headed for the Tree of Light. The raven, still attached to Dayanna's wrist and flying alongside the mount, released an excited *"Caw!"* The bird's eyes were glowing, reflecting the growing light. The light glistened off Dayanna's long, black hair, almost dry now from the ride. She realized the Light had brightened. She felt an emotion from it of sadness and desperation. It was summoning all its strength as though making a final cry for help before the Malbolians came to take it from its home. It was calling out for something. *For help. I feel you. I sense you.*

King Aremis, Dayanna's father and the king's elite guard had taken up defensive positions beneath the tree. They wore black kilts and leg wrappings to protect their legs from the cold along with black leather vests. Each wore thin dark strips of veil over their eyes. Her father left his position by the king. He looked at her sensing something was wrong. Looking around he suddenly realized Richard was not among them. The others showed welcoming but unsmiling countenances as they acknowledged the arrival of Prince Donachie and his personal guardsmen.

Eradrin dismounted from his stallion and helped Dayanna to the ground. He saw her father approaching and took a step toward him but Dayanna caught him by the arm and pulled him back.

"Dayanna. Where's Richard?" Her father asked. She kept her face turned slightly around from the tree that seemed to have brightened, thanking the Creator for the veil concealing the expression of her eyes. Should she tell him what happened? He turned her to the side and lifted the cloth from his eyes. She couldn't remember seeing her father so clearly than now...under the Light of the tree instead of a room filled with smoke and flickering torch.

He looked ever the same at 30 that he did a thousand years ago as his own father fought against the Malbolians. She had never seen how black his hair was. The only thing that gave away the age of an immortal was the glow of their eyes. The eyes darkened with age. His eyes were dark blue with a diminished light, darker than her own were. He was handsome. Well now, she would never have to wonder how it would be to be older physically than her father was. William Gatoria's face was filled with health of a young man but the eyes were darker. As an immortal, only an accident or violence could kill him. The body remained same age after the rite of Ascension except for the gradual darkening of the eyes and perhaps more sullen by all the experience that he had to endure from being defeated and being under the rule of the Malbolians for a thousand years. Could a mind have the capacity to contain all those memories?

All she knew for certain now was, in moments, those eyes will be crying, she thought. When she had grabbed Eradrin's arm, she wasn't going to tell her father about her brother's death with so little time left to live. But then, her father would never forgive her if they met in the hereafter that he had a moment to exact Richard's death upon the Malbolians coming.

"Richard died, Father." She said it so calmly as though predicting it would rain in an hour. Within her, there was no calmness. She was frightened and heartbroken with her chest tightening making it hard to gain her breath to sound words. Her eyes burned from the restraint of crying. In spite of this, she willed herself. Her father had taught her to always be poised in emotional states. It was prudent in political life. A display of emotions gave enemies mental weaponry that could be used against you. Moreover, if an enemy was the cause of a great emotional state, witnessing this was empowering to them.

"He died that I may go free," Dayanna said. "We were escaping through the tunnel system when we were caught. Eradrin was pulling

16

us out but Richard fought the soldiers that I may have a chance to be free. He died with honor, Father," she said. Her voice broke then.

"Richard is dead?" Viceroy Gatoria asked. He looked at her for a moment in disbelief. His composure slipped. Slowly, he reached up with a trembling hand to touch her cheek as if to verify that this was not a dream, lifting the cloth above her eyes he searched deeply within her and saw that what she said was true. In that moment, they shared their grief and pain as only a father and daughter could.

Dayanna did not have the heart to say that sentence again, one she had never imagined having to say.

"They're coming!" a soldier warned, pointing up toward the air above the knolls.

"I love you, Dayanna. No father could have a better daughter. We die in honor," he said. Closing his eyes, he leaned forward. For the first time she could remember, he kissed her lips. He turned, glancing over her with a final look over his shoulder before pulling the wrapping over his eyes. She tasted the salt of fallen tears from her father's lips.

The Raven was becoming impatient, flapping its wings harder, and attempting to force the Dayanna to the foot of the tree. She allowed the bird to lead her as she watched her father slip into formation with the other soldiers.

Eradrin waited for her. The light emanating from the tree glistened on his chest padding that was adorned with the Donachie Family coat of arms, which displayed a claymore with a pair of raven heads on the handle against the background of a blazing sun.

Even in the bedlam, Prince Eradrin was a magnificent figure. He stood more than six feet tall and his thick black hair, now free from the helmet he had discarded, reached halfway down his back. A braid of hair hung down his left side, inlaid with gold thread. His clear blue eyes concealed now beneath the wrapping, were a clear blue in stark contrast to the black hair and, his skin, although untouched by sunlight, was as golden as a natural tan.

"Ready!" King Aremis ordered.

They watched the brightening glow of Light from the other side of the three rolling hills. From above, the Light illuminated a hundred winged advanced guards flying slowly 50 yards off the ground.

Prince Eradrin took Dayanna's free hand to run the rest of the way to the tree. The snow-covered ground crunched loudly as their breath turned to mist in the cold.

"Glory to the Ravenites!" an elite guard shouted.

"Light into darkness!" another answered back.

The soldiers began to cheer, and then suddenly hushed. They turned their attention from Dayanna and Eradrin to the sky, which now seemed filled with the airborne Malbolian Knights. Through the Descension ceremony, these warriors had achieved spiritual wings that allowed them flight for several minutes. Persons spiritually devoted to their source of light, whether day or night light, could attune themselves to a vibrational sphere of wings. It took much training to develop the ability and mental concentration to maintain the mental hum of a vibrational state and have other thoughts at the same time. Great discipline. The Ravenites had possessed this ability before the loss of the Sun and the Light of the Moon of Day. To achieve the calling forth of wings was so exhilarating and spiritual, yet to see your enemy approach airborne was terrifying.

To continue this mental vibration during battle seemed impossible. Yet, the winged warriors hovered, exchanging positions with those on the ground as their powers gradually lessened. Dayanna doubted she would live long enough to see another change of guard. It seemed inevitable that the warriors would release their gleaming, silver-spiked spears at the Ravenites on the ground.

Dayanna looked up, hoping for some miracle. Maybe the Great Creator would rip the sky in two, come down, and rescue them. However, the sky was cloudy and brooding. The moon was within minutes of complete darkness as it was almost engulfed in a brooding cloud of storms. The airborne Malbolians were much closer. At any moment, the ground troops would appear over the last knoll. Eerie shadows rose into the air from the torches that many carried.

The cacophony of war broke the night's silence. Drums grew steadily louder. Wisps of snow fell from the Tree of light. Dayanna's heart filled with despair. Even the raven flew back to her shoulder.

"Caw!" The raven looked upward while flapping its wings. In spite of all the sounds, fury, and clanging Dayanna suddenly became aware of the ravens overhead. Their caws pierced the air over the wailing horns of the winged warriors. Streams of ravens were forming a ring overhead.

"Draw your swords, men!" King Aremis commanded. He was wearing a helmet shaped like the head of a raven that included the hooked beak. The plumage of feathers signified him as king and his visage was that of an elder Eradrin. "Archers, aim for the airborne!"

Five bowmen lifted their bows.

Five against two hundred wingmen? "Creator, save us! Give us the strength to defeat." Dayanna prayed aloud, though she wondered if even the God or Goddess that could create a whole universe would have the power to prevail over such a massive approaching army.

The first wave of Malbolian foot soldiers began to flow over the hill like an encroaching white sea. Their weapons gleamed from the reflecting light off the snow. They dropped their flickering torches to the side for now the Tree was shining even brighter. Malbolian wingmen flying above reached for their quivers and prepared to string their bows. The light falling snow created a strange beauty that was oblivious to the approaching bloodbath to be created by bleeding and dying bodies.

Long haunting wails sounded from the horns. The rhythmic beating of the drums vibrated into everything and everyone. *Thump... Thump... Thump... Thump...* One of the Ravenites' elite guard dropped his sword and started to flee. However, the other guards helped stilled his nerves and he slowly picked up his sword again.

Eradrin reached for Dayanna and held her face between his trembling hands, realizing that this was possibly the final moments of their lives. He was going to die, along with the beautiful woman that was supposed to have become his wife. Instead of sharing a life together, they were going to share a cold grave. That is if the Malbolians even bothered to bury them.

"I love you, Dayanna," he whispered against her ear, reaching inside his breastplate and producing a silken cloth. He unfolded the cloth and revealed a pendant with an iridescent stone, reaching quickly to tie it around her lovely neck.

"It has the colors of a raven," he whispered. "This was for your wedding day," he said hurriedly.

Tears welled in Dayanna's eyes, staining the cloth concealing them. She shouted above the noise, "I love you, too, Eradrin," reaching to kiss him on the lips.

"Now, you must go," Eradrin said, bending and forming his hands into a foothold. Dayanna placed her foot in the stirrup provided by

19

her lover's hands. One of the priests reached to take her hand and help hoist her into the tree limbs as Eradrin lifted from below.

Priest Ramon, was donned in his ceremonial purple robe and hood. The Light coming from the tree seemed to have brightened and rising to a blinding blare. The priest's forehead glowed bright in the Light's reflection. The darkening of the pupils from age was never so apparent. The drumbeats were much louder and could be felt through the tree. Batches of snow fell from the branches in cadence to the drums. The raven perched on the leather band of Dayanna's arm as though he understood what they were about to do even before she knew for certain. Her eyes widened with terror as the front line were poised on top of the last knoll.

"The Light now!" Her king shouted.

The Priest seemed frozen.

"Ramon!" Dayanna shook him by the arms.

"Get it now," Dayanna said.

Priest Ramon lifted his clothed eyes skyward and was startled by the hundreds of ravens that were cawing high above. He performed the sacred Raven Cross starting with his finger touching his forehead. Then the priest moved his finger down a straight line to form a U, representing the claw of the raven and the Trinity of the Creator's essence.

Dayanna glanced back at the knoll and saw the great white chariot carrying the Malbolian Emperor Shabael El Qui. He raised his hand high up to give the signal to attack.

The drums stopped. Even the world seemed to be holding its breath. All was still but the trickling down of snow and ravens circling above with Light of the Moon gleaming off their wings.

"Now, Ramon!" Dayanna urged.

"I…..I can't. This is blasphemous! God will strike me down!" His hand hovered over the Orb of Light cradled within the bowel of the tree!"

Suddenly the air was rending with cries. The frightening sounds of war thundered loudly. The emperor had dropped his hand. The Malbolians were charging.

Dayanna seized the Orb of Light and yanked it free from its place in the tree.

The Tree of Light went dark.

The sudden darkness disrupted the advancing army. Dozens of wingmen lost their concentration and fell before the foot soldiers.

"Remove the bindings! Fire!" King Aremis shouted, pointing upward.

The bowmen released a fury of arrows. The archers fired rapidly into the 200 winged men. They were momentarily blinded and collided with one another. Arrows tore through wings and struck bodies. The concentration needed for flight was broken and all fell earthward, falling in front of and on the advancing foot soldiers, who were almost recovering from sightlessness.

King Aremis cried out. Dayanna saw her father and beloved on each side of the King as they raced forward to take advantage of the disorientated army.

King Shabael's great horses reared as he shouted to regain control of his army.

Dayanna watched from her place in the tree. The two armies clashed and consumed one another into one massive metallic and leather cluster. King Shabael El Qui, himself was leading the army in quest of the retrieval of the flame. His forces were too many and too well armed to be repelled by the Ravenites. It was 100 against 2,000. The Malbolians had killed every man, woman, and child they had encountered on their way to the Light. Due to their haste to reach the ancient oak where their advance scouts had witnessed the priests and a small group of soldiers gathering earlier in the day, Ravellona Castle had been bypassed.

Dayanna took the cloth that had covered the pendant Eradrin had given her moments earlier and wrapped the light in it. Then she quickly tied the cloth to the leather thongs attached to the raven that was still perched on her wrist.

Dayanna knew in her heart what must be done. She and all those she loved would die at the foot of the Angel Oak. The only victory she could achieve would be to set the raven free with the Orb of Light and watch him fly away with the treasure that the evil Malbolians were so determined to own. She hoped she was dead before having the chance to witness the fall of the Tree of Light

"Wait? What are you doing?" Priest Ramon sounded exasperated. He grabbed for the Light. But even as his fingers touched the fabric of the cloth, Dayanna heard the arrow whiz by her head and saw the steel point drive into the priest's cheek. Ramon's beginning cry turned into a shriek of pain, spewing several teeth and blood. His long black robe flapped like a raven's wings as he teetered off the large branch and fell backwards.

Some of the Malbolians were tasked to lighting torches and scattering them on the ground to give the warriors better sight. Torches were tossed along the ground

The Malbolian soldiers were breaking through the ring of defenders and the scene had become surreal for Dayanna. The movements were staggered with the flickering of torch flames. The Ravenites were moving back to form a ring around the tree. Everything was moving in slow motion. Several of the torches were tossed back to keep from endangering the tree. One of the Ravenites was consumed in flames, screaming, and running. Her father clipped the man with his shoulders so that he would fall and roll, letting the snow out the flames. He rose to his feet then raised his sword at an approaching Malbolian. Dayanna watched as her father blocked his opponent's sword. However, he fell onto his knees as he was slashed from behind by a Malbolian solider. She reached to her waistband and withdrew her brother's pointed dagger, Dragon Fang. Gripping it by the tip, she threw it with all her strength at the Malbolian soldier, who was bringing his blade up for another slash at her father. The needlelike point of the dagger found an opening in the armored plate and disappeared to the hilt in the man's chest. He looked up, his eyes going empty, and the last thing he saw was the face of a pale girl holding a flapping raven.

"Go ahead, release the raven!" Eradrin shouted as he realized what Dayanna had in mind. Then he turned to face an attacker, slashing mightily with his sword, taking the head entirely off one of the enemy warriors.

Dayanna scrambled higher in the oak, seeking an opening through which to allow the raven to escape. As she stared upward, she saw hundreds of ravens attacking the winged Malbolian soldiers, pecking at their unprotected eyes. She found an opening in the branches and screamed, "*Go!*" The raven flapped its wings and began rising. But just before it cleared the tree, the cloth holding the Eternal Light became entangled in a branch. The raven continued flapping its wings, but wasn't strong enough to tear its burden free.

Above the tree, the flock of ravens appearing to number in the thousands was circling, forming a funnel that appeared as an inverted tornado cloud. Their deafening cries made the fighting sounds below obsolete. The Malbolian soldiers were rapidly surrounding the trunk of the huge oak. Only a few of the Ravenites remained to challenge them. The Malbolian king stood in his chariot, his skin tinted pale blue by the moonlight. His hair was white, reaching to his waist and he wore a cloak of eagle feathers. Several more feathers were attached to his hair. The image was a magnificent one although he was vulnerable in the chariot, standing above the action swirling around him on the ground. Nevertheless, he wasn't concerned with his safety. His focus was on the Eternal Flame and the raven struggling to free it from the oak's clutching branches.

King Shabael put down his bloody sword and reached for an arrow in his quiver. The muscular king, standing six-feet, four-inches tall and weighing more than 250 pounds, was an imposing sight in the half-light of the moon. Despite his size, his facial features were almost delicate and his eyes were an amazing pink and burgundy that became illuminated with emotion — anger or enjoyment. His movements were graceful like those of a fencer or a dancer. He raised the bow and drew a bead on the girl fighting to free the raven from the tree branch. Masora, his great white raven, was perched on his left shoulder. It moved its gaze from the bow to the girl in the tree and nodded its head. Shabael felt the raven's feathers against his cheek. He drew in a deep breath and pulled the bow back with as much tension as he possibly could.

Eradrin, fighting for his life, slashed an oncoming solider and looked up to see the king preparing to fire the arrow. He screamed a throat tearing "NO!!!" as the arrow was released and began its spiral though the air. Dayanna was tearing at the branch holding the Eternal Flame. She had managed to rip it free just as she was struck by a blow from behind that knocked the breath from her body. Her hand fell from the tree branch as she glanced down to see an arrowhead protruding from her chest. Oddly, she felt no pain and tried to find Eradrin with her fading vision, but everything around her was dying …

The raven freed its burden from the final grasp of the tree branch and joined its mates in the dark funnel. King Shabael screamed his frustrations as the Eternal Flame disappeared into the mass of birds. Then the king watched in stunned amazement as a hundred of the huge birds swooped toward the ground. His soldiers cried out in fear, but the birds ignored them, swarming around the dead girl in the tree.

King Shabael watched the scene unfolding before him in stunned amazement. For what may have been the first time in his life, he was speechless. He found it inconceivable that the Light had escaped him. A large group of ravens broke free of the swirl and began diving downward. His soldiers cried out in fear, falling to the ground, covering themselves. But the birds did not attack, they came within inches of striking the ground and turned upward, flying straight up the tree, whizzing by branches and darting over the body of the girl. The movements were so darting it looked like a black stream of feathers. The air was electric with caws. For a second time, Shabael was rendered into a state of amazement, watching the body of the girl disappearing ... piece by piece ... until her bones were picked clean. She was skeletonized ... and the circle of ravens continued from the funnel to the ground, back up to the tree, to the funnel above. The bones began to disintegrate. Within moments, even the bones were gone.

Shabael stood speechless until the flash of light and rolling thunder reclaimed his attention. The funnel of ravens seemed to be imploding ... sucked into this black hole in the center of the swirling. Shabael could feel the hairs on his arms rise, and the smell of ozone was thickening in the air. Something major was about to happen.

"Masora! After them!" His large white raven had been taut and ready. With one mighty swoop of its' wings, it jettisoned upward, straight for the eye of the funnel above. Shabael jumped up, his spiritual wings blooming and extending so quickly and hard that they literally snapped open. He rose several feet and cried out again, *"Release the Darklings! Now!"*

Cage doors flew open. Darklings tore the air with their high-pitched screams and gnashing claws. Streams of Darklings leapt from the trampled blood-soaked battleground. Darklings were a combination of black hole and ever shifting as smoke showing only glimpses of leather and talons and eyes. The remnants of a dead Darkling were black dust, bone, leather fragments, and a sulfuric stench. They drew in Light or when attacking their victim, they sucked life force out of them. . One never saw a Darkling in total. Only snatches appeared in their smoky black whiffs of smoke that were no bigger than the size of a large bird.

24

Streamers of Light from the torches followed the Darklings as they gnashed their teeth in anticipation of Ravens. They did not have arms, but long spiny fingers for the skeleton structure of their wings. On the mid-top of the wing were their thumbs, which were razor sharp and could extend outward several inches. They rose in a chorus of screams, causing the warriors to drop their weapons and clutch their ears.

Darklings entered the spiraling funnel of ravens. These creatures, known as Darklings, were a breed of vampire bats mixed with dark magic. Since the ravens were their natural enemies, the Darklings' lust for raven blood drove them into a wild frenzy. The Darklings were difficult to see and appeared be like a moving cloud of dark mist because Darklings could never be seen totally.

Streams of the Darklings flew toward the funnel. The first of them ascended and disappeared into the flow of ravens. Suddenly there was a blinding flash, a brilliant wave of light and simultaneous eardrum-shattering thunder. Then nothing. The extreme of the two was violent to the senses. The sky became clear, leaving all in the vicinity in a state of shock and awe.

"*No!*" Shabael cried out, thrusting his hands into the air. "No! The Light is mine!" Only silence answered. The sky was clear. Stars twinkled.

Between the Moon of Day and Skyeden, a ring of fire ignited. Through the ring emerged the raven clutching the Orb of Light. Behind this raven, a stream of its kin followed, bunched so closely together that they seemed to be one form. The ravens swirled and continued to mingle until the figure of a woman began emerging. More ravens joined the mass and behind them came the Darklings that Shabael had ordered into the fray.

Back on Skyeden, the Moon of Night was consumed in dark clouds that transformed it into a darkened red pupil-less eye.

Another ring of fire appeared; and, the raven still clutching the Eternal Flame flew into the ring. He vanished along with the still forming figure of the woman. The Darklings followed.

CHAPTER 2

BLUE RIDGE MOUNTAINS, NORTH CAROLINA

The huge yellow moon had only just risen above the spruce pines, casting eerie twisting shadows upon the terrain. Mica twinkled in the exposed gray rock that jutted unevenly among the knee-high brush that grew alongside the path.

It was the old medicine woman's favorite time of the evening, when the moonlight touched the heart-shaped white moonflowers and bathed them in a ghost-like illumination. Red poppies mingled with the moonflowers, appearing dark grayish in the moonlight. The air was filled with a honey fragrance, much like that of morning glories.

The old woman savored the moment, but as much as she enjoyed it, that was not the reason for her being there. Her Indian name was Makanda, which means one of magical powers. It was given to her several weeks after her birth because it was determined that she would have different colored eyes. One was blue and the other was green. As a child, the tribal medicine woman had taken a special interest in Makanda and taught her how to perform tribal medicine. Even though she was only 14 years old when the medicine woman died, Makanda assumed the role of the tribe's medicine woman. Her now frail body stiffened as the first clearwing hummingbird moth appeared and she smiled. The glowing six-inch moonflowers were an irresistible target for the hummingbird moths, which hungrily hovered above them.

"*Shhh.*" The old woman put a finger to her lips and alerted her eleven-year-old adopted daughter Mansi to the presence of the moths, tapping her lips with a forefinger, then pointing to the neon-lit moth that was alighting on the moonflower. The moths were easy to capture as they sat upon the blossoms. When the moths were dried, the dust from their wings and bodies could be used to spread on one's face to create a neonic glow that was reflected by the fire during spiritual dances.

The medicine woman prepared to reach for the moth when a movement in the north sky caught her attention. She raised a hand to quiet her daughter and pointed to a ring of fire appearing in the sky above the mountain. The young girl gasped as a sudden roll of thunder crashed and the circle of fire brightened. There was a swirl of dark beings in the light; and, some of them appeared to be falling from the sky. Suddenly, a much larger black shape emerged from the circle and began rapidly dropping to the mountaintop.

The medicine woman sat down the basket of ginseng she had gathered earlier and reached for her young daughter's arm. "Come! This way, Mansi." She led the girl up the path that climbed to the summit of the mountain. The girl followed, taking a moment to reach out and grasp the unsuspecting moth, then crushing it in her fist and dropping it to the ground. A cruel smile curled her thin lips.

It was almost a mile up the steep, winding path and the old woman kept Mansi moving briskly. They neared the peak and found that the temperature had dropped considerably. The perspiration on their faces felt cold in the mountain breeze.

The old woman and the young girl came around a turn in the path and the medicine woman stopped so suddenly that the girl banged into her back. "Wait!"

There were rustling sounds coming from the thick spruces overhead. Something small and dark. A bird perhaps. Another one on the opposite side of the path leaped from one branch to another.

Reaching back, the Medicine woman tugged at the girl's arm to continue.

A beautiful young woman stood in the path, long black hair flowing in the breeze. Her eyes were wide with fear and she seemed on the verge of a panic attack. Even in the moonlight, her eyes were as neonic as the clearwing moths, glowing with a brilliant, almost phosphorous blue.

The old woman took Mansi's hand and pulled her toward the transfixed figure. The nude body glowed white in the dim light and the medicine woman noted that the panic-frozen figure was holding something dark in her arms. She moved a step closer and saw that the black bundle being clutched was not her clothing, but what appeared to be dead birds, their feathers soaked in blood. There was also an arrow in the bundle of dead birds. It had notches and appeared to be made of metal than stone, stained in blood. The feathers at the other end were white. The girl's body was also bloody, reminding the medicine woman of a newborn baby having just been delivered from its mother's uterus. The girl appeared young, probably still a teen-ager. Something horrible had happened to her. Though covered in blood, the girl seemed very healthy and unharmed. She held herself with great poise. Her eyes gave a faint blue glow. They were mesmerizing. Was this one of the Gods?

No. She is human, the woman thought to herself. She started to reach out but something drew her attention to the trees behind the girl. Something was watching them. The movements in the trees were very still now. She reached a hand out to the terrified girl and spoke in the Cherokee Indian dialect. "Are you all right? Have you been hurt?"

The girl turned her glowing eyes to the sound of the voice and croaked, "Where am I?" The voice was weak and cracking from the effort.

"You are on Highest Mountain. Who are you and how did you get here?"

The girl was obviously confused as she continued to stare wide-eyed at the wrinkled old Indian woman. She suddenly realized she was holding something in her arms. When she saw the dead ravens, she collapsed to her knees. Several fell free and plumped onto the ground.

"No. No. No." She reached out to gather them back into her bundle. The heads lopped downwards.

"Child," the old woman said, going down on her knees also. "Here, here, I will help you. Mansi empty your basket. Let's put the ravens in it."

Dayanna looked at the woman questionably then back at the Ravens that were slowly removed from her grasp.

"We will honor them in the morn, child. I will have a platform built to lay their bodies upon to offer the Raven Spirit.," said the Medicine woman as she placed a dead raven in the basket. "What

28

caused them to die? Her hand stopped from pulling the arrow next. "Whose arrow is this?"

Pulling it free, she held it out to the young woman, whose eyes widened, then brow fretted.

"I can't remember. All I know is walking down this path. I don't know who I am or from where I came. I don't know why I am holding dead ravens. Please help me. I am lost."

Her eyes seemed to brighten. It startled the old woman. Mansi gasped from behind.

"Sometimes when bad things happen the Creator takes the memory away," the older woman said.

Unconsciously, the young woman reached to a spot about an inch from the center of her chest. It was red like a burn mark. Her fingertips gingerly touched the area. When she saw her fingers were stained in blood, she examined her hand then looked back to the Medicine woman.

The medicine woman quickly glanced around, trying to see beyond the shadows. "Are you alone?"

"Yes."

"We can give you shelter, clean you and warm you. We have food and water there. You can live with me as a daughter. Come," she said, her voice soft and reassuring. "We're going to help you. Our village is near. Until you remember your name, I am going to call you Raven. That will be your new name."

Mansi moved closer to the young woman while moving her opened palm close to the Raven's face to look at the blue reflection of light on her palm. Neon dust glistened in her hand from the clearwing hummingbird moth that she had squashed earlier.

"Are you the goddess of the dead?"

Raven did not answer. She stared at the girl and a single tear ran down her cheek. "You fell from the sky," Mansi said. "You must be a goddess. Goddess of Death who brings dead ravens. Will you teach me the mysteries of death?"

"Mansi! Silence!" The medicine woman pulled the child back. "Please forgive, Raven. Children have little wisdom. Mansi is my adopted daughter. Mansi means plucking flowers. All of her tribe were found dead but her. Several of our warriors found her sitting at the edge of the woods with plucked flowers around her. Seems I have two girls now in my care," Wakanda said.

29

They rose to their feet and started down the mountain path. Mansi led the way with Raven in the center of the progression.

"Mother, I forgot the basket of birds," Mansi said. "I'll get it!" Before the old woman could protest, Mansi was already disappearing around the bend where they had just left.

As Mansi reached for the basket, something swooped downward, causing her to fall back on her haunches. A big, white raven stopped midair, spreading its glorious wings with moonlight glow before it perched on the handle of the basket.

Do you hear me?

"Yes…" Mansi answered in a whisper of awe.

Do not tell the others about me.

"Yes…." She whispered back in a hypnotized whisper.

We will talk later.

"Yes…."

Return to them now.

"Yes…."

The white raven lifted on its legs, spread it wings wide, and then lifted back into the darkness of the trees.

Mansi ran back to the others, suppressing the smile on her face.

WEEKS LATER

Mansi. Wake from sleep. Open your eyes. Look at me.

She opened her eyes and scanned the dark interior of the dwelling. Her adoptive mother was sleeping, curled up in a blanket. Raven appeared to be sleeping. If that were so, who called her?

I am behind you.

Her eyes widened. Terror seized her.

No need to fear. I am your friend.

It is all right. I will come around to you.

She heard something moving lightly. Something white was coming around her feet. She started to scream.

Sssssh. I am a friend.

At first, she thought it was a cat and tucked in her legs. Instead, it was a bird. A white raven that made a little hop, then stopped. It nodded its head up and down several times.

Can you hear me?

Slowly, Mansi nodded her head.

Ah, you can! This is good. Very good. You do not have to speak. We can talk inside our heads.

What are you? Birds cannot talk, Mansi thought to herself.

The bird hopped up and down in excitement. *I do hear you. My name is Shabael.*

I am dreaming.

I could peck you if you like.

No!

Mansi drew herself into ball and looked at Raven and her adoptive mother.

I was teasing. Here. The white raven spread its wings and turned in a full circle. *Have you ever seen a white raven?*

No, Mansi answered, curious now.

I am King of the White Ravens in another world. I have chosen you to be the Empress of Darklings.

Empress? What are Darklings?

Ah, friends to serve you. They are your leathered night birds that are always surrounded in a dark mist. They cannot be in sunlight. Light kills them. They can be outside during the day, but only in the shadows. At night, they become more powerful and are able to move about freely. They will do your bidding.

Can I see one? she asked.

The white raven nodded its head and hopped over to the edge of the dwelling. It pecked at the bundle of rolled fur by her feet. Something dark moved along the outside of the fur. Its shaped wavered and gave her a glimpse of leather and claws.

Instead of fright, she smiled. *Like a shadow.*

Yes. To live they must eat Light. They can stream in the Light but cannot be exposed to it. They draw in Light and consume it but cannot be touched by it on the outside. Do you understand? The white raven took several hops toward her.

The Darklings serve you. You must be very careful with them. They also must be fed. They get hungry just like you.

Yes, Mansi said, her eyes transfixed on the forming yet formless dark mist. It slowly moved toward her. She caught a glimpse of a black eye, a claw, and a snatch of leather. Closer and closer, it inched up to her. The smell of the thing was a little harsh. It made her eyes sting.

Slowly, she outstretched her hand to touch it. When her fingers were two inches away, she spied a quick flash of sharp needle teeth matched by a quick withdrawal of her hand.

31

Shabael knew it would take some doing to get the young girl to feel any kind of working relationship with them. Darklings were frightening creatures. He would had never predicted her next move, she curled her finger and brought it to the edge of the Darkling's mist like one does when attempting to befriend a dog.

Then even more surprising, the Darkling's dark mist rolled over her hand several times affectionately. The girl giggled.

In another world, the world of Skyeden, King Shabael leaned back in the Sphere Seer's chair. Ten spheres were encased in glass consisting of three vertical rows. Each Sphere was black with fluid. An extended arm from the sphere sat a Seer on the other end. The arms can move 360 degrees around the spheres. Each sphere contained a bluish neon light that roamed beneath the inky fluid, which would rise to the sphere's glass and produce images. A different vibrational rate was attributed to each sphere.

When possessing the conciseness of Masora, it replaced Shabael's own sight and was projected on the huge inky Seer Sphere before him in the low neonic light on the glass wall. His priest, Calibri placed a hand on his shoulder lightly not to break the fragile connection between the King and his white raven.

"Sire, this is more than fate, for she is truly the Darkling's Empress."

A long moment passed before the White Raven spoke again, partly out of awe and fascination. While the Empress was melding with her first Darkling, others found passage through the dwelling. They eased toward her in reverence then caressed her body lovingly, sensuously, adoringly. Never had Shabael witnessed this. Nor had he heard of this ever happening before.

There are several things you must do to continue their existence, Shabael said through the white raven. *They must have a home, a special home, a Tree of Dark. You must prepare their home or soon they will die.*

Tomorrow night you must take Raven's arrow and the white branch. There is an old oak tree an hour walk from here. I will go with you. Once you find the tree, shoot the tree with the Raven's arrow. This will turn the tree into a Dark Tree. Do you understand?

I do, Great One.

Tomorrow night, then. When the time is right, we will get the arrow and go to the tree. So return to your sleep.

The white raven stepped back until it receded in the shadows. Mansi lowered her head and closed her eyes. She dreamed of magical things.

The following day Mansi anxiously waited for any signs of the white raven. She stayed close to the hut and had to be told twice to do a task for the medicine woman. She was distracted for her eyes were constantly scanning the edge of the woods around the village. She had to take several jerkins to wash in the river. After dipping the jerkins in the water to wet them, she would then hide along the tree line to wait for the white raven to reappear.

The medicine woman was particularly busy this day. Two women and a child were brought to her very ill. They were vomiting. Raven returned with a wooden cage containing three chickens that were to be prepared for a noon meal. She was told to stand several feet away as the medicine woman moved sage smoke along their bodies and chanted. One of the women slipped into unconsciousness. The child, a young and beautiful girl began retching violently. A small crowd began to gather.

The mother of the girl began humming and rocking on her feet, using the hum of song as a meditational prayer.

Calmness and deep concentration was the medicine woman's usual countenance, but with the one woman unconscious and the child now choking on her own vomit, she was becoming frantic. She turned the child on her side and kept looking at the unconscious woman who was apparently dangerously close to dying.

Raven placed the cage of chickens on the ground. Then she cradled the dying woman's head in her lap. While the old medicine woman was slapping the child on the back, she began speaking in a foreign tongue.

Without warning Raven screamed. The chickens panicked, clawing at the wooden bars of their cage. Going over backwards, Raven fell over and tried to distant herself from the unconscious woman while shaking her own hands as though desperately trying to rid them of some kind of painful sensation. Suddenly she thrust her hand out toward the young girl, and then screamed again. She stared at her hands as if they had transformed into wild creatures. Jumping to her feet, Raven lunged forward, diving onto the ground, thrusting out her arms before her.

The chickens silenced.

"Raven?" The Medicine woman inquired. Everyone was silent now, even the birds and insects in the surrounding area. She checked the child quickly. The retching had stopped.

"Raven?"

She didn't respond but her eyes were opened.

The unconscious woman gasped and sat up, looking at everyone around her, and wondering why they were there and staring at her.

"Are you alright?" the old woman asked again.

"Yes," Raven answered weakly.

"What happened?"

"I do not know," answered Raven. "I got sick."

Medicine woman didn't wait on the answer but slowly walked up to the chicken cage. The chickens were dead.

In all the commotion and sudden silence, Mansi forgot about the white raven. She started walking toward the center of the crowd to find Raven being tended to. The chickens in the cage were unquestionably dead.

Anger flared in the pit of Mansi's stomach like burning coal. Why were they so concerned over her? She was an outsider. She doesn't even know her name nor where she came from. Most were gathered around Raven. Those who had been gravely ill were now getting up from the ground and joining the others in the gathering group.

By the front of her dwelling, Mansi caught a glimpse of a white bird landing on the ground. The white raven turned her way. After seeing Mansi had spotted him, he hopped into the hut. Now was the time.

Mansi lowered her head and started walking to the hut. Her heart was racing. She felt important. She felt herself soon to become the Empress of the Land while these unknowing, pathetic people of the tribe stupidly idolized this stranger just because she was…. prettier? *I'm as pretty as she is. It's those blue eyes. She is possessed with an evil spirit and has cast magic on them. I'm not born from the tribe. Her magic does not work on me. Momma does magic but it is weak magic and only used for healing. I am an Empress. I will use my magic and become more powerful. I will show them. Mindless frogs, all of you.*

Hurry, Empress. No time to dally, the white raven said through thoughts. His head was poking out of the hut.

When Mansi entered the hut, the white raven waddled quickly to Raven's bedding. Mansi dropped to her knees and began unrolling the deerskin that contained the arrow. It was a curious piece with a metal tip and short narrow feathers cut into the wall at the other end. She then took the white branch in the palm of her hand. It felt funny. She wanted to fling it to the floor but resisted the urge. It seemed to have vibrated and made her a little nauseous.

Yes! Good! White Raven said. *Now get your bow. Hold all this down by your side so no one can see it as you go into the woods. Just follow me. I'll be in the treetops.*

Her mother was telling the people that gathered around Raven there was no need for their thanks and that they should continue with their day.

As the people began leaving, the Medicine woman was lifting Raven by the arm and moving toward the cage of dead chickens.

Now, Mansi. Now while their backs are turned, the white raven urged from a tree at the boundary of the village.

"Mansi?" her mother called while supporting Raven by the arm.

Mansi froze. She felt terrified. Had she been found out? With a quick glance, she saw the white raven recede in the shadow of a tree. She felt encouraged by this. Turning around, she gave a big smile. "I was going for a quick hunt."

Several nearby women laughed.

"Hunting is for men, my little one, but do your hunting quickly. Raven is ill."

"I will," Mansi flashed a bright smile and dropped it when she stepped into the woods. The shadows of the trees gave her comfort. When she took that step through the tree line, even at her young age she knew it was like the new path of her life she was departing upon. For weeks, she seeped with jealously. It tasted of bile on her lips.

Come. Come. We have a ways to go, the white raven said in her mind as he flew several yards at a time leading her way. The path rounded, and then the white raven veered off where there was no path but trees and stones. Mansi climbed over several small boulders then began an ascent up the high, sloping mountain.

For a mile, she walked among boulders, wild flowers and bramble.

Finally, the white raven landed atop of a pointed boulder and gave a short caw. Mansi pushed through several bushes of foliage and stopped when she saw the large, old oak tree. Though she had been out in the world briefly with the tribe, she had never seen this tree. It was huge and rose above the others. Some of the limbs were so long and heavy they had long ago gravitated to the ground and had grown like a long root above the ground. It would take four of her to have one hand touch the other around the base of the tree's trunk.

Here you go. This, my Empress, shall be your Dark Tree. Now, arm your bow with the arrow and shoot the tree, the white raven said.

The weight of the arrow was heavier than any Mansi held before. The tip with its slanted slits in the metal looked dangerous. She moved closer to the tree. The raven flew to a branch over her head.

Go ahead. You can do this.

If she missed, the Raven would be disappointed. She fitted the arrow across the bow. Her line was too thick to fit into the grove of the arrow so she tightened her fingers to hold it on place the best she could. Lifting the bow higher, she aimed and drew the line back and let it loose. The line slipped off the notch of the arrow as it shot off the bow. The *whack* and caw response would alone told her she had hit her mark. Joy turned into a moment of ecstasy. Then she heard the tree actually wail. The branches seemed to flinch as a reflex and then became still. Dozens of area birds scattered in flight. From the shadows around her, she heard possibly shrieks of joy coming from the Darklings.

While all the vegetation was flush with mid-summer, the narrow oak's leaves began to turn brown and curl upon themselves.

Dark veins began appearing in the grayish-white trunk of the tree, spreading and running upward along the branches. The late summer leaves of the tree began to darken and wither. An odor of death permeated the air around the tree like an ominous aura.

Now approach the tree and very, very carefully break off the arrow's shaft, the raven said.

The sounds of the leaves curling into themselves and turning from green to brown seemed to crawl along her flesh. A black liquid oozed from the arrow's wounding of the tree. She reached out with trembling hands, gripped the arrow, and snapped it off.

Take the white tree branch and break off a small branch from the tree now. Rub them together to create a fire. You have done this many times before, the raven said.

As she gathered dried leaves and began making a pile, the raven continued talking. *This will be no ordinary fire. It will be a Dark Orb of Light. Once it is created, you can place it in the palm of your hand. I will have you repeat the sacred words. And once you have done this, you will place the orb into the trunk of the tree in the hollow hole of its trunk. Do you understand?*

Will it not catch the tree on fire, My Emperor?

The orb will do it no harm. "Creator of Dark and Dreams, Oh Absentor of Light

Repeat these words as you rub the branches together, the raven said. The words came into her mind and she said them aloud.

"All Powerful God, Conqueror of All
Bless us with the Black Eternal Flame
Blaze the Black Fire to glorify your name
Give Black Fire as the El Qui desires
Your servants, your people, Oh, Great One!
Give us Black Fire!"

As you say. Mansi said.

A curl of white smoke rose carrying with it a strange odor that she could not describe except sometimes as the air does before lightning cracks in the sky.

Suddenly there was a bright, blue-white flash of Light. She jerked back, dropping the small branches and became spellbound by the Dark Orb of Light that floated several inches off the ground. She could hear it buzzing. The ball of light was only light, but somehow physical to touch, or so it seemed. She looked over to the raven that nodded its head, seeming to be as spelled bound as she.

Ever so slowly, Mansi moved an extended finger to the orb. It was like a bubble of light, or a crystal stone but weightless. This was indeed magical. No one would ever believe this. The tip of her finger touched the Dark Orb. It was bluish now and a jagged line of light began from the center of the orb and connected to her finger on the other side of the surface. She felt a tingling sensation from her fingertip that began to spread up her arm. It frightened her and caused her to look back at the raven.

37

It will not harm you. It likes you. Now, place it in the tree, the raven said. It flew from its perch and landed on her shoulder, stretching its neck to look closer at the orb now sitting in the palm of her hand. Shadows shifted around her. Darklings were inching closer. The sun had dropped below the trees causing the whole world to darken.

As she approached the tree, she could feel the buzz grow stronger in her hand with the orb. The curled leaves leaned toward the orb, following its direction like flowers to sunlight.

When Mansi touched the tree, all the leaves stopped moving. She found her footing, climbed into the oak tree, and stopped beside the hollow hole. Even the tree seemed to hold its breath as she placed the Dark Orb inside its trunk.

The Dark Orb brightened. Bluish rays of pulsing light came out of the hollow hole fanning outwardly then down into a see through veil like dome.

Dizziness overtook Mansi. She lost her hold of the tree and fell to the ground. She heard the cry of birds as they flew into the air, faltered then fell to the ground. A deer sprang from its cover of foliage and toppled over, regained its feet and staggered drunkenly.

Back at the village, those that did not fall felt a loss of balance. Several of the young children vomited. Medicine woman was sitting on the ground inside the hut. She reached out with her hand to steady herself. "Something has happened," she said to startled Raven, who had felt the same sensation. As the old woman hurried outside, she had to catch herself several times to balance herself. She looked around, extending her palms outward to feel. She looked upward toward to the rising moon to the east. She felt the brightening dusk moonlight on her flesh.

"Great Mother, what is this? I feel a change." Some of the tribal men were sitting on the ground. Several mothers were crawling out of their dwellings with their babies that were vomiting.

This was particularly worrisome for the medicine woman. This change was in the very fabric of the Great Spirit. In her inner-eye, her spiritual vision, her imagination, she saw the world woven in silken spider-like threads that was vibrant with the Spirit's life force. Stones, trees, her people, the gray wolf, the soaring hawk, the salmon in the water were made of the threads. Even the elements of fire, water, wind, and earth were threaded. Each contained the vibrational effects of Mother Earth and Father Sky, of the Father Sun and Mother Moon. Since the time of Creation, she believed the harmonious vibrations made the song she heard in the silence. But now, the orchestra that played and created the sounding keys of silence had changed as if one of the musicians were slightly off key, varying the vibrational rate and tone. The shift seemed to throw every living thing off balance. Children were the most sensitive to the spirit world. The frogs and insects had even quieted, trying to shrug off the shift like a person who was about to faint tries to shake their heads and regain their clarity again. The difference was this was not a temporary event for the chance was in the fabric....the stream of the energy....the living force. She lifted her hands and face toward the moonlight. It seemed the feminine side of the Creator had somehow strengthened and created the slightest off balance.

"Drum circle," Great Mother announced. "We must hold one at once. Summon all to join. We will dance and drum throughout the night and give healing to the Father Light. "

Since the first existence of her people of the Raven Tribe, they had used drum circles for healing. This shamanic drumming was a ritual that she knew before she could speak. Drums were sounding at her birth.

The shamanic drumming aided the circle of people to focus on an object and build up energy to be released upon it. The drumming drew individual energies together, recombining and multiplying on many simultaneous levels. When synchronized the energy grew its strongest. The drummers alternated setting the tempo and leading the group.

Wakanda knew what tempo was needed. What was lost in momentum and vibration, she now sensed had to be compensated. Yet, she feared what influence a small group could do when the altered vibration was woven in the threads of the source itself. As if the Great Creator was sick, but that couldn't be. The Great Creator was pure. The Great Creator's breath and sound created the thread of webs in all things. This was what terrified her.

"Hurry. Gather everyone. Get the drums. We do drum circle now. Crawl if you have to. If not drumming, you must dance, including the children and elders. Bring all."

The people scattered and staggered about. Wakanda rose to her feet and looked at the crown of the trees. She could even hear a slight

39

difference in the sound of the leaves with the breeze. The leaves sounded less alive. Then she became aware of the silence of the insects and the frogs. This time of night right at dusk, the fireflies would be dotting the periphery of the village. The only sound was the patting of moccasins upon the ground, the wailing of several children and urgent whispers to others. The horses should be neighing and hogs grunting with the sudden activity. Instead, they were lying on the ground. She looked around and saw several of the dogs doing the same. She sniffed the air. She could even tell by that taste in her mouth that was similar to an hour old slice of apple.

She begin walking toward the east side of the village. Her people followed behind her. His wife and daughter at each elbow supported Chief Dancing Squirrels. He was 74 summers in age, hair whiter than the peak of Grandfather's Mountain. His yellowing eyes followed her. Moreover, as he moved to join her, Wakanda knew he probably felt the vibrational shift more than anyone else did with his bones brittle as summer dried fallen oak twigs.

"Here," Wakanda said by a small fire. She removed a leather pouch from the tie around her waist and withdrew a handful of sweet grass. She took a bowl by the fire and lit the sweet grass in it. The flame died but smoke continued to rise from the sweet grass.

When she lit the end of it, the tribe began forming a circle. Chief Dancing Squirrels was ushered up to the head of the line. The Medicine woman held the smudge toward him then waved her feather fan so the smoke drifted toward him. She did this to cleanse him of bad energy and spirits. After the cleansing, he could join the circle about to be created. The ritual of smudging cleaned the mind and the surrounding environment and opened the energy channels of the body. With the feather fan, she directed the smoke over the heart, throat, and face to purify the body, mind, and spirit.

Passing the smudge among themselves, the drummers smudged themselves along with their drums. Once this was completed, Wakanda thanked the plant whose body made the cleansing possible. She moved to the east side of the circle and faced east. She motioned all to face each direction in unison as she begin moving clockwise, East, then South, then West, then North, inviting each Direction to participate and aid in the ceremony. After she did this, she included Father Sky above and Mother Earth.

Wakanda began, "Great Spirit of Light and Fire, and color red, come to us out of the East with the power of the rising sun. Let there be light in our words, let there be light on our path that we walk. Let us remember always that you give the gift of a new day. And never let me be burdened with sorrow by not starting over again. You give us illumination.

"Great Spirit of Creation of Water and color yellow. Great giving Spirit water is our drink that sustains all life. With the bowl of our desires, your water contains the materials. May our dreams and desires flow upon the earth to nourish and grow what we so seek. Send us the warm and soothing winds from the South to comfort me and caress me when I am tired and cold. Unfold us like the gentle breezes that unfold the leaves on the trees. As you give to all the earth your warm, moving wind, give to me, so that we may grow close to you in warmth. As leaves and blades of grass always reach for you, always seek to face you, may we do so. Man did not create the web of life. He is but a strand in it. Whatever man does to the web, he does to himself. Bring warm winds that spread the Great Spirit's breath so that it moves through all things. So that it lifts the birds, our spirits, and our dreams. Lift high the eagle of our spirits so that we may be close to you.

"Great Life-Giving Spirit and color black, we face the West, the direction of sundown. Let me remember every day that the moment will come when my sun will go down. Never let me forget that I must fade into you. Give me a beautiful color; give me a great sky for setting, so that when it is my time to meet you, I can come with glory. Great Water-Giving Spirit, your gentle breezes soothes us when we are tired. Unfold us like spring leaves and flowers teeming with life, dancing and ever lifting. You are the wind that lifts the eagle high to Father Sun. Carry our desires to the ends of the earth to manifest.

"Great Spirit of Love and Earth, come to me with the power of the North, make us courageous when the cold wind falls upon me. Give us strength and endurance for everything that is harsh, everything that hurts, and everything that makes me squint. Let me move through life ready to take what comes from the north. May we use wisdom as we move in decision while considering with the patience of a mountain's slow moving so that our answers are true and right and carry the weight of the mountain in truthful, right resolution. It is here the substance in our waters, our desires, which manifest onto

41

the earth. Your place is for sleeping and dreaming, solitude and spiritual introspection. With you, we communicate with Spirit and unseen worlds.

Wakanda then lowered to the ground on her knees and touched the earth with her hands. "Mother Earth, you give us life and means of substance to live. You give us waters, foods, and shelter. We praise you and seek ever to respect and protect you. We are made of your elements, as are all things of you. We are One with all living things and blades of grass, and mighty trees, and waters and fire.

Then she rose to her feet and lifted her hands to the sky. "Great Spirit Father Sky, you contain all. The stars, our Sun, are your radiance. We are all your children. Guide us and protect us."

The Medicine woman now turned slowly around and said, "We feel the change of your heartbeat. We feel a great disturbance Great Spirit. With our drum circle, we will begin with the rhythm and time of the eagle's flap of wing then quicken this to compensate for the slowing of your heartbeat. We will dance and raise our spirits with great life force and emotion. This we shall give to you to restore and make right all that has changed. We will regain balance and walk straight again."

Turning to the drummers, she began to sing to the beat of the eagle's winging as the facilitator to set the tempo in a steady, metronome-like pattern with precisely regular intervals, three beats per second to carry their intention, prayers, and awareness into the spirit world that sustained their physical reality.

"Ah nay, Ah nay, Ah nay." In unison, the drummers struck their hand drums on each of the "nay."

Throughout the night, the drums sounded in cadences of vibrational rates faster than the Mother Moon's light vibrations that the Medicine woman had sensed through her opened palms and upon the flesh of her face. She sought to counter the lower shift of vibrations of Moon. The vibration was slower and more powerful when the sun was far away and weakest of influence.

The dancers were moving in a clockwise pattern along to the drumming. Everyone was focused. The tempo was a steady, metronome-like pattern that created the sensation of inner movement. It was almost a hypnotic sensation that carried the people to a greater awareness of their spiritual plane and carried their prayers to the spirit world. It was a surreal scene.

Wakanda heard the lead drummer find his "sweet spot" where the drum began to sing and hum then resonate with all the other drums. A moment such as this always gave her elation. This was the moment where they became One with the Great Spirit. They sought to hold this moment long as possible. The dancers whirled and dipped, moving faster and faster in a circle, sounding yelps and cries of passionate joy. This climactic phase eventually began to wane. Medicine woman thrust her arms into the air and cried for them to stop. The drum leader pounded his beater into the drum with four thunderous beats. The drummers stopped.

Their hearts raced in the sudden silence. The drumming still echoed in their ears. The heightened energy seemed to give the world a white glow in Wakanda's eyes. Then the drums started their own thing again. This was the usual the point where she signals for the end of the first round of drumming with four thundering beats. She cried out to stop.

Thump! Thump! Thump! Thump!

After a long pause, the dancers motionless, Wakanda began to sing but stopped when from the corner of her eye she saw Raven standing outside the circle. She wanted in. One of the elder men did a smudging upon her.

Raven stepped inside the circle and stood by one of the dancers. When she looked at Wakanda, they both exchanged smiles.

Wakanda began with the pulsating lub-dub, lub-dub of a regular heartbeat rhythm, two beats a second. "Ay-nay, Ay-nay," she sang to shape all their energy into a powerful vortex that spiraled out into the fibers of Mother Earth's web, racing along the threads until it found Father Sun. Enlivening it. Quickening it and restoring its regular beat.

However, no one moved. All eyes were on Raven. She was standing on her toes with her arms thrust in the sky. Wakanda looked at the drummers and with her hand motioned a slower beat.

Raven nodded to the drummers, and then she took a long step and slowly made a slow turn, lifting one knee up to the level of her waist and lifting up so that other heel was off the ground. She made a sudden leap forward, pivoted again, then slowed and spread her arms as wings of a graceful eagle rising on a warm current of wind. She then flowed into a series of moves Wakanada had never seen in dance. The girl had somehow transformed herself into the embodiment of the Spirit. And even though the tempo of the dance had slowed, the

43

energy had not dissipated, but had maintained and now was growing, almost surging.

"Heyap!" Raven cried out then increased the speed of her moves like an eagle in descent. The others cried out in joy, fell in line behind her, and mimicked her moves. The drums quickened, and then leveled in a harmonic ecstasy. The world to Wakanda became infused with white light. Seconds passed, then a minute. Then more time passed, until at last, the harmony began to break up.

Wakanda cried out for the drums to stop. All gathered visualized the same completion of their energy delivered. Wakanda motioned for them to continue singing to the cadence of the eagle beat for several more minutes. She gave her final halt of the drum beating and all those gathered gave thanks as Wakanda moved counter clockwise giving thanks to each direction then released the circle.

It took all of them great effort to perform the circle. Many lay on the ground. Several of the children began to cry from exhaustion.

"Mother," Raven took Wakanda's arm and walked several yards from the crowd.

"Raven. Where did you learn to dance like that?" Wakanda asked.

Raven paused, and then a tear ran down her cheek. "I do not know. I just knew it somehow. But toward the end I no longer was thinking, I was just in the flow of it."

"You danced in Spirit. Never have I seen Dancing Spirit. I believe I had given you the wrong name," Wakanda said.

When they stopped, Raven leaned against the trunk of a pine tree. "Did it work?"

Wakanda looked at Raven's hand against the tree. "I fear not. Maybe a little, yes, but it is still strong this," she hesitated a moment then placed both hands on the tree trunk, and then she leaned her ear against it. Raven studied her with great interest.

"Daughter, now place your ear against the tree and place the palm of your hands against it. Tell me what you feel? What do you see in your mind's eye?"

Raven did what she asked. It reminded her of something. Yes, like a seashell that had the spirit of the sea within it. Then a great sadness fell upon her. *When did I hear the sound of the shell? Why would I know what this sounded like unless I had heard a shell? But where? When? I've forgotten this too?*

"Listen," Wakanda said, detecting Raven's distraction.

Pushing her thoughts away, Raven strained to hear more. It was the same sound but slowly she became aware of a barely detectable vibration. She thought of webs and threads and in her inner eye began to see a network of faint glowing threads of light. It was so beautiful.....it was emotional light of Love and...then she saw it....in the midst of thousands of white thin threads ran a black thread. She strained and focused on this within her mind. It was strange. It gave black light and absorbed white light. It drained the white light. This was the cause of the slower vibration. She jerked away from the tree to look at Wakanda.

"You see it too. I knew you would. Something has entered into the web that runs through all. Never has this happened. We must not tell anyone right now. I must do my prayers and ask for knowledge. Pray the Great Creator to be healed and the earth be saved."

"I will."

At the Dark Tree, Mansi regained her balance upon her knees. The White Raven regained his stance on the ground. Hopping several feet over, it gained a clear view of the moon still low in the sky. *You felt the shift of balance. We now must locate the Orb of Light. With this orb, we can vanish the sun and the world will be forever in darkness. Our power will grow. One day we will have a gateway open again between our worlds and we shall rule both. You, Mansi, will be the reigning Malbolian Ruler by the power granted by me, Shabael, High Emperor of Skyeden. Let the Dark Tree be your home.*

The White Raven hopped over to stand before Mansi who was still on her knees and said within her mind, *I will teach you words of vibrational power. You will create a protection aura upon the Dark Tree that no one but of Dark vibration may see. Here, you shall make your home beneath its roots. Command your darklings to tunnel into the earth and make you a home worthy of your station. Once the darklings begin their work, you shall return to your village and continue as if you are one of them. And when the time is right, you will begin the path of your destiny. So listen carefully for now we will teach you the sacred vibrational words to control the darklings and incorporate the energies of the Dark Tree's spheres.*

We must find the Tree of Light. I am sure now that the union of the White and Dark Orb will throw off the balance; and, the Dark shall reign here as in Skyeden. You will reign as Empress of your world. And one day, we shall learn how to create a portal between us. We will have conquered two worlds.

"Then I shall find the tree with this orb," Mansi said.

The drumming has stopped. Return to your village. Pay attention to your surroundings for any sign of the Tree of Light.

"I will, Great Spirit."

The White Raven flew into the branches of the Dark Tree and seemed to meld into the darkness as it receded deep within its crown.

"I live to serve you," Mansi. "I live to love you."

SLAUGHTER ON HARVEST DAY

Slowly the days moved. Mansi sent a party of darklings out each night to search for the Tree of Light. The White Raven and Darklings were sensitive to the force of the Spirit, especially to the workings of the White Spirit. All was woven in Spirit Essence just like a spider web. And when there was extraordinary workings, it quickened in vibration and brightened the threads. The Darklings were literally like hound dogs always hunting, tracking, attacking wherever they caught the Light energy working.

Yet even with the Darklings' supernatural senses, they could not find the Tree of Light. They could feel its pulsating and lightening of the threads that always led north of the village. However, after several miles instead of growing in strength, the Tree of Light's essence waned then faded completely. Shabael and his priests reasoned the Tree of Light had created a force that veiled its location similar to the magic used to veil the Tree of Dark from the villagers and woods traveler.

Within the village, there were great indicators of a great White Light energy. However, if a Darkling approached the village, it would begin to lose its essence and fade. A Darkling could not cross the river to the village without dissolving into nothingness. Only the White Raven could enter because it did not have the Darkling essence within it. Each day for weeks following the arrival of the Raven, the White Raven visited Mansi. After the creation of the Dark Tree, the Darklings dug a cavern beneath it. This provided a private place for the White Raven to visit Mansi. If he needed to speak to her, the White Raven would get Mansi's attention by flying along the edge of the woods while cawing loudly. Then Mansi would sneak out of the village to go to the Dark Tree. The young girl spent much of her free time there.

Years passed. Mansi grew into a young, beautiful woman. Yet inside her, jealousy and resentment grew over Raven. Her stepsister had ruined her life. All of the tribe deemed Raven to be a Spirit herself because it was said that she truly came from the Stars. Moreover, the most remarkable thing was it seemed Raven never aged. She looked the same as the day that she was found 12 years ago. What really poisoned Mansi's blood with hatred was Raven had some great power of healing. Mansi would seethe with anger when one of their people or even other tribes that have heard of Raven, came to her sister for healing. They would completely ignore her and go straight to their mother, the Medicine woman, to ask for her permission to be healed by Raven. This made Mansi killing mad so she would pluck a lot of flowers. She observed all the healings that she could. She watched how Raven drew the sickness or injury into herself then cast it off onto another living form to receive it. Mansi hoped by learning the workings of the Light magic that she could find a way to sabotage it. Rats, opossums, and fish were sometimes used but Raven mainly sought to use living things that were a danger to people and could not be used for food or clothing. Many times she saw Raven crying and praying to the now dead things that had taken in the sickness. That was so pathetic, Mansi thought. The cages were usually covered so you didn't see the creatures dying. Then an idea came to Mansi. Maybe one day she could put Mother in a covered cage and let Raven cast the sickness onto her and kill their mother. Now that would be so sweet, she thought. With all the time that had passed with searching for the Tree of Light, Mansi learned to be patient. Her time would come.

Then one day, White Raven came to her in the middle of the night into her hut. It pecked her check to awaken her. He told her that his head Priest had a vision of the future, which showed the ending of the world. Their great Kingdom in Skyeden would fall. There was a stirring of the White Spirit to rebalance; and, they must prevent this. If and whenever they found the Tree of Light one day, they could then trigger an event in her world that could keep the unbalance in place.

Mansi said she understood. When pale faces approached Chief Dancing Squirrels the next morning; she took this as a sign that there was a way for a Dark Victory. And if it came blazing, if it responded with its strongest energy, would it not come from the Tree of Light? Would it not leave such a brightening along the webs that perhaps….just perhaps… the Darklings could track along the threads and at last find the Tree of Light? She knew one thing for certain, if she could create the event that she now sought, her life would be changed forever.

Two young warriors encountered several men on horseback headed in the direction of the village. When the men saw the warriors, each held one hand high. Their weapons were tied securely on their horses. One of the two was dark skinned. He wore a round brim hat with a feather tied into his long hair and rode ahead stopping a safe distance away from the two warriors.

In Lakota, he called out. "We come in peace. We seek to talk with Chief Dancing Squirrels."

"Stop at the river crossing!" one of the warriors ordered. He spoke in a low voice to his companion then galloped across the river. Minutes later, several more warriors came to the river. They motioned for the three men to approach. The warriors circled the men as they were led across the river, followed the path, into the woods that eventually broke into the clearing of the village.

People joined the progression as it moved toward Chief Dancing Squirrels' lodge. When the group stopped and settled, the Chief emerged with two of his adult sons.

The dark skinned guide introduced himself, speaking in Lakota. Mansi edged close to the crowd but back enough to observe everything that was happening. The guide said a yellow stone had been found south of the river. He said white man placed value on this stone but it was worthless to Indians and said in the Indian's language these men were fools but dangerous. The men had guns and powerful medicine. It would be wise to trade the land by the river for the goods these men offered.

The Chief invited them to stay overnight. They would be fed and the following day would give his answer. Mansi studied the men and knew the tallest was the leader. His name was Ferrel Morgan. What distinguished him from the rest in first impressions was the long, red coat he wore. It was inlaid with gold thread on each side where it was divided in the center. The sleeves were narrow but widened out like flowers blooming. This coat was like Chief's Dancing Squirrels' headdress that signified him as leader of the tribe. It was a beautiful coat that possessed much spirit that was not Light Spirit, which had always felt harsh to her sensitivities. This man was Chief of Dark Power. He shared the Malbolian Spirit as her Chief Shabael, White

Raven. Yes, she knew with all certainty this man could be instrumental. He was powerful and his men followed him, watched his reactions before they shared his as their own. Such a man might prove hard to sway, but....at that thought, she smiled, cutting her eyes to the right to see....yes, there it was, a sign she held great magic, two young men of her own tribe were looking at her. There was yearning in their eyes. There was surrender of souls for trade to possess her body and passion. It amazed her when it came to the young men. It seemed the more disgust she expressed to them; the more they wanted her. She knew by the gaze in their eyes that they had dreamt of her, ravishing her, crying out their warrior victory cries as they came to completion with her held down by their strength and masculinity. *Fools. I can tear you apart without a second thought. With my Darklings and I ....our teeth and claws are long. And as they are eaters of Light, I will be the eater of your life. Yes, I will take your Spirit in, not you to force upon me or in me. I will rip it out of your heart; eat it with your blood dripping from my wet lips.*

Twice now, she had drawn a boy to the edge of the protected ring of the Dark Tree. She had seduced them with promises. How sweet it was to overpower them, to be wolf upon them, to spend her fire of ecstasy upon them then shred them to ribbons with the Darklings lapping up the blood spray until every piece of the boy had been devoured. She had felt their life force's frantic escape of retching body pains swept into her soul's energy with the Darling left tossing over the ground. Whining and moaning as their souls departed their bodies.

Oh, you are mine, Red Bird. She thought as she looked at the man the following day, clearly disappointed and agitated over the Chief's answer that there would be no deal.

She waited 30 minutes before taking her horse and going in the general direction of Red Bird and his men. White Raven appeared upstream from where she had emerged from the woods to the river. She sat quickly on her horse and looked around to see if any of her tribe people were about. White Raven flew a wide circle then landed on her shoulder making two clicks with its beak that meant "yes." Shabael was not present within the raven. She gave her horse two quick kicks to the side and hurried upstream.

The men she followed seemed to be in a hurry to get home but had another half day of travel left when the sun begin its descent in the sky. They pitched tents and prepared two chickens given to them by the village. After they had eaten and were drinking firewater, she

49

strolled into their camp and said to the Red Byrd's guide. "You shall have your yellow stones."

From those spoken words, Mansi knew her life would be changed forever.

In two weeks was the Harvest Day Festival. All the tribe would be gathered in the field. If Red Byrd returned with a large group of armed men, they could surround the field and open fire. The land would be theirs and she would wait with her Darklings for the brightening of the threads of the Light Spirit to come rushing in to counter the Dark event of annihilating the tribe. She and her Darlings would backtrack the path of the Light Spirit that she had no doubt would lead her to the Tree Of Life.

When the day finally arrived, there were several things even Mansi's wildest imaginations would never have predicted. It was the day she became immortal as an eighteen-year-old girl without a tribe.

CHAPTER 3

WELCOME TO MY WORLD

The Present - Silverton, North Carolina, Excerpt from Dylan's diary:

How many times have I sat dreaming of imaginary places of cinematic proportions as the central character in a dramatic event? I'm standing on a battlefield, looking as mighty as William Wallace does when victorious after facing astronomical odds to survive. On my held-high claymore is wrapped a strip of cloth sewn by my true love. The sound of my name rings in my ears as the army chants my name.

Then I open my eyes, look through my bedroom window at the backyard still covered in the leaves I'm supposed to have already raked. And my younger brother, Robert, is standing there, holding up the rake I'm supposed to be using with one hand and shooting me the bird with the other.

Welcome to my world on the day before my eighteenth birthday.

That was earlier this afternoon. Now I'm crashing. School again tomorrow. My senior year. Wow! Kindergarten to the 11th grade is a slow-motion treadmill that seems to be infinite. Then, in a light-year warp, it's your senior year and you have this kind of surreal feeling. I'm a senior in high school and I haven't a clue what I want to do with my life.

I'm nothing special, just an average teen-ager. I'm five-foot-eleven with blue eyes, black hair that hangs to my shoulders (much to my father's chagrin), a skimpy little mustache, and a strip of beard about the width of my finger down the

51

center of my chin. That look seems to work for Johnny Depp, and besides, I call the chin strip my thinking scratch pad. Some of the girls kid me about my "soul patch", but I'm not even sure what that means.

I'm not really an artist, but I do like to sketch things. I chose Art and English as my majors because they seemed to be a lot easier than anything else was. No, that's not exactly right. It's more like I'm terrible at math, I don't know a thing about plumbing or using a hammer and if I do have a skill, it hasn't found me yet. I came by all this ineptitude honestly, though. I inherited it. If my dad ever did anything around the house more mechanical than working the lever on his recliner, I never had the privilege of witnessing it. If something around the house breaks or springs a leak, Dad just calls somebody to fix it.

Oh yeah, my dad. He's one of those good ol' boys whose father made a lot of money doing some things that the family doesn't discuss a lot. My grandfather was part of the good ol' boys political machine and my dad was elected sheriff a few years ago. I think he said something nice to me once, when I was about three years old, but for the life of me I can't remember what it was. Like I said, my forte is reading and drawing pictures. My father thinks that makes me a sissy. So I read books to get out of my cramped little world and my dad just stares at me like I'm some kind of bug. The only expression I've seen on his face in the last couple of years is a smirk.

My younger brother, Robert, who is as tall as Dad at six-foot-two and only about forty pounds lighter than Dad's two-forty-five, is the spitting image of the old man. And he's at least as good as Dad is at the smirking and acid remarks. I'm not sure what my mom had to do with that conception, but there sure isn't much of her evident in Robert.

Robert is a carbon copy of Dad and they do everything together. They play catch in the yard. They go bowling. They hang out at the firing range and Robert is already planning a career in law enforcement. Yeah, he's sixteen years old and we're looking at Sheriff Robert already.

Here I am, hoping to be a writer and maybe an artist someday. Then there's Robert, throwing curve balls to the old man and putting .38 rounds on top of each other in a bulls eye. Not a hard choice for Dad to pick a favorite, I guess.

And, oh yeah, Robert, the sixteen-year-old, rides a Harley-Davidson and is president of a motorcycle club. Me? I ride my Schwinn and deliver the morning newspaper.

But life isn't all bad. There's my mom and she's one beautiful lady. I like to thumb through her old school yearbooks and photo albums and see what a happy young girl she was. She was always smiling, the kind of smile that made her everybody's friend. But she's not that way now. Those aren't smile wrinkles beginning to show on her lovely face. You look at her now and you think, "That's a lovely woman, but something's broken inside." It's as if the wind-up key to her inner music box has been lost. She's like a beautiful full-blossomed flower, but with all the color drained from the petals. I can remember her smile that used to light up the room. But I can't remember the last time that happened. She reminds me of the birds she watches in the backyard diving from the branches of a tree, searching the ground for a worm or a tidbit of some kind, grabbing it with their beaks and then fleeing as if the devil was after them. Or maybe just our big, fat black cat, Paula.

Mom has that edgy look, as if any moment she's expecting her security to be snatched away. She's been lied to, had promises broken, her heart smashed and her dreams shattered. Why she's still living in the same house with Sheriff Spencer Morgan is a mystery to outsiders. I know why, though. She loves her two sons and refuses to give them up.

One night when she and I were home alone, she told me about her first heartbreak. She was fifteen and desperately in love (she thought) with her boyfriend, seventeen-year-old Albert Jenkins. One hot summer day they decided to run away and she packed a couple of old grocery bags with a few of her clothes and slipped out of the house that night to meet Albert at the local Greyhound bus station. Only problem was, Albert got cold feet and didn't show up. I've often thought how I wished Albert had kept that date. I wouldn't have been born, but at least my mother might have known some happiness in her marriage.

Dad and Robert go out almost every night. Sometimes together if Robert wants to ride in the patrol car or hang around the Sheriff's office. If Mom doesn't have some church function to attend, she usually stays home. I'm in my room, reading of other worlds or painting pictures of places I've never seen and probably won't ever. She's lost and I'm lost. And even we are in different worlds. My world is make-believe. Her world is all too real.

I do have some friends, of course. There's Freddie, my best friend forever. Freddie's kind of a nerd, right down to carrying a comb in his shirt pocket and having a calculator attached to his belt. His father is an auto mechanic and Freddie is destined to follow in those footsteps. Freddie doesn't know exactly where his mother is. She ran away with a truck driver a few years ago and he's never heard from her since. She met the truck driver while Freddie's dad was working on the sixteen-wheeler's timing belt.

I have one more special friend, if you can call a bird that. I'm not even sure if it's a male or female. All I know is that ever since I can remember, I have this raven that's been around for about all my life. Mom says she first saw Ravenous on the day they strolled me out of the hospital. I know ravens can live 40 or more *years and stay in one place; and, I heard that Ravens are territorial and usually have life mates. I don't know what's Ravenous's situation is. Who knows? When I go out in the morning, it's dark but the porch light is on. Some of the surrounding birds are chirping. Ravenous waits on a limb of our front yard birch tree for me. I spoil him with sausage and eggs every morning. He stays behind while I start my bike route. And every morning, when I am about at the same spot on my route, Ravenous finds me and follows along off to the sides, perching at different trees, then hangs in the woods by the school bus parking lot or flies back home. If I'm home before dark, I always look for him. When I'm in my room with the window curtain open, he's there in the big oak tree yards away.*

Jeez, this is like the longest day log I've ever done. Guess with eight months of school left you just kind of reflect on a lot of stuff. Well, it's time for goodnight, all. Got those newspapers to deliver in the morning before school. Another exciting day in the life of Dylan Morgan.

Dylan closed the log and placed it on the bedside table. He turned off the lamp and stared at the ceiling, enjoying as always the reflective solar system there. The lighting had been a gift from his mother for his thirteenth birthday; and, it was his most prized possession, glowing with more than a hundred stars, planets with rings, two moons and shooting stars. He liked to pretend that he was lying on the ground of another world. In this world, he could stare at the sky and sense a feeling of the Divine. In his mind, the Divine was always a woman, a living being who perhaps possessed a soul of her own. He often closed his eyes and played out the scene in his mind. It was so real that he could actually feel the soil with the palms of his hands, the smell of the fresh air, unspoiled by the stench emitted from automobiles or factories, clean air the way he imagined it had been before America had been discovered and taken from the Indians. He could smell the fragrances of exotic wild flowers and the sap glistening like emeralds on the pines. Fireflies played in swaying fields of holly. He watched the clouds scurrying across the sky and sensed the breeze moving them and coursing through the branches of the huge oaks. It all seemed to be moving to an unheard mesmeric symphony. Dylan's favorite part of this dreamland experience was always the rising of the sun. Something about the rays of light made him attuned with the Creator. And it was this security blanket that he had been going to sleep under for almost five years.

He was sleeping with the deep untroubled sleep of youth, but there is a strangeness to the night. While he shifted restlessly in the bed, lightning from a distant storm flashes across the sky. A variable wind rises and falls. Clouds race across the night sky like dogs playing in a park. A raven appears at the bedroom window and perches on the sill, screwing its head from side to side, seemingly trying to peer inside the bedroom. Gnarled fingers reach out in the darkness to seize the bird and it lets out a startled cry and darts upward, out of reach of the long branches of the old oak tree that brushes against the window as a gust of wind passes. On the roof of the house, a second raven is perched on a lightning rod. Sitting. Watching. Cocking its head alertly from side to side.

It's almost morning and Dylan Morgan will soon enter his final day as a seventeen-year-old. He wouldn't be able to legally have his first beer but he could vote or join the army and give his life for his country. He had thought a lot about that … joining the army. Join the Army and be all you can be. Or join the Navy and see the world. See some of those mysterious places he had read about. It was an alluring idea for him, but not for his mom. Mom is set on her oldest son going to college. Adamant, in fact. Dad was ambivalent. To Sheriff Morgan, college was just a waste of valuable time and good money. If Dylan wanted to go to college, Dad said, fine, save the money from his newspaper route and then get a job to pay for his tuition. *Yeah, go to college if you want, son. But you pay for it. Not me.*

Money wasn't the problem, of course. The family was financially set. But for Dad, it was the principle of the thing. You wanted something; go get it. Just be prepared to pay for it. Mom, on the other hand, had been putting money into a college fund since the day she learned she was pregnant with her oldest son. She didn't tell Dylan that he could choose the college he wanted, but she did assure him that things were going to work out. Still, he saved the money from his paper route and wondered if he would really be able to pursue his dream of writing and painting.

The alarm sounded at exactly four-thirty a.m., a screeching video of a backwoods woman with missing teeth screaming, *"Get up! Get up!" Get your ass out of bed, you got things to do! Get up!"* And all the while banging on a tin pan. It was a video he had downloaded the afternoon before thinking that it should have him wide-awake enough to not even want to sneak a few more minutes of pillow time.

55

Before Dylan could pull on a pair of jeans, his father burst into the bedroom. *What the hell?!* Sheriff Spencer Morgan yelled. He glared round the room, finding it empty except for the startled Dylan.

"Sorry, Dad, it's just a wake-up recording," he mumbled. "I didn't realize it was going to be so loud."

"No shit, dipstick, you think it might be a little loud? Get rid of that piece of crap today! If this happens tomorrow, you and that shit both get your asses kicked out of the house!

"Christ, you're going to be eighteen years old tomorrow and you're still screwing around with toys. You know what? You're going to be eighteen, why don't you join the Army. You could just drop out of school and you'd be out of here in a couple of weeks and learn some kind of job. The Army will have some loudmouth sergeant to wake your young ass up about five a.m., so you'd probably love that. Jesus Christ, boy, I almost came in here shooting!"

Sheriff Morgan was a ludicrous sight standing there in a T-shirt and knee-length boxer shorts with deputy stars on them. There was a little bulge of belly fat showing beneath the shirt and the shorts and he didn't present the authoritative figure that he was so proud of in his starched uniform and pointed black boots.

Dylan stifled a giggle and sat on the side of the bed to pull on a T-shirt with an angry eagle on the front and his Reebok sneakers.

Sheriff Morgan made an imaginary pistol with his right hand, pointed the index finger at his oldest son and said, "I'm gonna go back to bed, boy, and I don't want to hear another sound from you. Jesus Christ!"

As he sat on the side of the bed and laced the sneakers, Dylan flashed back to an argument that he and his dad had recently had about money. Dylan mentioned that for his sixteenth birthday, Robert had been presented with the Harley-Davidson bike, while for his own seventeenth birthday he had been given sixty bucks for a video game. Dad went off, of course, ranting that while he might be the oldest son, Dylan wasn't worth the spit in a spittoon. "You're nothing but a dreamer and you're never going to be anything else. You got no skills, you got no grit, and you got no pecker. Ain't no fight in you, boy. So go play your video games while Robbie and I go to the shooting range."

That was the day that Dylan made up his mind that he'd never ask the sheriff for anything ever again. If he could somehow get into college without using the money he had saved, he'd buy his own motorcycle. But it wouldn't be a Harley. Everybody rode Harleys. He would be different. A rebel cycle. He would do it somehow even if it meant finding a second job after school.

So Dad didn't think he had enough grit, huh? *"Okay, well dear ol' Dad, if we were drinks at a bar, you'd be piss and vinegar, and I'd be a rare cognac."* Just because he wasn't punching people out after school like Robert didn't mean he was some kind of weakling or coward. A man of honor fought those who were worthy. To succumb to an idiot's berating was only giving him the power to hurt you with words. Dylan denied others that power and if his father saw that as a weakness, then so be it. Scuffling with half-drunk, redneck, beer-bellied losers was not something a true warrior did. When a true warrior fought, it was for a cause worthy of death.

Dylan couldn't see himself as an intimidator like his father, the sheriff, or Robert, the spitting image. He didn't threaten and he didn't bribe. Way back in his elementary school days, Dylan had been a safety guard, wearing the bright yellow shoulder strap and belt with pride. And even then, the year-younger Robert had called him a sissy for asking the other kids to follow the rules.

He may have been a sissy to Robert, but to many of the other kids who were constantly being bullied, he was a hero. A sort of avenging angel. When he saw a bully about to ruin some kid's day or face for a month, it was Dylan the Safety Patrol to the rescue. He was seldom as large as the bullying kid was, but he was faster with his hands, having proven that a few times to bullies who were attempting to intimidate him. And while the bullies had little respect for the uniform, they did have respect for a kid who was willing to look them in the eye and face them down. The bullies inevitably backed off, made some smart remark to save face, and walked away.

Dylan's mind was as quick as his hands and feet. The witticisms that he at times tossed at his father and brother were, if detected, not often appreciated. He had a way of "twinkling" a sentence with partially concealed sarcasm and, while many of the little innuendoes passed right over Robert's head, he occasionally detected the insult even if he didn't quite understand it.

Dylan often thought of a poster from one of his English classes that had read "Rebel Without a Clause". He loved that phrase and thought it fit him to a tee. He often created stories of heroes facing insurmountable odds, who through sheer courage became victorious.

School was so boring that he felt forced to make up those stories. He dreamed of being a knight in a secret martial arts school; his history teacher was Yoda from Star Wars. The math teacher was Data from Star Trek. The principal was Mr. Spock. The P.E. teacher was Spartacus. The football team he named the Spartans after the movie, "300."

And Freddie? Freddie was Lady Gaga. Ha-ha.

Dylan chuckled at that last thought, then rose from the bed and went to the window to check the weather. There were a couple of little dinks in the glass of one of the panes, as if someone had shot the glass with a BB gun. What the ...? On the sill outside, he noticed a tiny twig, so white that it almost seemed to be glowing in the early morning light. Underneath the twig was a black feather.

Dylan raised the window and picked up the twig and the feather. The feather was too large for one of the birds that were always in the tree outside. It must have come from a crow ... or a raven. "A twig is just a twig," he thought, but there seemed to be something different about this one. It was a pure white, through and through. And the feather, now that was a different matter altogether. It triggered a memory of a dream during the night. There had been a raven in the dream, staring through the windowpane at him.

And now he was holding a black feather in his hand. Eerie. An early birthday present?

CHAPTER 4

"BORN TO BE WILD"

Dylan pedaled his Schwinn and jammed with the Black Keys on his MP3 player as he rode through the neighborhood tossing papers onto dew-covered lawns. The morning air was cool on his face and when he inhaled, it awakened the inner linings of his lungs. He loved the burn in his leg muscles as he raced downhill after having made the climb up a steep incline. He was nearing his home and most of the one-hundred and fifty newspapers had been delivered. Most were simply thrown toward the houses, but several had to be inserted in boxes by the curb. It was late September and a slight hint of fall chill was in the air. He could see a gathering of clouds on the western horizon.

Rain by ten, he thought. He flipped a paper in the direction of their neighbor, Mrs. Jones, who was dressed in a robe and obviously awaiting his arrival. She waved, her robe revealing a portion of her newly enlarged breasts, and he waved back. He liked Mrs. Jones. She always paid for her delivery on time and she always gave him a nice tip. And on some days like today, the view wasn't half-bad, either with a breast tip. When he had mentioned that to Freddie, for the next two weeks, Freddie joined him on the paper route never really saying why but Dylan had an idea.

Dylan reached for another paper in the basket behind him and felt a movement. It was something soft and feathery, but there was also something hard and sharp back there.

"Caw!"

He turned his head and saw the raven, black feathers and talons gripping the basket to keep its balance.

What the...?

"Caw!"

"Jesus! Ravenous!" The bike wobbled as he almost lost control. *"Dang it!* Everywhere I go either you or your girlfriend is always following. You should have had the starring role in Alfred Hitchcock's 'Birds.' Maybe you'll understand this, "Nevermore!"

The raven showed no fear and simply gripped the basket and stared at Dylan.

"Caw!"

"*Caw* back at you!" Dylan said and waved a hand to shoo the bird.

"You!" the Raven answered back in imitation.

Dylan could have sworn that the raven had spoken. Was he losing his mind? He looked over his shoulder again at the bird. *I'm going crazy.*

Dylan threw another paper onto another lawn and the raven still remained perched on the basket, cocking its head to one side and giving him a '*What's wrong with you?*' stare.

"Don't give me that look," Dylan said, laughing at the idea of carrying on a conversation with a bird. "I know you know what I'm saying. You've been watching me all my life, lurking in the window, spying on me from telephones poles, sneaking bites from my sandwich by the open window in my room. Why don't you just come in at night and sleep with me?"

"Really? I like you too," The voice coming from the sidewalk startled Dylan. The speaker was Jenny Albright, a pretty high school freshman and neighbor. Embarrassed, Dylan kept pedaling, pretending he hadn't heard the girl, who was wearing a huge grin. Jenny was cute, but he was a senior and she was only a frosh. He liked Jenny, but only as a neighborhood friend. A child for crying out loud. And now that child must think he was senile, riding his bike and talking to a bird perched on the basket. He waved at Jenny and kept on pedaling.

The Morgans' house was next in the cul-de-sac and Dylan, as always, marveled at the beauty of the place. Sheriff Morgan had spared no expense in erecting a monument to himself, spending almost half a million bucks on the mansion that neighbors referred to as the "White House." Even the sheriff called his study the "Oval Office. Joke around the station was that if the White House was ever hit by a terrorist attack, they could fly Obama down for a live shot interview before the Morgan house to say everything is all right.

As he prepared to heave the paper into the yard, Dylan noticed that Robert's prized Harley-Davidson boots were sitting on the porch. A Jack Nicholson grin lit up his face and he heaved the rolled-up paper toward the boots. The throw was strong enough, but off line. Just as it appeared the paper was going to sail past the boots, however, a streaking black blur blew into the picture, and the powerful beak of the raven seized the top of one of the boots and dropped it into a puddle of rainwater in the yard.

"*Caw!*"

"Yeah! *Caw* right back at ya, Buddy!" Dylan shouted. "Way to go!" He pedaled faster and continued throwing papers.

The front door of the white mansion opened and Robert stepped out on the porch. He stretched and checked the still cloudy skies, then bent to pick up his boots. Only one boot? He glanced around, then saw the other boot lying in the puddle of water. He frowned, muttered something to himself, and walked into the yard to pick up the boot.

"*Caw! Caw! Caw.*"

Robert looked up and saw the raven perched in a nearby dogwood tree.

"*Are you laughing at me, bitch,*" Robert glowered, picking up the boot and threatening to toss it at the bird. A hundred yards down the street, Dylan was pedaling furiously and trying hard not to look back at his angry brother. "Hey, douche bag, why don't you get a real bike," Robert shouted after the fleeing Dylan.

Sheriff Spencer Morgan heard the commotion in the yard and came out on the porch. "What's going on?" he asked of his spitting image. The sheriff was dressed for the image he always tried to portray. A caricature of an Old West lawman, right down to the holster on his hip and the gold badge glistening on his chest. He ruined the image by wearing his blond-just-beginning-to-show-gray-at-the-temples hair in a crew cut. On his right cheek was a scar in the shape of a three. When he became angry, the corner of his right lip would rise slightly and tremble. When this happened, it partially hid the bottom line of the three and made it into a two. Dylan called it the countdown; three, things are neutral; two, he's not liking this; one, that's when he's shouting and the three scar turns into a one.

"Yeah," he drawled, "see what you mean, Robbie. You know, there are two kinds of males in this world, boy. Men with Harleys and punks with Schwinns."

Sheriff Morgan made no attempt to hide the derision he felt for his oldest son. He had his reasons. Though Dylan was a godsend in helping make some things happen in Spencer's favor, he hated that kid, despised him. The kid was born premature with his head too large compared to the rest of his body. The kid looked like a freaking bug-eyed gaping featherless baby bird. Even his baby cries sounded like chirps. There were times when the sheriff's hands shook from wanting to reach down into that crib and squeeze the ugly mass of wrinkles so hard that its eyes would pop out. Reflexively he reached up and touched the scar on his face. The scar transformed from a three into a two.

Dylan had been a "surprise baby". He had been born a month premature. It was exactly seven months after he and Sally had slipped off to the next county and got married. Hell, because the dumb bunny had been too ignorant to use birth control, she had gladly accepted his offer to marry her.

Thank you, Almighty, for giving a guy a break, he thought to himself sarcastically. After the little bird was born, he had been placed in an incubator. While wifey prayed for her little "accident" to survive, Spencer prayed just as fervently that the bird would shrivel up and die. Gawking bug-eyed, neck all stretched, head bobbing, chirping. *God Almighty!*

Then eleven months later, the Almighty seemed to have granted Spencer a blessing with the birth of Robert. Now that was a strong baby; came out strong as a stump and quickly became a reflection of his own macho ego image.

Deputies at the station called Robert, "Sheriff Junior." The sheriff's own little mini-me hand puppet. Spencer loved the kid. They were inseparable. Spencer did grow a little concerned that maybe things were taken a little too far when Sheriff Junior at age six came into his "Oval Office" with a Boy Scout knife in his hand and his cheek dripping blood, saying, "Dad, we're the same now, see?" Junior proudly pointed to three lines carved into his cheek. That was a little too weird even for the macho sheriff, so the Spittin' Image underwent some plastic surgery. Though the grooves were no longer there, they were thin white lines.

When someone asked Robert about them, he said they were "hereditary from Dad," No one dared to point out that wasn't exactly right.

Spencer sometimes wondered why he had never thought about having a little plastic surgery himself, but quickly realized that he liked the scar. For one thing, it reminded him of how much he hated Dylan. Hating Dylan was one of the sweet pleasures of life. He couldn't kill the ugly little bird, so he would just make his life as miserable as possible.

Yeah! Spencer Morgan thought, Robert was one strapping baby boy who developed muscles before he was walking. *That's my boy!*

Sheriff Morgan reached into his pants pocket and pulled out a money clip bulging with bills. He counted out five twenty-dollar bills and handed the cash to Robert. "Here, take this and treat your biker club tonight. Now don't get drunk and crazy. I don't want one of my deputies having to haul your young asses in for something stupid. Thing is, I may need you fellas to do something for me soon and I want to keep y'all happy. Keep it easy, rider." He waited half a moment to see if his son caught to play on words. No brain intended.

The Spittin' Image folded the bills and stuck them in a jeans pocket. "You got it, Marshall Dillon," he said, grinning. Robert was wearing jeans and a white T-shirt; and, his hair and eyes were a perfect match for his father's. No doubt whose son this was. They not only looked alike, they moved alike, shared the same characteristics and were usually on the same wavelength. When either of them focused on another person, their eyes narrowed into slits as if they were staring down a pistol barrel during target practice.

Robert picked up his motorcycle boots, used a hand to swipe the water off the one that had been dropped in the puddle, and carried them indoors. Today he was wearing black, pointy-toed cowboy boots. Just like Sheriff Morgan. He went to the garage, kick-started his Fat Boy Harley and gave the throttle a twist to get a window-rattling roar from the powerful engine before pulling out into the street. As he rode toward school, four other bikers joined him. His buddies were always waiting nearby.

Stewart remained on the porch for a moment watching Robert ride down the street. "Marshall Dillon," he mumbled. "I love you son, but you got a brain size of a rat turd floating in a jar of formaldehyde. Least you got one thing right, God, we'll be dead before I can see what the fuck he does to my inheritance."

Dylan had thrown his book bag into the basket of the bike before delivering the papers just in case he decided not to go back home. Now he wanted to make sure Robert was long gone before going home. So he decided to ride by Freddie's house to kill a few minutes before they rode to school. It was just a few minutes past seven a.m. but Dylan knew where to find his friend. He rode his bike to the garage, leaned it against the building, and rapped on the door. Seconds later the garage door began rolling up and seventeen-year-old Freddie "GaGa" Sanders stepped out. He was wearing an auto mechanic jump suit covered in grease stains and his ever-present glasses. His dark hair had the wet look that came from using that nerdy cream dressing. Sideburns ran below his ears and came to sharp points aiming at his nose. As usual, he smelled strongly of Old Spice aftershave lotion. He loved that stuff so much that he kept a bottle in his school locker so he could refresh the scent during lunch breaks.

Dylan gave his friend a huge smile and immediately began giving him grief. "Freddie, man, you're a geek with a serious twank of nerdum. How's it going, Buddy?"

Freddie flashed the million dollar grin that he called his "Tom Cruise". That grin had saved him from countless confrontations with people who didn't really dig his act. Freddie would never be called handsome. However when he flashed that electric grin and the freckles on his cheeks lit up, you knew he was one of the good guys. Girls liked him despite his nerdishness — or maybe even because of it. He was naturally shy, but covered it with the always-ready grin and some witty patter. He was smart in class and math was his Top Ten song of the week.

"Well, how's the almost birthday boy?" he asked, his eyes twinkling. "The dude is eighteen tomorrow and STILL a virgin, huh? High five, amigo. You get my jive? Yeah, I'm the baddest greasiest monkey in town!"

"Grease monkey, dopey," Dylan said, laughing. "Greasy just sounds sleazy. Come on man, you've got to change clothes before we go to school. And, by the way, you really need to get some sunlight to help that garage tan."

Freddie just grinned, then unzipped the jump suit and stepped out of it wearing jeans and a light-blue short-sleeved shirt. "Quick change artist," he said. "Let's go, Slick."

"I'm Slick?" Dylan said. "You're the grease ball."

The boys mounted their bikes and began pedaling toward the high school. They had gone only a few yards when they heard the rumble of a Harley coming from behind them. Big Scott, one of Robert's biker buddies, roared past them on a low rider, spitting a white glob in their direction. He came so close to Freddie's bike that he swerved off the street, almost hitting a mailbox.

"Well, wonders never cease to amaze me," Freddie muttered. "Looky there, Dylan. There goes a hog riding a hog!"

"There goes another statistic just waiting to be printed," Dylan said. "Guys like him have no clue. No dreams. No brains to make a nickel worth of chitlins. A little hog humor there," Dylan said.

"Suey!" Freddie called out. "Snork Porkin', mud slurpin, curly tailed, pink nosed, stump legged, belly dragging, bowling balled sized testicles with a little weee weeeeee, born to be dumb-umb-umb, lipless, fat back, pork chopped, meatless piece of bacon!" He finished up with his glasses askew and fist pumped.

"You get em, tiger!" Dylan cheered.

The boys laughed and continued pedaling, nearing the school.

"So, how's it feel being seventeen for the last day?" Freddie asked. "Must be awesome. I can't wait till I turn eighteen."

Dylan watched Big Scott disappear around a corner before answering, his voice tinged with uncertainty "You ever feel like you're nothing? Ever just feel like life is passing you by and you're not even being noticed?"

"Careful, you're talking about my life," Freddie joked. "Yeah, sometimes maybe. But that's when I pull an engine and get greasy."

"No, I'm serious. The last couple of weeks I've just had this surreal feeling. It's like something big is going to happen and I don't know what or when. All week I've been having the weirdest dreams. Sometimes I'm flying, and in others, I'm alone in some dark woods and the wildlife is fleeing from something that's coming. Something that's hunting for me. I don't know what it is, but it's something evil. I can sense it lurking in the shadows. I can smell its breath. And man, could it use a Cert!"

Freddie started to laugh, and then thought better of it. "Hey, Slick, they say dreams of flying are related to sex. That thing in the woods is probably your guilt getting ready to devour you for your impure thoughts. Besides, you know we'll be leaving our nests in a few months. It's enough to make anyone feel a little scared."

"Yeah, I guess that makes sense. But every day it's the same old thing, you know? I deliver newspapers, I go to school, I go to football practice, and I go home and try to stay out of everybody's way. Look, I graduate this year and go to college for four years. Then I get a nine-to-five job somewhere and then I'm sixty. I'm sixty years old, I'll probably die no more than ten miles from here, and I've accomplished nothing. There's gotta be more to life than just living."

Freddie threw his friend a puzzled look. "Hey," he said, "is this part of turning eighteen?"

"I don't know. It's just that I feel like I should be planning on doing something. Something more important than just hanging around waiting for something to happen. I just feel totally out of place. Guess I can thank my dad for a lot of that. It's just that I'll be an eighteen-year-old nobody and I really want to do SOMETHING!"

"Yeah, well, we all have our little egos, amigo," Freddie said. "We're all the center of our little worlds. But the reality is that Earth has three billion people all living in their own little worlds. That's a lot to stand out from if you feel you've got to do something important. I figure that's pretty much the deal with terrorists, you know. Big bangs get noticed. But there's lot going on out there, man. Look at the Internet. Voices are getting heard. Everybody has a stage on which to express their thoughts. I don't mean to go all philosophical on you here, but the world's a complicated place. We're all so connected that no event is isolated anymore. Something happens; it spreads all over the world in minutes. But, it's got to be sensational, like *bang*."

"I just want to do something that counts," Dylan said, "I mean, knocking one of my big bad-ass brother's boots into a puddle is sweet, but it isn't going to change my world. Maybe I've been reading too many books and playing too many video games with high drama. But you know, it's like I order a cream soda and they keep giving me a glass of tap water."

"Ah, the Metaphor Kid is on the loose again," Freddie laughed. "Man, born to be a writer."

The first class of the day was shop as well as Dylan and Freddie's homeroom. Dylan was still feeling philosophical. "No offense, Grease Monk," he said, "but just thinkin; twenty years from now where do you think you're going to be? You know, I see you with a wife, two-point four kids and you in your backyard auto repair shop under the hood of somebody's old Chevy. Seriously, man, is that a gasket you just pulled? You know, that's probably all right for you. I think you might even be happy with that. But don't you want more than spending your life under a car, listening to some goofy radio show. Oblivious to what's going on in the world outside. Work eight to ten hours, go inside, kiss the wife and two-point four kids, grab a beer, wolf down your meatloaf, watch another rerun of Two-and-a Half Men, then wash off the grease and hit the sack."

"Wow, Slick, you really make that sound kind of idyllic."

"Yeah, see what I mean. You're hopeless."

Freddie looks around to see if anyone is noticing, then stuffs a metric wrench and a couple of wires into a pants pocket.

"Really, Freddie. You're shop-lifting now?"

"Aw, c'mon. This is for a homework project. I do this all the time and bring the stuff back the next day. As for my future, don't sweat it. I'm good to go, man. I'm a simple guy with simple goals. Makes life simple, you know? Now you, you're turning eighteen tomorrow and you're starting to feel your age. Shoot, I remember when you were still looking for Camelot or something. Remember? You were always pretending to be King Arthur or Sir Lancelot or somebody. Then you kinda grew out of that and took on your James Bond persona or that old TV show, Highlander. You've always been somebody else rather than yourself. You know what I mean, Johnny Depp?"

"Huh?"

"Now you're sounding like my brother."

"Now me, I'm just me. But you do know that I can do a mean impersonation of Buddy Holly with a few Michael Jackson moves thrown in."

"Yeah, Greasy, you and your dead guys. Just so long as you don't give me your version of the Pee Wee Herman Tequila Dance. No matter. You're still my best bud."

"Best bud, blood brothers, Sir Samurai."

"Jeez, Freddie, you're the weirdest guy I've ever seen. But you're about the smartest too. You could build a Chevy engine with Legos, but you still forget your street address."

"Yeah, I resemble that remark," Freddie said, grinning. "But I remember the tree in our yard had ten thousand, three hundred and forty-eight leaves on it, so I never get lost. That is if I also calculate leave minuses accounting for weather, wind, bird activity...." Freddie continued mumbling his leaf counting variables as they entered into class.

As the morning classes ended, the two friends left for the lunchroom. Dylan bent over and picked up a small broken branch.

"I wish I could have been a great Barbarian warrior or like one of those Samurai guys in our video games." He made an imaginary sword thrust with the branch.

"Yeah? Well, maybe you ought to just join the Marines."

Dylan stopped walking. "Funny, but that's what my dad said this morning. The sooner I'm gone, the happier he's going to be."

"Aw, the sheriff is just a hard-ass. Don't let him get to you. He's been handing you that junk all your life."

Dylan closed his eyes, feeling the gentle breeze waft across his face. "I don't know what's going on, Freddie. I'm having those dreams that I'm flying and down below there's all these campfires burning. I'm waking up in the middle of the night with my heart racing. You ever feel like there's something big going to happen in your life and you don't know if it's good or bad? Just something profound."

Freddie laughed. "Yeah, every time I get the urge to whack off..."

"Oh, shut up! I'm serious!"

Sherry Parker strolled up. Sherry was a longhaired blue-eyed blonde cheerleader with a bubbling-over personality who had made a career of ignoring any boys other than senior star athletes. No letter jacket, no Sherry.

"Hi, Dylan." Sherry was bubbling in his direction.

Dylan's jaw dropped. His dark complexion and lean, hungry countenance had always attracted girls, but Sherry had never paid him any attention. But, oh yeah, he was slated to be a starting wide receiver on the football team this year. Hmmm.

"Uh-oh," Freddie hissed. "Looks like one of those profound moments to me."

"You want to meet at the Pizza Palace after practice?" Sherry bubbled.

"Sure, Sherry, that sounds great." Dylan cut his eyes over to Freddie daring him to make another remark.

"I'll just meet you there." Her blue eyes were shining. Dylan was beginning to bubble a little himself. Sherry put a little cheerleader move in her turn away and her short skirt flipped up. Dylan felt himself blush.

"Eighteen and I'm legal like a beagle hot on her trail, going to ring her bell," Dylan chimed to Freddie.

"Please don't do that," Freddie said. "I may be a nerd but you smell like a tur-"

Robert had walked up. He reached out, snatched the branch from Dylan's hand, and snapped it into two pieces. "Why it's the fairy Pink Flamingo Biker Wanta Be's Club."

"Whatever, Dylan just got a date with Sherry,' Freddie said.

Dylan's shoulders slumped and he closed his eyes.

"Hey, Sherry," Robert called out to her huddled up with her girlfriends, "Dylan says, he'll pick up you on his Schwinn. The only thrill you're gonna get is if the seat cushion falls off! *Ha, ha ha.*"

Sherry smiled, waved them off, and returned her huddle. The girls laughed.

"*Really*, Robert? I know you're abnormally bigger than I am," Dylan said, "but what's your problem? Why don't you go bully someone else with a forty IQ to appreciate your stupid jokes? I'm your brother. Remember? We're supposed to be on the same side."

"Oh, right. Gotcha, Bro." Robert turned his attention to Freddie, riveting him with his target practice stare. He reached into a jeans' pocket and pulled out an illegal switchblade. Freddie's face paled. Dylan couldn't believe what he was seeing. Robert pushed the button and the long blade snapped open, the metal glistening in the sunlight. Robert moved the knife so the light reflected into Freddie's face. "Think maybe I feel like whittling a little," he said, smirking. "I've heard bone makes a blade really sharp."

Freddie didn't back off an inch. "I'm not afraid of you, Robert," he said, his voice not quite convincing.

"Then you've just proved something impossible, geek; you're even dumber than you look. Let's see, if I make a move on you what are you gonna do? You gonna try some of that Sherlock Holmes movie stuff? You gonna visualize your moves in slo-mo? You going Matrix on me, Geek Boy? Well, let's see you visualize yourself out of this." He tossed the switchblade from one hand to the other and edged closer to Freddie.

"*Stop it!* Now!" Dylan's voice was angry and firm. "That's enough, Robert!"

Robert moved his menacing glare to Dylan and turned away from Freddie. "Okay, brother. But remember this; you may be older, but I'm bigger and meaner." He spit a white glob onto the ground, closed the switchblade, and began walking away. "See you at football practice" he said, more of a threat than a statement.

CHAPTER 5

ENGLISH CLASSROOM

Dylan heaved a huge sigh and felt the tension begin to fade away as he entered the English classroom. He liked and respected Mr. Jackson, only three years removed from college and possessor of a youthful passion for literature.

The class was studying Lord Byron and Shelley and Dylan loved it. There had been no television or even movies in the 1880s, but Byron and Shelley were the equivalent of movie stars in that era. Their poems were as epic as the blockbuster movies of more than a hundred years later.

Only the day before, Jackson had directed the class to read "Alastor", a poem written by Shelley relating to a young man who was attempting to find what his life was missing, visiting the "Eight Wonders of the World", and hoping to find "It." Whatever "It" was. Along the way, he took a nap beside the road and dreamed of a beautiful girl. Jackson began reading from that point:

"A vision in his sleep
There came, a dream of hopes that never yet
Had flushed his cheek. He dreamed a veiled maid
Sat near him, talking in low solemn tones.
Her voice was like the voice of his own soul
Heard in the calm of thought; its music long,
Like woven sounds of streams and breezes, held

71

His inmost sense suspended in its web
Of many-coloured woof and shifting hues.
Knowledge and truth and virtue were her theme,
And lofty hopes of divine liberty,
Thoughts the most dear to him, and poesy,
Herself a poet. Soon the solemn mood
Of her pure mind kindled through all her frame
A permeating fire; wild numbers then
She raised, with voice stifled in tremulous sobs
Subdued by its own pathos; her fair hands
Were bare alone, sweeping from some strange harp
Strange symphony, and in their branching veins
The eloquent blood told an ineffable tale.
The beating of her heart was heard to fill
The pauses of her music, and her breath
Tumultuously accorded with those fits
Of intermitted song. Sudden she rose,
As if her heart impatiently endured
Its bursting burthen: at the sound he turned,
And saw by the warm light of their own life
Her glowing limbs beneath the sinuous veil
Of woven wind, her outspread arms now bare,
Her dark locks floating in the breath of night,
Her beamy bending eyes, her parted lips
Outstretched, and pale, and quivering eagerly.
His strong heart sunk and sickened with excess
Of love. He reared his shuddering limbs and quelled
His gasping breath, and spread his arms to meet
Her panting bosom ... she drew back a while,
Then, yielding to the irresistible joy,
With frantic gesture and short breathless cry
Folded his frame in her dissolving arms.
Now blackness veiled his dizzy eyes, and night
Involved and swallowed up the vision;"

The young teacher paused, his breathing ragged. He had allowed himself to become caught up in the passion of the poetry and he struggled to regain his composure.

"Okay, anyone, can you tell me what Shelley was describing?"

Billy Hampton, a senior cut-up sitting in the rear of the classroom, raised his hand. "I'm not sure exactly, Mr. Jackson, but after hearing you read that, I think I need a cigarette."

While the class roared with laughter, Dylan opened his composition book and began sketching the raven he had seen in his dreams, using his imagination to give the bird a human face — a beautiful girl's face. It was a simple sketch, using a lead pencil. He gave her black hair and a pair of Angelina Jolie lips. As the sketch took shape, his heart began pounding with emotion. The girl's face was beautiful, but something wasn't quite right. He reached inside his backpack, took out a prismacolor pencil, and quickly gave the face a pair of startling blue eyes.

Mr. Jackson's voice brought him back to reality. "This isn't an art class, Dylan," the teacher said. "Now, what do you think Shelley was describing?"

Startled and embarrassed, Dylan flipped the composition book shut, drew a deep breath, and struggled to compose himself.

Dylan blurted out his thoughts quickly. "I think he's describing unconditional love. Love so deep that it can see all of you — your faults, your strengths — and still accept you for who you are. I think it's about someone who really gets you and who understands the poetry of your heart. I think it's kind of like being a lone raven that caws in the night and hears another raven answer."

Someone made a "caw caw."

Several snickers sounded around the classroom as Dylan glanced around the room. The guys were snickering and the girls looked at him trying to make eye contact.

"That's very poetic, Dylan. Maybe you were listening after all."

The final period ended and Dylan headed for the gym to dress for football practice. The first game of the season was coming up on Friday night; and, he was eager to begin his senior season. His speed and elusiveness made him an excellent wide receiver and an occasional running back. The focus today was on running offensive plays and working on the timing of pass plays and options.

Robert, of course, was already dressed and on the field. As soon as the players had completed their limbering up exercises, his younger, but much larger, Neanderthal brother grinned as they took their positions in formation for the first play. They lined up side by side for the play, which was designed to have Dylan fake taking a handoff, then cut outside for a quick-hitting pass from the quarterback. Robert's role as fullback was to spring Dylan free with a block on any player rushing in.

Robert was envious of his brother's growing role in the offense. He noticed that one of Dylan's shoelaces was coming untied and looping onto the grass, so Robert decided to mess up the play. Instead of coming off the count to block an onrushing defender, he sidestepped slightly and used his cleat to pin the shoelace as Dylan made his first move.

At the snap, Dylan exploded from his position and ran to the open spot, raising his hands to catch the pass, and then suddenly fell flat on his face as he tripped on the dangling lace. The football sailed out of bounds as the defensive players howled with laughter. Coach Mathis wasn't laughing, however.

"What the hell was that, Morgan? Did you fall out of bed this morning, too?"

"Sorry, Coach," the red-faced Dylan apologized. "Won't happen again." He glanced down and saw the loose lace, instantly realizing what his dumbass brother had done. On the sidelines, he saw Sherry and a couple of her cheerleading friends looking his way and laughing. "Great." The practice session ended without further incident and the still disgruntled Dylan headed for the locker room where he found a seat on a bench beside Freddie.

"Nice move on that first play," Freddie mocked. "What do you call that? A nose-dive in the flat?"

"One more word, Freddie, and you're a dead man."

"Okay, okay, I'm good. Say, ol' buddy, do you mind if I tag along with you to the Pizza Palace? Promise not to bug you. I'll just take my slice and my laptop to another table and leave the new lovebirds alone."

"Yeah, that's cool. Ain't no lovebirds gonna be there, though. Just sharing a pizza and some laughs." Dylan slapped Freddie on the shoulder pads and forced a smile. The smile died just as quickly a moment later as he saw Robert come into the locker room accompanied by their father. The sheriff often came by to watch his sons practice and even occasionally cheered a good play by Dylan. He was much more intrigued by the play of Robert, however, who played both offense and defense. The Spittin' Image was a fullback on offense and a linebacker on defense. He had made the all-conference defensive team as a sophomore and was being highly touted by his coaches for the coming season. Robert saw Dylan and whispered something to his father, who glanced at Dylan and then laughed.

Dylan saw red as he realized that Robert was telling the sheriff about the loose shoelace incident. "You did that!" he shouted, rising angrily from the bench. "I've had enough of your crap!"

Sheriff Morgan was still laughing, but Robert was taken aback by the look on his brother's face.

Dylan walked right up against Robert and grabbed a handful of the bigger boy's jersey, yanked it up under his chin and slammed him against the row of lockers. The impact sounded like a gun going off. The other players looked on in amazement. They had never seen the mild-mannered Dylan in a rage before.

Sheriff Morgan grabbed Dylan and separated his sons. "Whoa!" he said. "Back off, boy. Hey, Robbie was only pulling a friendly little joke on you."

Robert said nothing. He just stood there, wearing a leering grin.

Dylan loosened his grip on the jersey and stepped back. "Yeah," he said. "I'm really feeling the love." He turned his back on his brother and father and returned to the bench beside Freddie. Sheriff Morgan and Robert turned and left the locker room.

"Okay, what was that all about?" Freddie asked.

'What was what about?" Dylan replied. "You didn't see anything happen. Seriously, that stupid brother of mine tripped me up on that first play. He's such a zero."

"Dang," Freddie said, trying to suppress a grin. "I wondered what happened there. I thought you were taking a new course in face-planting."

"Okay, wise guy, have your laugh. It's just that Robert is such a dork. I think he stays awake nights trying to think of something to tick me off. What I want to know is whatever happened to brotherly love? I swear I think Robert hates me. And my dad is just about as bad. Did you see them laughing at me?"

"Yeah, nothing like that good ol' brotherly love thing," Freddie said, sarcasm dripping from every word.

The boys finished dressing into their street clothes and walked outside. In the parking lot, Robert and Sherry Parker, the bubbling cheerleader, were engaged in conversation. Robert glanced back, saw

Dylan coming, and casually slid an arm around Sherry's waist. They continued walking to where Robert's Harley-Davidson was parked and Robert handed the girl the passenger helmet. Sherry laughed, tossed her mane of blonde hair, and climbed onto the back of the motorcycle. The short cheerleader's skirt showed off her tanned legs. Robert revved the powerful engine; and, as he made a turnout of the parking lot, he slipped Dylan the middle finger.

"Crap!" Dylan said under his breath. A few parking spaces away, Sheriff Spencer Morgan climbed into his patrol car, a wide grin on his face. Ol' Robert had struck again. "That boy is all mine," the sheriff smirked as he pulled away.

Freddie could tell by the look on Dylan's face that this was not the right time to make a smart remark. "Wow," he finally muttered. "What a class act. He probably told Sherry that you were standing her up. I think you're right, Bro. I think this guy really hates you. Why do you think he's like that?"

"Don't worry about it," Dylan said, trying to hide the disappointment of losing some quality time with his favorite cheerleader. "I think its inherited behavior. I like Sherry, but if she's that easy for Robert to distract, she's not my kind of girl.

"Actually, I'm kind of favoring those black-haired beauties these days anyway," he said, throwing his buddy a smile. "If you could see some of the dreams I've been having lately, you'd understand why. Man, it's like this raven comes to me and we go flying together. But then she's not really a bird; she morphs into this beautiful girl and I can feel this Great Spirit inside her. I get this sense that she really cares for me; that we're soul mates."

Freddie stopped walking and gave his friend a serious look. Then he burst out laughing. "Man, I never know when you're putting me on anymore. If you're talking serious, then I'm talking about being seriously worried about you. Yeah, I cannot wait to hear what the school shrink tells you about these dreams you're having. Jesus! I thought I was the one who needed a girlfriend!"

"Seriously man, like the other night. I had a dream of flying and following a blackbird. I woke up in the middle of the night. I went to the window to get some fresh air and there must have been fifty or more perched in the oak tree. I swear they were looking at me. It's weird. They all were watching me. But what freaked me out was, when I stepped to the side it's like all their heads moved at once."

"Dude, I'm going to start calling you bird brain. You and the ravens."

"Shut up, Freddie," Dylan said. "You've got no idea what I'm talking about." He pulled the composition book from his backpack and showed Freddie the sketch he had drawn in Mr. Jackson's class. "Look, this is what she looks like. When Mr. Jackson was reading that Shelley poem, I saw the soul of it and this is what it looked like."

"Uh, you ever see her, Bro? Do you talk to her?"

"I'm not crazy. It's more of a feeling really. Of all people, I thought you'd understand." Dylan sighed.

Freddie knew when to back off. "Yeah, well, you artists see things in a whole different way than us mortals," he said, trying to lighten the mood. "You're a romantic … a Don Juan Samurai. Actually, you are more like raven mad. Get that? Raven mad. Anyway, ol' pal, happy pre-birthday to you, Birdman. I'm outta here. Caw! Caw!"

Dylan flipped his best friend a quick bird.

"See, there you go with the birds again," Freddie grinned.

"Ohhhhh," Dylan groaned. The boys mounted their bikes and pedaled until Freddie turned off on to the street that led to his home. Dylan executed a quick U-turn, and pedaled a mile to the Farmer's Market located on Main Street.

"That's all?" the clerk asked the boy as he placed the ear of corn on the counter. "One ear?"

"Yeah, thanks," Dylan gave the clerk a dollar, pocketed the forty cents in change, and walked back to his bike. He used the quarter to pry a few kernels from the ear of corn and placed them in his pocket. He tossed the ear of corn across the road, got back on his bike, and headed home. It suddenly dawned on him that he had no idea why he had just done this. "That was weird." He shrugged it off and turned his bike toward home. He was suddenly ravenous. Hunger had a way of redirecting thoughts. He was homeward bound.

CHAPTER 6

DYLAN'S BEDROOM

Dylan was lying on his bed poring over his world history homework when his mother knocked on the open door. Sally Morgan was still a young woman, only eighteen years older than Dylan, who had been born when she was sixteen and still in high school. Blonde hair, blue eyes with a still attractive body that belied her 34 years of age.

Dylan motioned for her to come in and she stood by the bed. "Well, tomorrow's the big day," she said, flashing the smile that he loved but saw all too seldom. "Eighteen years old. My baby's all grown up."

"You got the baby part right," Robert said from the hallway. "What you doing, Mom? Changing his diaper?"

Dylan ignored his brother. "Thanks, Mom."

Mrs. Morgan held out a hand and opened it to reveal a necklace with a half-moon attached to the chain. "This is something that's very special to me," she said. "This represents the unfilled dreams that I hope will one day come true for you, son."

Dylan held the chain in his palm and ran a finger along the jagged edge of the moon. It was heavy in his hand for something so small. "It's beautiful, Mom. Can I wear it now?"

"Of course you can. Let me help you fasten it. I am giving it to you early because it has so much meaning for me. I want it to be special."

"Thanks, Mom. It is special. I'll never take it off."

There was a calm sadness on Mrs. Morgan's lovely face. "This was given to me when I was younger than you," she said, holding out her hand and letting the chain uncoil to reveal two round silver pieces, one half covering the other. The upper piece was a deep black and covered half of the lower piece. Slots in the metal allowed the halves to move, covering or uncovering the other half.

"There's a piece missing, though," his mother continued. "It's built so that when both pieces are moved together, the dark halves are hidden and only the silver ones show. The meaning is that without each other, your hearts are dark. And when you're joined together, everything is complete with the light of joy. I've always imagined that the pieces are moons."

Dylan's eyes widened with a sudden realization, "Mom, did that boy in high school — Albert something — did he give you this?"

She glanced nervously over shoulder to the hallway, then pressed the medallion next to her heart. "He did," she said in a low voice. "I want you to promise me that when you find that right girl, you'll have a jeweler make the other half and give it to her. I want this to represent your unfulfilled dream that I know will come true for you," her mouth trembled and her eyes glistened with tears as she took Dylan's hand and placed the charm in his palm.

"I don't know what to say." It was not just the weight of the piece but also the emotion of it that coursed through the skin of his palm, up his arm, and straight to the heart. "I promise I will."

"Here," his mother took the chain and medallion from Dylan's hand, placed it around his neck, and fastened the clasp.

Dylan could feel the intense emotions raging in his mother. His heart went out to her. "Mom, what happened? If you two loved each other so much why didn't it work out?" he asked. She raised her face with her eyes closed. Her fingers touched her bottom lip as though remembering a kiss from so long ago.

"I don't know," she said, the remark sounding almost like a question. "We were supposed to meet at the bus stop on the highway. Oh God, I was so young and naïve. I had two grocery bags full of clothes and about thirty dollars in my purse. I was wearing my prettiest Sunday dress. Blue. Curled my hair that morning. I wanted to be beautiful for him."

"And he never showed?" Dylan asked.

"No," she answered, sniffing. "Never saw him or heard a word from him after that." She drew a deep breath. "I just stood there by the road. A couple of guys rode by and honked but I just ignored them. I just stood there. I just knew Albert was going to come. Then the bus came and Albert still had not shown up. The driver opened the door and I remember him asking, "Miss? Miss? You coming on board?" All I could do was shake my head. When those doors closed it was like the prison doors of life clanging together, shutting off my dreams forever."

Dylan leaned his head down. "I'm sorry, Mom."

"It's okay, sweetheart. For an hour after the bus left, I just stood there. It started raining; and, a few minutes later your dad drove up and told me to get in the car. I knew him very well, of course, although he was a few years older than I was. He had been asking me out for a long time, but I wasn't interested. Plus my parents said he was too old for me to date anyway. I was only 15, you know, and I was true to Albert. I didn't answer him. I just stood there. Oh, yes… I was wearing a little blue hat too. I remember that now. It was the first time I think I ever wore it outside of church. The rain ruined it. Spencer waited a few minutes, then got out, took my arm and put me into his car. I started crying then, must have cried for an hour, and Spencer just kept driving around, waiting for me to get control of myself." Sally reached out and placed a hand on Dylan's shoulder.

"I think something broke inside of me that day, son. Had it not been for Spencer's kindness and his family taking me in, I probably would have died in some alley that night."

"And you couldn't go back home?"

"When I was leaving, I told my father that I was going away with Albert. He got really angry. He was ranting and raving. He said if I walked out that door, I would never find it open again. So, I never went back."

"I'm really sorry, Mom." Dylan hugged her around the waist. She placed a hand on his head.

"You're a man now, Dylan. I know Spencer and Robert have been pretty awful with you. However, you just keep being strong. The moment you were born, I felt there was something very special about you. You were born with your eyes open; and, the first thing I said when I saw you was, 'He's going to change the world.' "

80

"Well, I'm not feeling very significant these days", Dylan said, feeling frustrated. "The problem is that I have no idea what I want to do. I'm in my last year of high school and I'm a lost soul. I know I love to read, write, and do art, but I don't know what I want to do with my life."

"You're young," his mother said. "There's plenty of time. Follow your heart, Dylan. Just do not end up like me. Be true to yourself. " She squeezed his shoulder. "There's something I must tell you tomorrow, sweetheart. I've waited eighteen years to tell you."

"What?" Dylan turned to face her. "Tell me what?"

"If I can wait eighteen years, you can wait a night," she said, her voice teasing. "Get some sleep. You have a big day tomorrow." She opened the door and glanced back over her shoulder, showing a sad smile.

"Oh, that's so not fair, Mom. I'll be wondering about it all night."

"Tomorrow, young man. Goodnight," She blew him a kiss and shut the door.

As soon as the door closed, Dylan hopped out of bed and stood before the dresser, staring at the medallion round his neck. "Two moons make one. Okay, where are you, my Alastor?" He moved to the window and stood there for a moment, then slowly raised it, feeling the cool air against his skin. He sighed, drew in a deep breath, and stared at the bright moon. The full moon's glow highlighted parts of the old oak only a few yards away. The tree was a beautiful creation with its branches reaching for the sky, but sometimes — like this night —when the light created shadows and a gentle breeze moved the branches within the crown, it could appear a little sinister. As a child, Dylan had dreamed that the branches of the oak were inching their way toward the window. He had watched the scenario many nights with an eerie fascination. As he waited for the long, bony fingers of the branches to wrap around his body and pull him outside into the bowels of the tree, he would have to fight the urge to scream for his parents.

He had outgrown those childish fears, of course, and no longer felt threatened by the tree. Or had he? He shivered and forced a smile. *Hey, I love trees. Almost all of my paintings have trees. What's wrong with me? Am I still seeing boogeymen?*

Returning to bed, Dylan tried to fall asleep. He stared at the constellations of stars he had placed on his bedroom ceiling a few years earlier and once again began trying to count them. That task was easier now than it had been when he first installed them. At least half of them had faded out and disappeared. Movement at the window caught his attention and he watched as the shadows crept across the glass and into the room. With his eyes slightly closed, he was just about to drift off to sleep when a quick movement outside the pane startled him awake.

Tap. Tap. Tap.

"Dylan."

Tap. Tap. Tap.

"Dylan."

Dylan blinked his eyes and strained to hear what the bird was saying.

"Dylan."

Sliding out of bed, he walked barefoot to the window.

"Come," the raven said, beckoning with its head for him to move closer.

"Hey, who are you? You're not Ravenous, but you have blue eyes too. And we can't be talking?" Dylan said aloud." I mean, I don't hear you. I'm imagining this!" Dylan raised the window, opened the outer weatherproof pane, and leaned closer to the raven, who showed no fear from his presence. He stared into the startling blue, probing eyes and sensed an intelligence that surprised him.

"Caw!" The raven lifted in the air. "Come with me."

"Sure. You want me to hop on? I can't fly. And you can't talk."

"Yes, you can. Yes I am. In dreams, you can. Come. She waits. "

"Who?"

"She waits."

"Who?"

The raven shook its head no as a sign of impatience and came back to the ledge. "Tired. Long way. You must see her. Ark! Too late! Too bad. Must go now." The bird actually sighed and shrugged its shoulders, then suddenly perked up.

"Say, do you have the corn?" The raven beat its wings and hovered by the window.

"The corn? Huh? Wait. How do you know about the corn?"

"Ark! Talk too much. Weary. Dreary." The bird's voice was a half croak, half-human squawk. *"Corn. Now. Ark!"*

Dylan, moving as in a trance, picked up a kernel of corn from the top of the desk. Then he tossed it to the bird who caught the corn in its beak.

"This is crazy," Dylan said aloud. He cautiously cranked the window open as wide as it could go and then pulled himself into a crouching position on the ledge, holding on to the window to keep from losing his balance.

"Crazy. Crazy. Crazy. I'm going to break my frickin neck for my birthday." For the first time he noticed another raven perched on the ledge to his left. It was Ravenous. Ravenous with the same glow-blue eyes like the Raven he had just given the corn to. He reached out and stroked Ravenous' head.

"Alastor," Ravenous croaked.

"What? At last her? What did you say?" Dylan was awestruck.

"Look," the other bird said. "Look at me."

Dylan looked at the raven.

"Close eyes."

"Seriously? I'm on a ledge."

"Close eyes."

"I'm going to bed," Dylan started to get back in.

"*ARK! EYES! CLOSE!*

"Shhhhhhh! Alright. Okay." Dylan scooted back around, holding tight to the window frame, his legs dangling over the side, and closed his eyes.

"Open," the raven said.

Dylan opened his eyes. He gasped but it sounded like a croak. Suddenly he was no longer in his body. He was looking at his own body, sleep walking back to his bed. Was this an out of body experience? *OhMiGod!!...No! I got claws. Feathers?! What's happened?*

"In bird," the raven answered.

"What?" Dylan hopped around and saw his Ravenous self with glowing blue eyes staring back at him. *I'm looking through Ravenous' eyes. OhMiGod! OhMiGod!*

"Come on. Don't just sit there. Fly. You know, spread, and flap. You can do it."

This is nuts. This is a dream. Do it. You've flown in dreams before. Yeah, bodiless. OhMiGod! Do it. Just do it. It's just a dream, right? Right?!

Dylan dropped from the ledge and flapped furiously. *I'm flying!*

There was a sudden sensation of being airborne although he could see his body on the bed. It was an eerie feeling as he realized he was no longer in his body. He was floating, rising above the trees and the houses while seeing the world below through the raven's eyes. He risked a glance to the side and caught a glimpse of a large black wing. *His wing! Jesus! I'm a bird! I'm flying!*

"I'm crazy!"

"Caw!"

Dylan turned to look at the raven who was acting as his escort. The bird was flying easily, flapping its wings leisurely, seemingly without effort. *Okay, let's try this wing-flapping thing and see what happens. Wow! That's pretty cool.*

The raven began to climb higher into the darkness of the night; and, Dylan followed, flapping his wings and veering to miss the electrical wires. *Gotta stay focused. Don't hit the wires. Stay with the raven. Oh my God, I'm flying! I'm flying! There's my street down there. Wow!*

The raven continued to climb and Dylan followed, working his wings until he was able to keep an even pace. He glanced at the terrain below and realized he was being led away from the neighborhood. The raven quickened the pace, and then went into a glide before beginning to flap its wings again.

Flap…glide…flap…glide. They rose higher into the sky. Dylan could tell they were heading west. His heart was pounding with excitement. They were so high now that if his wings should fail and he fell, he knew that he would die.

The bright stars formed patterns in the sky. Lights from the houses and streets below him were beginning to look like stars. He felt as though he was blanketed between two layers of star. Even with all this excitement, in the back of his mind, he hoped that he would be returning back to his own body at the end of this adventure. However, that wasn't important now. He was flying. He was free.

As he soared higher, he could feel the temperature variations and how they affected his flight, creating slight rises and falls. For the first time he understood what all the fuss about riding a motorcycle was about. The total sense of freedom! But riding a Harley couldn't really be like this!

Feeling more confident by the minute, Dylan felt a new breeze and attempted a rollover. It was exhilarating and he felt no dizziness. The move had cost him some speed, however, so he had to flap his wings to catch up with the speeding raven. They had flown for miles when Dylan realized that he had gained a distinct sense of direction. He knew that they were flying northwest. Far below, a major highway formed an artery with the cars flowing like glowing cells. Night flying was dangerous.

The raven climbed again with Dylan following. At this elevation, it was easier to glide which allowed them to travel much faster. The slightest flex of a wing or his neck was enough to change direction. It was if they were sailing in a sea while the moon rising on the eastern horizon appeared as a new click mark on his inner navigational system.

The raven came to an abrupt halt, apparently buoyed on an updraft, and turned its head toward Dylan. "Caw! Up ahead! Come on!" Then it flapped its wings and surged ahead.

A mountain loomed ahead with a grouping of small fires that emitted richly chromatic flames. Dylan turned to follow the bird and had to make a couple of strong flaps to keep up with the new pace. As he drew alongside the raven, it spoke to him inside his head: *Remember, key is vibration. Say nev- ...*

The screaming, white-gray thing came out of nowhere. The glaring eyes were wild with a crazed intensity and black rage. It emitted a crazed *EEEEEEEEEEEEEEEE*! Dylan threw his tail of feathers forward to brake his flight and felt a burning pain in his left wing as the assailant's talons tore into his shoulder/wing. The attack whipped him around in mid-air and the talons from the other foot were poised to send their needle-like points into his chest.

"Back home! Go! GO! *GO!*" the black raven cried.

Dylan's left wing burned from the injury, but he forged ahead.

"*EEEKKKKK*!" The white raven flew at the black one but missed the quickly shifting target. Dylan increased his wing beat in an effort to go faster, speeding over the treetops.

"*EEKKKK*!" This time the white raven's claw grabbed the black raven's shoulder, but lost its grip because of its momentum. The black raven appeared to lose its rhythm momentarily, but then regained it quickly. *"HURRY! GO NORTH THEN ZIG TO SOUTH. HEAD HOME!"* the raven's cry echoed in Dylan's head.

There. My house. I see my house. There's my window. I can see me!

"*EEEEEEEK*!" The white raven thrust upward, its beak pointed straight for the underbelly of Ravenous.

"Cawwww!" The other black raven entered the battle, striking the attacking bird from the back and sending the three of them into a downward spiral. Dylan was flung out of the tumble, swirling round and round and …

A wild-eyed Dylan was sitting up in his bed, hands grasping at air as if to keep himself from falling. *Rap-rap-rap.* The black raven at the window struck the pane so hard with its beak that a fleck of glass broke away. Ravenous was still in the room. The window was closed. Ravenous flew to the window. There was a flurry at the window and the white raven appeared, seizing the black one from behind and yanking the bird back. Ravenous jumped back. The black raven broke free enough to peck at the glass again, leaving a drop of blood on the pane. It was holding a white twig in its beak.

When the attacking bird locked its talons into the black raven's wing, it managed to drop the twig onto the window ledge. The birds locked their talons into each other and battled, wings flapping violently, talons ripping at flesh as they rose to more than a hundred feet. Still locked in the death struggle, they had drifted away from the house and were over the fence separating the property from the street when they began to fall. The black raven forced itself above the white and began furiously beating it wings, creating as much down-thrust as possible. The fence, with its deadly sharp prongs along the top to ward off intruders, rushed at them. At the last second, the white raven rolled over, forcing the black one underneath it, and then used its wings to pin the other's wings as they hit the top of the fence. The speed of the fall and the weight of the two birds were enough to send the metal prongs plunging into the chest of the black raven. There was a shrill shriek from the dying bird and the white raven released its grip and flew back to the window.

Ravenous shrieked and struck the window.

"Oh, no," Dylan cried, pushing the window up. Ravenous escaped.

"Wait! You could get attacked."

Ravenous landed on the fence between the prongs by the impaled black raven.

Dylan wheeled around and slammed right into his father.

"What the hell is going on?" He was standing in his underwear, barefoot, and holding his pistol by his side.

"Birds, Dad. Fighting."

"At midnight?" He slid the windowpane up higher, sticking his head out the window. "Good, damn bird. Crucified."

Dylan stepped back as his father shut the window and left the room mumbling. When he heard his father's bedroom door shut, Dylan looked out the window and saw Ravenous nudging the raven on the fence as though checking for life. When there was no response, Ravenous flew to the lower branch of the oak tree and hunched down.

"Sorry." Dylan whispered, and then laid back in bed, closing his eyes. His eyes opened. *Wait. Was I dreaming? No. Ravenous was with me in the room. I let him out. Did you? Maybe I was dreaming until Dad woke me. But I was at the window.*

Gasping, he placed a hand to his chest and felt his heart pounding. The cool flow from the air conditioning vent made him shiver. He noticed that his body was covered with a sheen of perspiration.

Something had wakened him. There had been a noise at the window. He wondered if he had not awakened if he might have died from the fall he was experiencing. Wasn't that what they said about dreams? If you don't wake up before you hit the ground, you die? He got out of bed and went to the window. He felt the chips from the bird's beak. Wow! He noticed the drop of raven's blood on the pane and then saw the white twig on the ledge. He reached out and took it in his hand.

Dylan opened the window and stuck his head out. The black raven was impaled on the fence. He jerked back when he saw the white raven back on the fence. It rose its head and looked toward him. . Even though they were yards apart, Dylan felt pure malice from this bird. Its eyes were black as coals, contrasting with its white feathers. Its eyes reflected light back like eyes sometimes do in a photograph. Or, did that glow come from within? The way it lifted its head and looked directly at him, it reminded him of that creepy scene in the movie "The Shining" when Jack Nicholson is looking out the window with his face tilted downward and his eyes upward. That was pure evil, one-hundred percent devil-stamped and certified. It had the power to hold his gaze. It had attacked him in his dream. Or was it a dream? Was all this real? Was he dreaming now?

The raven that had spoken to him in the dream ... the one that had led him to the village on the mountain, had been impaled One hundred percent murdered.

The white raven suddenly shot into the air straight for Dylan. Instinctually Dylan quickly slammed the window shut. The raven's claws struck the glass. Its eyes were a clear bright reddish. *Tear Light out of you!*

"EEEEKKK!"

The white raven was suddenly pressed against the glass as Ravenous attacked it from behind, trying to pin the bird against the pane. Dylan knew Ravenous needed help. He grabbed for the pencil on his desk and lifted the window up, intending to stab it into the white demon's chest.

However, before he could get the window open, the white raven pushed off with its talons. Then it grasped Ravenous' claw with its beak and slammed the smaller bird against the window ledge.

"Nooooo!" Dylan cried as the white raven reared its head back to drive its beak through Ravenous' heart. He threw the window up, striking the large white raven and banging his own head on the windowsill at the same time.

"God!"

"EEEEKKK!" The white raven shrieked and flew into the woods as Ravenous quietly flew circles in front of the window.

Dylan ran downstairs to his father's office. He searched for the keys in the desk drawer and then opened the gun cabinet. Next he grabbed a 12-gauge shotgun, and then fumbled with two shells from a box in the bottom drawer. He slapped the shotgun together and bolted for the backdoor. The night was silent. Crickets were chirping. Frogs were croaking. Several fireflies appeared to the left and moved toward the fence where Dylan saw the black raven on its back, wings spread, dead. And perched on the fence beside the raven was Ravenous. It nudged the dead raven several times then lifted its head and made a long, low, "caaaaauuuuuuaaahhhhh," sound. It was the saddest cry of emotion that Dylan had ever heard.

A window opened from above. "What the hell? What's going on now, boy?" Sheriff Morgan shouted from above in his underwear.

"Birds at it again. I scared them off this time."

"Damn birds. Next time just shoot the bastards. Tired of them eating the garden."

"Yeah, okay." Dylan turned his attention back to the fence and saw that Ravenous had flown away. He walked to the fence, stillhearing the dead bird's voice in his head. It had been a friend and had wanted him to do something. *She was waiting… key in the vibration…????*

At last her….????

Alastor?

She waits.

Alastor??? He was saying Alastor. Oh, God, I'm not telling even Freddie about this one.

He stared at the lifeless raven. *You'll never fly again.* A gentle breeze stirred the bird's feathers. Dylan removed his tee shirt, pulled the raven free from the fence, and wrapped the shirt around it. I'll bury you in the morning. He knew he couldn't take the bird inside, but didn't want to leave it on the ground either. He spotted an old beer cooler that his dad had left on the porch, placed the raven in it, and closed the lid.

Back in his room, Dylan was pulling a clean tee shirt over his head when he noticed the pain in his arm. He stood before the mirror and curiously examined the two reddening puncture-like wounds on his shoulder. *My wing, not my arm. In my dream, not here. Didn't happen here.* His mind raced trying to recall if he might have suffered the injuries during the scuffle at the window. That had to be the answer. *You just don't wake up with injuries from dreams.*

Maybe it hadn't been a dream. Maybe it was real? Oh man, this is really freaking me out! Dylan laid down in the bed, turned off the bed lamp, and then turned it back on. He closed his eyes. A moment passed. He opened his eyes again. Looking at the ceiling, he brought his hands up and tried to make a bird shadow. *What am I doing?* He turned and pulled a pillow over his head. *"Ouch!"*

CHAPTER 7

SKYEDEN: SHABAEL'S OBSERVATORY

"Wake! Wake up, Master! The Light comes, Milord. We must destroy it! The tree lives. The bird must die or all is lost!"

"*CAW!!*" White talons tore into black feathers. The black raven shrieked, contorted its body to gain leverage, and struck back. Using its own talons, the black raven ripped into the attacking white raven.

"*Nooo!*" the white raven screamed. "*I will not die! Will not!*" Nevertheless, the force of the black raven's counterattack was fierce; and, the white was driven back as the two birds, locked in a death struggle, plummeted earthward. The black raven was controlling the downward flight, guiding the two birds locked in mortal combat toward the fence below. The fence's metal prongs were coming at them at what seemed the speed of sound.

"*No! I will not die!*" the white raven screeched again, and with a mighty effort thrust its body to the left, pumped its powerful wings for impetus and released the black raven at the moment of impact. The black raven was impaled on the fence with a metal prong ripping into the bird's breast.

Looking up, the white raven saw the young man at the window, and then noted the white twig in his hand.

"*The twig! Get the twig!*"

King Shabael sat upright, his eyes glaring, nostrils flaring. His face was starkly pale as if the blood had drained from it. In fact, blood was draining from his cheek and he placed a hand to the cut.

"Ahhh!"

"Milord!" Shabael's wife, Shawndeli, wakened to his cry and reached for his bloodied hand, pulling it from his face in order to discover what was causing the bleeding. She saw the cut in his cheek and screamed for the guards who posted outside the bedroom door.

Two semi-armored guards rushed into the chambers. Upon seeing their king with blood on his face and hands, they began a frantic search of the room for the attacker. Nothing. Nobody. Nothing out of place. The window was secure. Within seconds, the concern on their faces was replaced with questioning looks. They glanced at each other, then at the queen. There was obviously no one else in the chambers. Their eyes moved to the queen's hands and then back to each other as they saw the blood.

The queen was sitting up in the bed with one arm covering her bare breasts. Shabael glared at the guards and pulled the sheet up to cover his wife. "Get off the bed," he said to her. After she was standing on the floor, he ripped the coverlets from the bed and threw the large pillows to the floor. He continued glaring at the puzzled guards and snarled, "Summon a healer! Now!"

One of the guards left to obey the order while the other remained in the bedroom, still unsure of what he should do.

"I don't understand," the queen murmured. "What has happened? And how?"

Shabael ignored his wife and moved to one of the windows, checking the bolts that the guards had checked only moments before. With his forehead furrowed in thought, he turned and placed his right hand to the facial wound.

"The Priest Highest! Now! Bring him here now!" he bellowed to the remaining guard. The guard hesitated, wondering if he should leave the king and queen alone. However, the withering look on Shabael's face melted his resistance and he quickly left the bedroom.

There was movement at the door. Queen Shawndeli motioned for the guard returning with the healer to enter. She was a middle-aged woman with eyes so black they were impenetrable. She had been in her mid-fifties when she had Descended almost a thousand years earlier. Therefore, she would remain in that stage forever or as long as the Malbolians controlled the Light. Her black eyes were a trademark of the healer's profession. Over time, the absorbing of the injuries that she treated had caused her irises to change gradually from the normal pink to black. The woman was carrying a cage with two black ravens inside.

"Healer Janessa," Shabael said, "I need your services." He moved across the room to a huge chair and sat down, raising his face so that the woman could see the wound on his cheek.

"I live to serve," she intoned. The woman's hair was braided into one huge ponytail that hung down her back. She was dressed in a grayish-white robe that bore the emperor's crest. Tiny bells were woven into the braids of her hair as well as into the tassels hanging from her belt, the hem of her robe and from the bottom of the long sleeves. Each bell was believed to be attuned to a specific tone and vibration. The muted sounds were part of the aura surrounding the woman and the magic she created. She also emanated an aroma of mysterious herbs and spices that proved almost intoxicating. Her presence lingered for hours after she had departed a room.

Before being recognized as a healer, Janessa had been labeled a witch. A very powerful witch. She had become a healer by judicial order. This came about when Janessa the Witch had been accused in a plot to kill Shabael's mother, the Queen Mother. The story was that the Queen Mother was having an illicit affair with a councilman; and, the councilman's wife had hired Janessa to cast a fatal spell on the queen.

The king was furious, not at the queen or the councilman, because he knew that no man, especially a loyal councilman, would dare commit such an offense against his emperor. The king's wrath was instead directed at the offended wife and the witch. The wife was executed at a public beheading. Janessa the Witch was given the ultimatum of having her own head removed or transforming her powers to healing. Therefore, it was that overnight the kingdom lost a witch but gained a healer.

It was determined to be only a coincidence a few weeks later when the accused councilman was discovered to have been attacked by thieves and left hanging from a tree where he had bled to death after having a lower appendage surgically removed.

Shabael watched the healer with curiosity as she went about her rituals. There were times in the past when he had thought he had caught a flash of insolence or perhaps mischief in the woman's eyes. But through the years, he had never seen any evidence of ill intent during her healing functions. Whatever the woman had been, she was obviously now leashed, or bridled, as it were. The bells on her clothing and the mysterious aromas seemed to dull one's senses and make one feel privileged that she was granting her presence and services.

King Shabael would never admit it, even to himself, but there were times when he found himself sexually stimulated by Janessa's presence. There had been a number of times when he felt he wasn't alone in this feeling as he detected a flirtation in her methods.

Janessa gently touched Shabael's cheek and asked, "The source of this affliction, Sire?" The little bells on her sleeves tinkled and her scent made Shabael's nostrils flare. She noticed and gave him an inquiring look.

"It happened in a dream," he said, his voice low and guttural. "A black raven in a dream."

The strange black eyes widened just a bit. "Not just a black raven," she said, and turned to the guards and queen. "I must ask you to step out of the chamber. Forgive me, Emperor, but I feel this discussion should be between us alone."

Shabael nodded. "Do as she asks." He reached a hand to his face and ran his fingers over the wound. There was pain, but nothing abnormal.

"It was not just a black raven," Janessa said after the others had left the room and the door was closed behind them. "This came from a raven tainted with Light." She touched the wound with her fingers. "I can feel the heat inside. Even with my powers, I cannot heal you immediately. This will take longer to heal than an ordinary wound. I will heal you, but I need to know; where is the Orb of Light?"

The eagerness in the woman's voice cautioned Shabael.

"As I said, this happened in a dream."

"And where did this dream take place?"

The impudence of the healer irritated Shabael. "I don't know where," he said. "In my bed, of course." His heart was suddenly racing. He forced a quick smile and reached to touch the wound again. Had the scent of the woman suddenly changed? Something was different, stirring his senses. The aroma was a mixture of ginger and cinnamon mixed with an odor he was unable to identify. The scent was strong, almost overpowering, and it made him emit a small gasp.

He was conscious of his breathing causing the scent to enter his body; and, he felt a slight wooziness.

Janessa arched an eyebrow and withdrew her hand from his cheek for a moment. She went to the door and motioned to one of the guards, "Place the cage on the table here." The two ravens were hunkered down in the back of the cage, obviously frightened. The healer opened the cage door and turned back to Shabael.

The healer walked in a small circle around the Emperor. She stopped facing south. "Come ye dark, Come from South to here. Protect us Dark Creator. Bring forth your healing essence." Lifting her hands, the tiny bells tingled. She turned to the north, and then west, and last to the east, chanting the same lines. After the four directions were covered, she turned to face Shabael.

"Dark flow into my hands, inter your healing powers" The ravens grew silent. They appeared frightened and tucked their heads beneath their wings.

Janessa stepped toward Shabael. She lifted her pale hand and lightly touched the wound on his face.

"*OUT LIGHT! INTO THE RAVENS!*" Her voice thundered in the room. Releasing her hand from Shabael's face, she made a throwing motion toward the Ravens. One of the birds shrieked, sounding like shattering glass by a dagger.

"Ah!" Shabael flinched.

"Again! Dark power come mend the flesh and cleanse the blood. Heal your Descended, Creator, and demonstrate your overpowering love for your humble servants. Mend our Emperor El Qui. Grant unto him your healing powers. Where Light, dark show Let it be so! *OUT!*"

As Janessa spoke, she used her hands to make pulling motions from the wound on Shabael's face, pulling as one would on a rope, hand over hand. She was struggling with the affliction while pulling it from the king's body. With one final effort, she used both hands to pull. The healer then turned to the open door of the cage holding the ravens and flung the invisible offender inside.

The raven remained cowered in the back of the cage. Janessa frowned.

"I was correct," she said, turning to Shabael. Her black eyes even darker. "This is not a simple injury. It is Light-tainted and the healing process will take time. All that I can release has been done. It will heal because I have removed the taint, but you must be patient."

Shabael stared at the woman. He wanted to strike her. Yet at the same time, he wanted to pull her to him in an embrace. He fought the conflicting emotions. He wanted her to go. He was drunk by her aroma and exhilarated by the rush of Dark energy, then literally deflated when she cast the energy back out and hurled it at the remaining Raven. But she was right; the energy of Light was still in his wound. It stung like salt in the open wound.

"Thank you, Witch," he finally said, reaching out a hand to touch her arm. Janessa reacted by placing her hand on his. It amused her that he called her witch rather than healer. This was his way of showing endearment.

"Shabael," she said, stretching the syllables of his name as a chef might in reminiscing over an especially delicious course. She stared into his eyes and knew the fragrances of her special herbs were working on him. When she reached out to simply touch his injured cheek lightly, she knew he was seduced and had she picked her nose, it would had aroused him. In his eyes, he was seeing her as exotic, beautiful, and seductive. She leaned forward with her lips slightly touching his earlobe and screamed, "*Aye!!!*"

The guards immediately entered the chamber, their swords at the ready.

"*Aye!!!*" she shouted again while placing a hand on the king's head and moving in a circle around him. She paused, threw her head back so that she was staring at the ceiling, and closed her eyes. "What comes to us, Oh Great Creator? What comes from the ring of fire?"

The raven became agitated in the cage. He was gnashing at the wire with his beak and tearing at it with his talons.

"Stop!" the healing woman demanded in a harsh voice. The raven recoiled to the back of the cage.

Turning back to Shabael, Janessa spoke quietly. "There are forces stirring, mighty Emperor. She with the powder glows will bring you victory, but also many woes. Beware, my handsome King, the ravens are coming."

Shabael rose quickly from the chair and almost staggered. He felt somewhat intoxicated from the woman's aromas. There was a dizziness in his head.

Janessa smiled and backed towards the door, bowing graciously. "I will return later today to check on you, my King," she said. "And I will remove these black ravens from your presence."

"What forces? What woman that glows?"

"'Tis all I know, Milord. All that was said was all that was revealed."

"Curse your encrypted Gods," he said, half swooning. He sat back down.

Shabael sat in silence and watched the woman leave his chambers. The eyes of the raven seemed to glower at him from the cage that she was carrying.

The queen, who had returned to the room, moved to Shabael and placed a hand on his arm. "Rest until the High Priest comes," Shawndeli said. "The old woman ... she is melodramatic, is she not?"

CHAPTER 8

THE RETURN OF MAKO

Moments after Shabael, embodied in the white raven, had pinned the black one on the prong of the fence, his daughter, Princess Alie El Qui, asleep in a tower a thousand yards removed from the main palace, was awakened in her bed by a visitor.

"Alie, wake up! Come on. Hear me! Open your eyes!"

The princess slowly came awake and opened her eyes to find a young man sitting on the edge of her bed, his image wavering as she struggled to focus, feeling almost nauseous. She blinked to clear her vision and saw the stranger. However, even though she did not know this man who had invaded her sleeping quarters, she did not feel afraid. There was something comfortingly familiar about the visitor. His head was covered with curly black hair that clung closely to his scalp. He had a thin nose and startlingly blue eyes. It was ...

For a moment, Alie thought she was going to faint. Her mouth opened but no words were uttered. She clutched her gown over her pounding heart. Finally, she whispered, "Mako?"

The young man smiled, his teeth white in the dim light. The world seemed to illuminate for Alie.

"I'm going to faint," she said, her voice almost a moan. "Mako Lasoto! It's really you! Am I dreaming?" The princess wept with joy and threw her arms around the young man. She kissed him on the lips, the forehead, the ears, the throat, and the lips again. She ran her fingers through the closely cropped hair and breathed in the smell of it. She was ecstatic with unbridled joy. "Mako!"

"Aye ... yes, my love. It is me."

Alie sat back on the bed as Mako rose to his feet. She left the bed and stood facing him. They were almost exactly the same height. Their eyes devoured each other. Alie let her gaze wander over him, to his black boots, the soft leather pants, the white shirt with the sleeves blousing at the wrists. These were the same clothes he had worn as she had been forced to watch his ravaged body waste for so many weeks from starvation. She took a step back, a scream building in her chest.

Mako recognized the panic on her face. "Don't," he cautioned in a pleading voice. "Don't scream, Alie. I know this is a shock, but it is only a dream. I am visiting you and speaking to you in a dream, my love. Give me a moment to help you to understand. Please, my darling. I don't have much time."

Alie tried to control her breathing, which was coming in gasps. She wasn't sure what to do. Of course, this was dream. She had been sleeping and she would probably awaken any moment to find herself alone.

But this is so real! It is Mako! Mako! I heard his voice. I touched him. I smelled his hair!

"Please, Alie. I have so little time and so much to tell you," Mako said. He reached out his hand to her arm and gestured for her to sit on the bed with him.

Allie could feel the pressure on her elbow. "This is too real to be a dream," she moaned. "Go away! I'm going to scream!"

"Alie," he said, holding her hand as gently as if it were a bird with a broken wing, "please allow me to explain. A grimace crossed his handsome face and for the first time Alie noticed a splotch of blood blooming from his left chest on the white shirt. She glanced down at her nightgown and saw bloodstains from their earlier embrace.

"You're hurt?"

"I am either dead or dying," he replied, a small smile playing on his lips. As he spoke, a new spot of blood began forming on the right side of his chest. "I'm sorry I couldn't come back earlier," he said.

Alie broke. She dropped to her knees and began a sorrowful wailing. Mako knelt beside her, his shirt growing redder, the blood dripping onto the floor.

98

"But you promised me. You said you would come back. After you had left your body, I remained by your bedside. I tried to give you nourishment. Even as your body shriveled and your skin turned to leather, I kept vigil by the bed. I allowed no one to come near your body because I knew you would return to it. I believed that your spirit would find its way back and that I could heal you; make you whole again."

Alie wept and the tears ran down her cheeks, ignored. She pressed a hand to one of the wounds in his chest and tried to stop the bleeding. Mako took her hand and pressed it against his cheek.

"I had no control of my movements," he said, his incredibly blue eyes boring into her pink ones. "I was taken to a place far away and I couldn't return to you."

Alie touched her cheek against his, finding it strangely cold. "But you are here now," she said, "Thank you, oh Great Creator!" She threw her arms open and pulled Mako to her. "Now you will stay with me."

"No," he said. "I only wish that I could, but I must leave you again. I have always dreamed of finding a way to return to you but now it is too late. It will never be. I am only grateful that I was granted this final goodbye."

"What? What do you mean, Mako? What are you talking about?" She felt his hot tears on her cheek, joining hers and dropping onto her gown.

"I am dying now," he whispered, the words coming with effort as his voice wavered.

"No!" Alie looked at Mako's shirt and saw that the two pools of blood had become one. "No!" she shouted again. "You can't leave me now. You stayed away too long and now you must remain with me. I command you!"

"If I could, I would," Mako said. "You must believe that. Now, say no more, but listen, I have only moments remaining."

Alie moaned and held him, rocking their bodies back and forth, as they knelt on the floor. This is just a dream ... a terrible, terrible dream that I must wake from. But at least I have seen him again. I have spoken to him, held him in my arms.

Mako was speaking, his voice low and labored. "Please, Alie, for me, for all that is right in your sweet heart, protect the Light. Protect it at all costs. It has to shine."

Alie pulled back from him and looked into the dying blue eyes. "My grandmother did this to you, Mako. Why did you lie unmoving in your bed for all those weeks?"

"Listen to me, Alie. I told you on our last night together that you would find me sleeping for several days. Remember? It had to be. I took the Light, Alie. I took Orb of Light."

Alie did not understand. He was speaking in riddles.

Mako gasped for a breath. "My time here is almost done," he whispered. He tried to take another breath, sucking in air between clenched teeth. His eyes closed as he tried to gather all the strength that he had remaining. "For a thousand years your people have kept the world in darkness. You possess your Tree of Dark and its Moon of Night. You have your Descension that will not allow your bodies to die of natural causes and you have the power to enter the minds of the white ravens. Do you remember? On our last day together you promised you would take me to see the Orb of Light that none of my people had seen for a thousand years."

"I wanted you to see it because I loved you."

"I know, and I was eager to see it, too. But just before you were supposed to come to me, I took Cawly from his cage and was feeding him kernels of corn when he raised his head and stared at me. I mean really stared, as though he wanted me to listen to something he was going to say. He began pecking at the drawstring of my shirt and acted as though he wanted to crawl inside it. 'What are you doing?' I asked, and he stopped, looked me in the eyes and cawed, motioning for me to open my shirt and allow him to get inside it. And I thought, wouldn't it be something if we had the magic to talk to one another again as our people had been able to do before the Light was stolen?

"Then I had an idea. What if I took Cawly to the Light? Would we be able to talk to each other again? And if that happened, could it happen for all my people? Perhaps our God was not dead after all, and somehow we would be able to restore the Sun and the Moon of the Day. The powers of magic would be balanced again. You see, I had to try, Alie. I had to do my best."

Mako paused, coughed, and a ribbon of blood spilled from between his lips.

"I'm sorry." He coughed again and wiped his lips on a sleeve. "It happened, Alie. Remember when we entered into the room and you said you could almost feel the Light's vibration? I could, and so could

Cawly. At that moment, the raven's mind and mine melded. Then I knew I had to find a way to get the Light back home to my people."

Mako paused, his breathing ragged and painful.

Alie pulled back from his quivering body. "So, when you told me you would be sleeping for weeks and you didn't want me to be alarmed, you knew you were going to meld your soul and mind with the raven and would be left in an unconscious state? How could you do that to me? You knew how I loved you and yet you allowed me to sit by your bed and watch your body wither away."

Then a revelation struck the girl. "Oh, Mako, this means that my grandmother wasn't responsible for what I thought was your death. This was of your own doing?" Alie's mouth gaped open. "Oh no! I almost killed my own grandmother because of what I thought she had done to you. Do you understand, Mako? I almost killed the Queen Mother! That's why I exiled myself to this forsaken tower."

Mako grimaced and placed trembling hands to his bloodied chest. "I'm so sorry,' he repeated. "My plan was to return once I had delivered the Light, but I was so caught up in the moment in the courtyard that I hesitated and was captured and placed in a cage. It made me crazy, knowing that I was penned up inside with the raven's body while my own body lay dying back here. However, there was nothing I could do. My fate was sealed inside that cage. Perhaps that is why the Great Creator has granted us this final moment."

He gasped and reached for Alie's hands. She closed her eyes and felt new tears streaming down her cheeks.

"I know that our love is true," Mako said, his voice quavering with weakness. "I knew you would be confused and would grieve. I never planned for all of this to happen this way. Not an hour has passed that I have not thought of you. I lived in a cage. It drove me mad seeing the Light from the window above.

"When your father came with his army, I was taken by a lady who I had given the Orb of Light. She took me to the Tree of Light. They had placed the Orb in the tree. It was glowing but it had not ignited the sun as they hoped. She climbed up in the tree and tied the orb to my claw," he said as he struggled for each breath. The blood on his clothing continued to spread and darkened."

Mako closed his eyes and leaned his head against her shoulder, and then he lifted himself upright again with effort.

"There was Light….brilliant light. We came into a new place. It was a new world because the stars were different. "Oh, God…" he tried to continue speaking as he heaved, chest wrenching in pain. He swooned but she straightened him. She was speechless, overwhelmed by his appearance and by his words.

"The ravens had consumed the body of Dayanna but were able to merge her back together. She lives. And while she wandered, we remaining ravens followed from behind until she met a good woman. The Orb of Light was no longer with me. I don't know what happened to it. The other ravens began heading back up the mountain…then I lost consciousness or something…When I was able to think again and see, I was at another Tree of Light… except it was alive and shining as once it had in Skyeden. The stars were different. There was only one moon and one sun. Here I lingered among the ravens and tree. I could not communicate with the other birds as a human. However, it seemed it was our duty to protect the tree. We were different from the other birds. Other ravens steered away from us as did any other animal that ventured close to the tree.

"Then one day, I was drawn or pulled as water to the moon, to go to a location. I just followed this inner feeling, like a magnetic pull to a certain direction.

I know that sounds as if I am mad. I think Cawly died over there and somehow my freed spirit returned here, except I suffered the same wounds." His face paled, he started to fall over but caught himself Still, I have one last request that I must ask of you, my love …" He paused.

Alie opened her eyes, thinking he might have drawn his final breath.

Mako forced a small smile that appeared more like a grimace. He groaned, gasped for air again, and continued in a voice that was barely audible.

"The Light, Alie. The Light. You must not allow it to die. I know you feel angry and betrayed by me, but please, if for no other reason than our love for each other, never allow the Light to stop shining. A time will come my love, when the fate of the Light is in your hands …" A stab of pain hushed him and made him clench his fists. "Alie, I love you so much. Please believe me. Nothing I did or said to you was done as part of any plan to regain the Light. That only occurred to me when you took me to see it. Please, Alie, you must believe this. It is the only peace I can attain." His body sagged, but he raised his head and asked, "Do you have a mirror?"

"A glass? Yes." She rose and went to the dresser, returning quickly with a small mirror. "Here," she said, angling the glass so that he could see his reflection.

Mako's eyes widened and his bloodstained lips curled in an ironic smile. "It's been a long time since I saw my face," he said. "Almost forgot what a handsome devil I am."

Alie lowered the mirror, placed it on the floor, and cupped his face in her hands. "You are very handsome," she said, her voice sweet and loving. "I remember well the first time I saw you. You were wearing a red shirt, a black vest, and a funny little hat with a small bell on it. You were playing a stringed instrument and singing and I remember thinking you had the voice of an angel."

Mako smiled. "Yes, and I followed your touring group for a month just to keep catching glances of you." His breathing seemed to become somewhat more regular and he cleared his throat. "I can leave you now in peace, knowing that we still love each other." He tried to squeeze her hand, but could not find the strength The effort created no more than a gentle touch.

"You must believe me," he said, "that I took the Light to another place, a world much like this one, and I hid it so that it may never be destroyed."

"But how could you communicate with the raven?" Alie asked, a puzzled expression on her face. "The Sun and the Day Moon, and Tree of Light must be active to have your Light magic. You have to attain Ascension."

Mako's face contorted with pain, but he continued. "But don't you see? I obtained Ascension many years ago when we possessed the Orb of Light and the Moon of Day was still shining."

Astonishment showed on Alie's face. "You've been through Ascension? You ... go on. Tell me more."

"When I took the Light to Skye Castle in the form of the raven, I was placed in a cage and held there until your father and his soldiers arrived to reclaim it a month later. The Ravenites ... a beautiful girl named Dayanna took me to the tree where they had placed the Orb of Light. The battle was raging around the tree. When it appeared the Malbolians were going to win and regain possession of the Light, this girl tied the Orb of Light to my talon, and I was released. As I attempted to fly away, I was swept up in a stream of ravens that were swirling in the sky. There was a blinding ring of light and ..." Mako paused to conserve his dwindling strength. "I can't remember much of what happened for a while after that, but as I regained self-awareness, I realized that I wasn't with her any longer. I was lost in a strange place. Some things in this land appeared familiar, but it was very different. I do not know how many years passed, but there were paved roads made and carriages without horses created. There were houses that contained light without fire. And, Alie, there was Day. Sweet, glorious daylight."

Mako coughed weakly and wiped a bright smear of blood from his lips with the back of his hand. He gathered himself, summoning the strength and breath to continue. The wounds in his chest burned agonizingly. The taste of blood on his tongue was coppery.

"I remained at the tree where I had placed the light, rarely leaving the site, until one day I was commanded by this inner voice — not a mind-meld conversation, but from a deeper place within. This voice commanded me to fly and it whispered one word: 'Nevermore.' So, I flew. I flew for a great distance, not knowing where I was going. Just flapping my wings and relying on this unknown spirit for guidance. I flew until I came to a place with many towers and large windows."

CHAPTER 9

NEW YORK CITY, 1849

It was a balmy night in the huge city with temperatures hovering around eighty-five degrees as the black raven circled between the tall buildings. The bird was being drawn to a poet whom some of the ravens already knew. This was a man of great importance who would play a role in a play in which he would never know he had participated.

The raven approached one of the buildings, instinctively knowing it was the one he was seeking. Suddenly there were several ravens flying alongside him, steering him in the direction of the building, then veering off as they neared it.

The raven perched on the windowsill and stared inside. A man was sitting at a desk, his head, covered with wavy black hair, bent over a paper on which he was busily writing. A strong odor of smoke and alcohol drifted through the open window.

The raven fluttered through the window and perched itself atop an open door leading to another room. The man looked up from his writing with a quizzical smile.

"A messenger has entered through my window and landed on my door. Ahh, I look for inspiration and you appear, my feathered friend." The man leaned back in his chair and tapped the pen on the edge of the desk. "I am Edgar. What is your name?"

"Caw!"

"Oh, well nice to meet you, Mr. Caw. Let's see … I was about to write a poem. Hmmmm …" The man reached for the glass of whiskey and pulled it closer. He flipped the end of the large pen he had been using and swirled some amber liquid into the glass. Placing the end of the pen to his mouth, he regarded the raven still sitting quietly atop the door. "Let me see … a raven lands on my chamber door. There must be inspiration in this.

"What great message do you come bearing for me, my friend?" Edgar Allan Poe turned and stared out the open window. A cloud crawled across the moon, making the night darker. "Will we ever see the light again?"

"Nevermore," the raven croaked. *"Nevermore."*

"Ah, you speak. What an ominous word … nevermore." Poe's smile suddenly faded. "Ominous, as I will never again see my beloved Lenore." He blinked his eyes to ward off the potential tears.

The raven flapped its wings and seemed to broaden its chest. It left the door and settled on Poe's desk beside the large picture of the beloved and departed Lenore. It sat, unmoving, staring at the man.

Poe's eyes suddenly widened as he realized there was something more than just a birdbrain on the other side of those penetrating eyes. There was an obvious intelligence … a kind of knowing. The bird seemed to be able to see inside him, to know him, know his suffering, his sense of depression, the loss of his great love, the demons that made him try to drown them in alcohol, the madness that haunted his dreams.

A sudden illumination shone in Poe's eyes and he snatched up the pen and began writing …

"Once upon a midnight dreary, while I pondered, weak and weary …" Poe stopped writing. "Yes, this is it. Oh, I think we have the beginnings of a great work, my friend." He sighed with satisfaction and almost smiled. "May I ask your name again, that I may credit you as an inspiration for my work?"

The raven cocked its head to one side and regarded the poet. It moved toward the man and gently placed its head against the back of his hand. *"Nevermore,"* it said once again. Then the bird flapped its wings and moved off the desk, leaving as it had come through the open window.

Poe stared out the window at the cloud that had completely covered the moon. "Thank you, my friend," he whispered. "For the first time in my life, I have found a soul that understands mine."

He reached for the glass of amber liquid and raised it to his lips in a toast.

"I'll drink to that, my friend. Nevermore."

CHAPTER 10

TAKING OF THE LIGHT

Mako grimaced with pain and resumed his story. "I returned to the tree and it seemed an eternity had passed until that night when I was struck by a great urgency. I know not why or what compelled me, but I knew I had to do this. It was as though the Great Creator had beckoned me. I took a small twig from the tree and began flying, having no knowledge of where I was going. I flew until I came to this strange land and I seemed to know exactly where to go and what to do. I flew to an enormous white house and perched on the windowsill of the second floor. Inside I could see a young man and I knew this human was supposed to fly with me. I knew I was to lead this young man to Dayanna, the Ravenite girl to whom I had given the Light. She had been in the Angel Oak when your people attacked and the ravens had brought her through the funnel to the new place. I do not understand any of this, but as I was leading the boy to Dayanna, we were attacked by a white raven. We fought and I was impaled on a fence as we fell. Now I am dying from those wounds. I feel that I am no longer even speaking physically, but mentally, because my lungs are filling with blood. I go soon, Alie."

Alie was not sure what she was hearing. Her fatally wounded lover was rambling, his words not making sense to her. "You Ascended when your people still had the Light? Your spirit is a thousand years old? But I thought you were only two years older than I was. You have lied to me! You've never loved me! You've been calculating,

108

devious, and manipulative! You lured me into taking you to the Light so that you could steal it! Deny this if you can!"

Mako, struggling to breathe and trying to understand what she was saying, gasped, "Yes, I am older. But the age does not matter, Alie. I would have reacted the same to you no matter when or where we might have met. I love you."

His voice was no longer audible and he was speaking to her through his eyes and mind. "I don't know how or why, my love, but we were granted this final meeting."

An awkward moment of silence hung between them. Then Alie resumed caressing his hair.

"Shhh," she murmured. "Lay your head down. All will be righted. My heart is grieved but I am thankful we have had this final time together. You may rest now, Mako. Your heart can be peaceful as you ascend into the other world."

Alie bent over him and gently kissed his cheek. She used her fingers to keep his eyelids open and stared into his clouding eyes.

"It was not your Creator who granted this last meeting, my darling. It was mine. Do you think I am a fool? Did you not think I would wonder how it was possible for you to lie in bed and continue to live without food or water? Your body did not dry, decompose, and crumble. It did wither to a point, but remained there. Your hair and nails continued to grow; and, I groomed you. I bathed your body and turned it so that you did not suffer from bedsores.

"I wept a thousand times and I cursed the lives of my father and grandmother. As the days passed, I grew suspicious of your mortality. I had an artist sketch your face on cloth. I traveled to Ravenland with it. I disguised myself and searched among the common folk in an attempt to learn what I could of you. During my search, I came upon the Maid's Hand Inn; and, I was told that you were reared there. Your father was a traveling musician who had lain with your mother a thousand years before. They told me that the musician had promised to wed her, but had then run off and deserted her. They said that as you grew older, you were discovered to have the voice of an angel. The Ravenite king was so enamored that he took you into his court. They said you were granted Ascension to ensure preserving your beautiful voice. But then, they said, there was a scandal in the court and you were exiled, forbidden to return."

"But I did nothing wrong," Mako weakly protested. "I refused the advances of the queen's sister, who acted in jealousy and had me removed from the court."

"Aye, that was told to me. Apparently, you were something of a legend in the Maid's Hand Inn. Now you're telling me that you have been through Ascension? Ascension? By the Great Creator, you are yet only twenty years of age. Are you one of the immortals? Are you a thousand and twenty?

"I never dreamed that you had stolen the Orb of Day. I believed with all my heart that my grandmother had arranged for your demise. That somehow she had placed a curse upon you or given you a poison that would not allow you to waken. I know she hated you and was bitter that my father had no son to succeed him. She vowed that she would die a thousand deaths before allowing me to wed a street musician. I was so certain that she was responsible for your state that I rushed into the Inner Chambers with a dagger and the intent to cut her heart out. I wanted to give her the pain that she had given me. *I hated her!* You must understand that burning hatred gave me the courage to confront the most feared queen of our generation. I stormed into her chambers with my dagger raised, determined to plunge it into her heart. But what I confronted froze me. I saw terror in her eyes. This vile, monstrous woman whose commands have led to the slaying of half our world's population was no more than a scared old woman. I felt like a giant standing over her. I felt like a goddess looking down on a frightened old senile woman. She was pathetic. The sight of her disgusted me. I spat in her cruel face and the saliva ran down her cold, pale cheek. I understood that even with all the wrath and ire that burned within my soul, she was not worthy of my revenge. I leaned forward and screamed in her face. Then I walked out of the chambers, hearing her gasp for breath as I left. I will never forget the pure joy that I felt in that moment. I left her and went directly to my father. I put the dagger to my throat and demanded that I be granted Descension immediately. I knew that one day you would return to me, that you would re-enter your body and we would be lovers for eternity."

"I'm sorry," Mako murmured. "I didn't know ..."

"Yes," Alie continued, "Here I am, forever eighteen. I did this for my love of you. I withdrew from public life and vowed to live in the Priestess Tower until your return. I vowed never to have a child to preserve the precious bloodline. I vowed to let the El Qui Dynasty end with me.

"Look at me. Let my face be the final thing you see, the face of a woman broken and betrayed. Lied to! You had Ascended and you never told me. You only used me for access to the Light. You do not love me. You never did. I curse your soul! Writhe in agony, you spy! You betrayer! You heartbreaker! Die now!"

"Please," Mako whispered, lifting a hand and pointing to his mandolin that Alie had kept in her room. "Inside … look inside. Please…" His eyes closed.

Alie pressed a palm to his mouth, shushing, stifling him. Her hand began shaking causing her to jerk it away. She stared at it as though it was a foreign object unattached to her.

"I'm sorry, Mako," she said as her body was again wracked by agonizing sobs as Mako struggled to continue breathing. "Please don't listen to the crazy things I say. Look at me, Mako. I didn't mean all those dreadful things. You know I love you. Always loved you." She touched his lips with gentle fingertips. "Oh, I've gone completely mad. Betrayed. Loved. Betrayed! I am so confused. I don't know what to believe!" She bent over stroking his hair, pressing her face against his bowed head. She felt his hair tickling her nose and reached to brush it away.

"Caw!"

Allie opened her eyes to see her pet raven, Maliki, who had brushed its wing feathers against her nose. In the dark room, something vague and eerily ghost-like attracted her attention. It was a small orb of light that was moving toward the foot of the bed. Maliki saw the orb and moved quickly to intercept it, but it zigzagged and escaped through the open window into the ever night.

"Mako!" Alie screamed, throwing her arms wide. "Please come back to me!"

However, the orb of light was gone, disappearing from her view as she stared out the window.

Alie held out her arm and the raven perched on it, gripping lightly with its talons.

"Mako came to me. Did you see? He came back to me. He does love me. I know he's dead, but he lives in another form. My grandmother did not poison him.

"Still I do not truly understand his intentions. Did he really love me or just use me so that he could steal the Orb of Light? I am tortured by the lack of understanding." Her heart pounded as she straightened in her regal pose, trying to regain composure. "You have awakened me, Mako. You have shattered the shackles of my exile. It is time now to rise." She wiped the tears from her eyes and patted her hair into place. She tried to speak with a calm voice, like a martyr before the guillotine. "I am Alie El Qui, daughter to the Emperor Shabael El Qui and daughter to the mother, the Queen, who died during my birth. I have received the rite of Descension. I am El Qui. "

The raven still clinging to her arm cawed its approval.

"I am one hundred and sixty-eight years of age, but eighteen of body," she said to the image in the hand-held mirror. Seeing Mako as a twenty-year-old in the bloom of health was a much better way of remembering him than the memory of watching his body dwindle away as if eating itself from within. His body had become nothing more than a leathered husk wrapped taut like a bag of bones. His once beautiful eyes were sunken while his ribs protruded from the chest. The hands had become like sunbaked crab corpses with fingers/crab legs appearing ready to snap off at the slightest pressure. Yellowed nails on his hands and feet had continued to grow until they were longer than fingers and toes. Yet she had believed that one day his consciousness would return to his body, and then Mako would be healed. He would be revitalized and restored to the beautiful young man that he had been. They would love again. He would be made whole again. He would return. He had promised. Her mind raced in turmoil.

Eighteen years old for eternity. Even when she reached two hundred in actual years, she would remain forever young. Her breathing was rapid. Her breasts were heaving. Perspiration ran down the cleavage of her bosom. She tried to control her breathing by taking slower, deeper breaths. With each gasping breath, she felt a sharp, rib-snapping pain rising from her broken heart.

"*All this time …* " It was her grandmother's voice sounding in her head. "*All this time you have self-exiled yourself, Alie. You must accept the betrayal. He lied to you about his age and never revealed his Ascension. He never loved you; he only sought the Light. When he had it, he abandoned you. Now look at you … trapped forever in a child's body. One day you may become a queen, but what man will respect a mere girl? But that matters not to you. You have no sense of family loyalty. You disgust me."*

Alie's vision became clouded with swirling black dots and the room began to sway. She rose unsteadily and the mirror fell from her lap. She watched it fall and shatter as if everything was happening in slow motion. She thought the image in the shattering glass had looked like her mother. She was swooning from the after effects of the emotions she had endured in the past hours. Alie managed to keep from falling and steadied herself against the wall. She picked up the mandolin Mako had pointed at and then allowed herself to slide down the wall until she was seated on the floor.

"Inside," Mako had directed. She drew a deep breath and brushed her white hair away from her pale face. She sniffed and wiped a sleeve across her face to clear the tears from her pinkish eyes. Alie reached beneath the strings of the mandolin and ran a hand inside the instrument. She could smell the scent of the wood. When her fingers found the parchment inside, she worked her hand free from beneath the taut strings. She was careful, afraid she might damage the parchment, which felt fragile and crumbly.

Her hands trembling, she opened the paper and began reading:

Today: 1003 a.l Sixth Moon, 5 days.
"Today I saw my future wife. I, Mako, son of unknown mother and father. Stable boy at day, singer-poet by night. I declare this proclamation — I will wed this woman. I know that she is the Princess El Qui and that my dream might be more realistic if she were the daughter of a pauper. But it makes no difference. Our eyes met and we fell in love. I was singing when this carriage approached and the curtain was suddenly drawn open. There was revealed the most beautiful face I have ever seen. The girl lowered her wonderful pink eyes that appeared as the purest desert gems. I could feel her gaze burning my skin. Her complexion was that of a white satin sheet that has never been folded. Her hair was as white as her skin. I wanted to touch her but feared she might break like fragile glass. I was singing, but missed an entire verse and didn't realize it had happened until some among the onlookers began laughing. I was spellbound. I left my life behind on that street. Now I am sitting across the street from where I think she may be. I am playing the mandolin and singing. At least the dogs love my singing as they have joined in with their howling.
"I made a little money today so I'm going to celebrate with a leg of chicken and a tomato. The talk on the street is that she is leaving tomorrow *for her*

homeland. However, as long as I can stay within sight of her, I will have my chance. Somehow, I know that."

Alie flipped through the pages. It appeared Mako had chronicled every moment from that first day. His every impression of his *"White Princess"* had seemed to inspire a new song or verse. She recalled many of the incidents. It was fascinating and a little weird to read about herself. She touched her mouth with her fingertips, and then brushed the strand of hair that had fallen across her face. She was suddenly concerned about her appearance.

Finally, under the notation ... *"The Last Note: I am going to lie down and shift my consciousness into my raven. I have found places into which I can literally disappear. As the raven, I will simply waddle down the hall and slip between the bars. I have smuggled a leather strap with a small pouch attached in which to transport the Light. Ah, this strange Light. It is not solid, but it still clings together."*

Oh, Alie, I do love you so. More than anything in the world, but I have to do this. This act comes from the very soul of my people. There are so many meanings and symbolisms. This Light is a greater thing than I could ever be. It is the soul of my people.

"I do love you, Alie. You must know that. But the importance of this mission is immeasurable. My intent was, and remains, to wed you and rear children with you. But this Light is more important than my being. Please forgive me for leaving you and for taking the Light. I do not know if it will be discovered that it was I who took the Light. If I am discovered, I do not know my fate. But if I do return, it will not just be to reclaim my moldering body, but to make you my wife.

"Though your kingdom now rules, the Ravenites and Malbolians will doubtless enter war against each other in the future. All I care about is loving you and being loved by you. This is the one great deed I have been asked to do for my kingdom and, surely, I will not be asked to do more. I will deliver the Light to the Ravenites at Skye Castle, and then return to you.

"It is best that you do not read these words until after I have gone and I pray that you will not hate me or feel that I have used you. I fell in love with you and left my home in the hope that we could meet and form a union. Finding you was the greatest joy of my life. I love you, Alie, and I shall return. That is my promise to you.

"If I should die before you, I will wait for you. If there is a new world, a paradise that awaits us, I will search until I find you again and we will be together.

We will wed. We will have beautiful babies and wear silly little hats with bells on them.

"*Goodbye my only love.*

"*Forever, Mako.*"

Alie rose and went to the spot on the floor where she had held the dying Mako. His blood had stained the ornate rug. She placed her hands on the spot. "Forgive me," she sobbed. "I am truly sorry for doubting your love. How could I be worthy of such a love?" Tears streamed down her white cheeks. She collapsed onto the floor.

"I almost killed my grandmother. Oh, Great Creator, forgive me."

She thought of the grand old woman, a woman of great beauty, confident, an unstoppable force when it came to matters involving the family. The family was her religion, her faith, her God. She would sacrifice anything, even her own life, for the family. Moreover, the Queen Mother was haunted by the knowledge that her son, King Shabael, would never have a son to inherit the throne.

Alie sighed and placed a hand to her heart. It was racing, pounding against her ribcage. This must have all been a dream! But no, there was the letter from the mandolin and Mako had pointed her to it. This was much more than a dream. It had been real. A smile played on her lips. "I saw you. I heard you. I held you. I love you!"

A tinkling sound interrupted her thoughts. The raven left her arm, cocked its head to one side, then disappeared under the huge bed. The "ting" sounded again; and, the raven came from beneath the bed holding an object in its beak. It waddled its way to within inches of Alie's face and shook its head, causing the tiny bell to ting-ting-ting.

Moving quickly, Alie threw on a robe, rushed out the door and through the hallway, signaling to the lift operator to lower her to the ground floor. Once it had descended, four elite Red Gold Guards, so named because of their uniform colors, jumped to their feet upon the arrival of the princess, obviously surprised to see her. Was she ending her self-exile?

"Lead me to Mako's chambers," she ordered, and when they guards offered surprised stares, she added, "I command this. *Now!*" Her voice was strong and forceful. It resounded of that El Qui voice of royalty and command, which no Red Gold could ever ignore or question.

Outside the tower, Alie was struck how the world appeared unchanged. There was a sky, a sea, and the Tree on the hill above them. The kingdom sprawled as far as the eye could see. The period of exile had almost made her forget this world. Suddenly, life seemed to have new possibilities. She moved at a brisk pace, surprising the Red Gold with her energy. They travelled up the stony path that led to the Emperor's Tower and governmental offices within the first gate. A few minutes later, they arrived at the small enclave where Mako's bed had been placed. She needed to know if the body had changed.

After the Red Gold opened the door, she passed through the living quarters to the bedroom … and stopped in her tracks. Her eyes could not register the picture before her. She gasped, placed a hand to her throat to battle the nausea, and closed her eyes, trying to breathe through her mouth to avoid the stench of fresh blood.

She fought to regain control of her emotions and reactions. Turning to the Red Gold soldiers, she said quietly and firmly, "Please wait outside." They turned and left, and then she pushed the door closed behind them, ignoring the troubled looks on their stern faces.

Now alone in the room, she surveyed the scene before her. Mako's body was whole and appeared fresh. The withered, leathery flesh was no more. This body had been recently alive. Blood was still dripping to the floor from the body sprawled across the bed. The chest showed two puncture wounds from which the blood was still flowing. The head was hanging over the edge of the bed with an arm was outstretched, the index finger touching the floor where it had scrawled one word:

Inside.

"I found it," Alie said, lifting the lifeless hand back on the bed. "What will it must have taken for a soul to animate a lifeless body. You truly loved me, Mako. Thank you for letting me know."

Alie moved to the bed and pushed aside the chair. She had sat in this chair so many times while reading to the sunken-cheeked, leathery corpse of the only man she had ever loved. Raising his head, she then placed it on the pillow and folded the hands on the chest. She pulled the sheet over the body and stepped back.

It took a great effort to fight back tears; her chin trembled. She leaned from the waist and kissed him lightly on the cheek.

"I forgive you, my love."

CHAPTER 11

SKYEDEN: SHABAEL'S CHAMBERS

King's Guard Rageton rapped twice on the door and entered King Shabael's chamber. Rageton was one of Shabael's finest and most trusted knights. Viewing him always gave the king a higher sense of well-being. Rageton stood six-foot-eight inches tall and was almost another foot taller due to the helmet and horns he wore. The knight was a massive man whose face was covered with a dense beard, a rarity among the Malbolian race. The beard, worn in long, thick braids, was Rageton's personal badge of honor. Each braid was embossed with threads of gold and a tiny white feather. Many children and some adults were frightened by the appearance it created. King Shabael liked to tease his favorite knight that one day a hunter would mistake the beard for a bear and dispatch an arrow into it.

Shabael was very aware of the adage that a beard often concealed a man's true nature, but Rageton was as loyal and faithful as any guard who had served the king. He never questioned or doubted a command; listened carefully, then meticulously performed the duty assigned to him.

The agility and quickness of the huge man often surprised the king. During battle drills, it was astonishing to watch the big bear drop, sidestep and strike. Yes he was a bear; a giant dancing bear.

Very few people knew much about the hulking man beneath the helm of horns, although he had been a soldier in the infantry for all his life. Shabael had discovered Rageton during one of his inspection

117

tours of the troops. While visiting an army campsite during a weekend training exercise, he came upon a diagram of dots and connected lines being drawn in the dirt. He was staring at the drawings when a captain walking with him chuckled and said, "Simple minds, Your Grace, entertain themselves simply."

The large man, who had been creating the designs, rose from his crouch and upon recognizing King Shabael, quickly bowed.

"Remove your helmet," the king requested. "What is your name?"

"Rageton, Supreme Commander."

As the man removed his helmet, his thick, curly hair tumbled down to his shoulders. The eyes were a dark pink and the beard was long and unruly.

"How frustrating it must be to be called a simpleton by one too lacking in intelligence to understand or comprehend brilliance. Am I right?"

"You should know that better than anyone, Sire." Rageton smiled broadly in the direction of the red-faced captain.

Shabael did not attempt to hide his own smile. "Those are astronomical markings, are they not?

"Yes, Sire."

"Come to me after we've returned to home. I think I have a place for you," Shabael said.

Days later the emperor requested audience with Rageton. Shabael sent Rageton to several of his best warrior trainers. After he received their reports, Shabael summoned Rageton and made him Emperor Knight. His sole job was to protect the emperor. Shabael made all the institutions open for his Knight. Rageton took full advantage and loved Shabael for the access to knowledge that he would have never had a chance to learn.

Rageton bowed to the king and announced, "Emperor El Qui, the Priest Highest has arrived."

Shabael placed a reassuring hand on the arm of Queen Shawndeli as he rose. "I must speak to the priest in private," he said to her. "Make sure of that."

Shawndeli appeared puzzled, showing a familiar furrow between her eyes. That furrow would be the only wrinkle she would ever have if her Descension was carried out as planned on her 28th birthday, only months away.

"Yes, my husband," she intoned, a bit too obediently and with a knowing smile. However, realizing that this must be a matter of vast importance if the king was excluding her, she gave him a quick nod and left the room.

King Shabael watched his wife leave, admiring the fit of her dark red gown, tied around her neck, then around her waist, leaving her back exposed. Her long white hair was pulled over her shoulder, hanging down in front. He admired the curvature of her lovely back and enjoyed watching her walk. At times, she reminded him of a female panther.

"Alfie," Shawndeli addressed her chambermaid, "send for my sisters, then return and help me dress."

"Your Highness." The girl bowed, turned, and darted from the room. The 14-year-old Alfie, a slave from a band of rebels in the desert Nahbra Kingdom, stood out in the room because of her startlingly black hair.

Shabael waved to one of his guards to fetch Nolan Turner, the son of one of his fallen warriors. The youngster rushed in, pulling a jersey over his head.

"Fetch me a lounging robe and a glass of wine, boy."

Rageton raised a hand and announced, "Priest Highest Calibri!"

The priest entered, wearing a white silk robe bearing the emblem of his station within the El Qui family — a white sword beneath a full moon reflecting its rays upon the steel blade.

"Your Grace." Priest Calibri bowed and his eyes moved to the bandage on Shabael's cheek.

The lad returned with a royal blue robe, helped Shabael slip it on, then handed the king a glass of red wine. Shabael motioned to the High Priest, "Let's speak on the balcony."

From their view atop the Emperor's Tower, the two men looked down on the citadel of Pandora, the capitol of Neverland. Four walls divided the castle from the Emperor's Tower to the ground level. Beyond the gate was an expansive moor, then a complex of animal shelters and stables for the horses. Past this were the homes of the farmers and their pastures. From there, rolling hills led to the Red River and beyond. It was estimated that the view from the balcony overlooked more than a million people.

The moon was a half crescent, shining its blue neonic light over the world. Everything seemed black and white under its light. Objects that were white actually shone brighter than the moon itself.

"I was asleep," Shabael said to the High Priest in a low voice. "I did not seek contact. It came to me as if in a dream."

"Intriguing," Calibri said. "And what happened here?" He gestured toward the wound on Shabael's face.

"I saw through Masora's eyes ... a black raven landed on a window sill." Shabael motioned, his hands moving in graceful arcs, as if the black raven were going to form in his palms. "The raven was carrying a white branch ... it was glowing pure white."

Calibri studied the king's face. "Was there light where you were?"

"Yes, there was one moon, but it appeared to be further away than our own. It glowed white also; as bright as the twig the black raven was carrying. The thing is, I, or Masora, attacked the raven. There was no premeditation; it was purely instinct. Something within me took action. It was an urgency of life and death if that twig was given to the boy. I struck the raven; and, we fought in the air for a moment, and then began falling. The raven tried to impale me on a fence with sharp prongs, but I waited until the final moment, then sprang upward, twisting and flipping him over with my claws clutching his wings and driving him hard into the spikes. I felt his flesh tearing and was able to release him before I was also impaled."

"A true warrior, whether man or bird, Sire," Calibri said. "And the twig? What happened to it?"

Shabael threw his head back, staring at the ceiling as though seeking an explanation from the Great Creator. His long white hair swung loosely down his back to his waist. He lowered his gaze and met Calibri's eyes.

"I released the raven and went to the window as quickly as I could. But the boy had opened the window and was holding the twig in his hand. He had it! I panicked. I thought the world was ending! I thought now would be the time the Great Creator would strike me dead by lightning. I flew right at the boy. My claw ..." Shabael looked at the palm of his hand. "Calibri, I grabbed for the twig and actually had my claw on it. I felt the corrosion of its essence. I felt ..." He touched his palm with his fingers ... "a withdrawal ... no ... a kind of electric shock in my hand ... and suddenly I was thrown back. The window slammed shut. I was stunned by the shock and fell to the ground. That's when I awoke and found the cut on my face. The black raven did this. Even in this world, so far away Masora and I share our wounds. But regardless of that, the boy has the twig. I don't know what he knows; and, I don't know why he has been sought out by the black ravens."

Calibri pinched his jowl, a habit he had developed when in deep thought. He lifted his head and Shabael thought the priest's pink eyes were literally glowing with excitement.

"What? What are you thinking? Tell me," Shabael demanded.

"This branch, Your Grace …this is your evidence of the Orb of Light. It has illuminated the tree that houses it and has created a new Tree of Light. My thoughts are that the raven you attacked was giving the branch as an invitation to the boy to find the tree. The black ravens seem to have a great interest in this fledgling of a man and have a special relationship with the Ravenite girl as well as the tribe that she has adopted as her own."

"Yes. If you are right, Calibri, the Orb of Light and this tree are not far away. This is a great breakthrough. For decades, we have kept the tribe and black ravens under observation. Masora has personally watched the girl. The black ravens created that portal to steal the Light away. Those ravens devoured the girl, taking her, and then reforming her back into living human form. They have broken the boundaries of magic. They work magic outside the act of Ascension!" Shabael laughed. "They cheat, Calibri!"

"If so, Your Grace, it is reason for grave concern. However, if the black ravens have somehow breached the natural laws, surely we shall be as capable."

Shabael took a step toward Calibri, lowered his head, and spoke in a whispered way that always made Calibri marvel. The lower Shabael's voice, the more strength it harnessed.

"We will have this Light," the king said. "We possess it or we destroy the only real threat to our supremacy. We rule because our world is Dark. And we are granted the right to be its rulers, for so the Dark God commands."

Shabael was speaking with conviction, although he didn't really believe in a Dark God. He was aware that if this became the knowledge of the populace he would be the first of the El Qui rulers to be executed by his own people. He believed in a force … a force like the lightning that flowed in all things. He was the Dark God of

Skyeden. This he believed, for never had the Malbolian throne been set upon by anyone outside the El Qui blood.

Yes, Mother, Shabael thought to himself. *I know I DON'T HAVE A SON! Shawndeli will provide one. Have faith!*

"Your Grace?" Calibri touched Shabael's arm.

Shabael shook his mother's image away and looked at Calibri questioningly with his pink eyes. What was he saying? Then he suddenly remembered something else about his dream vision. "Wait, there is more. I remember now. I've been so occupied with the thoughts of the white twig, I almost forgot. Earlier, before I made my attack upon the raven with the branch, there was one more raven.

The first raven tapped on the window. Then, he went inside and laid down, apparently falling asleep. The raven was very still for some time. Several minutes later it seemed to shudder and cried out. I think the boy fell into a dream state and the raven caught his spirit like a dream catcher snags the bad dreams. He was fused with that raven. Then a second raven, which had apparently been waiting nearby, appeared and urged the first raven to follow it. I trailed them and soon realized they were headed to the village of the Ravenite girl. As the lead raven flew on, I suddenly realized that he was carrying a white branch. This is when I attacked."

"Why do the black ravens want this man-child to find the tree?" Calibri pondered. Shabael could almost hear the pages of ancient texts and scrolls crinkling as they turned inside the priest's head.

"This new world, it is not much different from our own except it has a sun and only one moon. The alignment of the stars is wrong. Even though I was in a dream state, I could smell the air... feel its difference." Shabael touched the side of his face. "I almost died tonight. You would have found my body in the bed with holes punched in my chest. I will feel better when Masora is by my side. I do not like that we are so far apart but still connected. I could be sitting on my throne with five thousand of my men there to protect me. Yet I could still be slain because Masora flew into a tree.

"This faraway place is familiar but it is not of here. I think Masora moved through time to a different age when we entered the ring of fire in pursuit of the raven that escaped with the light. Masora followed the girl to a village where she has stayed since their coming. And Mansi ... she will command the Darklings and find the Orb of Light.

"Yes," Calibri said. "This twig proves the Light is near. It lives in a newly made Tree of Life. This is indeed real evidence. This young man that the black raven tried to give the twig to must be of some great importance. The black ravens want him to go to the village." Calibri paused for a moment and rubbed his forefinger against his temple. "Perhaps, My Grace, if we observe and do not intercede, we will be led to the Light. With our spy there, we could regain possession of the Light to either keep or perhaps even destroy it."

"Its rightful place is in our vault," Shabael said. "I pray to the Creator that we discover how it was taken from us. Without control of the light, we will always be threatened by the loss of our power. This will never happen under my reign. I will not live to see that happen." He gave Calibri a reassuring smile. "Priest Highest, this twig ... if we were to gain possession of this twig, I could have Mansi rub a branch of the Dark Tree against it. It would create an orb we could place in the Dark Tree. This would create the power of the dark magic. With the magic, we could raise an army and conquer this new world. If we could find a way to create a portal as the black ravens have ..."

"You are right," Calibri said. "To spread the Dark One's essence to this new world ... what great work we would achieve for our creator." Calibri closed his eyes and sent a quick prayer to the Great Creator that this would happen.

"With an Orb of Dark in the Dark Tree, we can create Darklings and perform the rite of Descension to the people there," Shabael said, his brow creasing in thought. "We must find a doorway to this world. Go and prepare the observation globes. We have much work to do. I'll contact Mansi through Masora. Send one of your priests to Black Tower and have them connect with Masora and be ready for me to communicate with Mansi."

"It is done," Calibri bowed and began to exit. The king motioned for him to wait.

"Calibri, I would like to tap back into Masora's memory and replay the attack with the white raven."

"I will have the Seer ready, Your Grace. I will meet you in the Observation Chambers." Calibri bowed and exited the balcony.

Shabael watched the High Priest leave the room and drew in a deep breath. It was still very early in the day, but he had never felt more alive and aware. If only he could find a way to transport himself to this place called Earth. If he could create an Orb of Dark and possess again the Orb of Light, he could have the unheard opportunity of being the conqueror of two worlds. He opened the balcony doors and stepped back into the bedchamber to be greeted immediately by Shawndeli. If the Orb of Dark Light was created and placed in the tree, would it remove the sun from their world as Skyeden?

"Husband," she said, smiling. "I suspect you are about to have your second surprise of this morning."

"What do you mean?" Shabael looked across the room. Two of his guards were standing by the door, huge smiles on their usually stoic faces.

"Come on, Shawndeli, don't tease me. Just tell me what's going on.

"She is back, husband."

Who? Who is back? Shabael cocked his head to the side and leaned in closer to his wife. "Is this some kind of riddle you're teasing me with?

"Your daughter. She's come out of seclusion and seeks to speak with you."

Shabael turned to the chamber door. *"Alie?"*

"In the flesh and blood and out of the Priestess' chambers. She was very kind to me. You need to go to her, Shabael."

The king raised a hand to the bandage on his cheek. "I look a bloody mess. Why is she here at this hour? This is all beginning to feel surreal." He ran his hands over his robe, smoothing it, and pushed his long hair behind his ears.

Shawndeli reached out and helped him adjust the robe. "You look very handsome and strong, husband. Now, go see you daughter." She rose on her toes and flicked a loose strand of hair away from his face.

"It's been a long time ... too long," Shabael murmured, as though speaking to himself. He nodded to the guards and they came immediately to attention, each taking hold of one of the double doors, and opening them simultaneously.

The queen's hand rested lightly on his shoulder as Shabael began walking toward the open doors. He smiled at his wife, feeling a mixture of shame and happiness. *Dare I feel happiness?* Alie, who had been so perfect in every way as a true princess of the El Qui had literally fallen apart emotionally. He had been told how she had barged into the Queen Mother's chambers with a dagger poised to attack. It

124

was supposedly all about a young musician from the Ravenlands with whom she had fallen in love. She had accused her grandmother of poisoning the young man. Then she had come to him with the dagger at her own throat demanding that she be placed through the rite of Descension or she would kill herself. That had been the last time in 150 years that he had looked into Alie's eyes … the moment she had been Descended and become immortal at the age of eighteen..

Following her Descension, Alie had exiled herself in the Priestess Tower. Shabael visited her regularly, never entering her room, but sitting outside the door and talking to her. She never responded, but he knew she heard him as he told her of things from his day. He never glimpsed more of her than a shadow or silhouette while he longed to see her face once more. On many occasions he came close to losing his temper; and, he considered having his guards break down the door and bring her out to face him. However, he never gave in to that urge, realizing that she had to come to him of her own free will.

At first he visited the tower several times a week. As time passed, his visits became less frequent. He now averaged going about once a month and he was as frustrated as ever. He stood outside the door, pummeled it with his fists, stabbed at it with his sword, leaving gashes in the hard wood. Even though her door was sometimes ajar, she never responded. Shabael could have shoved it open, stepped inside, and taken her in his arms. But as much as he ached to do that, he resisted the urge. Alie blamed him and the Queen Mother for the demise of her lover; and, the El Qui were legendary for their tempers.

Shabael did not know what had happened to the young man his daughter obviously adored with such passion. He had visited the room where the boy's wasting body laid. His skin becoming more leathery each day. Although he didn't understand, he knew something unnatural was taking place. Watching him was like watching a grape become a raisin. There was no movement; he took no food and no water. The brightest physicians in the kingdom visited the room and could find no explanation for what was occurring. Had he at some time been Ascended? Was he one of the Ravenite Immortals who had Ascended more than a thousand years ago when they had possessed the Orb of Light? Regardless, Alie had vowed never to leave the compounds of the priestess' chambers and tower until her lover had returned. When his body and belongings were moved to quarters on the Tower's grounds, Alie had visited it daily at first, but as her father's visits had become less frequent over time, so had her visits to her lover.

What has happened that she has come to him now, Shabael pondered. *Had her lover returned?* God, the king hoped he had not. But had he? Would they be standing together, asking for his blessing in marriage? The Princess El Qui marrying a pauper?

I had rather see her dead, son. You ... without an heir of your own and your daughter marrying a Ravenite beggar? Draw your sword and strike her down, his mother said in his mind.

Shabael stepped back and leaned against the wall. His heart was pounding furiously against his ribcage as the Queen Mother's words resonated in his mind. *Shut up, Mother! This is all your fault! It is your actions that have made her this way!*

Queen Shawndeli was alarmed. "Look at me," she said, lifting Shabael's chin so that their eyes met. "Don't become so alarmed. Find out what Alie wants first. That she has come this far after all this time is a monumental act for her. Go to your daughter. Come." She gripped his hand and led him into the foyer, then stepped aside.

King Shabael lifted his gaze slowly, seeing the leather sandals with a ruby attached to each ankle. Her mother's rubies. The hem of Alie's robe was of red silk; not that of the traditional priests' robe. A thread of gold was woven around her waist. Her hair was neatly combed and hung loose, ending at her waist. Her skin was white, almost ghostlike. The thought passed through his mind that if he touched her his fingers might simply pass through her as an apparition. It was as if he were living outside of the moment, like looking at himself in a dream. He noticed that her teeth were pressed hard into her bottom lip. Then their eyes met and Shabael was struck by unbridled emotion. Empathy and love shone in his huge pink eyes. Tears formed and rolled down his cheeks. Before he could lift his arms to her, she was there, fiercely holding him, her hot tears wetting his neck. He felt the softness of her hair. The smell of her hair brought back memories of rocking her in his arms as a child while he sat on the throne. That familiar scent of her hair had always given him a sense of peace.

The king held his daughter firmly and made a silent promise to never let her go ... to protect her... to be her father. He suddenly felt faint; and, the world seemed to fade around them. Father and daughter dropped to their knees.

The alarmed guards exchanged glances. They had never seen the Emperor show any sign of weakness before, certainly never seen him weep. Shawndeli motioned for the guards to retain their positions. She was smiling, but wiped a tear from her eye.

Alie spoke, the first words she had uttered to the king in a hundred and fifty years. "Forgive me, father, for I abandoned you. Never again."

When Shabael looked into Alie's eyes, it was like looking into her mother's. He had almost forgotten his daughter's face. But now, only inches from his own face, he stared into her lovely pink eyes, such a simple thing, but one so long denied him. Not only had he lost a wife that he loved and cherished, but also a daughter that he adored. Until now. Now she had returned and the moment almost emotionally overwhelmed him.

It was as though the Great Creator had materialized Alie from thin air and placed her before him, answering his prayers, and easing the grief within his heart. Yes, there was the tiny mole beneath her left eye, no larger than a freckle. And in the eyes — flecks of lilac mingling with the pink. This girl was his heart, part of his own flesh.

"Father," the voice was wavering. "Sadly I must inform you that I know what happened to the Orb of Light."

Shabael startled, the words surprising him. "Tell me," he half whispered. "Tell me of this." He used a hand to gently push the hair back from her face.

"Oh, father, I have recently learned that I played a role in its disappearance.

"You? But how?"

Fresh tears appeared in Alie's eyes. She nodded and bowed her head, showing submission to the king.

"Don't. Don't do that," Shabael said placing a hand to her chin and raising her face. "Tell me."

There was a tremor in her voice as she spoke. "I gave Mako a tour of the Prisoner Tower and ..." her voice broke. "I allowed him to stand before the Orb of Light."

"Alie," Shabael was about to reprimand her, but caught himself. How would that help at this time? Besides, he knew that he had yet to hear the worst.

"I didn't know it, father, but Mako had concealed his raven and brought it into the Orb of Light's cell. Apparently, being that near to

127

the Light triggered a fusion between him and the raven. Later that night, Mako's spirit entered the raven and returned to the cell. He took the Orb and flew for days until he reached Skye Castle where he delivered the Orb of Light to the Ravenite woman, Dayanna."

What had already been a surreal experience reached new heights of absurdity for Shabael. The story that his daughter had just related explained what had been the mystery of the century in Malbolia. Not one of the brilliant minds of the nine kingdoms had conceived of such a theory of how the Orb of Light had been stolen.

And now, to have Alie, his daughter, involved even unknowingly, approached treason. The historians would assure that his legacy would be that of the ruler under whose watch the Orb of Light had been stolen. Alie was still talking. But what else could she add? Shabael forced himself to focus on her words.

"The Ravenites trapped Mako and placed him in a cage, father. That's why he was unable to return." Alie paused, attempting to weigh the effect her words were having on the king. She knew that what she had to say next would make him even more furious. "When your soldiers were battling the Ravenites under the huge tree during the invasion, the Orb of Light was given to Mako. He flew from the tree and was caught up in the huge swirl of ravens you described. From there, he was transported to another place." She finished the last words with a grimace distorting her beautiful face.

"Wait," Shabael said. "You're telling me that the spirit of Mako …" His voice rose an octave. "Is this what you are telling me, daughter?" The king drew a breath through clenched teeth and called on a thousand years of El Qui ruling experience to qualm the fury rising within his breast.

"I'm sorry, father." Alie was whimpering, her voice barely audible. She was like a five-year-old kneeling before him. Shabael bowed his head and closed his eyes.

"How long have you known this, child?" His words were spoken low and evenly, without revealing the passion that was boiling within.

"I only learned it today, father."

Shawndeli and the guards were leaning forward, straining to hear the words of daughter and father.

"He's here? Mako has returned?" Shabael straightened, glanced at the others in the room, trying to ascertain how much of the conversation they had overheard. Alie leaned toward her father, placing her lips within an inch of his ear.

"He came to me in a dream," she said. "He said he was at this other place and attempting to deliver a twig from a tree to someone."

Shabael was fully alert now, focusing on her words. His fingers touched the bandage on his face. "Wait!" He held up a hand, forefinger raised for silence, and turned to the others. "Please wait outside, I wish to speak to my daughter in private."

The guards bowed their heads and immediately exited the room. Shawndeli approached Shabael and Alie, placed a hand on their shoulders and kissed each of them on the forehead. "It's so wonderful seeing you two together again." She bowed and left them alone.

Shabael waited until the double doors had closed completely. "All right, Alie, continue."

"When Mako was attempting to deliver the twig to the boy, he was attacked and mortally wounded. As he was dying, his spirit was set free and he came to me through a dream. He begged me to understand that the taking of the Orb of Light was not planned, but was an impulse of the moment. He had planned to return here, but was unable after being captured and caged by the Ravenites."

Shabael shook his head in wonder. "The answer to all this was right in front of me and I didn't see it. After your Descension, I went to his room. I noticed the empty birdcage in his room but did not think anything of it. He had already been Ascended? He was an immortal? That's why he hadn't died. He's here now? He's within the castle?"

"No father. Well, yes. I mean ...," Alie was flustered, trying to explain, her words jumbled, stumbling. "I think when he died, his spirit was released from the raven, and it re-united with his body here. He is dead. I feel such a fool. I thought you and grandmother had something to do with his condition. He said the idea to steal the light only occurred to him while in its presence. He said he truly loved me. I found a diary; and from what I read, it seems to be the truth." she heaved a deep sigh. It was all said now.

Shabael was stunned by what he was hearing. He was having difficulty breathing. His entire empire, the dynasty of the El Qui, could have been ... or could be ... destroyed if the Light was used to return the balance of magic to the world. Of all the wars and thousands upon thousands who had died during his conquest of

Skyeden. After the darkness came ... years of war ... He had trampled eighty-percent of Skyeden himself. He was the first of the El Qui to conquer all of the world. Rage rose like a purple fog within him. His impulse was to draw back his hand and slap the messenger of this news. Had it been anyone else in the kingdom — even Mother — he would have had them drawn and quartered and fed to the pigs for such weakness. Allow a Ravenite to steal the Orb of Light? Unthinkable!

Cut her fucking head off! Give the Ravenite pauper something to really sing about! The Queen Mother was shouting in his mind. The muscles in his arms tensed. He squeezed his eyes shut and felt the sting of perspiration. He opened his eyes; saw the angelic face of his beloved daughter, and the rage left him like the air from a deflated balloon. He placed his hands on Alie's shoulders, staring into her beautiful pink eyes. It wasn't her fault. She was just a young girl in love. A one hundred and sixty-eight-year-old with a teenage crush. His thoughts turned to his mother, whom he knew was going to be unyielding in her wrath. She was staunch and unbending concerning matters of love or what was best for the royalty.

She may have cost us everything, Shabael! She's an idiot! Cast her in irons and throw her in the dungeons ... or at least defile her beauty, mar it, rake deep furrows over those lovely cheeks that no man, not even a blind one could love her, Mother said.

For God's sake, shut up! Shut up! Mother! Leave us alone! Shabael silently screamed back at the Queen Mother, ending the imaginary conversation. *No. No. No. Alie is my daughter, my heart. She is the very image of her mother who died during her birth. I love her. She is my eldest child!*

"Embrace me," he said to Alie, lifting his arms. She was hugging him instantly, weeping, tears streaming down her face. And Shabael knew at that moment that he would have given his empire to bring happiness back into her life. He knew that had his mother been able to read his thoughts, she would have proclaimed him incompetent, too weak to sit on the throne, and she would have done her best to will the resurrection of his dead father and brothers. An image appeared in his mind of his father's skeleton strung like a puppeteer, sitting on the throne with Mother pulling the strings and speaking in his voice from her hidden position behind him.

Then another vision appeared as he viewed it from the white raven Masora's eyes. He saw his claws seize the back of the black raven on the windowsill that he now knew was Mako. *Oh, my sweet daughter, it was I who killed your lover.*

"Mako said he was attacked?" Shabael tried to keep his voice neutral.

"Yes, by a white raven."

By me, my precious one.

.Let her smell your hands. His mother urged. Perhaps she can still smell the blood. Or better yet, since the two of you are such romantics, let her touch the wound on your face ... the place her lover touched. Don't you think that would be so sweet for her?

Shut up, Mother!

Alie was still speaking and he forced himself to focus on what she was saying.

"I am so sorry, Father. I have hurt you and I've been an instrument in the theft of your — the kingdom's — most important possession."

At least she understands the significance of her actions.

"Yes," he said, searching for the right words, "the Orb of Light is the source of our power to hold domination over the world. Since the beginning of mankind, more than a million lives have been sacrificed for it. I watched my father ..."

The look of despair deepened in Alie's eyes. Upon noting it, Shabael decided to not pursue the thought. He pushed the mane of white hair back from his forehead and reached to cup her face in his hands. "There is still the chance that we may reclaim it. I believe that you had nothing to do with the theft of the Light, my dear. But many, including the Queen Mother, will feel that your love for a Ravenite pauper is a weakness that has been exploited and will deem it as premeditated treason."

Alie's eyes widened as her father's words sank in.

"I personally think this self-exile, the demanding of Descension, was a strength of your convictions to what you love, Alie. Nevertheless, you are a princess. You are El Qui. It is not a role you can choose, it is *who* you are. You are the living kingdom. You are responsible for your people. You are part of the leadership of the greatest military force in history. It is our way to be conquerors and emperors of the world. You can have anything you want. However ... whatever you want, you must be sure is not a detriment to the kingdom. What choices you make will not only affect you but will affect the kingdom as a whole. I have taught you this. I raised you on my knee, allowed you to preside with me in the matters of court and even the strategies of war. You are El Qui! It is your choice — you can walk out of the gates of Pandoras and live as a commoner or you can be standing by your father's side and be Princess of El Qui. I loved you as a daughter and groomed you as a king does a son to assume his seat on the throne."

Alie raised her face to meet his eyes. "I was full of hate and rebellion mostly for grandmother," she said. "I ... well, you know I have always thought that she somehow killed my mother. I just know it in my heart. And I have seen the looks she has given Shawndeli. She hates her. In all this time, since my exile, you still have no son? I am shocked she still lives."

"Alie, watch what you say. Mother is cruel at times in her unbreakable will to always do what she deems right for the throne and family, but I cannot... I will not believe she would bring harm to her family."

"I can't be so sure, Father. Until tonight, I really thought she was responsible for Mako's death and I kneel before you corrected. I ask for your forgiveness and give an oath to always abide by your wishes and do what is always good for the kingdom. I abandoned you, Father. But now your daughter has returned and I will be as strong and true as the fist of your right hand." She bowed from her sitting position with the side of her face pressed to the floor.

Shabael held a trembling hand over her head, and then placed it on her. She rose and they embraced.

Meanwhile, two thousand yards away, four of the Dark Tree Priestesses were dead. Their bodies were concealed in a storage unit adjoining the Priestess Tower and their robes had been removed. A procession of one hundred priestesses was headed from their quarters to the Priestess Tower where they performed their nightly moonrise prayer.

Shabael stood by the double chamber doors and marveled at the presence of his daughter. "I hope you will remain here, Alie. Perhaps you can move back to your old room. It hasn't changed since the day you left it. I always knew you would return one day."

"My place is here, Father, in this tower, and by your side. Never shall I leave it again." She took his hand and pressed it against her cheek. "Your daughter has returned."

"Go find Shawndeli then; she will help you get settled in."

"And Mako's body, father?"

"I will have some of my men attend to that. I would ask that his body be buried outside Pandora's gates. Perhaps by that willow tree you so love by the riverbank.

"Thank you, Father." She smiled, and then stole a quick hug. As she turned away, he thought he heard a small laugh of joy. It was music to his ears.

"Oh, Father, I would like to attend this morning's ritual. Though I have returned to the court, I would like to continue the morning devotional."

"As you wish." Shabael closed his eyes. "The song is very beautiful. It's been so long since I've heard you sing. The voice of an angel you have."

"Then soon, I shall sing for you."

"I look forward to that." But first, he had to attend to communications with Mansi and begin the quest for the Orb of Light. He watched Alie headed out of the bedchamber. As she walked away, she let her hand trail along the wall.

"Guards! We go to Black Tower."

"My love?" Shawndeli entered into the chamber room from her dressing room. She waved her attendants back and they began excitedly talking to Alie. She cupped Shabael's hands. "Well?"

"We'll see. It will be wonderful to have my daughter back. She has given me some information ... she had a dream that seems related to mine. I may have seen events that occurred with Masora, which may explain why I have this wound. I don't have time to talk now. However, we have evidence of the Orb of Light in the other land. Do not breathe a word of this to anyone."

"No, my love."

"Spend time with Alie this morning. Help me get back into the life around her," Shabael pleaded.

"I plan to, of course. She wants to attend the morning prayers with her sisters. Afterwards I was going to refresh her on the sword. Though we are seven years difference, I feel like a kind of mother-sister to her."

"She has always adored you, Shawndeli. Thank you, my queen. I must be off." Shabael took several steps then stopped. Shawndeli was watching him, concern showing in her eyes.

"There's something brewing," she said, her voice quiet, "like the hint of a changing season. I heard what the witch-healer said. 'The ravens are coming.' I can even hear it in the raven caws. Watch them on the Dark Tree. They seem more active. Uneasy, perhaps. These past few years have been like a calm before the storm."

Shabael gave her a crooked smile. "It's been awhile since we've had a large battle." He stepped onto the balcony. The world seemed dark and unmoving. Soon, the Moon of Night would rise, illuminating the world in a pale white blue world with dark and shadows. The horizon held a purple tint, no stars glimmered until a quarter high in the sky. "Shawndeli, have my sword, Stormraver, brought here. There may be a storm coming. You know I can't miss my chance of dancing with the lightning."

"My Lord, are you not electrifying enough?"

"Love you too, my Queen." He smiled then turned to his guards. "All right. Let's go."

CHAPTER 12

OUTSIDE THE EMPEROR TOWER

"Calibri," King Shabael addressed the High Priest, "you are not at Black Tower? The king and his guards were already on the path leading around the mountain to the tower."

"No, Your Grace, but I have sent word ahead to the Seer. You have my mind racing with possibilities and our work is so sensitive that there are few with whom we can exchange thoughts and share the excitement."

"That's true, Calibri," Shabael said, giving the priest a pat on the shoulder. "This is why we are such close friends and comrades ... for the good of Skyeden and Malbolians."

The priest nodded. "And your daughter? May I inquire of her appearance?"

"Yes, and that's why I'm so pleased you are here." Shabael motioned with his hands for the guards to follow further behind.

"I dreamt of attacking the black raven, Calibri, and Alie dreamt of her lover, the Ravenite Mako. She said that he had died and his spirit appeared to her in a dream." The king then told the priest the tale that his daughter had related to him. "It was I, apparently, who killed Mako. But I didn't reveal that to Alie."

Calibri shook his head as if to clear it. "My mind is spinning with all these dreams," he said. "But it is my opinion that with her having shared a dream related to your vision which occurred at the same time, there seems to be truth to all of this."

It was a perfect pre-moon dawning and the western horizon kept its purplish hue with a hint of rising moon glow. As they walked along the winding path, the mountain was lit by fire-staff flames. Shabael nodded his head in approval. He wanted the storm to come, relishing the thought of the accompanying lightning. His hands ached for the touch of Stormraver. "Like the approaching storm, I feel magic stirring in the air, Calibri. A change is coming. I sense a motion in things. Forces are at play that we must understand and control."

"Yes, indeed, that is paramount," the priest said. "We must understand what is happening." Calibri was dressed in a flowing white silk robe emblazoned with the emblem of High Priest of the El Qui family.

As the men walked the path, little wisps of sound emanated from the silken pants legs rubbing together between their thighs.

"I have to say, the breakthrough with the orbs is beyond exceptional," Shabael said, placing a hand on Calibri's shoulder as they headed to the lift. "I feel we are on the cusp of some grand spiritual vibrational awakening. Your work with the tree's spheres to share a consciousness and to see images ... is to me as much a profound discovery as the rite of Descension."

"Your excitement brings joy to my ears," Calibri said, bowing his head slightly as they entered upon the lift. Calibri pulled the alert rope for the lift operator below. Within moments, the wheel above them began to spin as the rope was being pulled from below.

"I know I shared with you my emotion that day one hundred and fifty years ago, when the Raven carrying the Orb of Day escaped into that funnel and I ordered the darklings and white ravens to pursue," Shabael said.

The lift passed two floors as the momentum increased. No matter how many times Calibri used the lifts; he always felt his guts lurch with the movement.

"Ah, yes, the day I showed you the Seer Orb," he said. "It only took us since the beginning of our time to figure this out and then months to perfect before I wanted to present it to you."

"Oh, I think you exceeded yourself that day," Shabael said, and smiled at remembering the moment Calibri had produced the small orb from the sleeve of his long robe.

"Ha! You are right about that," Calibri nodded, seeming to share the same memory. Usually when the two walked from one tower to the next, it was casual and filled with intriguing talk. But today they walked faster.

"Until that time, a person could only see through his Descended animal. But the work with this plasma in a containment vessel around the vibrational orbs of the tree ... that was brilliant. With a fingertip against the glass encasing the orb, the electric plasma attaches itself creating a white glow around the fingertip. By moving the fingertip you can tune into the vibrational state of an animal ... see through its eyes, send it thoughts that can be communicated through telepathy to another." Shabael laughed. "Sorry, my old friend, I know I am merely repeating the workings of this out of amazement. You discovered this."

"Well, the other priests and I did accomplish a great feat," Calibri admitted modestly. "But your thoughts are greatly appreciated. It is our duty to understand the orbs of the tree, for each orb of the ten spheres of the tree is an essence of the Creator. It is the ladder for us to understand and transcend to strive to be godlike. To learn the spheres, to control the vibrational states to every aspect of all this," Calibri waved his hand, "is the way the Creator has provided for us for preparation and understanding when we shall be worthy of his presence."

"That day when Masora passed through the portal, I thought our connection would be broken," Shabael said. "But that evening, when I laid down and was half asleep, our minds linked. I saw through his eyes. I saw the constellation of stars unfamiliar to me. He was in the trees overlooking a village of a people that I was unfamiliar with. Then, that's when I saw her, the girl that I had shot with my arrow. No one could have lived with that wound. I watched her be devoured by ravens that then ascended through a ring of fire. And now... I am sure it was the same girl. It has to be."

In addition, through Masora's eyes he had seen Mansi for the first time. The girl was eleven years old then. How seemingly right it was that the first time he saw her, she gave him the knowledge that he needed. She had stepped out of a small hut made of mud and twigs. Mansi was carrying an arrow that she gave to the young woman. It was his arrow, with purple feathers and his name inscribed along the shaft. He himself had carved the wooden shaft from wood that had come from the dark tree. There was no doubt then; this was the same young woman he had shot.

Shabael told Calibri about the arrow again. It was a story Calibri had heard a hundred times before from his King, but he always showed interest as if it was the first time he had heard it.

Being able to see through Masora's eyes was in itself a miracle. Trying to pinpoint the consciousness of Darklings through a portal elsewhere, perhaps another world, was almost impossible. Had it not been for Masora, it would never had been done. What images they could receive were distorted and weak. Masora's communications were stronger but only Shabael received clear images. The images picked up by the Sphere Seers were always flickering and faint. The region of the sphere north had never shown activity until Masora's and the other Darklings that had passed through the portal tried to communicate.

Through Masora, Shabael found an ally. She helped create an inactivated Tree of Dark. She raised the Darklings and was his hunter for the Orb of Light. Now he had evidence that the Orb was in a tree. Maybe now they can find more clues to its location.

An hour ago, while looking through the eyes of Masora, he saw new star formations. This was the first time Masora had contacted him through dreams. When he connected with Masora, the images were better than in the Seer Spheres. There was another difference also. The Sphere images were simply looked at. However, Masora, in this dream, he was looking through Masora's eyes. He felt the coolness of the night, the smell of blood and fear. He felt the talons tear into the black raven, and even heard the sound of the prongs of the fence snapping ribs as they protruded from the black raven's chest. Shabael stepped back against the wall of the lift, lifted his head, and closed his eyes. "I remember them," he said, his voice incredulous. "I saw stars of a scorpion, a crown... "

Calibri stared into the king's eyes. The High Priest knew that all was well between them, but one did not peer into the Emperor's eyes without a feeling of trepidation. He had heard too many stories and seen the look in El Qui eyes when they ordered a dire sentencing upon an enemy, especially from the Queen Highest. The thought of Shabael's mother made him shiver. She was a woman of exquisite beauty and so greatly loved, although it was a kind of fear love. The Queen Highest was the personification of the Malbolian spirit. He often thought of Shabael as the blade and the Queen Highest as the edge that made the cuts.

"To think we may have been the first men to witness the evidence of another world or places of different vibrational states as one of your theories! I love our talks, Calibri."

"I, too, Sire." Calibri had been fifteen years older than Shabael when he took the rite of Descension. Both men's appearances belied their years of wisdom because once Descended the body remained ageless. Therefore, if a 120 years old Descended person was only twenty years old physically, he had the wisdom and maturity of man one hundred years older.

They reached the landing of the tower and walked to the backside. Four of Shabael's personal guards trailed them. Two guards were at the entrance that led into the priest's tower. They stood to attention with one hand poised on the hilts of their swords, the other hand, palm turned outward, by their face. The Red Gold guards were called that because they wore deep red kilts covered with paneled leather and leather-paneled vests and gold helmets. They were the pride of the king's forces.

Before entering into the White Tower on the south side of the Tree of Dark, Shabael and Calibri repeated a series of taps from their forehead to their abdomen that represented the ten spheres of the Tree.

"My heart always races when I see our Tree of Dark and these ten plasma spheres around her. God, I love the lightning. It electrifies me." Shabael spoke with the excitement and wonder of a young child.

"As the legend has it, it runs through the El Qui veins," Calibri noted.

"True, it does indeed. Sastorm El Qui was struck by lightning at the age of five. It is said he was marked by the Creator to become ruler of the Malbolians. Oh, to have such honor. One day I shall be anointed, touched by God's hand."

"I have no doubt," Calibri said, looking at the horizon. The Moon of Night was announcing its coming by the brightening of the approaching purple clouds. He thought he saw a flicker of lightning. "Your Grace, the way this day has already begun, it would not surprise me if this were to be the day."

"My daughter returns and I have evidence of the Orb of Light and its tree. We can possess it again or even destroy it to end our greatest threat of igniting the Sun here again. A fine day it is turning out to be.

And… Can you imagine, Calibri, if we can find the magic to create portals, we could have a new world to conquer."

The two men looked skyward and voiced in unison, "Oh, Great Creator, I commit to thee." Then they re-entered the lift and Calibri pulled the cord, signaling for the tenth floor. They began to rise.

"A glorious night it has been," Shabael said, staring out across the ocean, feeling the caress of the cool breeze beneath his hair. He could smell the briny sea and a vague hint of sulfur from the glassy slate stone shore that had been formed during a volcanic eruption before the first people came into being. Shabael placed the palm of his hands against the walls of the lift. "Tomorrow I will summon the council and priests to discuss the new developments. I can feel the vibrations. It always lifts my spirit."

"To live within the vibe, Milord, is to live within the Creator," Calibri said.

"I like that, Calibri. We should have that engraved on one of the buildings."

The lift came to a stop. Shabael stepped onto the catwalk and looked down. "You never realize how tall this tree really is until you are here," he said. "I feel like I am the King of the World."

"You are, My Grace." Calibri laughed. "Now we must take the inner lift down to the first level to the observatory deck. I want you to tell me what you see."

They reached the lower deck, made their way across the catwalk, and entered the enclosed observatory of the First Sphere of Skyeden Life.

"I always love how the hair on my arm and neck rises when I get this close," Shabael said. "The vibration makes my teeth itch." They stepped onto the glass observation globe. In the center of the globe was the first light sphere, humming and vibrating in a greenish hue. Beneath the sphere was a golden extended arm with a chair at the end of it. A Seer always sat in the chair. The arm moved three hundred and sixty degrees around the one hundred foot diameter sphere. A tuning fork was suspended from a harness attached to the glass above the sphere. The fork vibrated and created a wavering, humming tone that remained the same continuous note. The center orb of the top triangle of tree orbs contained the Orb of Dark. Pipes of glass extended from this orb and then connected the seven other spheres as adjoining triangles going downward. The electric threads of plasma flowed along the tubes and through each of the ten spheres.

"Sit in the chair, My Grace," Calibri said, and motioned for the Seer to rise and give the Emperor the seat. "By reversing the spin of the tuning fork we can replay the vibrations that have recently passed. In this extended arm, we have inserted a smaller sphere that was attuned to Masora.

Shabael looked surprised. "You are able to encapsulate an individual's vibrations? Well done, Calibri."

"As you know we have no way of seeing the first hours of this new place ... Earth," Calibri continued. "But after your viewing and discovery of the girl, we have maintained visuals through Masora, dedicating a Seer day and night and keeping an unbroken vibrational link with him. We followed Dayanna to a place that she began going to about eighteen years ago. She came every evening to the child's home, never entering, but observing. Since that time, we have continued a steady observation of this child. Nothing had really happened of interest for us until this evening. Before I could be alerted to the event, I was summoned to your quarters." Calibri leaned closer to the small orb positioned in the arm of the seat, then raised back up. "Look into the orb, Your Grace."

Calibri turned toward the Seer. "Replay the sequence of events you showed me." The Seer mounted a ladder and turned a wheel that was attached by a rope to the tuning folk. He stopped and nodded to Calibri.

"Watch now."

Shabael leaned forward, looking into the green glowing orb.

"Remember, relax, and allow your eyes to become unfocused toward the center," Calibri instructed. Shabael gasped as a black raven flew from overhead and landed on the edge of the building wall. Shabael seized the armrests, shot a glance to Calibri, then back at the raven that was only yards away. Seeing through the eyes of the white raven, Calibri watched the black raven and what the black raven carried in its beak. A white light grew before the black raven. The light seemed to be coming from a small branch it was holding in its beak and it was like white fire. It was so bright that it hurt the eyes.

"*Cawwwww!*"

The white raven cried out and made a dive for the black raven. White claws seized the back of the black raven's head, while the second claw thrust its talons deep into the flesh. The black raven's head slammed against the window so hard the glass cracked. Then there was a white blinding flash causing the white raven to shriek in pain, releasing its grip, flinging itself backwards, and falling downward. The black raven recovered quickly and latched onto the white raven with its talons. The birds flapped their wings and pecked at each other's heads, gouging at an eye, pulling free small feathers and flesh while their talons raked over each other, tearing into their chests. The black raven's remaining eye widened, noting something of importance. It screamed out and lunged with all its strength into the white raven, sending both birds backward, then down … then impaled. The black raven emitted a final cry of pain, then silence. The small sphere went back to a cloudy green. The image was gone.

"That's what happened!" Shabael said. *"That was Masora!* I was seeing through his eyes!" Shabael spun around in the chair looking at Calibri. "Tell me!"

"You are right. It seems the black raven was attempting to give the young man a branch of a white tree."

Shabael leaned forward, trying to read what was in Calibri's mind. "A new Tree of Light, you mean? You agree with me then."

"I believe so, Your Grace." Calibri said, and nodded.

Shabael struck the arm of the chair with a victorious slap. "So, this is evidence that the Orb of Light still exists and is in this other place. Is this what we can imply from what we have witnessed?"

"It is, My Liege," Calibri said.

"Awaken Mansi! Call to her now," Shabael demanded. "A hundred and fifty years, Calibri. It has finally revealed itself. If we can possess this one egg-sized orb of light, our dominance will never be threatened again. Change the spheres or whatever you have to do. I must speak to my earth witch.

"Mansi, oh, how important you are becoming to me."

Shabael entered the observatory, his personal guards standing rigidly at attention behind him. He motioned to one of the watchers to get out of his chair and took the vacated seat, bowing his head. The spheres acted as telepathic receivers that transmitted signals into images on their inky surfaces and were fine-tuned to receive specific frequencies in specific areas. The Darklings were the key to the complicated operation as they were programmed to sense vibrational frequencies and telepath the images through their own eyes. When a

142

connection was made, the watcher could see the images and communicate with the Darkling. The watcher was also able to transmit his voice through the Darkling, although the sound was raspy and cracked. This was one of the many gifts the Dark Magic had bestowed on the Malbolians.

Shabael focused on the Darkling that began to appear in the globe. A faint light arose on the surface but was blurry and weak. "Is this the best we can get with the Darkling?"

"Yes, Sire," the Seer said.

"Where is Masora? Release the Darkling." Shabael closed his eyes and touched the extended arm that held Masora's sphere. "Masora, it is I, Shabael, let me see through your eyes

After a moment, an image suddenly flashed upon the surface of the sphere transmitting from an underground cavern filled with metaphysical devices and huge maps. The king paused for a moment, he no longer saw the sphere or the others around him, he saw through Masora's eyes. And when he next spoke, what he said aloud before the sphere was spoken out of the mouth of the white raven.

"Mansi, awaken!" Shabael's voice rasped in Mansi's mind like reptilian scales slithering across ice.

The young woman, who had been dozing in bed, sat up. Her eyes blinked as she fought to shake off the stupor of sleep. She looked around the room for Masora.

"Mansi, here."

In the shadow beneath her shelf of clothes, she saw movement with glints of leather and teeth. Claws scrapped against the stone of her cavern floor. *He's talking through a Darkling. Where is Masora?*

She wished she had time to comb her hair, slip on a summer dress that accented her youthful 18 year old body forever in its sexually, ripe-for-the-plucking fruit. In biblical terms, she saw herself as the personification of the apple from the Tree of Knowledge. Though things went terribly wrong that day of harvest over a century ago, she had been gifted with a most powerful tool, a body of seduction. She learned quickly to use her tool not in the sexually acts of her body, but of the messaging to another how she gave a look and smile that said to another, she possessed the promises of untapped ecstasy, where a bite of her, this deliciously honey-dew dripping apple would give experiences…in a way… a kind of knowledge of such exquisite unadulterated pleasures it would be life altering, unveiling new perceptions of the world. It would be a climatic revelation so invigorating it would animate every code of the DNA strands in the man's body that would show him the true reality of the world.

Since the Day of Harvest, she herself was altered forever because she had gained Dark magic. She saw everything as vibrational with positive and negative or Light and Dark. She had felt the slowing of frequency in her vibration down into her very atomic level. There were two emotions a human experienced, fear and love. Fear was of a low frequency and love was higher. She discovered after that fateful day, with her lowering of frequency, she could manipulate from others, not just to lower another's vibe, but she could quicken it into a higher state of love vibration. With this power and the body she possessed, she doubted there was a man alive that could resist her.

As she rose out of bed, her bare feet touching the cool stone of the cavern floor, her thin gown slipped from her shoulders. Even through the eyes of a Darkling and a transmission of images from her world to the world of her Great King, she sensed the physical rods within his eyes going through the physical process of electric processes and chemical stimulations to produce her image within his mind. She had the ability to quicken his vibrational frequency to a higher state of love.

"Mansi," the raspy Darkling voice sounded again, yet softer, affected by her magic. She tried to suppress her smile and knelt on one knee.

"Yes, Sire."

As the King was looking into the Orb, he spoke to Calibri. "Look, it's so clear now, almost as seeing through Masora. This is good."

"Yes," Calibri said. His eyes seemed fixated on the girl's breasts. It took him a little effort to break away. "You no longer are locked into Masora's point of view, but within the Orb you can literally float around like a roaming eyeball. You can view from behind her to before her, from the ground and up to the ceiling looking down."

"It's magical," Shabael whispered back, and then he returned back to Mansi. He had become aware how the sight of her affected him. In some ways, it made him fear her.

"As you may surmise by my wound on Masora here," Shabael presented Masora's right side of his face, I intercepted a black raven a short time ago. The raven was attempting to lead the boy to your village. I prevented this from happening. Then, the same raven

144

attempted to give the boy a small branch of the White Tree. I killed the raven but the boy took the branch and closed his window, preventing me from taking it."

"Healing thoughts to your injury, My Grace," she said. Oh, how she wished she could see the man behind the white raven and that she could hear his real voice that was distorted through the transmission. She wanted to reach out and touch his wound, press her lips to it.

"It is imperative that we find the Tree of Light from which this branch has come," the seemingly disembodied voice said. "We must be alert to any sign that can lead us to the Tree of Light. We must possess the Orb of Light within it! Over a hundred years we have searched in vain and yet it still eluded us. On that Day of Harvest our chance to track back to the source was missed.

"Assemble your Darklings and keep a constant eye on this Dylan. The Light source we believe is seeking him out. Get a place close by him so you may respond immediately to any Light activity. Use your ability to see through the Darkling's eyes. We must find this last Light and the sacred tree that harbors it. When we do, you will combine the Orbs. This is the key to the imbalance. This I believe will take the Light from your world to a permanent state of darkness. Then the dark essence will become powerful and lead you and me to conquering this world. When the touching of the orbs is done, you must put the Orb of Light in a secure place that no one can find. For what gives us power... can take it away. Possessing the Orb of Light will assure our worlds of dark dominance. You understand this?"

"I do, Sire."

"Very well. I dream the day our worlds are dark. And we will find the key to unlock the pathway to one another."

"It is the dream we share."

"Yes. Now, heal Masora of his wound. He will accompany you."

Masora lowered its head, closed its eyes, and seemed to fall asleep. Mansi turned away and went to the cavern entrance, pushed open the door and emerged beneath a giant root of an ancient gnarly tree. The tree's limbs were filled with Darklings, their shapes barely visible in the dimness. Pulsing within the crown of the tree branches was a black fire. An arrow protruded from the tree's trunk.

Mansi faced the tree, her heart swelling with pride. It seemed so long ago that she had come to this place following the betrayal of her family and tribe. The white raven had come to her that morning, and whispered for her to follow it. It led her to the decaying old oak, its trunk pockmarked with rot. The memory of that day washed over her and she recalled how she had stolen the arrow and the small white branch that had belonged to Raven. She had driven the arrowhead into the tree and waited to witness its transformation.

She turned away from the Dark Tree and stared in the direction she had come from after the slaughtering of her tribe members. Her visage darkened and she screamed, "Why did you ignore me!? Why couldn't you have loved me, Stepmother!? Well, that's too bad! Now I am a queen with an army of Darklings at my disposal. I am a queen! Do you hear?"

She was so excited. How she wanted to spread the news to her friends and family of which she had none. Kawanda had said she did not remember the name of the tribe or if it had even been a tribe that Mansi had come from. A small party of warriors had taken the medicine woman to a mountain known for its lichens that she used in one of her medicines. The small group stumbled across the remainder of a plagued tribe; and, the medicine woman gave all the comfort she could to them. Still, half of the remaining few died that evening. A dying mother asked if she would take her child and the Medicine woman agreed. Two days later, everyone else in the camp was dead. The medicine woman directed warriors to burn the corpses and almost unbelievably, none of them caught the disease. Mansi, only five years old, was adopted by the medicine woman and taught to call her Grandmother.

Mansi whirled and faced the old tree. "I want more!" she shouted. "I deserve more! Oh, I will protect you as my Emperor has commanded. I will study the Dark Magic until I understand it. However, because of you, I must be isolated. I must live beneath your roots like a mole. Why have I been given the desires of love but only to be denied? Why was I enraged to the point of betraying my people to the enemy and watching them being slaughtered? Why did my own grandmother deny me the attention and praise that I wanted and deserved? Was it your will that I be tormented and changed into an unloved creature, doomed to seek what will forever be denied me? Oh, you have twisted my heart into a vile, venomous sac of scorn. Yes! I want to hurt the world! I want revenge! I want to rip the world into pieces and put it back together so that my actions will be acknowledged."

She paused, stared up at the dark sky, and murmured, "It's going to be all right now. My Emperor has acknowledged my worth. He sees my worth. It is he that loves me. I will live for the day that we can be together."

A feeling of freedom and absolution washed over Mansi. There would be no more humiliation from tribe members who had scorned the orphan. No more forced cordialness to the young woman she and her grandmother had discovered on the mountain trail that night. They had watched the ring of fire approach in the sky and saw the object fall to earth. The girl had been standing in the path, clutching a bunch of dead ravens and the arrow that now protruded from the tree trunk.

"Rise my Darklings. Follow me!"

She raised her face to the sky and shouted, "I am *Mansi*! I am *Queen*!"

CHAPTER 13

NEVERLAND — EMPEROR'S TOWER

"The Moon of Night is rising, High Priest," Shabael said to Calibri as he departed with his Red Gold guards back to the Emperor Tower. As he walked around the mountain, the sounds of his and the guards' footfalls sounded loud upon the cobblestone path. He looked upon the rising Moon as rising hope and sensed victory forthcoming. The signs were all there. His daughter had returned to him; the presence of the Orb of Light had been revealed. Queen Mansi was a gift from the creator that would carry out his will in this other land. He had no doubt that she would find the Orb of Light. It was a great morning. Perhaps he would surprise Shawndeli and Alie with a visit. Oh, and mother, he smiled.

"Wait," Shabael said. "Let's go to the Tower of the Priestess. We will surprise the Queen and my daughter and then walk them back to the Emperor Tower."

In the Tower of Priestess, on the highest deck on the other side of Black Tower, a hundred of the hooded priestesses were on their knees deep into their morning devotional prayers, a daily ritual that began each day before the Moon of Night rose from the other side of the Dark Tree. When the moon rose above the horizon, its rays ran upward through the branches of the tree. Though the prayers were made in silence, there was a sense of great excitement in the air.

The orator, singer of Praise to Light of Night, was Princess Alie. In celebration of her return to the royal court, the High Priestess asked if she would sing this morning. It felt like a moment of rebirth for her. She had erred in the belief her family had mortally wounded her lover. She had denied her father her love. In discovering her wrong, she swore she would never desert her father or people again. She would rise and stand by her father's side and his new queen. Her heart was filled with joy. How she wished her mother could see her now. Her presence was felt; she longed to see her late mother's face, to feel her arms around her. She glanced over at her stepmother, Queen Shawndeli, who gave her a supporting, comforting smile. There was pride showing in her countenance and what appeared to be genuine happiness. They had always gotten along, and had she allowed herself to trust Shawndeli more and sought her out. She would have expressed her outrage and sometime murderous thoughts; and, Shawndeli would have reasoned with her. However, that was long ago.

Alie turned to fully face the bowed priestesses in their red robes. Alie was also wearing red in an attempt to show that she would always feel a connection with her sisters. Only the men of the priesthood and royal family could wear the white robes of their faith, Dreamanity.

Their God and creator was "Dreamer". The Malbolians believed one's afterlife was determined by their dreams. Their consciousness continued out of their body but lived in a dream-created world based on the dreams of their sleep. If a person had nightmares, their afterlife would be a world of nightmares. The Dreamer had created all that exists. As children of the dreamer, they possessed the ability to create their own afterlife. The Moon of Night possessed the qualities of *dream light*. The Dreamer's creative thoughts were vibrations. His visions of Skyeden were created by his vibrational thoughts. And as the vibrations spread into the nothingness of space, solid physical forms slowly came into being. The universe was created with Skyeden at the center. This was their belief. So, when Princess Alie prepared herself to sing, she thought of the wonder of all around her and the greatness of her Creator, the Dreamer. Her raven, Maliki, was not feeling the spirit of the morning. His claws were extended. He was slightly crouched, turning his head from side to side in an effort to view everyone in the crowd of bowing priestesses.

Alie, feeling Maliki tense, glanced quickly to her raven and saw the short feathers of his head were standing up. She sent him a thought. *It's all right. It's just stage fright.* She lowered her head and drew in a deep breath. Slowly she raised her hood-covered head, letting her lungs open as she begin to sing,

"Blessed be the Light of Night
That sweetly comes arising
What joy brings the glorious sight
Of moonlight over the horizon

White Ravens in Light of Night
Dark magic beneath our wings
Purple skies in the moonlight
Like the heavens of our dreams

Blessed be the Light of Night
We are warriors of the Dark
Faith makes great our swords of might
To slay our enemies' hearts

White Ravens in Light of Night
Champions of Skyeden
White Ravens sworn to fight
Forever we shall be winging"

As the words lifted the spirits, the priestesses' spiritual wings opened. Like the delicate white evening glories that bloomed with the kiss of moonlight, the feathers unfurled like the flower petals. The priestesses rose several feet off the floor. Their bodies basked in the Moon of Night's rays of purple hues that filtered through the branches of the Tree of Dark. It was a glorious sight. The rays of purple light upon the glowing spiritual white wings created a dream-like blur of feathers and mist.

Alie's words floated across the air like the first moonlight ever to fall upon a drop of evening dew. The priestesses were lifted so high that their spiritual wings touched the ceiling.

This was unexpected for the four assassins who were kneeling on the back row. Normally the Princess knelt in the row they were in now. In addition to this, the Queen Shawndeli was in attendance, kneeling with the High Priestess up front.

CHAPTER 14

ATTACK OF THE SNAKE PEOPLE

Shabael stopped along the path, at the foot of the tower. "Listen. Isn't that my daughter?" he asked. "It is. I know it is." He lolled his head back and listened to Alie's voice that echoed off the mountain and seemed somehow enhanced by the branches of the Dark Tree. He opened his eyes and saw the rays of moonlight spilling from the Dark Tree onto the tower terrace above. He felt his heart rise in his throat and the threat of tears in his eyes. He exhaled, hoping to exude a little emotional release there rather than from his eyes, especially with his men around. He almost laughed. *So fierce a King was he.* When Alie's voice held a long note, he listened as if his ears were savoring the taste of a favorite wine. His daughter's scream jarred him back to reality with a rush like the shattering of a glass. His eyes flew open in time to see the figure hurled over the edge of the terrace and plummet to earth. The body made a sickening crunch-splat sound. He was struck with blood splatter and watched in horror as the first died in the attack.

The sight had frozen Shabael. Then he found his own voice, "Alie!" he cried, then lunged forward and scooped up the limp body into his arms. He yanked the hood back and saw it was a bareheaded priestess. He could tell from looseness of the body that the bones within her were shattered. The back of her skull was flat. An eye dangled down her cheek. Shabael released the priestess and wiped his

151

hands against the folds of his robe, then regained his feet and began running. He literally tore his sword from the scabbard.

"Move aside!" he commanded, sending the priestess guards at the entrance of the tower scattering. Men were forbidden to enter the Tower of the Priestess, but this was no time for protocol. The Red Gold guards followed behind their king.

The cries grew louder as Shabael raced up the steps. Women fought to exit the terrace entrance and two more of the priestesses fell past Shabael and struck the bottom floor of the tower.

"No!" Shabael screamed. "Move!" he shouted to the women attempting to flee down the narrow steps. The stone stairs were only wide enough for two people side by side. Another priestess fell to her death and the fleeing women still fled down the stairs. One of them collided with Shabael and had he not jerked to the side he would have impaled her with his sword. He shouldered his way upward. "One at a time! One!" He pushed upward against the wall, allowing room for others to move down the steps on his left side.

Five more floors. His heart thundered in his chest. Sweat ran into his eyes. The altitude was so high on the mountain that the exertion made it hard to breathe. His sandal caught on a jagged part of the steps, ripping it from his foot. He stumbled forward and felt the tip of his sword catch in the robe of a fleeing woman. It nearly yanked his sword from his hand. Members of the Red Gold guard behind him shouted for him to give them a chance to catch up and be in position to defend him.

Shabael was up again, ignoring the guards' panicked request and shouldering his way up the steps with one sandal missing. "To the side! The side!" He shoved the priestesses to the left of him. Two flights up. "By the Gods!" he shouted, summoned all the strength within him, and pushed again.

"The Queen!"

"Princess!"

Their names being shouted from within the terrace sent electric fear through Shabael. Finally, he grabbed the opening to the frame of the terrace doors and swung his body inward, knocking over two priestesses. His sword fell from his hand and clamored on the floor. He scrambled to reclaim it as hands grabbed him under the arms and hoisted him up.

"Alie! Shawndeli!" Shabael cried. There were dozens of purple-hooded robes scrambling and screaming. He whirled around, looking for the enemy. The only thing he could see was priestesses. "Where?" He jumped up on a table, trying to see above the mass of panicking bodies.

"They went this way!" a priestess shouted, pointing to the High Priestess passage.

Shabael jumped off the table. "This way!" he said to his guards.

One of his guards was yelling, "What is happening here?"

"Assassins!" someone answered. "Four of them. They chased the Queen and Princess. We tried to stop them, but there was too much panic!"

As Shabael plunged down the Priestess Tower stairs, he thought he heard the same voice scream, "Snakes! Snakes!" He hated snakes. To him every snake was poisonous. He replaced his sword in the scabbard and withdrew his dagger, still running down the stairs, taking three steps at a time. He reached the landing of the balcony and sprang through the doorway. The balcony was empty. He ran to the edge and peered down. Two of the priestess guards were lying on the ground. Then he saw Shawndeli's white waist band. There was a spray of blood on it.

"Down!" They're down here!"

Shabael jumped over the ledge and landed on his feet. He heard screams coming from the other side of the Dark Tree. The moon was over the horizon making it hard to see at ground level. On the other side of the tree was Black Tower.

"This way!" He ran ahead. Two of the Red Gold guards flanked his sides as they ran past two priestesses lying on the ground.

"In the tower!" a woman cried out. Shabael raced past the priestess, subconsciously noting a glint of metal. He slid to a stop as he rounded the Dark Tree. Priest guards were poised in defensive poses, but no one had come this way.

"Priestesses don't wear metal. Back! That woman! Stop her!"

"She went there!" a Red Gold shouted, pointing to a path leading down the mountain.

"Ahhh!" Shabael cried out in desperation. The path was narrow and rocky with thick brambles and branches on each side. It was a dangerous, dark descent.

"Run, Alie!" he heard Shawndeli cry from down the path.

"I'm coming!" Shabael shouted. "Desist, bastards! I'll kill you all!"

Shabael slipped, sitting down so hard that the breath was knocked from him, sending gravel and stones rattling down around him. He leapt upward, grabbing the trunk of a small tree, and swung himself around the bend of the path and slammed into the back of a hooded figure. The figure stumbled forward and Shabael drew his dagger back with his right hand and reached with his left to grab the hood of the robe and yank the assassin around. However, the hooded figure was already turning with lightning speed, sending Shabael forward with his own momentum. The king had a firm grip on the hood and refused to let go, yanking the head of the assassin back toward him as he fell forward. In the pale moonlight, he saw yellow eyes and narrow pupils and his knuckles brushed against what felt like scales of a fish. Then the thing hissed ... human lips ... but as he loosened his hold on the hood he felt something tactile and wet flick across his wrists. Then something caught in his sleeve, white and boney... and then he struck the ground. The hooded "thing" screamed as a sword from one of the Red Gold guards struck at it. Shabael grabbed at a branch of a nearby tree and regained his footing. The assassin whirled, literally spinning in the air with daggers flashing and struck down two of the Red Gold guards. Their swords and armor clamored against the stones as their death cries filled the air.

"Run!" Shawndeli shouted. Her voice sounded much closer. Shabael turned around and leapt downward, grabbing another tree branch for support and throwing himself around the next turn, slamming into another hooded figure. He attempted throwing his left arm around to bring the assassin down as he fell, but the enemy countered with a spin in the opposite direction. Shabael lost his balance and fell, bumping down two of the steps. He looked up and saw that he was at Shawndeli's feet. She had a dagger in each hand, pointing them in the direction of two assassins who were coming up the steps toward her.

The assassin that had eluded Shabael was crouched, holding a wicked curved blade aimed at Shawndeli. As the king approached, the assassin leapt forward to attack Shawndeli from the rear. Shabael sprang upward, his shoulder clipping the airborne assassin on the thigh as he collided. The momentum caused the assassin's body to swing around and it crashed into the bramble on the left side of the path. Shabael braced his feet on the ground for impetus and lunged forward. The assassin's knife clattered to the ground. The attacker's robe was caught in branches and thorns when Shabael's dagger struck the mid-section and he finished the thrust with a slashing pull on the blade. The agonizing shriek that ensued was that of a woman's voice.

Shabael's momentum carried him forward, taking the impaled attacker with him to the ground. As they landed heavily, she tore herself free and rolled across the path. Shabael made a desperate grab for her feet but the woman ducked beneath the foliage. She appeared to be slithering — a serpentine undulating — as she zigged and zagged, disappearing beneath the leaves and branches.

"AHHHHHH!" Shabael shouted in frustration and turned to thrust his dagger at the two assassins threatening Shawndeli. "Where is Alie?"

"She ran into the barn!" Shawndeli shouted. "Down there! Go! I can handle these two."

Shabael snatched up knife that the fled assassin had dropped and charged down the steps. "Rageton?" Shabael shouted without bothering to look for his faithful guard.

"Sire?" Rageton answered from somewhere along the path.

"Protect the Queen!" The guard did not bother responding, he just turned and ran toward the embattled Shawndeli.

The stonewall barn was yards away. The door was swinging as though someone had just entered.

"Stay back!" Shabael heard Alie cry.

"No!" Shabael shouted, hoping to distract the attacker as he charged ahead and slammed through the door, sending it banging against the inside wall. He paused to allow his eyes to adjust to the darkness of the barn. A second before the door slammed shut, he glimpsed the back of the attacker's head. The assassin's hair was thick and bushy and as vividly red as fire, falling free of the robe as the head was reared back. The dim light dancing off the woman's cheeks of flesh and scales revealed a wild-yellowed eye with a narrow pupil.

The still-swinging barn door created a bizarre scene of darkness … light … darkness

Suddenly, just a millisecond before Shabael reached the terrified Alie, something before him, reared its head back. In the shaft of light Shabael caught a glimpse of the side of its face. The yellow eye gleamed like copper. Then there was a glint of light shining off glistening long fangs just before the attacker struck like a viper. It was like two women kissing, except his daughter's scream that followed told otherwise.

Darkness.

Shabael grabbed a fistful of the devil's hair and wrenched at it with all his might.

A strange throaty stricken gasp sounded from his daughter. The attacker was twisting in his grasp. They were falling.

Light.

They struck the ground, locked in mortal combat.

Darkness.

Shabael roared, rearing his arm back and striking downward with a fist only to hit dirt as the attacker squirmed and whipped from beneath his body.

Light.

The attacker was a blur of robe as it whisked out of the doorway. The door swung back, catching the robe, and tearing it from the fleeing assassin.

The door remained open. Shabael crawled toward his daughter who was now sitting on the floor, her back against the wall. Her eyes were wide and frightened. A hand covered her mouth. Blood leaked between her fingers.

"My love, you're hurt!"

Alie's eyes were wild with panic. She was struggling to breathe.

"Breathe! Here, give me your hands!" Shabael pried her hands free. There was a puncture wound through her lower lip and one in the tip of her protruding tongue. She was gagging, struggling to breathe.

"Breathe through your nose!" Shabael shouted. "Come on! Breathe! Someone help me! Help!" Shabael cried out. He released Alie's hands and placed his to the sides of her face, trying to keep her mouth open.

Light.

Shawndeli burst through the door. "Is she bitten? Did they bite her?"

"Yes, I think they did! She cannot breathe. Her mouth … they bit her mouth and her tongue, I think," Shabael answered.

Shawndeli dropped to her knees and replaced Shabael's hands with her own on Alie's face, forcing the girl's head back. "Keep the door open!" she said. "I need … No, take her…take her outside.

Hurry!" Shabael lifted Alie in his arms and rushed outside. Shawndeli carefully placed Alie's head on the ground and turned her to best catch the moonlight.

Then Shabael hastily began arranging search parties. "Sound the drums! I want these assassins found," he ranted. "Send guards to find the Queen Mother and get her within these walls."

Shawndeli was desperately attempting to save her stepdaughter. "Give me....no..." the queen was flustered, her mind darting in various directions as she sought to find some way to help the beautiful girl, dying in her arms. She literally tore a strip of leather from her ponytail. "I'm going to have to remove her tongue," she said to Shabael, who was still hovering over the two. "It's swelling and her flesh is burning where the poison has entered."

"No. She'll die!"

"She'll die if we don't!" Shawndeli said.

Shabael jumped to his feet, wild-eyed, checking the surroundings. "I need fire," he said. "Get me fire! Shabael pointed up the flight of steps.

"Get fire!" the soldiers shouted up the line. Within seconds, a torch was being passed down.

Alie clutched Shawndeli's wrist in a death grip. She was shaking her head violently and wheezing as she sought to get air though her rapidly closing throat.

Shabael took the torch and placed it on the ground. He held the blade of his dagger over the flame, impatiently waiting for it to heat. He looked up at the Moon of Night, silently asking how this could be happening. Tears fell from his eyes and trickled down his cheeks as he questioned whether he could do what had to be done. The blade was glowing hot.

Alie's wailing had become guttural and animal-like. It sounded like a large wild boar, startled out of its natural habitat.

Shawndeli turned to the Red Gold guards. "Help me hold her still," she said, and two soldiers placed their hands on the moaning, shivering princess.

The blade of the dagger was red hot and glowing in the dim light. Shabael moved behind Alie and firmly gripped her head with both hands. The two guards knelt, one on each side of the girl, and held her convulsing body as still as possible. Shawndeli straddled over her with the dagger, its blade still glowing.

"Look at me, baby" Shabael said. "Look at me. It's going to be all right, my love." Alie stopped crying and Shabael saw determination in her eyes. He recognized the raw courage and his heart melted inside his chest as she nodded for them to proceed.

"Do it. Do it *now!*" Shabael said to Shawndeli, tears streaming down his face.

Shawndeli gripped Alie's tongue with her left hand and pulled. The swollen tongue was slippery with blood and she had trouble keeping it in a firm grip as she lowered her head and took the organ into her own mouth, sucking. "Ahhh!" Shawndeli gasped, dropping the knife and clutching her own throat. "Water! To me! Now!"

Shabael marveled at his wife as she released Alie's tongue and was trying to wave air into her own mouth, spitting a discolored stream onto the ground.

A guard arrived with a leather pouch and handed it to Shawndeli. "It's wine," he said apologetically.

Shawndeli drank from the wine pouch, rinsed her mouth and spat it out, filled her mouth again and gargled. She spat again.

"Ohhh ..." she moaned. "The poison I sucked out was burning. I'm okay ... I think. I didn't swallow any of it." She took a deep pull on the wine again and repeated the rinse and spat it out, then held the leather wine pouch up to be taken.

"All right, Alie,' she said to the terrified girl. "Once more, my dear. Stay with me. Look at your father, Alie. Concentrate on his face."

King Shabael kept a firm grip on Alie's face, holding her still as Shawndeli went about her grisly task. He fought to keep his eyes fixed on his daughter's face, trying to instill a courage that even he wasn't sure existed. The guttural sounds emitting from Alie's tortured throat were like mortal wounds to his soul. As the girl's body jerked and thrashed as spasms wracked it, Shabael had never felt more impotent. He was the Emperor of Skyeden where all heeded his commands or suffered the consequences as he saw fit. He held the power of life and death over his subjects. He could exterminate an entire culture. However, he was powerless now in this attempt to save his little girl.

Steeling himself and drawing from the inner strength that Alie was exhibiting, Shabael focused on locking his eyes with his daughter's. Together they bonded for added strength.

Shawndeli regained her grip on the girl's slippery tongue and moved the razor-sharp knife into position.

"I love you." Shabael said to Alie. Alie blinked and kept her eyes riveted to her father's.

Shawndeli made the cut.

Alie winced and suddenly went limp. Shabael saw the pain and fear in her eyes fade into unconsciousness.

Shawndeli removed the knife from Alie's mouth and used the bottom of her robe to swab at the flood running from the girl's mouth. "I can't reach it," she said, a pleading look in her eyes as she looked at Shabael.

"My sword!" Shabael shouted, loosening his grip on Alie's head. He stood, moved the exhausted Shawndeli to the side, and knelt beside Alie's inert body. "I can't see; there's too much blood."

Shawndeli quickly swabbed at the bloody mouth and bade a Red Gold to move Alie's head. "Keep her head turned so the blood can flow out," she instructed.

Shabael was frantic. "How can I do this?" he asked.

Shawndeli, fighting to keep her composure, placed a hand on her husband's arm to reassure him. "I cut to the root of the tongue," she said. "Just press the sword downward and to the very back of the tongue. But keep the blade angled down; you must not block the throat. Now, Shabael. *Do it now!*"

Shabael mustered all the strength and resolve in his body and mind and moved the blade inside Alie's mouth. Her body was still limp and unmoving. Shabael looked to Shawndeli, seeking even more support, and inserted the blade deeper. "I'm not sure."

"I'll help guide it," Shawndeli said, and placed her fingers around the blade, pressing it down and back.

"Ahhh!" Shawndeli cried, gritting her teeth, her body quaking with the effort. She suddenly jerked her bloodied hand free and brought it against her chest.

Shabael, his face a ghostly white, withdrew the sword from Alie's mouth and let it drop to the ground. His expression was one of pure horror. He moved to Shawndeli and placed an arm around her shoulders, pulling her close.

Shawndeli kissed him on the cheek, then knelt beside the still unconscious Alie and wiped the blood from her face and neck. She looked up at Shabael with tears streaming down her cheeks. "You did it!" she wept. "You did it!"

"Healer coming!" a Red Gold guard shouted from his position along the path. "Clear the way!"

Shabael reached a hand to Shawndeli and helped her to her feet. The all too familiar dinging of the bells rang in his ears as he watched his guards parting the gathered crowd on the path to reveal the Healer Janessa and one of her aides. The war drum sounded, tardily alerting Malbolians of an attack.

"She's unconscious," Shawndeli said as Healer Janessa knelt beside the Princess. Shawndeli and Shabael moved to give Janessa room as the bells on her robe jingled. The pungent odor of strong herbs almost took their breath.

Janessa took one look into Alie's mouth then quickly turned to the king and queen.

"She was bitten," Shawndeli said. "Poisoned as though bitten by a snake. The venom was burning her tongue, creating a hole in her flesh. I didn't know what else to do."

Janessa did not respond. She waved for her aide to bring the cage of rats and place it on the ground.

"I have her tongue," Shabael said, offering a bundled cloth in his hand.

The healer held Alie's mouth open and reached out her hand to be given the tongue. She unwrapped the cloth and placed the tongue back into the girl's mouth. "What is wrong with your hand, My Queen?" Janessa asked, still looking at Alie.

"I guided the hot blade to cauterize the wound."

"You did a very good job. The cut is clean and you did remarkably well with closing the wound." Janessa straightened, cupped Alie's jaw with one hand, and held the tongue in place with the other. She glanced toward the caged rats.

"Goddess Moon of Night,
Mother of Skyeden,
Dream weaver,
Spinning webs of crisscross destinies,
Before you, a Princess,
A child of Descension,
A being blessed of your gift of immortality
Heal your dream child,
May she have again a healthy reality.

160

Oh, I ask of Thee, Great Mother,
Let my body be a conduit to receive injury
and pass it on to the rodents.
We give thanks to those who sacrifice their lives for our healings.
I the conduit!
Injury come to me!
I pass it on!"

With each word, the voice grew not just in volume, but strength and clarity. It seemed to Shabael the healer actually raised off the ground. The air around her shimmered.

The crack and flash of thunder and lightning suddenly sounded overhead. Shabael jumped to his feet, raising his sword skyward.

"No!" Janessa yanked her hand from Alie's mouth and fell backwards. She grabbed Shabael's free hand and lifted herself to her knees.

The rats inside the cage were scurrying over one another seeking shelter from the lightning, apparently unaffected by the healing attempt.

Janessa looked at her hand, rubbing her index and forefinger, then checked the cage. She wrapped the tongue back in the cloth and said, "Emperor, speak to me over there," she motioned to a place away from the gathered group.

"What happened?" Shabael said.

"I've not felt the presence of Light this strong since last I healed an Ascended Ravenite. Whatever attacked the Princess is of the Ascension of the Orb of Light. But I am confused." She rubbed the tip of her fingers together and closed her eyes. "Not as powerful as the Orb of Light and certainly not of a thousand year-old Ascended."

"I don't understand," Shabael said, and noted Shawndeli looking at them curiously. He shrugged his shoulders.

"The attackers are Orb of Light Ascended," Janessa mused. "Yet, somehow different."

"Ravenites? But what I saw was not raven," Shabael said. "These attackers ... they had patches of scales and their eyes ... their eyes were yellow and their pupils were not round. They were ..."

"Narrow, like snake eyes," Janessa completed the sentence.

"Yes." Shabael said.

"Bring me one of the bodies," Janessa said.

161

Shabael repeated the request as a command and a Red Gold answered, "Sire, no bodies to retrieve."

"What do you mean?" Shabael sounded incredulous. "There were four of them. Not one?"

"Nay, Sire. It is as if they have vanished," the Red Gold said.

"Four assassins manage to escape the most highly trained warriors of the world!" Shabael's words were tinged with disbelief.

The soldiers on the steps above began stepping aside to allow a large bald man pass. He was wearing a red silk robe with gold trim.

"Malcolm, welcome. Come join us," Shabael said.

Malcolm stopped near Alie's feet and stared at the unconscious girl. "She's dead?"

"No," Shawndeli said, her face grim. "She's not dead. She is going to live. She had Alie's head cradled in her lap and gently held it as two soldiers arrived with a stretcher.

"Take her to my chambers," Shabael directed. "Malcolm, join me and Healer Janessa."

"We have no reports of an advancing army," Malcolm said as they began walking. "We are locked down. Gates and bridges are secure. No one leaves or enters."

"Seems there's a concerted effort to assassinate the El Quis," Janessa said, glancing at King Shabael.

"Two options I perceive," Shabael said. "Either someone seeks revenge for a personal grievance or one of the tribes, knowing their bleak chance of surviving an open conflict, has sought a more subtle, precision strike on the royal family. Whatever their mission, they have eluded us. Moreover, we know they are not wholly human. They have scales and fangs and ... they slithered like serpents. Whoever ... whatever they are; they are tainted with the Orb of Light. The injuries they cause can only be healed naturally. But with that venom, those of Dark Descendant will only have minutes to live."

"Are you speaking of snakes, Milord? Malcolm asked. He reached out and placed a hand on Shabael's shoulder, not realizing how close he came to losing that hand as the nervous Red Gold Guard reacted.

Shabael showed no sign that he felt the familiarity was an offense. "Yes. I saw and felt scales on their cheeks. I saw the fangs and how they reared their heads back to strike just as a cobra would. Their eyes were yellow with narrow pupils; and, they are lightning quick, faster than any human."

They reached the top of the stairs and began walking the path around the mountain that led back to the Emperor's Tower. Thirty Red Gold guards surrounded the group as they carried Alie on the stretcher.

Several flocks of white ravens were flying in different directions over the capitol and Malcolm pointed to them. "We have eyes everywhere, Sire. But it's as if they simply vanished."

"They have to be near. Perhaps they are hiding in the shadows, licking their wounds," Shabael said.

A messenger appeared and whispered into Malcolm's ear, who turned and spoke softly to Shabael. "The Queen Mother is safe inside her chambers."

"Thank the Creator for that," Shabael said, more as an expression than personal belief, a knowledge that he shared only with Shawndeli.

More than a hundred Red Gold Guards were stationed around Emperor Tower. Shabael's party avoided the foyer and entered the Royal members lift that went directly to the King's chambers.

"Place Alie on my bed," Shabael said. "Healer, do what you can. And coordinate with Calibri and his finest scholars to find a way we can do healings of those with the Orb of Light taint."

"I will, Sire," Janessa said, jingling as she bowed.

"Malcolm, I want regular updates from the High Commander."

"Done, My Emperor."

Nolan," Shabael motioned to the young servant. "Gather my armor. If they strike again, we'll be ready."

"My Emperor," a Red Gold Guard entered the chamber. "Rageton sends word there are neither indication of an impending attack nor any sign of the assassins."

Shabael glowered. "I want two hundred men to start from the Priestess Tower and move outward, looking in every shadow and crevice," he ordered. "These assassins are extremely dangerous and apparently possessing snake-like mobility. For any of these captured dead or alive, I will deed a parcel of land, present a bag of gold, and grant knighthood to those responsible. I want ravens in the air and double the Darkling scouts. Use Darklings as trackers. Have Rageton also send out fifty cavalry to the Black River."

"It shall be done, my Emperor."

"I will stay some time with my daughter and then join Rageton on deck."

"Yes, My Emperor."

"That is all." Shabael turned so Nolan could finish strapping his shoulder armor and Shawndeli placed a hand on the king's shoulder and whispered into his ear. "Forget not your mother."

Shabael looked at Shawndeli, feeling a kind of despair at the thought. "Thank you. So much going on." He waved Nolan off and fastened a strap on his wrist, saying to Malcolm, "Ask Queen Mother to come to our chambers when she is able."

"As you command," Malcolm said.

CHAPTER 15

THE BURIAL GROUND

Dylan awakened as though he had been electro-shocked. He sat upright in bed, feeling "juiced," as though struck by a sugary orange juice jolt that made him want to crow. Maybe it was a reaction from the combination of flight and fight from the dream and ...

Hello world, I'm eighteen! Whatever, this was a crazy cocktail effect he was experiencing. Dawn was minutes away. He slipped out of his PJ's and peered out the window wondering if somehow the world would look different at eighteen. At least he was old enough now to join the army as good old Dad had suggested so many times. He could vote now, too, although from what little he had gleaned neither of the two vying for the presidential seat would be any great thing for the country. Maybe it was too late for any president.

Strangely, he found himself thinking of politics. *Yeah, here I am eighteen for a couple of hours and already I'm thinking about changing the world.*

Jesus! Am I an idiot? I've still got newspapers to deliver and I'm looking for answers to the world's problems. I'm not Captain America! I'm just a teen-ager trying to learn who I am. I'm smart enough to know that America today is not the America of not so long ago. Everything is fragmented. Everything is offensive to everyone so nothing gets done. God has been removed from courthouses and classrooms. Even "ho, ho, ho," has become a bad thing to say in Australia during Christmas. It's all just confusing and disillusioning. My Dad certainly isn't religious. He goes to church because it's politically correct, especially if you're the county sheriff. Yeah, Mom is religious but, man; Dad sure does beat her into the ground about her faith when bad things happen.

Like the night Mom was sitting at the dinner table praying for a child that had been struck by a car. Dad came in, smelling of booze, and kicked a chair across the floor, causing Mom to halt in mid-prayer.

"Hey, Hon," he snarled, pulling his 45 Magnum from the holster and aiming it at Mom. "Would it be my bad if I pulled the trigger or… God's bad for not stopping me?"

That was the first time that I ever saw fear in "little" brother Robert's eyes. Even he was fearful that Dad just might pull the trigger that night. Robert sat frozen in his chair with the fork poised an inch from his opened mouth. Then Dad laughed, "Don't worry, Hon, I'm not going to spatter your lovingly prepared meal with your gore cause that ain't what eatin's for. Pour me a glass of tea. I'm thirsty."

There had never been a lot of talk about Spencer family history. Dad did have a line of ancestral friends, forefathers, and foremothers kind of stuff with the photos hanging in his home office … the oval office. They were grizzled, hard men posed standing with slain bears and some holding Indians' scalps draped over their outreaching arms like Spanish moss on cypress trees. There was his great-great grandfather, bearing the Spencer look, tall and bulky, as strong appearing as an oak tree. It was easy to see where my father and brother got their large hands. Thinking of their large hands brought back the memory of how his dad used to squeeze his head with his hand.

"Jesus!" Dylan could still feel his Dad's huge palm pressing down on the top of his head when he was a child. The fingers curled around and squeezing the skull, bringing tears to his eyes, leaving little purple bruises around his temples. And how Mother would always ask later what those marks were. Dad would say, "Oh, Babe, the baseball helmet. You can always tell a true ballplayer; ain't that right, Homer." Then, under his breath he added, "That's like in Homer Simpson, kiddo," and he would give Dylan a hearty slap on the back, showing Mom how peachy-keen everything was between father and son.

The first hint of dawn was showing through the woods behind the house. A light mist hovered just above the ground. The road would be a little slippery with the bike today. He noticed the feather he had found on the window sill last night, laying by the white twig on his dresser. Turning to the window, he saw the small spider web cracks in the glass and reached out to touch them. Why was it that when he had a good dream something bad always had to come? He recalled the exhilaration of flying, following the raven through the woods to the mountain of campfires. Then the cry of the attacking white bird sounded in his mind. He subconsciously rubbed his thumb over the scratches on his hand. He noticed specks of blood on the windowpane and looked downward where he had seen the raven impaled on the spikes of the fence. It all came flooding back …

Opening the window, he stuck his head out for a better view. He heard a sound behind him and turned. "Oh, no. Not you! What do you want?!"

"Yeah, me, Drama Queen. What's got your panties in a wad?" Robert was standing in the doorway of the bedroom.

"Oh, there were some birds fighting outside my window last night."

"No shit, Tonto? What you got in your hand?"

"Just some stuff I found on the window sill. What are you doing up so early. Wanna help me deliver the morning news?"

"In your dreams, weirdo. I just heard you moving around and wondered if you'd like to try shoving me up against the wall again?"

Dylan thought for a second about accepting the invitation, but decided to keep things civil.

"Look, Bro, I know you're probably not interested, but some weird things have been happening. Like I was dreaming of flying last night, following a raven to a mountain with campsites below and then another raven attacks us. Guess I had just heard them fighting and then dreamed about it."

"Little brother having a bad birdie dream again?" Robert said in an imitation of a little girl voice.

"Okay! That's enough," Dylan said. "You're hopeless! Just move out of my way so I can get dressed. I have to run my paper route."

"You want me to move? Move me! You're eighteen today, right? You're supposed to be a man now."

"You know what, Robert, if that brain in that Neanderthal skull of yours had grown proportional to your body maybe I could converse with you as an equal."

"Huh?"

"Think on it," Dylan said, moving past his bigger, younger, and dumber brother. He gathered up his clothes and dressed in the bathroom, hurried out to his bike and rushed through the paper deliveries, then cycled back to his home, finding everyone at the breakfast table.

167

He didn't stop, instead rushing upstairs and retrieving an empty shoebox from his closet. He was heading for the front door when his mother called out, "Hey, hold on, birthday boy. Breakfast first."

"I'll be back in a minute."

Robert rose from the table and stood by the window over the sink, munching on a cream cheese bagel. "Fool."

"Whatta ya mean?" Spencer asked.

"He's hopeless, you know," Robert said.

"What?" Spencer rose and went to the window. "What's he doing?"

"Oh, big deal, Dad. Dead bird. I guess Bro's going to give him a funeral."

"Jesus, he weeps for a broken blade of grass," Spencer said with ill-disguised sarcasm. "Really?"

"Oh, he'll be picking roses and writing a eulogy. May even dress up in his Sunday suit," Robert snickered.

"Stop it, please," Sally said. "You two have to understand. Dylan's artistic. He's different from you two, sensitive to the world and to others. There's nothing wrong with that."

Robert laughed. "Sorry, Mom, did you say he's autistic? It's just that damned tree-hugging pony-tailed Pole. He's hopeless," Robert said.

"That's Poe. As in Edgar Allan Poe," Sally corrected. "And watch your mouth, son. I don't like to hear you or your father cursing."

"Whatever," Robert said.

Sheriff Morgan stared out the window again, sucked through his teeth, put his cup of coffee down on the table, and went to his "oval" office. The room smelled of old cigars, bourbon, Old Spice, and old Sherriff Spencer Morgan's farts. He took a seat behind the huge mahogany desk and slowly spun his chair around so he could reach up to touch the old sepia photograph of his great-great grandfather with a group of men. The sheriff moved his fingertip along the group of raven feathers hanging from the stuffed bear's neck and spoke a single word to himself, "Haunting."

"Dad? Everything all right?" The Spittin' Image had followed him into the office.

"Just keep an eye on that brother of yours," the sheriff said. "That boy ain't cooking on all the units."

"Sure, Dad. You mean like police surveillance?"

"Yeah, something like that. Now get out of here. Have a good day at school."

Spencer rose from his desk and went to Dylan's room. He looked out the window to make sure Dylan was still digging the hole. Turning back into the room, he noticed the black feather and white twig and his eyes widened.

"Something's going on here." The sheriff reached up and touched the scar on his face. He found a sheet of paper and gingerly pushed the feather and the small twig onto it, folded the paper and returned to his office. At his desk, he placed the feather and twig in an antique pipe box then put them in his desk drawer.

He tapped the desktop, then turned and took a photo off the wall of him and five other men holding hunting rifles. The men were posed around a stuffed bear adorned with Native American headwear, and strung around its neck like a ghastly necklace were six dead ravens hanging by their claws.

The photo appeared to be about fifteen years old and beside it was another one. This one was a very old black and white. The men in the photo were bearded and also were posing with a stuffed bear with ravens around its neck.

Morgan reached for his cell phone and started punching numbers. "Round and round, here we go."

Dylan sighed and wiped tears from his eyes. He was surprised by the physical ache in his heart as he used the small shovel to dig the grave. Until a moment ago, he had never considered life without Ravenous. Suppose this was Ravenous instead of the strange raven. He had vivid memories of his first encounter with Ravenous, before he had claimed the bird as his own and named it. He was just a little more than two years old, walking out of the hospital, holding his mother's hand, when the raven landed on the sidewalk only feet in front of them. It was a detailed memory, right down to the blue coat and little hat with earflaps that made him look like a walking marshmallow.

When he saw the raven, Dylan pulled free from his mother's hand, squealing, flapping his arms like a baby bird; and waddled his way to the raven.

Sally let it happen. She allowed his tiny hand to slip from her grip and paused to watch the eerie scenario. She was intrigued, eager to witness what was about to happen between toddler and bird. She felt no fear that the raven might attack her son. Only curiosity. She paused with one hand raised as if about to call to Dylan, but simply stood and watched, her head cocked to one side.

Dylan reached out a hand and touched the bird on the head. The raven stretched out its neck and lowered its head, almost like a courtesan paying homage to a king.

"Eruk," the bird croaked.

"Eruk," said little Dylan.

The raven moved, almost appearing to do a short dance on the sidewalk. It stilled, then bobbed its head twice. Dylan dropped to his knees and leaned toward the bird. The raven's beak moved and Sally could almost swear she heard some words. She couldn't make out anything specific, but Little Dylan's eyes widened and his mouth dropped open.

Sally had seen enough. When she moved toward the boy and the bird, the raven took several steps backward, sounded a couple of "Caws!" and flew to a nearby tree where it alit on a branch.

Little Dylan rose to his feet, his mouth still open, a look of awe and wonder on his face.

"Well," Sally asked, "what did your friend have to say?"

"Cawer," Dylan said. Then he did something Sally would never forget. He turned to her, raised his index finger, and said, "One."

Actually, the strange encounter at the hospital came as no surprise to Sally. Since the first day that the tiny premature Dylan had been taken home from the hospital, there had always seemed to be at least one raven nearby. She would go to a window to adjust the blinds and a raven would be perched in one of the trees in the yard. And now, having witnessed the encounter between her little son and the raven, she sensed that the birds were his protectors. His personal angels. It gave her a peace of mind. Sally decided having ravens around might be a good idea. She always thought of that especially when Spencer went into one of his moods.

Entranced by the connection, Sally visited the library and researched ravens. Their habits, their appetites, their movements. The birds fed on fruit, nuts, corn … and dead things. When she approached Spencer about starting her own business, he callously waved her off. She didn't need to work, he reminded her. Hell, he didn't even need to work, drawing off the inheritance from his gold-mining and shady forefathers. Truth was he didn't want Sally out of the house. He had not forgotten that runty little bastard that she was all set to run off with on that rainy night.

But somehow, Sally pulled it off. She promised to hire a manager and a couple of high school students as helpers. Spencer wasn't half listening anyway. He was watching something on a small television monitor; he just nodded and waved her away.

The next morning, baby in stroller, notebook in one hand and pushing with the other, Sally went to the vacant store she had selected, checked it out though the street window, and called the owner. The guy was thrilled to rent the building to such an outstanding lady. And yes, he thought it was the perfect location for "Sally's Pet Store."

She returned home to find Spencer gone and the VCR tape he had been watching protruding from the player. The sheriff had obviously left in a hurry. Ordinarily, Sally wouldn't have dared do it, but this was "New Sally." Businesswoman Sally. She placed the invoices and bank receipts on the nearby table and pushed the VCR tape with Mayor John Tucker's name taped on it into the player. Her hand went to her open mouth as she realized that the hidden camera in the Honeybee Massage Parlor was revealing the illustrious mayor's rising and falling sweet cheeks over a very young masseuse. The Sheriff's Department was going to have no problem getting a generous budget this year. Sally turned the machine off, popped the tape back out and stored another piece of valuable information that she knew she would probably need some day.

Once the store opened, a winter day never passed without food for the ravens being sprinkled around the oak tree behind the house. The ravens were happy and fat, and should have been. Only a couple of hundred yards behind the huge white house was a growth of trees. Sally quickly learned this was where the birds gathered and rested. A small trail ran from those trees to a five-acre field.

The industrious Sally planted berries in a section of the field—strawberries, blueberries, watermelon, cantaloupe, honeydew, and several apples and peach trees. She knew the Ravens also had a taste for dead animal flesh so she brought them the remains of deceased pets from her shop.

Despite her new freedom, Sally still lived in constant fear of her husband. There wasn't a night she didn't hold her breath and cringe in bed until she learned that Spencer wasn't in that drunk zone that made him punch-happy mean. She feared one day he would kill Dylan or

171

her if the right formula came together to create that perfect storm. She knew he loved her in his own strange way, and yet he hated her because he knew he never really had her heart. He would die for her and yet would lash out at any man whose eyes stayed too long on her. And yes, he would kill her because he sometimes just got so pissed he wanted to blow her beauty through the wall with his sawed-off double-barreled shotgun.

The problem was that he knew she didn't really love him and he attributed that to her sickness. Never would he confront her about it because he really didn't want the words "I don't love you" to come out, to be real, to have to be dealt with. That was why, when he discovered the little covey hole in the back of the barn where she kept the airtight aquariums used to suffocate mice and rabbits, he didn't confront her. No. He would save this knowledge. An ace in the hole.

Shortly after finding the aquarium death traps, Spencer followed his wife when she left the barn carrying a small duffel bag across the butterbean field garden to her own little garden of berries. As he watched her, Spencer could only reason that this was some kind of madness.

He left her alone with her madness; as long as she stayed home and was the good wife, all was right in his world. Minus a few mice and rabbits, maybe.

As Sally watched her oldest son Dylan digging the grave under the tree, she thought it was funny how they had never really talked about the birds. She just knew — as did he — that there was something special … some kind of connection. She waited until Spencer left the kitchen before she went outside to Dylan. Placing a hand on his shoulder, she asked, "Is that Ravenous?"

"No. Ravenous has a long patch of blue on the left side of his chest. This is a really large bird. It's big as a cat. Have you ever seen one this big before? And look, Mom, look at the eyes." The dead bird's eyes were a luminous blue. Clear sky blue.

"I've never seen eyes like that on any animal. Such a shame."

"How did it get caught in the spikes? I mean, he must have fallen from very high to have those spikes driven though him like that. "You don't think Robert …?

A feeling of sickness and anger, hot like grease from a frying pan, rose inside Dylan until he could taste it, feel it burn, like stomach acid

172

at the bottom of his esophagus. "Oh," he moaned, shaking his head back and forth, "He better not have."

Dylan scanned the ground for any kind of evidence. There had been a light rainfall last night. Maybe there were footprints.

"Hey, look at this, Mom." Dylan knelt on the ground and picked up a white feather. He rubbed the white feather between his fingers, trying to identify the bird that had lost a white feather. Goose? Duck? Pigeon? He had seen none of those recently. He handed the feather to his mother and while she examined it, he studied the marks on the raven.

"Last night there were birds fighting out here, Mom. They hit my window so hard it caused a little crack. I thought they were both ravens even though one was white."

"Well, maybe this one was attacked by a hawk or maybe an owl. They have some white feathers."

There were several puncture wounds on the raven most likely caused by a beak. The left wing's spine looked to be completely severed. That had to have hurt.

Dylan gently touched the wing of the Raven and grimaced as a red ant crawled over his finger. He spread the wing open and held the white feather alongside it. The feathers had the same shape and length. Had it not been a white feather he would have guessed it had come from the black raven. A white raven? Was there such a thing? Jesus! He had seen the birds fighting. The white one had even tried to snatch the twig from his hand. But wasn't that just part of the dream. He shook his head to try and clear it.

"Look, Mom," he said, placing the white feather next to one on the black raven's wing. "What do you think?"

"Except for the color, they look the same to me," she said.

"Have you ever seen a white raven?"

"No. Never even heard of one." She looked out toward the grove of trees. "We've always had ravens around here, you know, but I've never seen a white one. I imagine they are a pretty rare breed. Seems we have a little mystery on our hands."

"Yeah, well, I'm going to bury this one by the tree."

"Okay. If we had time, I would have you walk with me across the fields. Something I'd like to show you."

"Ah, a day filled with mysteries," Dylan said. "Okay. Sounds good."

"Kind of a yucky way to start your eighteenth birthday, though. Anyway, have a good day, son.

"I will, Mom. But, you know, I'm kind of scared. I feel as if something bad is going to happen." He was kneeling by the tree now and looking at the large wings of the raven hanging outside the box. I know this is stupid silly and superstitious, but I've always felt that if I see a raven flying left it means good luck. From left to right is bad. And I really don't think finding one impaled is a good omen."

Sally chuckled. "It certainly wasn't lucky for the bird, was it? Well, just be careful on your bike. Hey, I'm not going into the store today. You can take my car if you'd like."

"Thanks, Mom, but I'll pass. I enjoy riding with Freddie.

"All right. Love you. Don't forget to eat something before you leave."

"Love you too, Mom."

Dylan glanced around the yard, half expecting to see ravens. Nothing. No Ravenous. He cocked his head, listened for a moment, and didn't hear anything. He gently placed the box in the hole. "You are a beautiful raven," he said, stroking the feathers on the wings as he crossed them to make them fit inside. "May you fly high in the afterworld, my friend." He patted the soil over the grave, went inside and washed his hands at the sink and then ate an egg sandwich that Sally had prepared. When he came back downstairs after getting his book bag, his mother called for him. She was standing at the kitchen window.

A flock of ravens was landing around the grave by the oak tree.

"Look, is that Ravenous?" Sally pointed at the low branch on the oak tree.

"Yeah. It's him." Dylan felt almost giddy seeing his old friend. *"Caw! Caw!"*

"Caw! Caw!" came a return from one of the ravens.

"Oh, my God, that is so crazy," Sally said.

Dylan was feeling great. Ravenous was safe. "Well, I'd better get over to Freddie's place. No telling what that grease monkey is into by now."

Sally was still staring at the ravens. "What a story you and Ravenous would make. I bet Oprah Winfrey would love to have you as a guest. Be careful."

"Always."

CHAPTER 16

THE BIRTHDAY GIFT

Dylan braked his bike to a sliding halt at the garage door and gave three loud raps on the closed door.

"Hey, Monkey, time to roll."

The garage door slid partially open to just above Dylan's hips and Freddie stooped to scoot under it. "Hey, Amigo. I got just one question to ask you?"

"Shoot."

"You want to Schwinn it or Indian it?"

"I don't get you, Einstein," Dylan said, curious as to why Freddie seemed so excited.

"Well, like a picture dictionary, let me reveal it to you." Freddie stepped back and, with a formal flourish, raised the garage door. "Ta-da! And behind door number three!"

The garage was huge, large enough to house four cars with room to repair them. However, today there were no cars, just two shiny motorcycles. There was an Indian head painted on one of the gas tanks.

"Uh, what's this?" Dylan walked to the first bike and ran his hand over the leather seat and up to the chrome handlebars.

"Yours, Best Bud."

"What?" Dylan looked at Freddie.

"Happy Birthday, Kingosabee. You have one 2001 Indian Chief, yellow and white. Teardrop road lights. Indian saddle bags, backrest, windshield, a flat tire kit with a 150 rear tire. Updated parts. New voltage regulator, coil, starter. Runs freaking sweet with a great 88-cubic inch S&S engine. Even got you some low fenders. She's got twenty- nine thousand, seven hundred miles on her, and your Chief is ready to haul your ass to the highways of Heaven!"

Dylan was so stunned that he sat down hard on the concrete floor. A hand went to his mouth and his eyes were tearing. "What did you do, Freddie?"

Freddie's father, Mike Sanders, walked up and placed a hand on each of the boys' shoulders. He was a broad man with a crew-cut haircut, wearing a blue work shirt, blue pants, white socks, and a nametag that read "Mike".

"Freddie's been working on these for a year now," Mr. Sanders said. "We found two Indian bodies on eBay and, as they say, the rest is history."

Freddie was almost jumping with excitement. "We're really cool now, Dylan. We are frickin' outlaws. Kings…well, Chiefs of the road. Happy Birthday. Go ahead, sit on her. She's yours."

Dylan threw his leg over the bike; put his feet on the clutch and brake. He rolled the accelerator and closed his eyes … dreaming of the highway. "You guys are serious?"

"Yeah, Dude. Serious as Obama with a tax audit on a Tea Party member."

"Wow! My heart is racing! Oh, man! Oh, wow!" Dylan couldn't find the right words so he threw out his arms and hugged the grinning father and son. "Gosh, I'm having trouble believing this. Heck, I'm having trouble breathing. Never have I ever even dreamed of something like this. I'm speechless."

"Well, if you're speechless, shut up," Freddie said, laughing.

"Wanna fire her up?" Mr. Sanders asked.

"Do I?" Dylan smiled. "Somebody try to stop me."

"Yeah, well just put it in neutral," Freddie said. "Now, turn the ignition."

The bike fired up on the first try and Freddie and his father high-fived. The bike roared as Dylan turned the throttle up a couple of times. He turned it off and looked at his best friend. "Freddie, this is so cool!"

"Well, what do you say, wanna play hooky today and learn how to ride these Chiefs?"

"Hey, it's your eighteenth birthday. I won't rat on you," Mike Sanders said.

"Okay, that does it for me," Freddie said. "Let's find a parking lot and practice. What do you think of the old K-mart that closed last year? Big lot there,"

"Sure, let's go," Dylan, still feeling giddy, said "Hey, what's our motto?" "On it. I own it. If it's a girl I bone it!" They burst out laughing.

"Jesus, help us," Freddie's father said.

They all three turned to look at the street as one of Robert's guys roared past on his Harley.

CHAPTER 17

THE PLOT THICKENS

Big Scott had a malicious smirk on his face as he rolled down the highway toward school on his Fat Boy Harley. He had seen something that Robert Spencer, a.k.a. Rob the Mob, was going to find entertaining. Most felt Rob was a pretty big guy, thick and unmovable. But Big Scott didn't have that nickname for no reason. He was a head taller than Robert; so tall he could walk up to his Harley and sit down on it without throwing a leg over it. It was hard lifting a heavy Fat Boy by oneself. But Big Scott could have worn one as a necklace. That was an exaggeration, but to everyone's mental photo of Big Scott, it seemed to be pretty accurate.

Rolling into the parking space at school, Big Scott switched the Harley off and stretched his legs so far out front that the points of his boots passed the front tire. He reached over to Robert sitting on his bike and gave him a little "get your attention" slap.

"What's up, Big Scott?"

"Well, something you're gonna find amusing."

"Oh, yeah?" Robbie leaned back, crossing his arms. He spit a white glob off to the side.

"Seems your little bro and his bud Sci-Fi got them a pair of Indians. Old, like made in the last decade but all shiny and new looking." Big Scott said.

"No way." Robbie was standing upright now, brows knitted. He clenched and unclenched fists so hard they made knuckle popping sounds. "Where?"

"Sci-Fi's place. Should be rolling up any second." Big Scot said, standing up and stepping back off the Fat Boy.

Robbie just shook his head. "Man, you're a tree. Look, my Dad wants us keeping an eye on Bro. You got the keys to your grandpa's truck?"

"I do, Tin Star." Big Scott said, slapping a side pocket of his jeans.

"Indians? Really?" Robbie asked.

"Chiefs. Looks like 2000 models maybe. All chromed out. Somebody done a real job on them. Real sweet."

"No way. If you're jiving me, Big Scott, I got a number eleven boot you ain't walking over."

"True is true, Boss." Big Scott looked over his shoulder. "Shoulda been here by now."

"You got me curious. Indians?" Robbie asked again.

"Yeah. They got the chief heads on the tanks."

Robbie spit again and huffed. "Yeah, I suppose Bro, if he got a bike, it wouldn't be a Harley. It's just that Indians are cool and I thought their ignitions were rigged with anti-nerdum. Well, Big Scott, if you're right, I think we're going to have a little fun."

CHAPTER 18

SKYEDEN — SHABAEL'S BALCONY

King Shabael El Qui walked out onto the balcony of the castle and stared at the blue-tinted moon hanging on the horizon of the early morning. Even the cool breeze couldn't wash away the taint of his daughter's blood. His hands trembled as he re-lived the moment when he had pushed the hot blade of his sword into his daughter's throat while his wife's bare fingers were wrapped around the flesh-searing steel as she guided it to the base of the toxin-laden tongue.

The sword had been bloodied by too many men to recall over the years, but his hands had never trembled before making the killing strike. In his mind, all had been justified kills under the visage of war. But now, when his sword had been used upon his beloved daughter, he wondered if he could ever use it again. "Oh, but I will! When we find those assassins, I will!"

Shabael surveyed the domain of his castle grounds. Hundreds of white steeples rose, impaling the cotton balls of mist that were rising to mingle with the low-hanging bruised clouds like wolf pups scurrying to their mother's breast. To his left, the moon was a quarter high in the sky, giving the clouds a fuzzy edge of burgundy.

The dawning was still; no drums sounding alarms; no clatter of swords; no cries in the dark. On a normal dawning there would be the sounds of an awakening castle, barking dogs, tolling bells; a cacophony of music he had always enjoyed. The smells of bacon, honey, and baking dough normally assaulted his saliva glands. Today.

Nothing. Quiet. Eerie quiet. The shuffling of soldiers' feet; an occasional clip-clop of a horse's hooves. The city was drawn into a taut knot of apprehension.

On this morning, the city was akin to a frightened hare lying low in its burrow, waiting for a stalker to pass. Who had dared attack the royal family? The thought made Shabael furious, turning his normally pale face red in stark contrast to the white hair. The rush of blood made his face burn. At times like this, Shawndeli had often said his face was as red as his eyes. He realized he had to regain composure and rubbed a trembling hand over his face, remembering the dry scales of the assassin's cheek, the glint of moonlight from a wet, curved fang dripping of venom before it pierced his daughter's face.

Who were they? What were they? Who was behind this dastardly attack? There were no people in Skyeden that bore a resemblance to these attackers. Were they in disguise? No. He had seen them up-close with his own eyes, felt them squirm and slither from his grasp. In addition, he had seen the harsh reality of the venom from the fangs.

No reports from his guards. Only a disquieting silence. There was not a time when he could recall this deathly silence in Neverland. It was unnerving. Even the white ravens were silent as they circled above the confines of the castle, broadening their search with each pass.

Where had the assassins gone? They couldn't have simply vanished. If they were still in the kingdom, they would be found. Every inch of Neverland would be scoured.

Do it now! He relived the terrible memory of his wife grabbing the red-hot blade and guiding it down Alie's rapidly closing throat. Shaken, he grabbed the rail of the balcony. No parent should have to do such a thing to a child. Alie had come to him begging forgiveness and he had failed to protect her,

Forgive me, Father, she said again in his mind.

Shabael realized his eyes were tearing up and was thankful that no one was there to see this. Now, of all times, the people needed their king to be strong Thumbing away the wetness, he bellowed, "Malcolm!", and moments later he heard the rustle of the man's silk robe as he hurried through the door to the balcony. As always, he arrived with scrolls tucked under one arm and a pen ready to record the king's orders.

"Your Grace?"

Shabael turned his burgundy eyes on the man. "Summon the War Council for a meeting this evening. We must discuss our future plans."

The red was beginning to fade from King Shabael's cheeks. His eyes glistened in the light reflected from the torches surrounding the balcony.

He continued addressing Malcolm, who became more uncomfortable with each word from his obviously troubled king. He hesitated, sensing there was turmoil raging within His Majesty. Political concerns, kingdom conflicts, and war strategy were items the king shared easily with him. It was the personal conflicts that were rarely shared. Those exchanges could only be with his wife or perhaps with Calibri, certainly not with the Queen Highest. Ah, the beauty that she was, receiving sympathy from that woman would be like placing the end of burning faggot against a block of ice and expecting to start a fire. One only went to the Queen for advice on some ruthless matter.

When Malcolm noted signs of distress in the king, he pressed for more intimacy. "Sire, how are you? You and the royal family have been through such an arduous ordeal with the grave injuries to our princess."

"We did what we had to do." Shabael said, his voice low and gravelly. "At least she is alive. Serpentine assassins? What were they? Where did they come from? Nothing of this nature has ever been seen in Skyeden. This reeks of inside betrayal, Malcolm. How did they get past the guards and gain access to the priestess robes? What were they? They were foreigners with local access. They obviously had information that could have come only from the highest office of the priests and priestesses."

Shabael shuddered and wiped his hands on his shirt, trying to rid himself of the sensation of the scaly reptilian figures that he had battled. Realizing that Malcolm was staring at him, he asked, "How many years did you serve my father?"

The question surprised Malcolm. He had made it his life study to know the thought process of the king he had served. He knew it so well that he could often speak the words before they had formed on the king's lips. "I was prepared as an advisory to your father even as he was a child being prepared for the kingship, Milord."

"You were Descended at the same time as my father?"

"I was."

182

"You attended the same lectures, the studies, the armed training, and you both received manhood on the same date. As a result of this, he drew upon you for advice. That is why I hold my own actions in reserve until I've held council with you. I know that in your heart you carry my father's spirit. "So, I tell you now that I am thinking of leading a garrison to track these attackers myself. What do you think my father would do?"

"He would be a king of his people and a protector of his family. You fought bravely, and had you not given your all, your daughter would be dead now. Your family is safe, and although your enemies are yet free, there is one person who has the knowledge to ferret out the underground information you need."

"Mother."

Shabael's visage clouded for a moment, and then he gathered himself. "Summon my council, Malcolm. In addition, advise my mother that I seek an audience with her. Now!"

Shabael stared up at the blue moon again, inhaled deeply, and turned to re-enter the palace. He walked along the hallway that led to his mother's chambers and found the usual four guards posted at her door. The guards were wearing full body armor and as he approached, their hands moved to the hilts of their swords.

"Step aside," Shabael gruffly commanded.

Trumore, Captain of the queen's personal guard, was unmoved. "My Emperor," he said softly. "You know I cannot." Trumore's reputation was unimpeachable. He had proven himself time and again on the field of battle; and his fighting skills were legendary. He was an intimidating figure, standing a few inches taller than King Shabael and built like a rock formation. On the field of battle, he had a reputation of being invincible while brandishing his "Cleaver", a five-foot sword that could cut a horse down with a single swing. He wasn't wearing the "Cleaver" in the royal chambers, but his short blade was quick and deadly.

"Excuse me?" a red-faced Shabael said.

Trumore held his gaze steady. "The Queen so commands. She is not to be disturbed."

"The queen commands?!" Shabael was losing control of his emotions. "She may be your matriarch, but I am the patriarch. I am supreme here. Now open these doors, you insolent pig!"

Trumore was surprised by the vehemence of the king, but he was not about to relinquish his position. He stiffened his pose and Shabael saw the other three guards becoming tense. "We cannot open to you or anyone else, my Emperor. And I have to inform you that another step will constitute an offensive move on your part."

Shabael leaned forward but did not take a step. He drew his dagger from the sheath at his waist and focused his stare into the guard's eyes. "You will not yield to your Emperor?" Trumore gave no answer, with only a nervous twitch of his cheek giving an indication that he had heard.

Shabael suddenly sheathed his dagger and smiled. "You may relax, Trumore. I was merely testing your resolve. I will wait until the queen is ready to receive me."

"I am very much relieved," Trumore deadpanned.

Moments later, there was a tap from the inside of the chamber door. Trumore opened the door and stood aside. "You are granted access," he said to Shabael.

"You are golden from armor to heart," Shabael said to Trumore as he passed. But the guard didn't acknowledge the praise.

Queen Mateah El Qui was sitting in the foyer surrounded by chambermaids who were polishing her nails and arranging her white hair. She had milky-white skin and her eyes were the same pink burgundy shade of her son's.

Shabael knelt before her. "Mother."

The queen waved a hand in dismissal of the chambermaids and they left the room. She extended a soft hand for her son to kiss.

"Creator of my life," Shabael began, "I have good news. Remember the reports we received of ravens from the tribe watching a boy-child?"

"Yes?" The Queen leaned forward.

"Well, I have had Darklings observing and only last night a raven delivered a white twig to the boy's window." Shabael tried to hide the excitement he felt as he received the visual images of his mother's facial changes as she interpreted the news.

"A white twig? Do you think …? The time must be nearing."

Shabael could barely contain the exuberance in his voice. "After one hundred and fifty years, Mother, we have signs of its existence. We are watching very closely now. Soon we'll know its location and we'll be able to destroy the tree that hosts the Light."

The queen exchanged her smile for a small frown. "And what of the Ravenites? Do they have any knowledge of this?"

"None that I am aware of," Shabael replied.

"This is good, my son. Once we learn its location and destroy the new tree that holds the Light, we will rule eternally. Skyeden will remain forever under the Dark Magic and we will always be strong and invincible.

"Just think, Your Royal High Emperor, we were so close to achieving this same goal one hundred and fifty years ago beneath the Tree of Light in Ravenland. We must not fail again."

CHAPTER 19

DEATH TO THE KING

150 years ago at the Tree of Light.

Eradrin fell to his knees, slowly lowering himself until his chest was resting on the ground. Above the din of battle, he heard Shabael commanding the Darklings to chase the ravens into the funnel. Placing both palms flat on the ground, Eradrin forced his exhausted body to rise until he was upon his knees. He scanned the huge tree but was unable to locate Dayanna. Nearing panic, his eyes darted about the bloody battlefield, searching for her body among the dead scattered on the ground. Nothing. Noticing his sword on the ground, he placed his left hand on the wound in his side and reached for the weapon. A huge boot was suddenly planted on the sword and Shabael stood over Eradrin. He kicked the sword to the side then reached out a hand and lifted Eradrin's chin.

"Son of Aremis," Shabael said, appearing ten feet tall to the kneeling Eradrin and measuring him with his burgundy eyes. He turned to a nearby soldier and ordered, "Send a healer now to tend this man's injuries." He touched the torn mail on Eradrin's side, and from his own chest plate removed a cloth. He pressed it against Eradrin's wound, then, in an unexpected act of kindness, Shabael lifted Eradrin's sword hand to hold the cloth in place. Eradrin complied but made no attempt to return Shabael's gentle smile.

Shabael took a step back and then walked over to King Aremis. He knelt on one knee and raised the fatally injured Aremis until he was resting against the tree trunk. The warriors gathered around them were silent. It was as though the whole world had been stilled.

Shabael reached out and the barely conscious King Aremis stiffened as if to brace for a blow. Instead, Shabael smiled and opened his hands in a show of peace. "I'm glad you are still alive," he said, placing a hand on the fallen king's shoulder. Aremis started to reach up and remove Shabael's hand but decided it might be best if he did not and let his hand fall back to the ground.

A light breeze lifted some strands of Shabael's long hair against the fallen Ravenite King's cheek, picking up some of the still flowing blood.

"A king should be killed by a king, not be executed later in a courtyard, but on the field of battle. I give you this honor, Aremis."

Eradrin attempted to rise but the quick hands of the surrounding soldiers held him in place. Shabael ignored the side action, focusing on the King before him.

"It has been so long, my friend. It seems it has been as long as the entire history of our world. It was inevitable, of course. Since the day of the lightning, we were destined to become enemies. Isn't it funny how whether it has been one hundred years or five centuries your memories of the past still remain as last night's dreams? I cannot remember a time when you were not my enemy.

"Yes, even a thousand years ago I remember what a worthy adversary you were. How close you came to defeating us. No army in the world's history had ever breached the Red River. I remember the fear you invoked in me and my people with your army, so massive and outnumbering our own by hundreds to one. We could hear the sound of your horns from our castle walls. No enemy in our history had dared come so close. I will confess to you, I saw fear in my father's eyes that day. You were a great warrior, King Aremis. But, alas, even with the greater numbers of men, horses, and supplies, you were defeated. And now, you steal the Light from us but barely present a defense? Surely, you knew I would respond. "

"It was an act of our God that brought us the Light," King Aremis spoke weakly through his pain. A trickle of blood ran from the corner of his mouth.

"An act of your God? What have you done so offensive that he would create an event that would bring my wrath upon you?"

King Aremis attempted a retort, but Shabael lifted his hand. "Shhh. The Gods play their games." Shabael lowered his hand and motioned for King Aremis to look upon Eradrin. "What departing words will you give your son before he ascends your throne?"

Eradrin strained to gain his feet, but was too weak. "Father!"

King Aremis gazed directly into the eyes of his son. "Be strong, King Eradrin. You have the Donachie blood within you. Do not mourn for me; it is my time to die."

It was eerily quiet, just the sound of the banners waving in the breeze, as the world seemed to be holding its breath. Eradrin felt his heart sink. Tears rolled down his cheeks. He felt numb. Everything was surreal. He stared at his father ... they shared the same handsome facial features including the square of their chins. Childhood memories flashed through his mind.

"Come on, son. I have you. Take that first step. I know you can." Aremis holds out his hands. "Come on. The first step of our future king, aye, he is."

Young Eradrin lifts a trembling foot and drops it. Then, he moves the other foot.

"And a King steps into the world!" Aremis announced to the world.

"This sword was given to me by my father as I now give it to you, my son. "As in three generations before us from Donachie to Donachie. It is yours."

Aye! Your first buck! Grand shot, son. What a proud father you make me!"

A dozen images of past events flashed through the prince's mind as he gazed on his dying father.

"Son. I, King Aremis Donachie, bequeath title and kingdom to you. Never forget the Donachie legacy. Be true to your heart and people. You and the land and the ravens are one. Serve our God and Light. Serve the people. Take care of your mother. Tell her I love her. And remember ... love is light. God is Light. You are the king of the people of the Light. "

Aremis's voice grew strong and loud, like that of a prophet. "The Light is coming. The Light and Word shall bring the balance. Then the darkness will be ..."

"Forever!" Shabael raised his dagger and slashed Aremis's throat.

"Father!" Eradrin broke free of the hands that held him only to be clubbed behind the head, causing him to drop to his knees.

King Aremis gasped. He brought his hand to his throat and then fell against the tree. His chin rested upon his chest and blood gushed between his fingertips. His eyes were pressed tightly closed. When he tried to breathe, air was sucked into the cut in his windpipe rather than his mouth. He desperately tried to draw in air, but the pain caused his eyes to roll back into his head. His hand fell from the gaping wound in his throat and his body began to convulse. Death relaxed the convulsions and the body grew still.

"Caw!" A raven with deep red feathers dropped from a branch in the tree and alit on the dead king's shoulder. With a bloodstained hand, Aremis forced his dying body to perform one last deed and he cupped his eyes as though being blinded by a bright light.

A faint ironic smile curled the king's lips. He raised his hand and stroked the bird's breast. Then he gasped and grabbed at his throat, falling forward. One of his eyes remained open and stared blankly at Eradrin.

The red raven gently nudged the king's cheek, issued a mournful cry. *"Cawwwww!"* Then the raven flapped its wings and returned to its perch in the tree.

Only the hands of the Malbolian soldiers held Eradrin upright. He felt as dead inside as his father. The open eye seemed to looking into his soul. And in a faraway voice, he thought he heard, *"I love you, Son. Now, you are king."* The words that followed held no meaning to him.

I love you too, Father.

Shabael turned to Eradrin. "Your father lies dead and so does your Viceroy. You have a kingdom of women and children and old men. Your precious capitol remains intact, however. Return the Orb of Light to me now and I will spare you any more tragedies."

"I know naught of the Light." His voice sounded very controlled but as taut as a pulled bow. *My father is dead. You killed my father. You! YOU!!!!*

"What sorcery was used? Where is it; the Light?" Shabael insisted.

"I don't know. I saw nothing of what happened. I was fighting."

"Enough!" The voice came from amid the gathered crowd, piercing like a dagger to a heart. The Queen Highest wore a red robe and white-gold armor. Her hair was long and white as snow. There was an air of royalty and arrogance about her. Had Eradrin seen the woman on the street he would have thought "Magnificent!" He understood why she was considered one of the most beautiful of women. Her eyes were almond shaped, lips deep red against her pale skin. She could have passed for a spectral in the night, a ghost of haunting beauty that created a kind of melancholy feeling, a sense of loss of a great love.

This was true except for one thing: he knew her from personal contact and from tales of her legendary acts of cruelty. Most feared her more than the Malbolian Army. Her son, King Shabael, was but an infant shadow compared to this woman. Within those beautiful eyes resided the vilest, most evil, living thing ever to walk upon Skyeden soil.

They called her the Red Dragon.

The surrounding warriors dropped to their knees as she approached. Her steps were quick and certain, making her abrupt stop dramatic as hair and robe swung forward then back from her body. Her attending white raven, perched on her left wrist, was adorned in a tiny red velvet vest. As Queen Highest straightened to her full stature, so did her raven. Only the Malbolian royalty merged with white ravens, while citizens completing the rite of Descension merged with Darklings.

"You know of my cruelty," Queen Highest said, her confident voice ringing as she addressed Eradrin. "I will ask you only once, and if I conceive that you are lying to me, I will boil every child in your kingdom, cut them to strips, and feed them to the Darklings. Then I will cast those images into your mind where that is all you will see until the day I have you executed. Think very carefully on what you are going to say." She placed a hand on Eradrin's chin, raising his head so his eyes met hers, leaned in a little closer, and searched his face for any readable signs of deception.

Eradrin was still traumatized over the loss of his father and Dayanna. Laid strewn around the Tree of Life was death, like a kind of macabre root system. His father's blood was still wet on the ground. Men he had known a thousand years, immortal to natural causes, were dead by sword and spear. He was so deep within himself because of the horror he had just witnessed that the Queen Highest's words were as meaningless as the patter of rain on a roof while he was sitting in the basement. A vicious shake brought him back to reality. The Queen was not accustomed to being ignored. The look she noted in Eradrin's face was a familiar one. It was the expression of once proud and strong man who has realized he has been defeated.

The shake served its purpose and Eradrin's blue eyes focused on the blazing pink pupils before him. He had to replay the words she had spoken in his tortured mind to give them meaning. His eyes widened. "The children?" He reached a hand out to take the queen's wrist and was conscious of a dozen swords being drawn. "I tell you the truth. I did not see the direction the ravens took. I was engaged in battle and my back was to them." His chin was immovable, held firmly in the queen's iron grip, but his eyes darted around, searching for Dayanna's body.

"You have no idea? What magic was used? *Where did they go with the Light?!*" She shouted this last question. A couple of nearby horses snorted.

"There was no magic. No plan but to reach the tree and make a stand."

"*Gah!* You know nothing of the funnel of ravens?" Queen Highest released her grip, stepped back, and placed her hands on her hips. Wrath blazed in her eyes.

Shabael was standing to the side, eyes closed and brow creased with concentration. "Mother," Shabael motioned her to lean closer, seeking privacy for his words, "I believe he speaks the truth. I was watching them and even I lost track. They appeared to fly through a ring of fire and disappeared high above with the Moon of Night behind them."

"A portal? Be conscious of any disturbance of your thoughts, Shabael, they may be a great distance away. Maybe still in transport. If your raven tries to contact you, it may be a weak connection. Pay close attention."

"I will," Shabael stepped back and watched his mother approach Eradrin.

"Yes?" she asked the prince, her eyes penetrating.

"Where is she? Where is her body?" Eradrin asked. He tried to stand but again hands found his shoulders and pushed him down.

"Who? Whom do you seek?" the Queen asked. She was tiring of this.

"Dayanna. She was in the tree with the raven."

"I pinned her to the tree with an arrow through her back," Shabael said. "Then your ravens swooped down and devoured her before they disappeared into the funnel."

"Devoured her?" Funnel?" Eradrin was questioning his sanity.

"Enough of this game!" Queen Highest turned her attention to the frightened prisoners around her. "Since there is no child among us…"

"I have a child, Queen Highest," sounded a voice from the surrounding crowd. A Malbolian soldier stepped forward, wearing the armor of the Skye Castle Guard. His attire was stained in red and still wet from what appeared to be the stink of sewage. The makeshift bandage wrapped on his cheek was blood soaked. He approached Queen Mateah with a young boy, a firm grip on the lad's neck. "Caught him escaping with Lady Dayanna, You Highness. This is her brother, Richard."

"Is it now?" Queen Highest asked. "Release the boy to me. And you… get your wound treated and bathe for all our sakes. It appears you underwent quite an ordeal catching this little mouse. Come to us this evening to the royal court and we will discuss this in further detail."

"I will, Queen Highest, as you so wish," the soldier bowed.

"So, you are Richard?" Queen Highest asked. "Beneath the muck I think there is a handsome young man." She reached out a hand and almost touched his head but withdrew and walked around him, her nose wrinkling in distaste. Richard's white jerkin was still wet and stained as were his leather pants. His face was discolored with darkening bruises.

The Queen Highest motioned for Richard to turn so that they both faced Eradrin. "It is a shame with all that you have lost this day, you lose your family, Eradrin. Richard would have made a great brother-in-law if you were able to wash the feces and stink off him."

"My father and my greatest love have perished this day" Eradrin said weakly. A wave of dizziness almost made him faint. "You have proved you are the conquerors. Can you not prove you have mercy?"

"It is your actions that have brought this upon you," The Queen Highest said. "It is your decision whether your love's brother lives or dies." She withdrew her long dagger. "This weapon is tipped in poison. Some observers have noted that the poison works faster than death from the bloodletting of the cut. Shall we observe and find out for ourselves? I am very curious."

"He's just a boy," Eradrin pled.

"Yes, a boy whom you have just condemned to death by your actions!" Queen Highest grabbed Richard's hair and yanked his head

192

back, exposing his throat. "Now talk! Tell me everything! I wish to know your plan of action and, most important, where the Light has been taken."

Eradrin was humiliated and powerless. He was on his knees, the hands of his enemies pressing down on his shoulders. The look of shame and hopelessness were reflected in the eyes of his remaining guard. He felt like a child in school brought before the other pupils by the schoolmaster. His mind wandered and he questioned the battle strategy of his slain father. Had he been king he would have met the Malbolians at the crossing of the river, destroyed the bridge and perhaps cutting Shabael and the queen off from the main force. That done, he would have happily slit their throats.

That chance had come and gone, however. His father lay dead in the pool of his drying blood. He himself was on his knees, expecting the decapitating stroke of a sword at any moment. He trembled with the desire to rip this woman apart with his bare hands.

"Speak now, fatherless prince," Queen Highest said, her voice dripping with sarcasm.

"I know nothing else. This is the truth!" Eradrin began, speaking with some difficulty through a parched throat. "After the Orb of Light came into our possession, the council met daily debating what we were to do with it. Many felt the legend is true that it can somehow bring light back into Skyeden, but all we could do was create fairytales. We had no idea what measures to take. We were at a loss. Then, when we learned of your presence only days before your attack, our discussions were scattered. I begged my father to mount a defense, even an offensive strike with me at the lead.

"My words held no sway. When we received reports you had crossed the River Divide my father still did nothing. Only this morning did Father order the castle guard to disarm themselves and leave the gate lowered. I urged him to overpower your stationed squads within our castle and throw them over the cliff. Still, Father said no. He would only take his elite guard to the Tree of Light and make a stand to show it was only the royal family, not the populace that stood against you. He was trying desperately to save his people.

"That is the truth. Dayanna decided on her own to retrieve the raven that had brought us the Orb. Richard went with her. I waited by the rear gate for them. We had no further plan." Eradrin looked at

Shabael and the Queen Highest, both seemingly unmoved by the heart-felt confession.

"She strapped the Orb of Light to the raven and released the fowl to flight," Eradrin said. "She died freeing the bird when its leg was caught by a branch. Her only instruction was to surrender the Light when you defeated us. What else she did was of her own doing," Eradrin said. "Feeling the situation hopeless and that we were all most likely to die, she set the raven free."

Richard moaned upon hearing of Dayanna's death. He had seen his own father lying lifeless at the foot of the tree. His own eyes were open but appeared unseeing as he battled the horror of the past few hours. His thin body was shaking, his chest drawn tight, his heart pounding.

Queen Highest looked at Eradrin, then at Richard, whose demeanor gave her pleasure. Her bottom lip bulged. "Ahhh, when you look at young Richard, does it not make you wonder what your own son would have looked like had your Lady lived?"

The words made Eradrin's body physically contort. Was Dayanna really devoured by Ravens or was this just a tale the Malbolians were using as part of their torture methods? No raven had ever fed upon a Ravenite. Was it all a lie? He had seen the ravens swooping down then going up again. He had seen Dayanna shot in the back with the arrow. Her body was nowhere to be found or any evidence she had been there at all. She was gone. No wife. No children. He would never be a father. Soon, there would be no Richard. Then it would be his turn to face the blade.

"This is all you will tell me?" Queen Highest asked, her pinkish eyes glistening. She adjusted her hand on the hilt of the dagger. Strengthening it. The Moon of Night hung low on the horizon, almost seeming to touch her hair. The bluish-white moonlight appeared to flow among the strands of white hair making her seem surreal and consisting of dream mist. How could so vile an evil come from such an ethereal angelic beauty as she? She could have been the image Eradrin had conjured up in his mind for an angel of the God of Light.

It was said that a man gazing at the Queen Highest would not feel the blade that killed him. The pinkish eyes, once gaining your attention, would not release it. Her skin was so pale the hints of blue veins could be seem. Her lips were of a pinkish hue that one could imagine dissolving if touched by your own. Beneath this fragile delicate theme of white resided what many believed the cruelest living soul that had ever existed in Skyeden.

Eradrin turned his gaze to the kneeling Richard, his mouth working as to speak, but unable find words that could possibly appease this angelic fiend. Oh, how Richard always reminded him of Dayanna. Anyone seeing them would know the two were brother and sister. Were! Oh God! They shared the same laugh and that upright stance they always held. He felt his heart sinking ever deeper into despair. The hopelessness of despair was encompassing.

"I have spoken the truth," he said once again. "I ask for your mercy on this boy. He is innocent of any wrongdoing. Kill me, but spare this boy!"

"I see," the Queen said, smiling. "And what of you, young Richard?" She knelt to be on eye level with the boy. She loosened her grip in his hair and gave him a consoling pat on the shoulder. Blinking her eyes and smiling sweetly, she said, "There is no point for such a handsome, young man to die. Oh, how I have wished for a grandson your age. Yes, such a shame. I would have been so proud and loved you so dearly. I would have given you the world, the best education, the best clothing, armor, and weaponry." She looked at King Shabael. "He would have made a fine son for you, would he not, My Emperor?"

"Ah, Mother, you never fail to impress me with your gift of lacing venomous words with honey," Shabael said. "Aye, who knows; he could have been a future King of the Ravenites had his sister lived." He knew that he was being taunted for having no male heir to the throne. If he were to die, the El Qui line to the throne would be broken. However, Alie, his oldest daughter could take the throne and rule as queen. Alie! Yes, she was definitely her father's daughter. She would be a wise ruler when the day arrived. He loved her fiercely and admired the strength she had shown despite the suspicion that the Queen Highest had been involved in killing her mother and poisoning her lover. His youngest daughter, Blanca, was a little egocentric hailstorm. Anywhere she and her sister appeared publicly, she was always asking who was the prettiest. Unlike Alie, Blanca adored her grandmother. Many times, he had found his mother spoiling her while the girl was thought to be playing alone in her room. God forbid Blanca gain the throne, she would mar every beautiful woman in the kingdom. If only Shawndeli could give him a son. *Now you're sounding like Mother.*

"Tell us, young Richard, what were your sister's plans? Surely she would have confided in her brother."

Richard sought Eradrin's eyes and spoke as though he was addressing the prince. "We were leaving the castle but Dayanna decided to turn back. She said it would only be proper to free the Raven who had brought her the Light. That ogre of a guard saw us fleeing from the aviary with the raven and caught me but Dayanna escaped with the Prince. That is all I know."

"All right, dear," Queen Mateah said. She rose to her feet and stepped to Richard's side, still holding onto the back of his hair so that his neck was most exposed. The right corner of her lip rose to form the wicked little smile wives make sometimes when their husbands have stumbled.

Eradrin sensed what was about to happen. "Wait! "Kill no more. We could have lied and told you anything. But we have told you the truth. I..." He stopped when he saw the Queen's hand tighten on the dagger. Her polished red nails now showed as her fingers curled around the handle.

Richard, knowing the end was near, began singing in a low harsh voice that made Eradrin weep, his shoulders convulsing. He recognized the song Dayanna had sung to her brother when he was only a tad of a boy and had lain afraid in his bed.

"Snow falls upon the woods,
"So pretty does it fall.
Covering the trees
And the mountains so tall...."

"Please, have mercy on this child!" Eradrin tried to rise but the strong hands on his shoulders kept him down. "There's no need for his death."

"Ah, well, you are right, Future King," Queen Highest said. "There really is no need to do it but only for my amusement. But, after all, isn't that enough reason?" She emitted a radiant smile and pulled the razor-sharp blade across Richard's throat.

"No!" Eradrin leapt forward, breaking free of the men that held him. He caught Richard just as his knees began to buckle. With one hand, Eradrin grabbed the top of Richard's head and with the other hand at the base of the boy's throat, he desperately tried pressing the ear-to-ear gash back together.

Richard was gasping. Air hissed through the blood spurting from his slashed windpipe. His eyes were wide and wild, rolling from side to side. Eradrin pulled his once future brother-in-law against his chest, feeling the boy's hot blood spray against his own face and neck and flow between his flesh and armor.

Eradrin wept. Holding the boy tight, he ran his hand through Richard's hair. "It's all right now. You'll be with your sister and father. And I expect to be seeing you all soon. The Light loves you. Just close your eyes. Shhhhh."

Richard's arms began to flail in the throes of death. Eradrin could feel the exhales of misty air through the cut throat against his neck that made a wet, wheezing, sound. "Shhhhh. Soon you can lie in that field of snow you were singing about. The sun will be overhead. You will feel the heat of the sun on your face for the first time and your sister's arms around you." Eradrin's words turned into a mourning groan as the boy's body relaxed in death.

"Dayanna will sing to you again. Listen. Can you hear her?" Eradrin held the boy closer and began to slowly rock him. He began singing in a low voice that cracked with emotion.

..."the sun is shining bright
The ravens are flying high
There's no need to fear
Sleep in peace through the night...
The new day is coming
Yellow sun and skies so blue
Rejoice the Light of new days
Will forever shine on you...."

Eradrin felt the invisible hands of Dayanna and his father resting upon his shoulders as he slowly rocked Richard's stilled body and was comforted by their presence. His eyes remained closed and he pictured the clear blue sky and the long-missing sun shining down upon a field of snow.

The hands suddenly tightened painfully on his shoulders and Eradrin was yanked backward as Richard's body was pulled from his grasp. He rested on his knees with Malbolian soldiers flanking him. It was his turn to face the executioner.

Queen Mateah released her hold on Richard's body, allowing it to collapse to the ground. She sighed as she noted her white robe and armor stained in the youth's blood. "Can I not go through one day without blood spoiling my clothing? Although, I must say, the blood look always seems becoming to a Malbolian, especially when it is that of a Ravenite." She whirled on the heels of her boots to face Shabael, who was attempting to bring himself back into the present following his mother's cruel shock-and-awe act of throat slitting. Her brutal actions and the broken words that Eradrin had sung had touched him in a way he did not think possible. This frightened him.

"You may resume your proceedings, Exalted One," the Queen said, bowing to the shaken Shabael.

One thing he could depend on; no matter her deeds, Mother always showed respect for his station. And now she was setting the stage for his presence. Shabael shook his head and thought how amazing it was that his mother always found a way to outdo herself in her little dramatic bloodletting follies with the enemy. The great woman was a natural.

The Malbolian soldiers were enthralled by her actions, no matter how severe or cruel. These people were the enemies, were they not? What would things have been like if the roles were reversed? Yes, she seemed to enjoy the bloodletting. In addition, it provided them with conversation during the victory celebrations that followed.

Malbolians were warriors first. As there were no worthy adversaries left in their world, they filled arenas with cheering fans. Riches were given to the greatest surviving warriors. Malbolians were born with a desire to dominate and live in the holy moments when animalistic blood lust possessed them. It took generations of training to become what they called the Red Rider, which was to perform with calm tactical mind offensive and defensive moves. No true Malbolian could master the Red Rider without having continuous repetition of strikes and defensive moves with perfect precision until it could be done without thought.

Perhaps it was the Queen Mother who came closest to meeting Red Rider perfection. Though she was not a sword warrior, her beauty and mind were her weapons. All that observed her knew the Red Rider was within her, raging as violently as any man on the battlefield.

She struck with her weapons of words instead of swords and they proved just as deadly. She had the insight to find the cruelest, most innovative ways to agonize her enemy. When she performed, she was the most beautiful, desirable woman a Malbolian warrior could imagine. Moreover, the men were smitten by her presence, loved her more than their king. They were enamored by her not only because she was beautiful, but because she was the purest Red Rider that the kingdom had ever known. When she rode, she inspired lust in the warriors' hearts to the extent that even their wives benefitted. Oh how happy the Queen Mother made those wives when their husbands came home from watching her performance on the battlefield that had set their loins on fire.

Still, Shabael was not jealous. His use of the willing queen to carry out the necessary cruelties shielded him from the gory image he might have obtained. In truth, she was the greatest weapon in his arsenal. Her presence created instant, paralyzing fear. Admittedly, there were nights when he awakened with icy chills and nausea from the feeling that it was actually she who ruled him; that under the veil of motherly love she bewitched him to believe her ideas were his own. On the rare occasion when he had held ground on a decision contrary to her own, some event always seemed to happen to bend his thinking toward hers. He woke up many nights with a racing heart, wondering if some dreadful punishment or act he had commanded was really his own. Shabael could not accept that he was the same evil blood-lusting monster as his beautiful mother. Where he dealt punishment swiftly, she sought the most heart-wrenching soul-crushing psychological torture prior to a man's death. She was the epitome of the Red Rider.

She was Mother and he thanked the Great Creator that she was his ally. Or was she? Alie was convinced Mother was instrumental in her own mother's death, but he had always thought the idea absurd. They were family, not enemy. However, there were things he remembered from the night his first wife had died after the birth of his second daughter. He had noticed that his mother never approached his wife's bedside during the labor and birthing. And moments before the child was born, his mother had spoken with a new post-partum doula. The child was delivered without complications. She was bathed and announced as a daughter. Shabael was delighted although he had truly wanted a son. He reached out to touch his new daughter when the doula cried out in horror. Shabael

199

staggered backward in horror as a stream of blood shot from his prone wife, making a crimson arch in the air before striking the floor. More powerful spurts followed and Shabael could not believe how much blood was being spewed from his beloved wife. It was at that moment, when he was swinging his gaze to the screaming doula, that he saw that uncontrollable little hitch in the corner of the upper lip of his mother.

The doula was a healer and had brought caged mice into the room into which to cast any injury or ailment. However, it happened too quickly, without warning, and the healer said death was instantaneous. She was helpless as there was no life to save.

For Shabael, the extremes of opposite emotions were bewildering. From the greatest joy to the depths of despair in a heartbeat. He pled to the Great Creator to bring life back to his wife while his mother continued to stand silently in the corner, showing no emotion or signs of sympathy.

The doula determined that the queen had died of a ruptured artery. She had died so quickly the healer had not even had an opportunity to lay hands on her.

It was an hour later when the other incident that was to give Shabael a thousand nightmares happened; something he had never spoken of to anyone. As he was leaving the room, one of the servants was removing the bloodied discarded clothes when an object clanged to the floor. It was a piece of very thin metal, perhaps an inch long and scroll thin, sharper than the edge of a sword. Later he dreamed of hearing the doula scream and turning around to see her holding his newly born child in her arms and speaking through clenched teeth, "It's a girl," with blood dripping from her lips and the thin metal piece between her teeth which she had just used to slice his wife's inner thigh. And the Queen Mother was standing in the corner with that little almost indiscernible smile on her lips.

Shabael never confronted his mother with any of his concerns. He thought it was better to leave it alone, because if what he suspected was true, one of them would have to die.

As for questioning the doula, that avenue was lost when she apparently leapt from her balcony later that night. Then, all those years later, Alie had as much as accused the Queen Highest of plotting the death of her Ravenite boyfriend. And, as much as he dreaded facing the truth, he had caught his mother eyeing Queen Shawndeli with disdain.

It seemed of late that every private conversation they had always came around to the topic of a son for his heir. It suddenly dawned on him that the slashing of the boy Richard's throat was his mother's way of demonstrating how he was cutting the throat of his own lineage of blood kings. *Alas, how Mother could make one action have so many meanings.*

It had taken all the courage he could muster, but Shabael had finally confronted the Queen Mother only a week earlier. He had caught her staring hatred at Shawndeli and, burning with anger and disgust, he had gone to her and whispered, "If she dies before I, so do you, Mother." Startled, Queen Mateah could not keep the shocked look off her face, but then that little uncontrollable hitch-of-the lip smile showed. Shabael walked away, unsure if he had helped or worsened the issue. It was then that he realized, of all the kingdoms of Skyeden and the unknown lands beyond the mountains to the west, it was his mother he feared more than any enemy.

What a day this has been! Shabael felt he had been so near to repossessing the Orb of Light and the failure infuriated him. Everything he could want in this world was his. There was nothing unattainable. There was no worthy enemy to oppose him. Yet, he felt despair for having come so close to obtaining the Orb of Light, only to have to watch it disappear in a flock of ravens. Sweeping through the Ravenites weak defenses had been so easy. There was hardly any resistance at all, with the only fighting coming at the foot of this tree. *Damn!* There was no way for the Orb of Light to evade his grasp; and, yet by some supernatural force the ravens had escaped with it.

There was no Moon of Day to activate the magic of the tree, yet magic had prevailed. It was infuriating. Then, adding to his woes, Queen Mateah had followed up with her display of ruthlessness and guile. While he planned strategies, leading his men, and winning the battle, she had performed an act of violence upon a prisoner that would no doubt be translated into some heroic deed that would become the most talked about action of the venture. There were times when he could have handled this, but not today. Today he had to prove he could be as ruthless as she. He would not let her steal the thunder.

He wanted to do something to show her he could be just as capable of producing horror in the minds of a people. He would prove to her that he was not only her equal, but superior. For the first time in his life he wanted to turn it all around. He wanted her to fear him as much as he had feared her. Fear was the language she had mastered. It was the only thing she understood. He turned to the still kneeling Eradrin.

"Future King, we have spared your kingdom's children because of you telling the truth," Shabael said. "We will keep our word. But, for every day the Orb of Light is not returned, I will have the eyes of one child removed."

"What? No! *Nooo!* This is evil!" Prince Eradrin responded, his eyes blazing.

"That depends on which side you're on," Shabael mused. "I am assigning Malcolm Vokin as your overseer. He will report to me your actions of each day. And the first offense I find toward me or my kingdom, we will find appropriate ways to punish your children and your women." Shabael turned to look at his men. "We'll have the army stay in Skye Castle this evening. Future King, you and your family may remain in your chambers. I will make you king tomorrow. Have your court prepare for the ceremony for mid-day. Dismissed."

The gathered soldiers and citizens began dispersing. The Queen Mateah stood with her hands folded, her eyes turned downward as if bored by the proceedings. Her attitude and arrogance infuriated Shabael. *That didn't get your attention? Well, maybe this will!* "One moment," he said and motioned to Rageton. "Have our archers in formation one hundred yards from this location facing the Tree of Light. Prepare them to use torch arrows."

Audible gasps issued from both Ravenites and Malbolians. *That made you take note.* He could not recall having ever seen a shocked expression on her face before. And for the first time in his life, he felt the corner of *his* lip raise in a Mateah smile. Yes, he finally had her attention! What he had just commanded was an unthinkable act. The original Tree of Light and Tree of Dark had never been attacked. Up above, the circling ravens and Darklings of both armies sounded shrill alarmed cries. Either they understood what had just been ordered or had simply picked up on the high emotions of the people. No one in the crowd moved. It seemed to the stunned Eradrin that the whole of Skyeden, and perhaps even the ever-expanding universe, had been frozen by the audacity of King Shabael's unthinkable proclamation.

It was believed by all the populace of the kingdoms of Skyeden that the two trees were where the physical and spiritual worlds met. The trees represented duality of those worlds to the Great Creator. Each tree channeled separate essences of the Creator and the forces and energies created a balance.

Prince Eradrin could never have imagined he could be more shocked than having suffered the loss of his father and his love Dayanna. However, Shabael's order had accomplished the seemingly impossible. He could actually feel the blood draining from his face. When the Malbolians had captured the Orb of Light, they had triggered something that had destroyed the Sun and the Light of Moon. It was a day of terror for every person and beast in Skyeden. The Sun and Day of Moon vanished from the sky, leaving only darkness. The magic of the Light faded. The Ascension of Light, the act of dedication of one's soul to the Light Essence, which granted immortality to natural death, could no longer be performed.

That event was deemed by many to be the end of the world. Hundreds of men and women in Skyeden died of fear. Some committed suicide and others simply went mad, their minds unable to endure the presumed horror that awaited. Hours, days, weeks, and months that followed gradually reduced the anxiety, but there was no longer daylight. The world was in a permanent bluish-white neon-like state when the Moon of Dark was making its orbit. But when the Moon of Dark set, the world became without light, except for the faint illumination of deep blue sky spread evenly above the horizon.

No one could begin to imagine what might happen were one of the trees destroyed. It was generally speculated that a huge black hole would be created, sucking in all that existed. To strike down one of the trees was considered the greatest offense to the Great Creator. Surely, it would mean death or eternal damnation to the offender.

"Exalted Highness," Prince Eradrin cried out, trying to keep his hatred for King Shabael from erupting. No matter the personal cost in pride and integrity, he had to attempt calm reasoning with the one person he hated above all others. At that moment, Eradrin would have gladly given up his own life for the chance to slay Shabael. It took all the effort and control he could muster to speak in a reasonable and calm voice.

"The destruction of the tree could bring doom to us all and damnation to the offender, Your Majesty, even to your own people.

For it is your kingdom that will do this deed, and for that you will risk damnation of yourself and your people."

There was a stirring of unrest among the soldiers from both armies.

Could I get one of them to turn? Eradrin stared at the near-panicking people. *One of them could throw a spear and end it all. Could I possibly have the power of persuasion to bring the El Qui down? If so, they will have me lead them and will praise me when I order the death of the Red Dragon.*

Some among the on-lookers fell to their knees as if awaiting a bolt of lightning from an angered Creator. But even through all the chaos, Shabael heard two whispered words that struck him with the impact of a sledgehammer.

"Your Father!" Queen Mateah spoke from twenty yards away. An instant silence spread across the people. The archers, who were already moving into formation, halted. A soldier withdrew the torch he was about to dip into a vat of tar for the archers to use to ignite their arrows. All eyes turned to the queen, hoping and praying she would stop this madness.

Until that moment, Prince Eradrin had not realized the extent of the power the Red Dragon held. Her whisper could silence thunderstorms. He suddenly began to realize what her people already knew. The woman was impregnable. Had the two of them been alone in a room and he had been armed with a sword, he would have dropped his blade when she looked at him.

Shabael was having much the same experience. He felt as though an assassin had stabbed him in the back. It was uncanny how Mother not only knew the one chink in his armor but how so skillfully and accurately she impaled him with words. She incapacitated him. He opened his mouth. He closed it. What he didn't say orally, his eyes revealed.

"Need I say more?" asked Queen Mateah, the Queen Mother, the Red Dragon of the Red Riders.

Shabael attempted to impale her with his eyes. It was blasphemy to use his father's death before his men as a means to manipulate him, especially with what she implied. The monarchy's story to the world was that his father had sacrificed his life so that Malbolians could live in a world of dark, where Dark Magic reigns and the Light force was destroyed. That was the official El Qui story. What really had happened was quite another story. It seemed from the moment his father had taken the Light from the Tree of Light, the Queen Mother was at his ear whispering, tempting him; encouraging him with seductive images of becoming as powerful as a God if he did this one thing that no man had tried before. *"Take an orb in each hand and unite them,"* Mother had urged his father. *"You will be made a God."*

You killed him too, Mother. For someone dedicated to protect the throne you certainly do have that black widow spider love going on. Could you be responsible for the death of my first wife, my father, the exile of my daughter? Why am I still alive? Is it because you think me weak and controllable? Or do you need me? Because without me do you fear you will lose the power of the throne? I must really frighten you, Mother. Made you use your trump card, did I not? Now are you afraid? Does the puppet suddenly frighten its master?

A portion of the gathered men began to step aside and Queen Shawndeli, borne by a magnificent stallion, made her way to where Shabael stood. She was followed by a double formation of her one hundred women warriors. The sight of his beloved wife brought Shabael joy. He motioned for Rageton to dismiss the archers. Shawndeli's white horse pranced to a stop, gently reared, and dropped down with a flick of its mane.

"Your Grace," the queen said.

Shabael clapped his hands and spread his arms to warmly receive her. "Ah, our Queen and her Red Death Sword Dancers. You may have just saved the world, my love." He ran a hand over the horse's nose then reached up to help his young wife down, suddenly aware of how her presence had such a mood-changing effect. He loved her unconditionally and seeing her approach, the glory of her pose, her beauty, her spirit, as through the eyes of a common man or warrior, was scintillating. Shawndeli was the first El Qui Queen who had insisted in participating in battles. In accordance, the greatest weapon experts of the world had trained her. Oh, what a sight for a Malbolian King to see his Queen with her squad of her red-clad Sword Dancers.

Shawndeli's first love was dancing and she had worked her art into her weapon katas. There was no wasted movement, for on the battlefield one had to strike quick with intent to kill. She and her Sword Dancers were mesmerizing when they went into action and well earned the name Red Deaths. They were reminiscent of the myth of sirens off the coast that reportedly mesmerized sailors into drowning.

Oh, how the king loved her, and he made a special show of it when Mother was around, knowing that compassion and expressed affection made her cringe. He dropped to a knee and took his wife's hand to kiss. Nodding toward the still kneeling Eradrin, he said, "My Love, this is the future Ravenite King, Eradrin Donachie."

Shawndeli presented a bow that created audible gasps among the soldiers. The Queen Mother's mouth was agape. No Malbolian royalty had ever bowed to the conquered. Shabael didn't have to look at his mother to detect her disdain.

"I am honored to be in your presence, Prince Donachie," Shawndeli said. "My heart grieves for your loss this day. I know you must hate us and wish us dead, but please know there is nothing personal in what is transpiring here today. It's just the way of the world; those that rule and those that obey; those that live and those that die. If your family experiences any discomforts, please let my entourage know." She reached out a gloved hand and placed it on Eradrin's head. "May the Creator comfort you."

Shawndeli gave a bow to Shabael, who was still discombobulated by her bow to the prince, and moved to stand by his side. The king glanced at his mother, seeing her rage as red as her eyes, and laughed. It was a hearty laugh — a roar really — that started deep inside his belly and simply exploded. He slapped his knee, and then slapped the back of one of his soldiers. The soldiers, finally able to release some tension, also began laughing. It was so contagious that even some of the Ravenites laughed, if not out of humor, for relief in the realization that perhaps their world may have just been saved.

"I will not allow war to turn us into barbarians," Shabael said, and straightened to face the gathered soldiers and citizens. "Despite what some of you may think, Malbolians do have codes of honor. We do not seek to crush you; we ask only that you acknowledge us as your rulers. You may keep your culture and customs intact. We have no desire to change your beliefs or way of life. Of course, we are claiming your armed forces as our own and will begin an immediate, indoctrination period. Shabael paused, then moved to Eradrin and extended a hand to help the prince to his feet. "Come, take my horse to the castle, and have a healer attend to you. I shall ride with my wife."

Eradrin was in a state of utter confusion. How could this King and Queen possibly think they could console him after slaying all he had loved, as though they were friends visiting to show their support for his lost ones, as though they had nothing at all to do with their deaths?

The young queen's arrival had obviously had a dramatic effect on the Malbolian King. The interactions between the Queen Highest, Shabael, and his wife were like trying to listen to music of discord, climatic notes, and surreal undertones of rhythmic melodies that made no harmonic sense. He imagined it was like a prisoner being questioned by three interrogators using opposite emotional appeals in search of a confession. Then, as if someone had turned on a lamp, it dawned on Eradrin that his life had just undergone a dramatic change. His role as the young prince, heir apparent to the Ravenland throne, had ended. His father the king was dead. *Long live the king! And that king is I.* Eradrin loved his people. He loved this land and the sacred Light. He suddenly saw himself as a spiritual knight of the Light and King of his people. Though beaten down, humiliated, bleeding from a stab wound, and having witnessed the deaths of those he loved, he had never stood so tall and proud of his name, of whom he was, and what he must do for the people and the Light.

"I thank you, Exalted One, but I ask for the sake of my dignity that I ride my own horse back to the city," Eradrin said. He glanced toward the young Queen Shawndeli, hoping Shabael's answer would be influenced by her presence.

Shabael looked first at his mother, then at his wife. One face frowned disapproval; the other smiled approval.

"Yes, I understand," Shabael said with a slight nod and a little smile. "Let us return to Skye Castle."

CHAPTER 20

SKYE CASTLE: ERADRIN'S CHAMBERS

Eradrin threw his wine goblet against the wall and the silver chalice clamored to the floor. His father, his love, her father, her brother and hundreds of his people were dead, their blood spilled like wine from the cup. He swung the balcony doors wide and stepped outside onto the balcony and into the sounds of drunken soldiers and the occasional cry of a woman.

A woman screamed, the sound dying just as suddenly as it had begun. Eradrin covered his ears with his hands and staggered backward. "All is lost," he whispered to himself. "Great Creator, have you abandoned us? Is your Light gone from the world? We were your people! Why have you turned your back on us? We are slaves to the Darkness? Why? Why my father, my love, my king and my people? Why do you do everything in your power to induce me to hate you?"

Another woman's cry rose from the streets below and Eradrin scanned he dark streets, hoping to locate the source. The attempt was futile, however, and he raised his hands to the sky in frustration. His people were huddled in their homes, praying their doors wouldn't be kicked in and the premises ransacked.

"This is enough!" he suddenly shouted, and threw the door open, startling those in the lounge area adjoining his stateroom. His mother and brother rose to their feet and it was that moment that he realized the full impact of his father being dead. When he entered the room, his family and guards looked at him — not at him — but to him. He was to be king now, ruler of their lives. Hell had befallen his people, who were experiencing inexplicable horrors beyond his control at this moment. He searched for words that might be worthy of the situation

"What King am I?" he cried, ripping at his high-collared jacket. "Our women and children are suffering at the hands of these ruthless, vile men; and, I do nothing? We just sit?" No! I cannot stand down! How can I live a day letting our people be submitted to this? My conscience forbids me."

"What would you have us do, Brother?" Thomar asked, holding out his open hands.

"We gather our men and we stop this madness! I can't bear the cries," Eradrin ran his fingers through his hair. "Why are we the Royal Family? What is our purpose? Is it not to protect our people? But we cannot. We are lost. These Malbolians treat us as subhuman; lower than dogs. If we do not take a stand on this, of what value are we?"

"It is the way of the world when you are of the defeated," Eradrin's mother, Queen Juliana, said, her gaze fixed upon the floor. She was leaning against the wall, her arms wrapped around her waist, internalizing the pain.

"No," Eradrin said, smoothing out his hair and taking a deep breath. "No." Then more emphatically, "NO!" We will not take this! I would rather us die now, this night, standing as a people with dignity, than to be subjected to this. No!"

"Eradrin, please, you are upset now," Juliana said, pushing away from the wall and reaching out a hand to console him.

"My sword," Eradrin said to his guards.

Thomar placed his hands on Eradrin's shoulders. "We are under guard, brother. The Malbolians have declared a curfew this evening. Anyone found outside their abode will be punished by death."

"Then make me a martyr," Eradrin said.

"Your people need you. Your family needs you. I know we are beaten down now and are suffering at their hands. But for the Great Creator's sake, you are to be our king. You are our hope. The Donachie bloodline must live on for the people."

"Then if I die, Brother, you shall be king and your son assures our continuing bloodline."

"Eradrin, you must not talk this way," Queen Juliana urged. "What is happening is horrible. What you have endured today — all of us — is unthinkable. And this is why we need you alive. We need your strength and your presence."

"Strength? What strength? We huddle in our palace rooms while our people are being subjected to barbaric atrocities. I will not stand for this! It is unthinkable that the Malbolian king allows his army to do this."

"It is the Malbolian way, my brother," Thomar said. "They are a warrior tribe that has ruled the world for a thousand years. They have conquered all that stood against them. They hunger for blood and incite their defeated to fight just to slaughter them again. I would not be surprised if it were they who gave us the light only for an excuse to fight us."

"Why pretend they need excuses?" Eradrin asked, his voice perplexed. He looked at the guard holding his sword, and realized it was the weapon that had been carried by his father, the slain King of the Ravenites. The pommel featured two black raven heads that had been hand-sculptured in wax from which a mold was created. Molten bronze had then been poured into the mold to create the pommel; followed by copper plating. A chemical process had then been used to turn the ravens' heads black. The sword had been forged for the first Ravenite king and had been passed along to each king in succession.

"I can't just stand here," Eradrin moaned. "My father, my love Dayanna, and our kingdom have been lost. No! I refuse to accept this defeat." He snatched the sword from the hands of the guards and strode toward the door.

"Eradrin, stop!" Queen Juliana cried out with such urgency that her son halted in mid-stride and turned to look at her. "We knew if ever we were found to have the Light that this would happen," she said. "My son, there is not a Ravenite in the Kingdom who would not die for the chance of regaining the Light … the Sun … a day again. Listen to me; your father sat on the throne for many years. Hard years. But never did he act on impulse. He was a mountain that moved sparingly, but mightily. He moved with prudence. If you seek vengeance for this day, then you plan actions that have everlasting consequences. With your father gone along with the kingdom's heart, Dayanna, our people need you more than ever. You now have the seat and the weight of the throne and you must act accordingly."

"In ceremony only!" Eradrin argued, "King Shabael presides in the place of my father. A Malbolian gives me the throne? He and his witch mother? And this Malcolm, who acts as their eyes and ears, is to direct and advise me? How can I be called King?"

"Listen and heed me, my son. Because you have the blood of your father and me and you are the eldest son, it is your right to be king. Now listen to me; lay your sword down for now. Your people need you. When they see you ascend to the throne tomorrow, they will at least have hope. A remnant of something to hold onto and believe in. You are the future, Eradrin."

"Yes," Eradrin bitterly replied, his head down, staring at the mosaic floor, "a King without his Queen. Am I to forget that it was Shabael who killed Dayanna? Am I to forget the slaughtering of young Richard? The ruthless slaying of my father? My first act as king will be to declare a day of mourning for all those who lost their lives in this battle. I will build statues to Father and Dayanna so they will forever be remembered."

Eradrin dropped his sword and embraced Queen Juliana. "What about the children, Mother? Do we allow them to mutilate a child a day? We do not know where the Light is. An entire generation of Ravenites will be blinded.

"Oh, Great Creator, may the Light save us.

CHAPTER 21

RAVENLAND PRESENT TIME

King Eradrin Donachie closed his eyes as he leaned against the Tree of Light. He was resting in a place between two large roots that ran from the base of the trunk. The leaves on the old tree were much sparser and smaller than they had been in the time of the Light. Many of the old leaves were preserved in the cathedral. One leaf remained that had been used during the Ascension rites before the Malbolians had attacked. King Donachie tried to recapture the smell of those leaves, as they had been when the crown of the tree was lush and thick with them.

Today marked the one hundred and fifty year anniversary of the battle with the Malbolians underneath this old tree, but Eradrin remembered every moment of that day of infamy. Each year since, he had come to this spot and relived the happenings of that day. There were battle scars still remaining on the tree's thick trunk. It was here that his father had been driven back and wounded ... and murdered.

As he mused over the events of that awful day, he fingered the jeweled iridescent stone that hung around his neck. It was a cut from the same stone he had given Dayanna beneath the tree all those years ago. It had been the final time they would touch. One hundred and fifty years ago ... His thoughts wandered back to when he had relinquished his father's sword to his mother on that awful night, and had lain in bed wondering if he would be in close enough proximity to King Shabael during the crowning ceremony that he might kill him.

Such a long night that had been...

CHAPTER 22

UEYS IN THE PARKING LOT

It was hard to look cool and be a little scared at the same time, but Dylan gradually brought the speed of his birthday cycle up to fifteen miles an hour, just getting the feel, learning how to lean into the turns. The Kmart parking lot was large and empty in front of the shuttered store, but it was from the lots of the adjoining stores that a car periodically came barreling through to get on the highway. One was coming toward him on the right and he slowed the bike as he prepared to make a tight U-turn. Despite the lack of speed, or perhaps because of it, the bike began tilting over. Dylan panicked. There was no way he was going to let this bike get scratched! His left foot found the old tarmac and even though he couldn't stop the momentum of the bike going over, he was going to let it down with the gentleness of a mother's first kiss on her newborn.

God! This was embarrassing! However, other than his red face, all was good. He let the bike down slowly, while he was still standing. The bike lay on its right side, the engine purring quietly … until Dylan forgot that he was gripping the accelerator, and rolled it forward as the weight of the bike pulled it toward him. The powerful little engine roared and the bike did a 360 on its side. Dylan quickly realized his mistake and shut off the accelerator. The bike stopped its crazy spin immediately and the motor shut off. Dylan quickly glanced around, hoping no one had noticed. No such luck.

"Are you all right?" Freddie pulled his bike alongside the embarrassed Dylan, concern showing on his face.

"Yeah, nothing's hurt but my pride. Jesus! I'm going to die if I've scratched her up."

"Hey, man. Everybody lays their bike down." Freddie's voice was consoling, no Grease Monkey scorn evident. "If you ever meet someone that says they haven't, they're lying. Let's lift her up."

They hoisted the bike upright and found a couple of scratches on the crash bar.

"Thank God for the bar," Dylan said.

"Yeah, you want me to go get Dad's truck? We can take her back home."

"No way! I'll break this stallion. I'm getting right back on her," Dylan said. "Got too slow in the turn, that's all."

"The secret to making a uey with a bike is, whatever direction you're turning, you look as far over your shoulder as you can so you see ahead of the turn."

"Got it."

"Well, you go then, Major Dude," Freddie said. "Hi yo! Ride 'em cowboy."

Dylan straddled the Indian, gave a thumbs up, took a deep breath, and started the engine. He circled the parking lot for several minutes, stopping and starting; making tight U-Turns. His confidence was building with every loop he made and he was beginning to feel as one with the machine. He was loving it.

Freddie signaled him over. "Want to take a little ride? Maybe up toward the mountain? Not much traffic, just long country roads."

"You mean skip school?"

"Yeah. It's your eighteenth birthday. We got Indians, Dude. We're officially a couple of bad asses. Shit, man, everybody would be disappointed if we didn't do something bad-ass today."

"Yeah, I dunno. There are sheriff's deputies all over the county. One of them sees me, Dad's gonna hear about it. But you know what? Why not? Let's do it, man. Let's blow this joint. Let's do the mountains and bust that Blue Ridge Parkway wide open."

Freddie began, "We're on it," and Dylan chorused, "We own it. If it's a girl, we bone it!"

The AWOL buddies high-fived, twisted the accelerators, and hit the road.

Side by side on the edge of the highway, the sun in their faces, the powerful roar of engines throbbing in their ears. Heaven. A raven cawed from its perch on a power line across the road.

"Caw!"

Dylan wasn't sure if it was Ravenous, but he wasn't about to take his attention off the road. Another *"Caw!"* and Dylan playfully answered the blackbird with a loud *"Caw!"*

"Jeez, this is sweet," he said to Freddie. "It's like flying. I feel like a Raven; wings spread and flying high."

"Yeah? You and your birds. You know what the last words of the hockey bird were?"

"No?"

"Oh, shiiiiiiitttttttt!" Freddie said and roared ahead.

The AWOL students rode for some twenty miles before Freddie motioned to pull into an old general store with one fuel pump.

"We get about a hundred and fifty miles a tank. Let's fill 'em up here and we won't have to worry about it anymore." Freddie said. "How's it going? You okay?"

"Yeah. I'm realizing I don't have a motorcycle permit and no insurance to be riding it, but other than that, yeah, I'm great, man."

"Well, you can take care of the prima donna stuff when we get back. Right now, you're total badass ... a real outlaw. Heck, if you weren't already Kemo Sabe, I'd call you Jesse James. "Tomorrow is plenty of time to worry about all the red tape."

"Wow! Nine bucks and I've got a full tank. Sweet!" Dylan tightened the gas cap. "Hey, how far is Raven Rock from here?"

"You mean where that old Indian tribe lives,"

"Yeah. Let's go there.

"I dunno ... I guess maybe thirty miles. But that's a lot of riding. Thirty miles up there, then fifty back home."

"It's a special day; one I want to remember. Oh, man! Can't believe I'm straddling a frickin' Indian. No one's got a better best friend than you, Monkey Man. Let's do it. I feel like I've already been up there in my dreams."

"You and your freaky ravens," Freddie, said, rolling his eyes. Then he turned and pointed. "Dang, Dyl, you've got a fan section."

Dylan followed Freddie's pointing finger and saw three ravens sitting on the telephone wire. As he watched, two more joined them and began an animated cawing.

"I can't tell if they're cussing me out or happy to see me," Dylan said.

Freddie frowned. He was beginning to feel guilty. He knew they were asking for big-time trouble from both the school and their parents. This was supposed to have been a short joyride, not an excursion. *Jeez, it's going to be after dinner before we get home if we go to the village.* Dylan was supposed to be the sane one, what the heck is he thinking? "Hey, Dyl, maybe we should head back. We don't want your dad calling the school and finding out you weren't even there."

"Crap! Maybe you're right. I have football practice, too! No! No way! I'll call the coach and then call home. I mean when they hear I've got an Indian and with it being my birthday, I don't think they'll get too worked up."

Freddie shrugged and they parked their bikes by the store entrance. They stretched their legs, went inside, ordered a couple of Mountain Dews, and then came outside to enjoy the sunshine. Nothing like high-octane caffeine. As they downed the sodas, two girls wearing cut-off jeans and tank tops walked past. A willowy blonde and a curvaceous brunette. A perfect pairing. Two packages with all the wrappings. "Cool bikes," the brunette said. Dylan fell in love. Freddie was awestruck.

"Be right back," Dylan said and followed the twin dynamos into the store. He pasted a half-mocking smile on his face and ordered a pack of Marlboros. Mr. Cool. Eighteen years old and ordering smokes. Lot of brass. The middle-aged Asian man behind the counter didn't even give him a second look; just took his money and rang up the smokes.

"Let's see how cool we can look," Dylan said after returning to his bike, grinning at Freddie, and giving him a cigarette. Freddie, put a lop-sided grin on his face and removed his glasses. They straddled their bikes, attempting to portray their best James Dean images. "Okay, Freddie, you can have the Dean look. I'm going with Marlon Brando. This is definitely my wild side."

The door opened and Dylan put a match to the smoke, took a long, slow drag, and began gasping, then coughing, his face red from the spasms. He caught his breath, fought the tears in his eyes, and embarrassedly saw that the girls were watching.

"You all right?" the blonde beauty asked. "Yeah, I remember my first cigarette, too."

Freddie, holding his unlit Marlboro between his lips, snorted.

"No, no, I'm fine," Dylan said, wiping the tears from his cheek. "Just had something go down the wrong way."

"Yeah, like your Mr. Cool image," Freddie said, giggling.

"Well, it's a shame we have to go babysit," the brunette girl said, tossing her hair over her shoulder and extending her chest. Freddie almost choked when he noticed she wasn't wearing a bra. The nipples of her proud, young breasts strained against the fabric of the thin tank top. She wasn't paying attention to him so he chanced a little longer investigative stare, not noticing the blonde with her hand on her hip looking directly at him.

"Hey," the brunette said. "See that yellow house across the road? We're babysitting some brats, but we'll be through about eight o'clock. Why don't you guys swing by and we'll go for a ride," She did a little wiggle, her breasts dancing, the nipples singing. "Oh, I do love straddling a bike."

Dylan felt his heart pulsing. "Ah, I'd love to but ..."

Freddie rode to the rescue, "We have a club meeting tonight. But we'll be back this way. Real soon."

"Oh, okay. It's a shame," the brunette said and turned to walk away. The breasts followed. The blonde was still staring at Freddie, her lips curling into a sneer. "Pervert," she said, then dropped her stare to the crotch of his jeans. "Little winkie."

Dylan stifled a giggle.

"Let's get outta here," Freddie said, his face reddening, the James Dean persona forgotten.

"Let's ride, Winkie."

"Shut up!"

They revved the engines and hit the asphalt, headed up the highway to the mountain tribe. The only clouds were a few white puffs and the visibility stretched to the horizon, which appeared as rolls of purple and deep blue among the mountains. *This is one of best moments of my life. What a birthday!* The wind in Dylan's face made him feel as though he were flying. He could smell the roadside honeysuckle and feel his ears popping with the rising altitude. Below, the tall pines in the valleys appeared to be maybe a quarter-inch tall. The ever-winding road traversed upward around the range of mountains whose peaks pierced the drifting clouds. He loved the sound of the bike's pipes and that throttle of power. He was eighteen and still a virgin, but he wondered if having sex with the hot brunette with the surging nipples could be any better than this. Nothing in his short life had ever given him this much pleasure. He patted the bike. *I'm gonna give you some kind of sexy name and treat you like a queen.*

Grow up and get a bike, you little Schwinn-pedaling fag! Robert's sarcastic voice sounded in his mind. Okay, so most hard-core bikers frowned upon anything that wasn't a Harley. But an Indian! That was an exception. A classic ride anywhere in the world. Dylan twisted the accelerator and closed to about thirty yards behind Freddie.

Freddie pulled into an overlook and Dylan coasted in alongside him.

"See there, that's Mt. Mitchell. Over here is Raven Rock. It's about fifteen miles away. Half that as the raven flies," Freddie rolled his eyes. "Seriously, what the fudge?"

Dylan turned to see what Freddie was pointing at and noticed about twenty ravens settling into the branches of a spruce pine across the road. He turned and looked back across the valley at the foot of mountains and saw the river. *Déjà vu!* He had seen it before ... all of this. But it was different in the daylight instead of the hazy night of the dream. Yeah, it had been a dream, no matter how real it had seemed. *It was just a dream.* He remembered the bend in the river, recalling the reflected blaze of moon upon it.

"You okay? Look a little haunted," Freddie asked.

"Altitude I guess."

"We're in the mountains. We're riding our bikes," Freddie said excitedly.

"Heck yeah, we are," Dylan agreed. "Thanks for the best day of my life, Podner."

"Hey, we've been best buds since kindergarten," Freddie said, removing his glasses and wiping them with a handkerchief. He held them up and stared through the lenses. "You know, they say you can see five states from the Blue Ridge."

"Yeah it's a view all right. Nice and cool up here, too." Dylan drew in a deep breath. "I can smell the pines and fresh air. But I'm ready to roll. You ready?"

"Ready."

The road, becoming more winding by the minute, continuously climbed and the temperature seemed to drop a degree each mile. They rode through two short tunnels, blaring their horns and revving the strong little engines, feeling the reverberations from the rock walls. Raven Rock three miles, the sign read. The pines appeared bare and black on the top of their trunks and the road straightened, ever rising to Raven Rock. Up ahead, the boys could see where the trees ended and a roundish rock jutted into the sky. And atop the rock, there were trees again. The scene appeared as though someone had run a razor all the way around the neck of the outcropping and left the crown with hair standing up like a longish crew cut. It reminded Dylan of a Native American hairstyle he had seen in an old sepia photo somewhere.

The teenagers cruised past the state park office and a restaurant, and then made a wide circle around the peak of the mountain until they reached the parking area at the top. Two large totem poles with sacred ravens stood as permanent sentries. The parking lot was full, but they found openings large enough for the cycles. At one end of the lot, another pair of totem poles led into a Native American village where potters, weavers, stone workers, and glassmakers displayed their skills and offered the finished products for sale.

"For a beginner, you're a fast learner," Freddie said, not trying to hide the admiration he felt for his friend. "C'mon, let's check this place out. Wow!" Look at all those women. Whoa, wait a minute. Is that an ironsmith? I love the old days where you had to really think to figure out how to make things."

A group of children gathered near the totem poles suddenly began pointing and talking excitedly.

"What's goin' on?" Freddie asked. "What are they looking at?"

Dylan turned and saw several ravens dropping down to perch on telephone lines that led into the village. For some reason, the birds' presence gave him a comforting feeling. He quickened his pace to catch up with Freddie and one of the blackbirds made a *"wruk wruk"* call. Startled, Dylan thought he recognized the distinct caw of Ravenous.

"Wruk wruk wruk! Wruk wruk!"

Dylan stopped in his tracks and stared at the ravens. He couldn't tell if it was Ravenous for sure but the bird was certainly excited, hopping up and down on the wire while the other birds remained perched. As he watched, more black birds joined their mates. Now there were more than a dozen. Dylan shrugged and caught up to Freddie.

"Look over there," Freddie said, pointing to a small crowd gathered a couple of hundred yards in the other direction staring upward at a white raven circling.

"Wow! How about that? You know, I found a white raven feather last night outside my window. Before then I didn't even know they existed."

"Looks like they do, Dyl. Albinos, I guess. You know there are white squirrels up on Black Mountain."

A rapid, worried murmur of indiscernible words emanated from the perimeter of the small gathering. It was an old Indian woman speaking with another Indian woman, her voice anxious and animated. The women continued pointing and whispering. A third woman brought a hand to her throat and did shooing "go away" motion with her hands in the direction of the strange bird.

This has to be rare, Dylan thought, as the brazen intruder perched on one of the totem poles. "It really is a white raven."

The group of ravens sitting on the telephone lines appeared to be gathering into either a defensive or offensive posture. They hunkered low on the wires, leaning forward in what appeared to be some kind of pre-flight dive position.

The white raven rose on its legs and spread it wings. Gasps sounded from the onlookers. Suddenly, the white bird emitted a high-pitched screech, flapped its wings, and lifted into the air, flying north from the village.

The black ravens reacted like cheerleaders at one of Dylan's high school football games, jumping up and down on the wire and croaking hoarsely.

"Wow, look at that," Freddie said. "Racist ravens."

Dylan laughed. "Next thing you know, they'll be wearing KKK hoods."

"Hey, I'm going to check out the blacksmith," Freddie said.

"Okay, I want to look around. I'll meet you back here in fifteen minutes.

Dylan wandered over to a woodcarver who was ... wouldn't you know it? ... painting the face of a raven on a section of a new totem pole. A glint of light caught Dylan's eye. He turned and saw the flash had come from a necklace being worn by one of the Native American women who was running a hand over a woven doormat.

"Beautiful," Dylan said aloud. A smaller, older woman who was standing in front of him, turned around.

"Why, thank you, young man," the old woman said, smiling broadly. "You're not bad yourself.

Dylan flashed a smile and turned to walk away when he spotted the girl across the road. His breath caught in his throat. He felt as if he had been hit by one of the falling boulders common in the area. He felt goose pimples crawling up his spine. He closed his eyes and shuddered. And when he opened his eyes, she was gone. Just like that. A mirage in a desert. Where could she have gone?

A panicky moment later, he spotted her again. She had paused to watch an old woman weaving a tapestry. He walked until he was parallel from her hoping to get another look at her face, but she had her head down. He marveled at how the sunlight seemed to turn her black hair blue. *Hair as black as the color of a raven's wing.* The girl raised her head and stared directly at hm. Their eyes locked. Her eyes were an almost iridescent blue and even from fifteen yards away, he could tell they were like none he had ever seen. Realizing she was holding the gaze, his mouth opened like someone who had not figured out how to breathe through his nose. He blinked, straightened, and felt his cheeks burning. The girl smiled as she turned her eyes away and then began walking.

Dylan didn't know what to do. His emotions were raging and his hormones weren't far behind. He watched her walk away as a tremor surged through his suddenly hot body. *She smiled at me.* He threw a quick glance over his shoulder to make sure that some other guy wasn't standing there and that he had interpreted her look the wrong way. He turned back and the vision was gone. *Jeez!* Panic set in. He quickly moved onto the path between the vendors and breathed a soft sigh of relief as he found her again. She had stopped to look through a box of beads. She began moving again. Dylan noted that the other tribespeople extended little bows of courtesy to her as she passed. *Is she some kind of tribal princess?* She continued to move along the row of vendors and he followed, determined not to lose her again. And then, just like that, she was gone. *Where'd you go this time? Are you some kind of princess ghost??* He sighed and there she was again. How did he keep losing sight of her? It wasn't like this was some kind of crowded city sidewalk, for crying out loud. She looked at him, flashed a smile, and then disappeared behind a nearby hut. He hurried across the road and rounded the dwelling. *Okay, fun is fun but hide and seek is for kids. You're playing with me.*

A blur of movement caught his eye; and, he saw her between two huts, walking toward the nearby woods. Dylan gambled and took his eyes off her long enough to try to find Freddie. No Freddie. Back to the vision, who was still on the path leading to the trees. Dylan's heart was pounding. Was she deliberately leading him away from the village? Was this really going to be the best eighteenth birthday in the history of the world?

Quickening his pace, Dylan made a turn on the path and found himself at the edge of a cliff. It was sheer, a thousand-foot drop over the precipice. And the vision was gone again, nowhere in sight. He walked around, checking behind the bigger trees. He even searched among the overhanging tree limbs.

There she was! Some two hundred yards away he found the beautiful blue-eyed temptress, on the other side of the chasm. Waving at him. Oh, she was having fun. As he watched, raising his hands in a helpless gesture, she blew him a kiss, turned, and disappeared among the trees.

Dylan returned to the bikes and found Freddie talking to a girl.

"There he is," Freddie said.

"Hey, sorry… I wandered off. Hi," he said to the girl. She was in Indian dress, obviously one of the tribe.

"Oh, this is Summer. Summer, Dylan."

"Hi, Summer. This is really a cool place."

"Thanks. It's fun meeting the tourists."

"Yeah, Summer's going to be a biologist." Freddie said. "She's going to Appalachian State this summer."

"Is that so? Sweet. I'm still checking out my application forms. Gotta send 'em out soon."

"Yeah, Super Jock here is still waiting on a football scholarship," Freddie interjected.

Summer smiled. "You should think about ASU if you like the mountains."

"It's definitely on my list."

Freddie grinned at the girl and shot a menacing look at Dylan. *Keep off. No trespassing.* "I'm pretty sure I'm going to ASU, Summer, and I'll hang onto your number. You'll definitely be hearing from me."

Dylan decided to salvage his friendship with Freddie and let the girl know he was not available. "Look," he said, his eyes earnest, "I saw this girl a little while ago that I'd really like to meet. She has long black hair and amazing blue eyes. She's about your age, maybe a little older. Pretty tall. She was wearing a necklace with a stone in it and a traditional dress like yours with beads woven into the sleeves."

"Dude, you took a mental photo of her?" Freddie laughed.

"Don't know who you're talking about," Summer said, turning away abruptly. She paused and looked back. "You can call me, too, if you like, Dylan ..."

"Huh?" Freddie looked at her then back at Dylan. "Wha ...?"

Dylan felt terrible as he literally watched the air deflate from his friend. "No, buddy," he said. "She didn't mean it like that. She was just being friendly to me; she likes you."

"Are you sure?" Freddie asked.

"Heck yeah. Don't worry so much about it anyway. You've only known her for five minutes. You must have really impressed her, though. Uh, huh, bringing her by the bike, sealing the deal, you old wolf."

Freddie grinned. "You're a lousy liar, but I know you're really my friend. It's all cool. One day I'll meet my other. She'll be smart and have glasses like me, but when she takes them off and lets her hair down, she'll be a natural beauty and she'll love me like the old Charlie Rich song — 'Behind Closed Doors.' "

"Yeah, that's the way it should be." Dylan answered distractedly as he scanned the village one last time in hopes of seeing the black-haired goddess. He felt his blood surge as he pictured her, then he shrugged, closed his eyes and felt the sun on his face. He drew a deep breath. "Wish you could have seen her, Freddie. Hair down to her waist. Blue eyes you wouldn't believe. In the dark she'd probably look like the night elf on World of Warcraft."

"Yeah, we're just hopeless romantics," Freddie said, sighing.

Dylan laughed, turned, and pointed at his bike. He patted the seat and chanted, "We see it.! We own it!"

Freddie laughed and chorused in, "If it was a girl, we'd bone it!"

Just two buddies out for a day of fun and anything else fate might throw at them. "Seriously, Freddie, this has to be like the best day of my life. I'm still in shock over the bike and I can't believe what you and your dad did. I can't believe we rode to the mountain on it." He threw his arms skyward. "We're on top of the world!"

"Actually, only five thousand, three hundred and twenty-five feet, Kemo Sabe."

"Thanks Data. Come on; let's descend back into the inferno of life below."

Freddie threw a leg over his bike. He hit the crank and threw his head back. "Oh, I love it!"

"Maybe we can come back in a day or two. I'm on a quest of finding my Indian Princess now."

"Well, you can have your mysterious princess; I'm just going to try to heat up Summer," Freddie said. "Seriously, man, it's like this has been the first day of our lives."

"Yeah, well, let's don't get into the drama. Let's go, Mr. Winkie!" Dylan grinned and gunned the Indian's engine, kicking up a spray of gravel from the parking area. Freddie followed, only feet behind.

They were only halfway through the first downhill curve when common sense overcame exhilaration and Dylan slowed his bike. He put the bike in neutral and found it still coasted fast enough that he had to apply brakes.

Freddie pulled alongside. "Feels like freedom to me!" he shouted. He raised his hand from the handlebars for Dylan to give him a high-five.

Freddie dropped back and honked his horn. Dylan checked him out through the rearview mirror and Freddie gave him a thumbs up.

CHAPTER 23

TO HELL IN A PICKUP

The pale greenish-blue pickup truck was on Freddie's rear wheel before he even knew it was on the mountain. Three men were standing in the bed of the pickup, holding onto the cab. There were three other men in the cab.

All of the men, including the driver, were wearing hooded masks with huge eyeholes cut in them.

Startled, Dylan felt his front wheel swerve off the pavement and onto the strip of grass that grew between the road and the sheer drop-off. For the first time, he realized there were no guardrails at this point on the seldom-used road, which was still the property of the Indian tribe. He quickly corrected the steering. This was not the time for getting sloppy.

Why wasn't the jerk driving the pickup passing? They were only doing maybe fifteen miles per hour. Dylan raised his left hand from the handlebars and signaled for the truck to pass. Behind him, Freddie was doing the same thing.

Instead of passing, the truck lurched ahead, to within inches of Freddie's rear wheel. The truck horn suddenly blared, the sound causing Freddie to do his own wobbling. The driver held the horn and had the nose of the pickup almost against Freddie's rear wheel.

"Hey!" Freddie shouted. "Back off, already!" He could hear the pistons working in the truck and the ominous rumbling of fat tires. "Back off!" Freddie yelled again, and then goosed his Indian, pulling

226

alongside Dylan. Freddie mouthed some words, but Dylan couldn't understand what he was saying. Freddie dropped back behind him.

They rounded a curve and approached a short tunnel, the three vehicles so close they were moving as one. Inside the tunnel, the pickup driver blared the horn to a mind-numbing decimal level. As they cleared the tunnel exit, Dylan heard Freddie screaming. There was a grinding of metal on asphalt and the squeal of rubber, all eclipsed by the screams from Freddie.

A motorcycle tire bounced crazily past Dylan who checked his mirror and saw this tumbleweed of metal slowly coming to a stop behind him and a pale green pickup racing past it.

"What the …!!!"

Dylan turned his gaze back to the road only to see that he was entering a curve entirely too fast to make it. Instinct took over and he laid the speeding bike down. Rubber squealed on the road. Sparks flew as the metal of the bike slid along the pavement. Everything was happening too fast. Dylan, still holding onto the bike's handlebars, slid and spun toward a foot-high asphalt curb and directly toward a large outcropping of rock on the edge of the cliff. He closed his eyes, expecting the impact of his head with the rock, but the spinning motion of his body saved him from the crushing blow. He reached out, desperately trying to find something to grasp but there was nothing. The rebuilt Indian bike and mangled teenager sailed over the edge of the cliff together.

Then a funny thing happened along the pathway to death. When you are about to die, there's something like an automatic trip line when the brain knows it's been screwed. A part of the brain goes into this Matrix Movie Mode where even sound seems to stretch and bend. This was what Dylan was thinking with great clarity as he observed himself flung off the side of the mountain with his arms doing windmills and the Indian several feet below him, still right side up, wheels spinning, and the engine starting to gasp for gas. *"Wow,"* he thought, *"the bike's four times heavier, yet we fall at the same rate."*

"CaaaCAWWWWWwwwww!" A black blur sped past the falling boy, then another. How many seconds did it take to drop five thousand feet? More black blurs swept past. Suddenly, Dylan was consumed in a mass of flapping wings, feathers, and talons. The sensation was like being struck by black lightning with a thousand caws sounding inside his brain. He could no longer see, but could still

227

feel the sense of weightlessness as he plummeted earthward. Then his mind accepted death and mercifully went blank.

Dylan regained consciousness seconds later and felt his body being eased gingerly to the ground. He remained still, keeping his eyes closed. *I'm dead. I died. I don't want to open my eyes.* It was eerily silent except for a distant whir. It was like being underwater, knowing all he had to do was rise and break through the surface to the light and world. But he was dead. He should be dead. Had he just received the answer every thinking person ever born on the earth has asked; is there conscience after death? *I must be in Heaven because I'm not burning.*

Rise. Slowly. Carefully. Something has to be broken. He began to feel warmth on his flesh. *Sunlight?* He could feel the hair on his arms moving because of a cool breeze. He heard a nearby bird chirp. An insect buzzed by his face. He smelled earth and heard the trickle of water. Slowly, he let the tip of his tongue run between his lips.

Testing. I am alive. I am alive! Okay — the easy part — open your eyes.

The harsh sunlight made his eyes water. He raised a protective hand and realized his left arm was okay. His right arm was beginning to throb, though, and he wondered if it was broken. He attempted to move the arm up and a stabbing pain suggested that wouldn't be a good idea.

He raised his eyes and saw treetops swaying in the breeze treetops. And that's when he remembered Freddie.

The truck! Freddie's down. Curve. Cliff. Falling. Alive. Okay, I'm going to scream now.

Deep down within him he felt the scream building, the one he should have emitted as he was going over the cliff. It was that primal scream that the brain's trip-line mechanism always prevented from firing.

"Ahhhhhhh!"

While he was still screaming, Dylan re-opened his eyes, saw the cliff above him, and whiffs of dust floating in the sunbeams. And in his peripheral vision, he could see blurry black spots with flapping wings merging into more solid defined objects that disappeared in the woods around him.

The hoarse scream suddenly stopped, its echoes resonating for a moment. Dylan gasped and slowly wriggled his fingers to make sure they worked. He lifted his hands, touched his face, and ran a hand along each arm. He felt the back of his head and the skull seemed intact. Finally, to verify he was still alive, he pulled at the ground, squeezing his hands and feeling the gravel in his palms. The reality of the gravel and the stinging of his palms shifted his brain back into the present mode. He remembered the wheel of Freddie's bike that had rolled past him and the awful sight of the rolling metallic rolling ball that the collision with the pickup had created.

"Freddie!" Dylan clambered to his feet. He started toward the side of the mountain, and then realized what he was about to attempt — climb five thousand feet up like a monkey. *And what was that?* What were those black-winged blurs he had seen? He remembered falling and the sensation of a cloud of wings and claws and beaks and overtaking him.

The next thing he remembered was the boom and explosion of his bike, then settling onto the ground. But there hadn't been a boom. There should have been a boom, like all the movies when the car or bike goes off the cliff and explodes. *What just happened? Why am I alive? God? God, did you have something to with this? Deep breath. Sit down. You're stunned.*

And Freddie is dead.

Dylan sat back down, gasping. He could not logically understand what had just happened. He turned his gaze up the face of the mountain, then looked behind him and realized he had not dropped to the base of the mountain, only down to the next level. Okay, he would have to climb about twenty yards up to the road then head up around the ascending curve to the loop of pavement above. He checked out his bike and marveled at the lack of damage. The bike must have hit the tree branches and fallen slowly to the ground as it appeared intact. The front fender was bent, the foot bar was bent, and part of the arm of the clutch handle was missing. However, other than that it seemed fine. No explosion and pieces flying in all directions. *Maybe that was what happened. I struck a treetop on the way down that caught my fall. That's it. No. That was pure and simply God's intervention. Even if that did happen with the tree catching my fall, I would have gotten scratches and bruises. Jesus Christ! Get off your ass! Freddie!*

Trying to gain a perspective of where he was and where he wanted to go,

Dylan surveyed the situation. A hundred yards down was the lower road. He could get there easily and run up the rest of the way back to the spot of the wreck, to Freddie. *Take the bike. That's stupid.*

No way it's rolling. But the bike didn't really look that bad. *No way, no how.*

Still, he lifted the Indian to its wheels and rocked it back and forth. The clutch was workable. The motor was dead, but when he tried to crank it, it roared to life on the first try. Dylan was stunned. The bike was as intact as he was. *Nothing serious. Good to go. Let's get to Freddie.*

He pushed the bike to the lower road and mounted it. The front fender was within a hair of touching the front tire. It couldn't be helped. Let it scrape. *Got to hurry.* He had already wasted too much time. Every second that passed could mean life or death for Freddie. The foot clutch wasn't quite right but he managed to get it dropped into first and raised the acceleration. "Yes!" The bike's motor whined as Dylan tried second. He toed the gear up higher and caught third, causing the bike to lurch and work hard with the incline of the road. Finally, the speed caught up to the gear and the riding smoothed out until time to shift. There was no feeling of a fourth gear as he brought the clutch bar as high as he could with his foot.

The battered bike wasn't going to win any road races, but it was serving the purpose. It sputtered and jerked like an old man's death convulsions. And then it gave a final tremor and the engine died. Dylan laid the bike down and began running, imagining himself looking like of one of those Walking Dead zombies doing the *I gots me some meat a comin'* shuffle.

As he approached the crumbled heap of metal in the road, the world swung back and forth into light as though the sun was a huge lantern being swung by a railroad man. Several people had gathered and they parted in order for Dylan to pass. Somehow they seemed to know he was connected to this horrific scene. He passed the discarded wheel with its spokes gleaming and striking his brain like ice picks. Next was the huge bulbous headlight, glass shattered, chrome gnarled up as though the world's biggest bulldog had been gnawing on it. Then he saw the metallic tumbleweed that once had been a proud Indian, tilted to one side. The front wheel forks were pointed upward. The handlebars were bent inward. Wedged between the rear brake lever and handle bars were five brown-leathered things that he suddenly realized were Freddie's gloved fingers.

Freddie was still on the bike. Or in it. But that could not be possible. Of all the photos Dylan had ever seen of a motorcycle, he had never seen one with the frame bent so severely. It was as if some five-year-old God in diapers had reached down and pinched the bike from both ends. The Indian had rolled up like an armadillo. The sight seemed to draw Dylan inward like a movie special effect where the background goes further away and the foreground object zooms up. The world took on this surreal quality again. There was oil pooling on the ground beneath the crumpled bike, or was that blood? He saw the foot pedals of the bike with the bottom ends of Reeboks showing, attached to feet, with Freddie's characteristic untied laces dangling. The shoes were attached to legs and where the large headlight had been was the back of Freddie's head, he was bent over the handlebars, pinned down with the back end of the seat hiked upwards and the rear wheel was actually bent up and over. The bottom frame had snapped, bending so drastically that the front end was trying to meet the tail end like a crazed dog that had at last caught his tail between its teeth.

Then Dylan heard the most precious sound of his young life. Freddie moaned. A low guttural sound. And the world that had been wrapped in a flimsy gauze was suddenly unwrapped. Black and white became colors again. Sound engulfed him. The scream that had been building since he was hurled off the cliff rose up into a gut-wrenching articulation. "Freddie!" Dylan reached the twisted metal and body and stopped, staring. *Jesus!*

Freddie's face was pinned against the front of the bike. With no wheel left, his face was pressed against part of the motor that had to be red hot. The smell of burning flesh and gas was an odor Dylan knew he would never forget.

"My glasses. I lost my glasses." Freddie was actually conscious. He was talking. Mumbling and almost incoherent. But talking. Alive.

The impact of the bike with the asphalt when it had flipped had caused the gas cap to pop off. The fuel had poured over Freddie's chest and down the front end of the bike. Behind Freddie's leg and the seat, a small pool of gasoline had gathered and it was almost ready to spill onto the motor.

Dylan swiped at the fuel with a hand to keep it from spilling. When he raised his eyes, he saw an Indian holding a beer with a lighter in one hand and a cigarette between his lips.

"Noooo!" Dylan sprang forward and this crazy lunatic voice sounded in his head, *Look, Coach, great tackle, right? Shoulders beneath the waist!* The Indian sailed backward, beer, lighter, and cigarette arching up in a perfect juggler's circle. The beer bottle shattered when it hit the pavement.

"What the fuck?" the Indian gasped.

"Gas leak!" Dylan yelled, rolling to his feet and rising. His skinned knuckles were burning. He turned to the crowd and pleaded, "Help me! Help me get him loose."

"There's an ambulance on the way," a woman said.

"Freddie, hang in there, buddy. Hang on. Help is on the way." Dylan reached out with trembling fingers and lightly touched Freddie's hair.

"My glasses. I can't fix this without my glasses," Freddie said in a distant, dreamy voice.

"Here." A man handed Freddie's glasses to Dylan. One arm was broken and a lens was severely cracked.

"I've got your glasses, Freddie. It's all okay. Relax, okay? You took quite a tumble there, buddy." Dylan looked at Freddie's hands and how they were broken at the wrists and poised like a "Hey, there!" There were new bulges around the elbows and the jagged point of what must have been the humerus had ripped through the leather sleeve.

Lowering his gaze, Dylan noted that most of one of Freddie's kneecaps was missing.

"Truck coming, Dylan. Watch out..." Freddie said somewhere in a dream.

"I'm safe, Winkie. I'm okay." Dylan reached over and pulled back the front of the leather jacket. He fought a surge of nausea at the sight of the broken rib protruding from Freddie's chest.

"I can't fix this. No glasses."

"Here," Dylan said, trying to fight back the tears. He placed Freddie's one-armed, shattered-lens glasses on his nose. "Okay, buddy, you have your glasses."

"I have them?" Freddie asked weakly.

"You do," Dylan said.

"I can fix this now?" Freddie said in a fainter voice.

"Yeah. You can fix it now. You have your glasses."

"The ravens are coming."

"Yeah. The ravens are ..." Dylan suddenly realized what he was repeating, but the sound of a siren from an approaching ambulance interrupted.

"What did you say?" Dylan asked.

Freddie didn't respond. Maybe he was losing consciousness. A blessing. Dylan moved a hand to Freddie's forehead and pushed the hair back from his eyes. His hand was trembling. "Freddie, hang on, buddy. It's okay. You'll be okay now. Come on. Open your eyes; make a sound. Do something! Squeeze my hand! Come on, Winkie. Don't you die on me, God! No! Hang on! Hang on, buddy!"

The ambulance arrived and the doors swung open. Dylan felt a hand on his shoulder and backed away.

Freddie whispered something.

"Wait! He's saying something," Dylan pushed through the restraining hands to lean closer.

"Promise you'll forgive me, Dyl. The ravens are coming," Freddie said.

"What? Huh?" Dylan felt himself being pulled away.

"You know him?" The tech asked.

"Freddie Sanders," Dylan said. "Don't let him die. Please."

A highway patrol car arrived with its siren ending in a "whoop."

"Move that Jaws of Life over here," a rescue worker said.

"You better step back," another worker said to Dylan.

"Sir, do you know the victim?" the highway patrolman, with Newman on his nametag, asked.

Dylan wasn't listening, though. He was focused on the firefighters using the Jaws of Life. It reminded him of this villain cartoon character in Mad Magazine, the one with a long black beak.

"Sir ...?" the patrolman asked again. "Sumbitch, you're the sheriff's son, aren't you?"

"Yeah. Dylan."

"Saw you at the fireman's fundraiser barbecue last month. You're having a helluva senior year in football, by the way. You gonna play for the Mountaineers next year? Say, what happened here? You know this victim?"

The patrolman walked to the rear of the bike and pushed the warped metal aside so he could read the tags, bringing his hand radio to his mouth.

"He's Freddie Sanders. We're friends, both from Silverton."

"Well, what the beJesus happened here?"

"It was crazy. We were on our bikes and this truck came up behind us. Six guys, but couldn't tell who they were. They were wearing hoods over their heads. They rammed into Freddie and then came after me. I went off the cliff with my bike over there," Dylan pointed.

"What color was the truck?"

"I don't know … it was green, no, blue. It was a weird greenish-blue, I think," Dylan scratched his head.

"How about you? You hurt? Damn, you must have hit the curbing and then that big rock. Guess the rock saved you, boy."

"No. I …"

went over with the bike and this cloud of black feathers was flapping and cawing and they kind of swooped me up then let me down without a scratch. Wasn't that something? Then they kind of morphed into black ghosts and disappeared into the woods.

"I'm … I'm not sure," Dylan said.

"You guys speeding?"

"No, sir. We had just left the village and were heading home. I was in the lead and I had the bike in neutral. "

"Let me see your license."

Great. Here we go. "Sure." He handed the officer his wallet.

"Ready? You got him?" the rescue worker by the bike asked. He poised the Jaws of Life to cut the handlebars.

"Ready," said another worker.

The sharp steel jaws cut into the handle. "Okay, keep that arm held up. Going to cut the pedal so we can get his foot free," said the jaw operator.

Two county sheriff's cars pulled up and Dylan recognized the deputies.

"What's going on?" Deputy Jed Hamilton asked.

"A truck carrying a load of Ku Klux Klanners rammed into Freddie and ran me off the cliff."

"Yeah? We've had some reports the last couple of weeks of them shooting at cars and burning crosses," Hamilton said. "Wait till your Dad hears about this."

The bike was lowered onto its side and the freed Freddie was lifted onto the stretcher.

"Damn, Dylan. That's Freddie Sanders, your pal?" Hamilton asked.

Dylan nodded assent and moved with the workers as they rolled Freddie to the ambulance. "Hang in there, Freddie."

"He's out," a tech said. "Excuse me, Sir, you need to give us some room. Pulse and blood pressure are falling."

Dylan stepped back and watched as Freddie was being loaded into the ambulance. *"He's going to die."*

"Wow, if he makes it to the hospital it'll be a miracle. Did you see any body part that wasn't broken?" Deputy Hamilton asked an EMT.

Dylan placed a hand on the deputy's arm. "Can you give me a ride to the hospital?"

"Yeah."

"Hey, son" Patrolman Newman called from his patrol car. "Mind coming over here, please?"

"Yes sir."

Dylan saw the skid marks from both tires of his bike where he had laid it down. The rear light signal and mirror had been ripped off and were lying in the grass by the roadside. He remembered Freddie saying something about this being the first day of his life. *His last?* Little sparkles of sunlight flashed on the looming boulder on the other side of the curb. *Wow!* He had just missed doing a head-bang with that monster by inches.

Patrolman Newman propped a foot on the curb and peered through his binoculars for several seconds. "Hmmm ... a thousand feet."

"I'm sorry?" Dylan wasn't following.

"Had you missed that rock, you'd be dead, son. Straight drop-off from here. A fall that far and you would've left an impression on the rock."

Patrolman humor. Great. "Really?"

"Here, look," he pointed to the space beyond the rock. "You're one lucky son of a buck."

"Yeah, I know. Look, I don't want to be rude, but is that all? I'm really concerned about Freddie and I want to get to the hospital."

"Yeah, all right. I imagine you do. In fact, I'm surprised they didn't take you in an ambulance. You look pretty banged up. Guess you football guys are pretty tough, huh? Go ahead. I'll finish my report with you there later."

"Thanks."

Deputy sheriff Hamilton tooted the horn on his car. "Dylan, you ready? Your daddy and mama are going to meet you at the hospital. "

Dylan slid in the front of the car. "The medics say anything about Freddie?"

"I'll be upfront with you, son. The techs don't think he'll make it to the hospital."

The ambulance was still parked at the emergency room entrance, its rear doors open. A roll of tape and a pair of surgical scissors had fallen to the asphalt. The attendants had been in a hurry. Dylan glanced in the vehicle as he walked past and saw red-stained gauze, several loose tubes and a blood pressure cuff. Three more sheriff's deputies were standing near the emergency room admitting desk and they all waved at Dylan, mouthing various forms of, "Are you okay?"

"Dylan!" his mom called out from behind. "Dylan?" Sally Morgan came in with her arms open to embrace him. Sheriff Morgan trudged in behind her, giving the deputies a look as if to ask, "Why are you here instead of on patrol?"

"Oh my God, Dylan! Are you all right?" his mother asked.

"I'm fine, Mom. I got off my bike before it wrecked. But I'm worried about Freddie. He's messed up."

"What I want to know," Sheriff Morgan asked, "is what the Hell you were doing on the reservation during school hours. And where the Hell did you get those motorcycles?"

"Wait! Dylan was riding a motorcycle?" Sally backed up and gave him a questioning look.

"It's my birthday," Dylan sputtered, thinking how lame the excuse sounded even to him. "Freddie and his Dad rebuilt two Indians and gave me one for my birthday."

"Oh, Lord, it's a miracle you're not dead," Sally said, closing her eyes and voicing a silent prayer to God for the protection of her son.

"I want to hear more about a dumbass guy who gives a motorcycle to a teenager without even consulting his parents," Sheriff Morgan ranted. "Somebody's got a lot of questions to answer."

The sheriff was interrupted by the sudden entrance of Robert, who came trudging in with several of his leathered-up "brothers". He spotted Dylan and paused, a confused look on his face. He shook his head like a dog that had just heard something that tickled its brain, then moved up to within inches of Dylan's face.

"You stupid fool! What were you guys thinking, anyway? Bikes are for men, not pansies like you two. You missed football practice, too.

Coach said tell you that you won't be starting in the game Friday night. You're benched, Mr. All-Star."

"I'm fine, Robert, thanks for asking." Dylan turned away.

"Huh? Don't walk away from me, Bro. I'm talking to you." The scowling Robert clamped a big hand down on Dylan's shoulder.

Dylan reached up, gripping the intrusive hand, and for a moment there was a little battle before Dylan dipped his shoulder, freeing it from the grip.

Robert leaned forward and whispered in his ear, "Know what, Bro? Wish that was you in there instead of pukeface."

"Well, at least you're honest," Dylan said, not looking at his brother and moving across the waiting room to take a seat next to his mother. Sally reached over and patted his knee. Robert was still glaring at him from across the room, but Dylan ignored him. Robert stepped back and whispered something to his leather-clad buddies that made them chuckle.

Freddie's father, Mike Sanders, entered the waiting room, his face pale and drawn with concern. Sheriff Morgan glared at him. Robert and the wolf pack seemed to bare their teeth, then turned and filed out the door. Mr. Sanders motioned for Dylan to walk with him.

"Tell me what happened," he said as they entered the hallway, and then listened intently as Dylan relived the horror of the incident.

Mr. Sanders' face grew paler and grimmer. "Hopefully your father will find out who caused this," he said.

"I hope so, Mr. Sanders. Those guys in that truck had every intention to kill us. How's Freddie? Is he conscious?"

"Well, they were afraid to give him anything for pain when he went into the ER, and when they started working on him he slipped into a coma."

"Oh, God."

"It's bad, but it's a miracle he's still alive. At least he's breathing on his own. But, to be honest, I think it's just a matter of time, Dylan. They have tubes sticking in him everywhere. They haven't even tried to set his bones. They think he's broken all his ribs, both arms at the wrists and higher up. His kneecaps are literally gone, both legs, both ankles, and possibly his hips are broken. The right side of his face is missing a layer of skin where it burned. It's hopeless, I'm afraid," The man's shoulders buckled and he wept. "He's all I've got …. I never should have helped you guys get those bikes."

"He's going to make it," Dylan said. "Freddie is a fighter. He has to make it. As for the bikes, Mr. Sanders, we were so happy. Freddie said today was the first day of his life."

Dylan and his parents returned home where he showered, assessed his few bruises, put on a much-needed change of clothing and marveled over his luck. He could have been following behind Freddie. Borrowing his mother's car, he returned to the hospital where he found a haggard-appearing Mr. Sanders in the waiting room. He rose, welcomed Dylan with a hug, and motioned for the boy to follow him into the Intensive Care Unit.

"He's in a coma, you know," the middle-aged nurse cautioned. "Please keep your voices down and don't bump the bed or touch him." She checked her watch. "Five minutes."

Freddie looked like a mummy, his torn body bandaged literally from head to toe. "If they can get him stabilized, they're going to try to set some of the fractures," Mr. Sanders said. "In fact, they're hoping he stays in the coma until they've done some of that. At least, he's breathing on his own."

Mr. Sanders paused and watched a tear run down the unbandaged side of Freddie's face. Mr. Sanders' body shook with silent sobbing as he turned and left the room.

CHAPTER 24

TOO SLICK TO DIE

Dylan felt hot tears streaming down his own face as he stood helplessly by the bedside. "Oh, Freddie," he croaked in a hoarse whisper. "I'm so sorry, man. I should have done something. I saw them coming behind you but I never thought they'd run you over. I should be dead, Freddie. My bike and I went over the cliff and I didn't get a scratch. I'm not even sure what happened. Maybe I was in shock or something, but I can't remember everything. It's weird. But look, Winkie, you can't leave me and your Dad. I need you around to always let me know I'm not the lowest point on the human food chain. I love you, man. Hang in there. You're too slick to die, Greasy." It suddenly became hard for Dylan to breathe and he walked over to the window.

"Caw!"

Something slammed into the glass -- a white raven. The bird clawed furiously at the closed window and struck it with its beak, leaving spots of blood on the glass. It was obviously trying to attack Dylan.

"No sun. No moon. Run, Dylan. They come for you!" Freddie was out of the coma, struggling to sit up, his eyes wild.

Dylan left the window and moved to the bedside. But Freddie was gone again. *Did I dream that?* Freddie was laying still, eyes closed.

"What the ...?" Dylan went back to the window and checked the pane of chipped and blood-spattered glass. Looking outside, he saw a

239

large oak tree with a flock of ravens that appeared in constant motion as they rose in the air then settled back in the tree.

No sun. No moon. Run, Dylan. They come for you!

The florescent lights suddenly flickered in Freddie's room in the Intensive Care Unit of the hospital. Dylan backed away from the window. The green glowing digits on one of bedside monitors winked out, and then back on. 89.1. Blacked out. *Run!* Blacked out. 89.1. *Run!*

Dylan moved toward to the door and the ceiling lights flickered and seemed to dim. Light from the florescent bulb seemed to be pulled away as though it were a shimmering see-through movie screen, moving along the wall to the window. The bulb grew dimmer as the movie light was drawn from it. Then it began to narrow and move down the side of the wall toward the blackened window. Streams of green light moved from the monitor, floating through the air like one of those Disney cartoon scenes depicting the aroma of food.

Dylan was overcome with a spell of dizziness. His head was swimming as though something within him — his essence — perhaps his energy, seemed to be sucked from him like a tide under the influence of a full moon. Reaching back, he took hold of the doorknob to help steady himself.

Aye, Captain, we've reached warp speed, a voice sounded in Dylan's mind that sounded like Scottie on Star Trek. All that had light and energy seemed to be drawn toward the black window in a vibrational, shimmering blur. Dylan suddenly became aware that it wasn't the window that was black but something from the outside that was attached to it. He tried to bring the thing into focus but it was a blur that continually shifted, revealing a glimpse of claws and flesh that looked like old leather. The body of this thing of black did not appear to be solid, but instead seemed to form a black hole. Yes, it was a black hole, but it was a living thing of anti-light that was drawing light inward. *A living air-sucking black hole.*

Dylan fought the sensation of feeling he was being drawn through the wall. His tortured mind recalled a late night radio talk show with Art Bell where abductees were recounting how they had been lifted from their beds and moved through the ceiling and roof and into an alien spaceship. What laid in waiting for him at the other end of this horrific suck was not going to be a stainless steel table with a smiling alien holding a foot-long probe. No. There would be darkness. *Nada. Nothing. No light. No sun. No stars to dream upon. Just black on black.* Dylan felt his heart pounding against his chest, felt his blood running cold as his arteries constricted. This was true fear. Not even going over the cliff that afternoon had been this terrifying. Whatever this was, it was anti-God. This was terror in its bleakest form.

No Sun. No Moon to dream upon. Run, Dylan! Run!

Dylan shook his head, trying to clear it from this maze of horror. He closed his eyes and began backing away from the window toward the door, feeling his way with his hands. His grasping hands found the door handle and he backpedaled through the door and into the hallway. The pulling sensation was severed and the center of his chest felt like a black hole. He could actually feel the release from the black thing's power as energy seeped back into his body. He left the ICU area and hurried to a nearby lounge. A table lamp was burning between two sofas. He went to it, cupping his hands around the hot light bulb, and letting the warmth flow through his hands and into his body, absorbing its energy. The internal draining had stopped. He gasped for breath, trying to gather air to replace the energy that had been depleted from him.

"Sir, are you okay?"

A nurse wearing a white doughnut-powder mustache rose from a chair in the corner of the room. Her fingertips were pasty and white in the lamplight as she dropped the half-eaten donut she would never finish this night. She approached Dylan and placed a hand on his shoulder.

"Are you okay?"

Dylan removed his hands from the hot bulb in the lamp and stared at her as if she had spoken in a foreign language. He tried to focus his eyes, blinking them rapidly.

"Sir?" The nurse reached out and placed a hand on his arm. Dylan's eyes finally became focused upon her.

"Oh, sorry. I'm okay. It ... " Dylan started to tell her what he had seen, then realized how even more crazy it would sound to the person hearing it. "I'm sorry. I didn't mean to scare you." He nodded at the lamp. "That was kind of a religious thing with the light bulb. I just got a little spooked thinking of my best friend lying in there dying and being alone in the darkness." He wasn't sure what he was saying sounded logical. Wasn't even sure he was making sense. *Jesus!* Had he hallucinated the black-light-sucking-blob on the window to articulate the fear he was trying to depress?

"Look," the nurse said, her tongue flicking at the white powder on her lips, "perhaps you'd like to sit in the family lounge just outside the ICU. Maybe being closer will help you feel better. In fact, go in and be with him if you like. I'll be checking on him in a moment and I'll come back and talk to you."

"Yeah, sure. Okay." Dylan backed out of the nursing lounge. He walked to Freddie's unit, drew in a breath, and opened the door. The view from the window was unobstructed. No hidden forces were pulling at him. The only sound in the room was that of the machines working to keep Freddie alive. The florescent light was steady, lighting the room. The monitors were making their normal rhythmic beeping.

I'm losing my mind" Dylan took a tentative step toward the window and noted the darkening sky. Taking deep breaths to steady himself, Dylan went to the window, slowly reached out, and touched the pane, half expecting his fingers would somehow pass right through the glass. A young woman standing near the oak tree in the yard seemed to be staring directly at him. She was wearing an ankle-length white dress and had a shawl around her shoulders.

"Sir?"

Dylan jumped as the nurse from the lounge entered the room.

"I'm going now," he said. "Goodnight, nurse." He nodded at the woman and went out to the nearby lounge to find his mother there. She rose and hugged him tightly. Mike Sanders was sitting in a chair, his head resting on the back and his eyes closed.

CHAPTER 25

SHADOWS AND DARK THINGS

Dylan went to a window and opened the blinds, but the woman by the oak tree was gone. He felt dumb for even thinking about it, but there was a sense of uneasiness about the woman. The way she seemed to have looked directly at him standing at the window. Whatever it was ...

"I need some air," he said to his mother and left the lounge. Breaking into a trot, he negotiated the halls, found the main lobby, and headed for the rear parking lot. No woman in white. Just some ravens roosting in the oak's branches. He stopped and scanned the area but the girl was not to be found. Something — a shadow — moved along the trunk of the tree. Or maybe not. His mind was playing tricks on him again. There was no one there. However, something ... a raven? The girl? No. Maybe a squirrel or a stray cat. He shivered.

There it was again ... a shadow on the trunk. The lights were on in the parking lot but shadows seemed to encroach from all directions. The tree's trunk seemed to shimmy with dark movement.

"Wrup. Wrup." It was distinctive caw of Ravenous. His personal raven. Dylan felt better and issued a sigh of relief. The hairs on his arm lay down. Several other ravens sounded low, short caws. Dylan remained still, watching the dark shapes on the tree trunk. Were those the same shapes that had attached themselves to the window earlier? A thread of light suddenly appeared in the dark mass, appearing to be

drawn from the parking lot light. God! Whatever these things were, they seemed to draw light and energy from electrical sources. Would they attack him? How about the ravens, who were remaining calm, only occasionally flapping their wings? Dylan moved toward the oak, waved his arms, and shouted, "Shoo! Go away!" But the birds ignored him.

Three dark shapes suddenly leapt from the tree trunk and floated toward him. He saw them coming, turned and began running back to the hospital. He glanced over his shoulder and saw that the forms were about twenty yards behind. They were moving quickly with trails of light like ribbon streamers from a Fourth of July festival.

His tennis shoes made a slap-slap-slap on the pavement but the sounds he heard were those that were rapidly growing louder and nearer, sounding something like a dog's nails walking on a tiled kitchen floor. The clicking of claws and teeth. The sounds were gaining, too close to look over his shoulder. It was like reliving a childhood nightmare of being chased by a monster. It was still twenty yards to the hospital door; and, even with his wide-receiver speed, he was losing ground. There was no security guard at the door. He had to make it inside on his own. The clicking was closer, louder. But he could make it. He had to make it.

Then Dylan felt the energy being sucked from him. His movements slowed until he felt as though he was running through air made of syrup. The back of his head began to tingle. He could feel the synapses in the back of his brain begin to misfire. At any moment, he was going to start flickering like the florescent lights. He could actually feel the loss of control of his voluntary and involuntary functions. At any moment, he felt he was going to drop to the pavement and perhaps have a seizure as the last bit of life was drawn from him. He felt himself falling, almost dropping to his knees before gaining control. He prayed for the electric impulses of his brain to move his legs. The light at the hospital entrance began to flicker.

Something grabbed at the leg of Dylan's jeans. The final control of his legs was wrenched from him.

A terrible, high-pitched screech electrified the air. Dylan's feet were yanked from beneath him and he was sent sprawling forward.

An ear shattering *"Caw"* suddenly chorused with the shrieking. Wings flapped and fluttered. Dylan slammed chest-long into the pavement.

"Have you lost your mind?" Sheriff Spencer Morgan groused. "Damn, boy, can't you walk?" His father was standing over the prone Dylan. "Shit, you can't run on the field or even walk and you think you can ride an Indian? Jesus H Christ, you oughta be in that ICU with your freaky little friend."

Dylan rolled over, sat up, and looked down at his feet, half expecting them to be missing.

Jesus! Everybody thinks I'm losing my mind. Am I? He looked around but there was no sign of anything having been chasing him. *I really am going crazy!* Then he saw them ... what looked like claw marks in the pavement and several black feathers that appeared as though they had been yanked out of living birds with bits of meat and blood attached to the spines.

"For God's sake, stand up!" Sheriff Morgan rasped. "You want somebody to come along and see you like this?" He gave Dylan's leg a not-so gentle kick. "Are you on drugs, boy? Do we need to do urine tests on you and your nerdy buddy? Hey ... nerdy buddy ... have to remember that one."

Dylan rose to his feet and for a moment thought he was going to fall again as his trembling legs almost betrayed him. Thought commands and electrical nerve messaging were still askew. He turned to face his father. "Why don't you just leave me alone? All my life all you have done is spew hatred toward me. I'm tired of it, Dad. Now just get out of my way."

The sheriff was shocked. Neither of his sons had ever spoken to him like this. "Just shut up and let's go inside. I'm looking to have a serious conversation with that old grease monkey in there."

"Look, I'm serious, Dad. Leave me alone!"

"And just what are you going to do about it?" the sheriff said, pulling himself to his full height and puffing out his chest. He grinned, sending the scar on his face into contortion spasms. "You gonna hit me, chicken shit?"

"Spencer?" Mrs. Morgan called as she stepped out of the sliding doors to the hospital. "Is everything all right?"

"Sure, Sal. Peachy cream," Spencer said. "We were just playing a little question and answer game. It was Dylan's turn, that's why I said hit me. Ain't that right, boy?"

Dylan didn't answer, instead turning to his mother. "Anything new on Freddie, Mom? Is he having a problem?" He purposely ignored his father.

"Oh, no, honey. Freddie is resting now. His father is even going home for awhile. We all need a break. Let's go home. They'll call us if anything happens. Let's go home. What an awful, terrible eighteenth birthday you've had."

As the Morgan's two cars pulled out of the parking lot, Mansi stepped out of the shadow of the small ventilating unit on the roof of the hospital. She was greatly intrigued with Dylan Spencer. After all these years this night was the first time they had shared eye contact while she was in human form. The incident had made her heart race. Something about this young man was greatly valued by the Light. It made her want to fling herself through the window, seize him and devour him. There was a brilliant aura around this boy. The Darks could sense the presence of a Light and vice versa. However, Mansi wasn't even sure Dylan was aware of that ability. The ravens knew, though. Wherever he went, the black ravens sensed him like some shiny sparkling thing on the road. She had never found him without a raven hovering around. Moreover, her companions, the Darklings, were just as sensitive to him. It took all of her mental prowess to keep them restrained.

As Shabael had taught her, the original Tree of Light and Dark possessed the purest of their Light/Anti-Light. With each new generation of Light-carriers and Anti-light carriers, the magic of each grew less powerful.

Shabael had told her that before the trees were moved to the opposite ends of Skyeden, the other tribes were given a branch. These new trees flourished, but were not as powerful. Those utilizing the magic of the new trees would never be as powerful as those blessed with the force of the original trees.

But how could someone like this boy possess the Light and its magic without the direct influence of the Tree or having achieved Ascension? Ah, but, neither had she. She had gained her magic and dark force by invitation, seduced into it in a way by King Shabael. Seduced. Yes, seduction was such a nice word and her most powerful magical force of which she seemed to be a natural. Her contact with people was very limited, yet she made a great study of the art of seduction. When the young man saw her through the window, she had known that he would come to her.

Magic was brewing in the air. Events did not happen by chance. Forces were gathering. It could be felt in the wind, heard in the uneasiness of the ravens. Elements were moving into place for the perfect storm. Days ago a white raven came to the dark tree. Hours later, a second white raven came. New white ravens arrived daily. A spiritual war. A mortal war. *I feel you. There are others worlds than this. Shabael, I serve thee. Yes, the forces are at play. I have an idea about how to find your tree, my Emperor.*

Mansi stepped away from the light, blending with the shadows, and watched the parking lot exit. A moment later a group of white ravens emerged from the shadows. One white raven followed Sally Morgan's car. Following the car, like a black exhaust fume was a darkling. As it followed the car, streamers of light were released in its path.

CHAPTER 26

BY THE TREE OF LIGHT

The eternal blue-tinted world had seeped through flesh and manifested in Eradrin's brain like a film of algae on pond water. It shadowed his mood, his life, his kingdom, the world. Even the air he breathed was tainted. He looked up into the crown of the tree at the small-shriveled leaves. Those leaves once were the size of his palm. They had been a wonderful color of green with blue veins that glowed in the light of the setting sun. When the Sun had shined after a light rain, the leaves had twinkled like emeralds. When the Orb of Light was in the crown of the tree and the Sun and Moon were in place, the tree hummed with life. It vibrated and produced the colored spheres. It enlivened and connected one to the vibrational lifeline of the Creator.

I am an ineffective defeated king. How many days had he been here now, two or three? He glared at the few remaining strips of dried meat; the only food he had brought with him. It had been one hundred and fifty years since the attack of the Malbolians. Yes, they were still alive, but at times, the existence was more like a life sentence. The Ravenite kingdom was intact, but it was not really alive. It merely existed. *Just as the Light has gone from Skyeden so has the life out of the Ravenites.* There was never joy. Just a blue depression. Once there had been Light, near immortality, transference healings, the glorious Ascension, and the merger of your tribe's totem animal. Once, after he had gone through Ascension, he had ridden with his Father to confront an advancing army of Malbolians on the southern border of Ravenland a thousand years ago.

It had been more than a thousand years since the armies had confronted one another and now it was happening again. Oh, Eradrin remembered the glory of that day, when their army had been at least equal if not superior to the invading Malbolians. Their banners waved proudly and the sky was filled with supporting ravens. And there was their mightiest weapons, their mascots and pride of heart, the Dravens. How majestic and powerful these magnificent half dragon, half-raven creatures had been as they rode them into battle. The stab of pain he felt for the loss of his father and brother was no greater than that for the loss of Magonite, his personal Draven.

Eradrin looked at the palm of his hands, closing his eyes, trying to remember the leather and scales of Magonite's skin. The bound power of Magonite's muscles, his insanely racing heart, his mighty roar that could generate avalanches and scorching jettisons of fire. Who would not feel a conqueror of the world saddled upon Magonite?

Inspired by the memory, Eradrin leapt to his feet and pumped his fist into the air as an act of defiance to any that challenged. The moment was intoxicating — the tremendous feeling of being astraddle Magonite, riding beside his father over the River of Great Divide with the glorious Sun above them and the Day of Moon rising over the horizon. They were the rulers of the North.

That was the glory. That was the feeling of freedom. *Yeah!*

Eradrin pumped his fist again, his heart still racing. He finally relaxed and leaned against the tree trunk, closing his eyes. Cherishing the memory of happier days. He opened his eyes to the blue-tinted world that was reality and saw a figure walking his way, just cresting the hill. The man was in no hurry, walking slowly with the aid of a long staff.

Eradrin squinted his eyes and recognized the man as Aribon, one of his nephews. This walk was too long for such an old man. That he had made it this far from Skye Castle was surprising and a testament to the man's will.

Funny how this old man was like the son Eradrin had never had. When Aribon's father, Thomar, passed, Eradrin had adopted the boy as his own. This old man wasn't just his nephew, he was his son. Waiting, he smoothed his hair, tightened the band that held his braided hair and straightened his clothing. A king should at least appear presentable.

Eradrin reached out to embrace Aribon when they met. "My nephew. Why, would you make such a journey without a horse?"

"Second Father, My King, I come not as a folly but out of long deliberation. This is something I have planned a long time." He gripped Eradrin's arm with a frail, shaky hand. The once long slender fingers were knotted with arthritis. The simple task of gripping a man's hand caused insufferable pain.

"It's good to see you. Come, stay with me awhile beneath the tree. You can ride my horse back and I will walk alongside you."

"You are kind, Second Father. I do wish to be with you beneath the tree."

"So shall it be. Actually, I'm glad to see you. In truth, I was reminiscing about riding Magonite along with my Father yours; and, after the reverie, I find myself a little depressed."

Aribon placed his hand on Eradrin's shoulder as they walked to the tree. "Thank you for coming out to meet me. I'm not sure I could have made it the rest of the way. I can walk a mile. It's just that when my destination is more than that, my joints start their protesting."

They reached the tree and Eradrin spread out a blanket and propped a makeshift pillow against the trunk of the tree.

"I have some beef sticks left if you like?"

"No, no, no. I had my last meal only two hours ago."

Eradrin gave Aribon a puzzled look "Your last meal?"

"Yes. Which leads me to the reason I am here."

Eradrin studied the familiar face. The skin was thin and stretched with tiny crow's feet around the lips and eyes. Those once brilliant blue eyes were thick with tumors. The left eye was particularly milky with cataracts. The once thick, black hair was now a few wispy white strands pulled over from one ear to the other.

"It is time for my passing," Aribon said.

"No. Not now, you are my closest friend, a son to me. You're a Donachie of the First Family."

"I know. Nevertheless, my health is failing. The healers say it is only a matter of days."

"Then I will make you comfortable in your bed and I'll not leave your side. We'll ..."

"Wait. Listen. For a thousand years, we have lived under tyranny and with the loss of freedom. "Right there," Aribon pointed with a shaking hand," I saw my grandfather — your father— slain. I want the honor to at least have the control and freedom of choice for my death. It's a matter of dignity and pride. I'm not eternally thirty years of age like you, nor am I Ascended. I am one hundred and fifty-six years old. I was six when grandfather and father died.

"I remember."

"Allow me to die beneath this tree with dignity and peace."

"I love you, Aribon, as a son. I will stay by your side," Eradrin said. He placed an arm around Aribon's thin shoulders. "I will not know what to do when I have need of your counsel."

Aribon smiled weakly and tapped Eradrin's chest over his heart. "I will always be there with you. Just listen for me; I will answer."

"What of your wife and children?"

Aribon pulled out a folded parchment of paper. "Will you give them this for me?"

Eradrin reached for it, then stopped. Taking the letter would be an act of affirmation.

"Take it. Go on."

Eradrin reluctantly accepted the document.

"It's a beautiful day, and I feel wonderful," Aribon said, allowing a small smile to appear on his wrinkled face. "Tell me, my uncle the king, what is the one day of your life you will never forget? "

"You mean like the first time got yourself got drunk, donned that god-awful wig, and went into the brothel?"

"Oh, don't remind me of such foolish behavior. No, I'm not speaking of myself. I want to hear you describe the most memorable day of your life; every detail of it."

"I guess it was the day I was crowned," Eradrin said. "But that wasn't a happy day. Let me ...""

"Oh, yes," Aribon interrupted, "that's the day I want to hear you speak of. I was there, but I was only six years old. My memory is sketchy, to say the least. Please. This is the perfect time and place."

"Very well, I will tell you of it. However, let me say this one thing before I begin: No matter how or when you die, Aribon, you will always be a man of honor. As King, I do not think there was another in the kingdom that could have made me more proud than you have. The two of us have always shared a special bond. You were only a child, but you were with me on the day of the crowning. Your father was a handsome man and the three of us stood as proud Donachies. We were as strong as our name has ever been. Your name and legacy will always be a pillar that the Donachies may lean upon."

"Thank you. I hope soon that you shall take a wife and have children. It has been too long. Too many chances must be taken and your death could leave the throne empty. I know you will never love from your heart again after the loss of Dayanna, but you should find a wife. Marry a princess from one of the western kingdoms and have her bear a child, an heir to the throne. Your sister's proposed marriage into the graceful and intelligent Hicool people will be considered a great success. So do it! Marry a western princess. Solidify the kingdom of Skyeden and win back our freedom."

"I will live for that day," Eradrin said.

"Good. Now tell me about the day of the crowning."

CHAPTER 27

ONE HUNDRED FIFTY YEARS AGO

Eradrin stopped and stood in the hallway before entering the throne room. The black jacket he wore had belonged to his father who had worn it on the day of his crowning as king. Standing on each side now were his brother and sister, his mother directly behind him. Following at a respectful distance were council and officers of the court and with them the High Priest.

Standing back flush against the walls were Malbolian soldiers. Eradrin glanced over his shoulder at his mother and noted that she was standing straight, always filled with pride and honor. He had never seen her slumped in defeat and now her eyes were shining with a quiet defiance.

The ceremonial drums sounded in unison with a double beat switching to single. Eradrin thought it sounded like the cadence of a man approaching something that he had a building angst to strike. It seemed to be the perfectly timed metronome to the building fury and contempt he held for the man that was about to crown him.

Thrump. Thrump.
Thrump. Thrump.
Thrump.
Thrump.

The twenty-foot tall carved-wood doors to the throne room swung open. At the end of the room on a raised platform was the throne that had been created from the bones of the greatest of

Dravens and hundreds of ravens. Each arm of the chair was a wing pointing forward. The back of the chair rose thirty feet with the Draven's head positioned as if to survey the whole of the throne room. The floor and walls were carved from granite and marble with engraved swirls. These contained the invisible threads of the Creator's essence that were woven in all that existed. On the back wall was an image of the Tree of Light made of gold. The vibrational spheres consisted of huge emeralds that had been found by the pioneers who had come to the mountain and carved Skye Castle from the stone.

The Malbolian guards stepped back from the doors to the throne room.

"It shouldn't be this way," Eradrin's brother Thomar said as they moved through the room to the terrace. He was several inches shorter than Eradrin and many pounds lighter. Still, they shared the characteristics of the Donachies with their strong chins, thick hair, and mannerisms.

"It is what it is," Eradrin replied, forcing a small smile.

Six year-year-old Aribon had accompanied the men through the great room and onto the terrace and now stood on Eradrin's left. "Is it true?" the boy whispered, "that their King sees through the eyes of the Darklings?"

"Yes" Eradrin said. "He has that ability. Just as a long time ago, we had the ability to see through the eyes of the black raven. We lost that ability but they still possess it. There was a time when we ruled with white magic. So there had been balance until, as the legend has it; the Eclipser slew the light of the sun and made it our moon. The balance was broken and with the white magic gone so was our immortality. Only the Light of the Eternal Flame is said to have the power to restore the light to make our moon into a sun again. "

"Who is the Eclipser?"

"King Shabael's father. It is said he sacrificed his life to the Creator so that the world would be rid its Sun and Day of Moon. When this happened, our Sun and Day of Moon vanished forever. I shouldn't speak of this for I know it is fearful for one as young as you."

"I'm not afraid! I am a Donachie! But I do find the Darklings scary, Uncle Eradrin."

"As do I."

Aribon had a puzzled expression on his face. "Where did the light go when they took it?"

Eradrin gave the boy an inquisitive look. "You are going to be a very smart man. With a good sword arm and your smarts, you'd make a great king. But enough; I must focus now on the ceremony."

"Yes, my King."

"Thomar," Eradrin turned to his brother. "At any moment we're going to be summoned. If something happens, protect your son. He is too precious to lose. If something happens to me, you shall be next to the throne and then Aribon." He gave Thomar a sheaf of papers. "Here, these are to be read upon my death. I have bequeathed you heir to the throne."

Thomar frowned. "Nothing is going to happen to you, brother. I will defend you till my own death." He accepted the folded parchment with the waxed Donachie seal and slid it inside his robe.

"No. If something happens to me, you stand down," Eradrin said. "We must not let the Donachie line be broken. "

"You remember that advice yourself," Thomar whispered. "Don't do anything foolish. We need you to guide us through this. You are much more suited to this than I. You are able to speak in the high tongue and inspire us."

"You give me far too much credit, my brother. I am ruined within. I am dangerously close to drawing my swords even knowing it could mean death for us all."

"Then all hope is lost. You must not break now. Get through this day and we will plan our strategy for a war."

"War?"

"We will prepare."

"Yes, and they will kill us all," Eradrin warned.

"No. Not if you are king. You are the Chosen One. You are wise and cunning, brother. Keep the political peace for now and we will find ways to strike back at them."

"For a thousand years they have been building an arsenal and an army that is far superior to our own. They have the Dark Magic while our Light has abandoned us."

"Yes. That is true," Thomar said. "So?"

"We cannot survive forever living in darkness. If the Creator fates me to be King, it is my obligation to find a way for the Ravenites to live with Light. When we bleed, do we not leak blood and Light? I had

255

a vision last night in which a raven brought the Light and father spoke to me. He said we should not lose our faith and that we will have the Light again."

"Father spoke to you? Is this real or a dream?"

"I wasn't dreaming. I was awake. It was the last thing he said before he was killed. I believe this to be true."

"Then this will inspire our people. We have spoken of small attacks upon the Malbolians, just enough to keep them on edge and let them know there is civil unrest. We can accomplish great things."

"Yes. You select your men, but do it quietly and make sure you can trust those you approach. This must be of the upmost secrecy. The El Qui can never link these attacks to us; do you understand?"

"I do, My King. I've not felt this excited about something since Skyeden had a sunrise."

"I too, my brother. I can hear the songs of freedom in the treetops and the excited cries of the ravens." Eradrin lifted his head to feel the wind moving across the terrace. People below were scurrying about, preparing for the funeral ceremonies that would commence soon after the crowning.

"So, three shall come on raven wings," Thomar mused. "Three. Three what? Three Lights? What else did he say?"

"He said nothing else, except to remind me to keep faith. Now, I must get my thoughts together for this mockery of a crowning ceremony. I miss father, Thomar, but I am beginning to feel that without his over-riding caution, we may be able to initiate some plans for our future."

"Aye. I did not want to voice that, but I feel the same, brother. I am tired of this mind-numbing subservience. I am burning for vengeance, Eradrin. As soon as this coronation is finished, I will start gathering my men. We will begin immediately."

"Where?" Eradrin asked.

"I understand the El Qui are leaving mid-afternoon tomorrow. We will leave during the funeral and set up an ambush by the Great River Divide."

"That's two days ride from here."

"Yes."

"Your absence will be noticed, especially at the funeral services."

"I'll attend our father's service, then slip away. "

"All right," Eradrin agreed. "But as many men and horses as you're taking, you're going to have to be very careful not to arouse suspicion. I'll announce that as the new acting Viceroy you are holding surprise inspections."

Thomar stepped back and gave Eradrin a long head-to-toe perusal "The Donachie Brothers. We will make a formidable team!" Then he raised his right arm in what looked like an arm wrestling challenge. Eradrin smiled, grasped his brother's hand and they embraced.

"It is our time now, Brother. What we start today we must never let falter until we have achieved victory," Thomar said.

"We will keep the faith until the ring of fire and the coming of the three on raven wings," Eradrin said.

Thomar stopped at the doorway to the Eradrin's bedchambers. "If something should happen to me, would you take Aribon under your wing?"

"Yes, I will be honored. But you will come back."

Thomar winked and grinned at his brother. "What did all the other lads call me during the competition games?"

Eradrin smiled. "The Comeback Kid. You were never going to quit. But you know that what we do from this moment forward will be the cause and effect that will not only affect the kingdoms, but the spiritual realm of the Light and Dark. We cannot lose ourselves in the petty egocentric immediate circles of our little worlds and forget the war between the Light and Dark. All that exists will break if there is not a balance. Remember, our mortal lives are here but an eternity awaits us where there may exist a much larger battle."

"You're right, of course," Thomar said, his lips curling in a mischievous smile. "But you need to prepare yourself now. See you at the funeral ... er ... crowning."

Eradrin stepped to the balcony rail and looked down on his people below. His heart was heavy as he thought of their fears and doubts. He stood in thought for a moment, then left the balcony and went to the queen's chambers where servants were busily helping his mother prepare. "Alfie, is the Queen dressed."

"Yes, my Prince. Oh... I'm sorry, please forgive," she bowed profusely, "My King."

Eradrin smiled and nodded his head.

CHAPTER 28

A RELUCTANT SUCCESSION

The Malbolian guards tapped their staffs twice as a signal for the procession to the Throne room to begin. Eradrin felt a surge of bile building in his throat as he followed the directions of the enemy soldiers. He had thought he could be tolerant of them, but he had to fight the urge to rebel. He stared straight ahead, managing barely to keep the disdain and hatred he felt beneath the surface of the facade he presented.

"This is blasphemous!" Eradrin whispered to Thomar. "Crowned by the tyrant that killed our father. What kind of king am I?" He kept his eyes lowered so as not to see the Malbolian King Shabael, Queen Shawndeli, and the Queen Highest, not out of fear or submission, but to avoid showing the hatred and revulsion he felt toward them. *Father! I am supposed to be above this!*

Thomar reached out and placed a hand on his brother's arm. "Control your emotions," he said. "I know you're in a living Hell right now, but get through it. Receive the crown. Then we'll have our revenge. Go, now. Be crowned."

"It seems more like being damned," Eradrin whispered, drawing a deep breath to compose himself. He forced a quick smile for Thomar's benefit and took his first step.

The doors to the throne room opened fully. The drums grew louder. The choir began to sing.

"Glory high the new king comes
Oh, hear the Kingdom's bells ring
Glory high the new king comes
Majestic upon the raven's wings"

The Malbolian High Priest Calibri and Ravenite Priest Belthine stood on the first step. Calibri was dressed in an all-white robe and Belthine was dressed in a black one. Both wore chains bearing the symbols of the kingdom they represented. They stood; and, each was holding long candelabras.

A Malbolian Court Guard announced, "Here ye the Lords of the Donachie Tribe; Lord and Prince Eradrin Donachie; Lord Thomar Donachie; and, the young Lord Aribon. Hail to thee, High Royal House of the Ravenites."

A silence fell upon the gathered. The court was filled with twenty ascending rows on each side. Murals depicting Ravenite history adorned the walls. Above the murals were stained glass windows, which had admitted the light when there had been day. Now torches, candles, and lamps illuminated the court.

Eradrin glanced to the right at his mother, who acknowledged him by touching her heart with her hand. Beside her were her mother, sister, and two brothers. Behind them were the rest of the family members.

Seeing everyone gathered in the same location sounded an alarm for Prince Eradrin. If Shabael or his mother had decided to end the Donachie rule, this was the perfect setting. They had the whole bloodline under one roof. He averted his eyes from the group so as not to draw attention to them.

Priest Highest Calibri stepped forward and bowed. "Glory. Glory. Glory. In the name of the Great Creator, the powers of Light and Dark, as named and deemed worthy by the Emperor High Shabael El Qui, and so acknowledged and writ in approval thereof by the Ravenite High Court, that Lord and Prince Eradrin Donachie, of true royal blood and heir to the throne by rite of passage proceed in the ceremony to be king of the North, ruler of the Ravenites.

"Lord and Prince Eradrin Donachie, do ye accept the right of seat upon the Ravenite Throne?"

"As my Father and those in our bloodline who have served as king, I do," Eradrin said. He still kept his eyes lowered, staring at Shabael's boots.

Priest Calibri moved to the first step of ten that led to the throne. "This row I stand upon represents the earth plane. With each ascending step, you acknowledge the virtues of each and give oath to abide by the specific holy laws governing each of the human conditions. For to ascend the tenth spire you thereby say in action you have made passage through each of the human conditions and now obey the law of the Creator. Is this so?

"It is." Eradrin answered.

"Please come forth to take your first step," Priest Calibri said.

Eradrin began walking toward the throne. With each step his heart pounded. The drummers began their *Thrump. Thrump. Thrump.* With each step, it felt as though he carried a mountain on his shoulder; a mountain of immense density filled with anger and sadness.

Slowly, he let his eyes rise from the King Shabael's boots, stopping at Shabael's waist where he held before him the sword to be used for anointing and crowning.

What the prince saw sent a red cloud of rage surging through him. The sword was stained in blood! It had not even been wiped clean after the slaying of his father. The heathen! That same, bloodied sword was to be used in the ceremony to make him king. What an outrageous gesture! He was to be crowned king with the sword that had slain his father? Was this some symbolic show to establish that the El Qui were conquerors and masters? *My father's blood? Really? I am to accept this?* Eradrin tried to draw in a breath but found he couldn't breathe.

The hatred for those responsible for the humiliation, the display of callousness, congealed and grew within him with each step he took toward the Malbolian King. He could feel every eye upon him. It had been more than a thousand years since a Ravenite had been crowned and this was to be a mockery.

Not this way. Eradrin's eyes moved along the blade of the sword to Shabael's hand that was gripping the offensive blade. The left hand cupped the point; the right hand held the sword by the hasp.

Each step was synchronized with the drumbeat, making Eradrin's footfalls sound as if he carried a heavy weight. The choir's voices sounded in spirit for such a glorious occasion. *Not this day, this moment.* All attention was focused on him. Many of their hearts cried out in the realization of what their prince must be feeling as he went through this insulting, demeaning mockery of being crowned.

For one thousand years, the Ravenites' King Aremis had done nothing but surrender to the will of the Malbolians. Deep within the heart of every Ravenite was the dream that one day their new king would rally them to rise and stand against the Malbolians. Now they were at last getting a new king; and, his reign was being christened with a sword that still bore his father's blood. Was their fate to be another thousand years of living under the Malbolian hand?

Creator, help me. I know not what to do. Eradrin reached the ninth step, one below the towering Shabael and the terrible sword. He raised his head to look into Shabael's face and a tear ran down his cheek.

"Kneel before me, Lord and Prince Eradrin Donachie," Shabael ordered.

Eradrin was an arm's length away, his body trembling with emotion. His right hand began to tremble.

"Kneel," Shabael said, his voice louder and commanding.

Thomar was standing with his mother on the first row to the right of the throne, his hand resting on the hilt of his sword. He cast a nervous look toward the Malbolian soldiers and noticed that they also seemed to be tense.

Do it! Do it now! It was his father's voice, but Eradrin thought it also sounded like Thomar.

Grab the sword from him and drive it into his chest!

No, my son. Do that and the guards will kill you as soon as you move. Even if you kill him or just wound him, Queen Highest will strike back with such a wrath she will make the Inferno seem a courtyard playground.

Don't listen to him! For a thousand years, he did nothing but placate the Malbolians. Now his death has given you this opportunity. This is our father's legacy to you. Servitude to the Malbolians. Strike the tyrant down! This is the only chance you'll ever have. For the Ravenites. For Skyeden! Sever the head of the snake!

Eradrin glanced again at his family. His mother was motioning with her head for him to kneel, while Thomar was urging him to do something quite different ... anything. Eradrin smiled in their direction, then turned back to face the Emperor.

Thomar felt a moment of dizziness and anchored himself by gripping his mother's elbow.

Eradrin met Shabael's eyes for the first time as he began his descent to one knee. There was a collective sigh in the room. The Queen Highest smiled proudly and glanced around the court, drinking

261

in the looks and emotions of every Ravenite in the room. This was pure and total victory, a submission to their superior, supreme rule.

Shabael spoke loudly, confidently, "I, Supreme Regent of Skyeden, by the powers invested to me, and by blood of El Qui, bestow to ye, Eradrin of Donachie, the right to the Ravenite throne. Do you swear an oath to serve the Highest Regent of Malbolina, never with malice but always with servitude?

With servitude? Really? Eradrin was fuming. *Creator, why have you forsaken us? Why I am to be humiliated. Haven't my people and I suffered enough?*

Shabael: "What say ye?"

"I ..." Eradrin's eyes moved to the sword again, fixed on the dried blood of his father.

With lightning quickness, Eradrin lunged for the sword. His hands enveloped Shabael's and he yanked at the weapon. It came free so easily that Eradrin, expecting resistance, teetered on the heels of his boots and almost fell down the steps. He regained his balance and thrust the point of the sword forward with the razor-sharp blade slashing through Shabael's white silk jersey and skimming the flesh of his chest and abdomen. The king fell backward to elude the blade and Eradrin sprang forward, arching his arms up with the sword to drive it downward.

A powerful force suddenly struck Eradrin in mid-thrust and he was propelled to the side, the sword clanging to the floor. Eradrin struggled as he and Rageton, the Malbolian Superman, rolled on the floor, but he was no match for the huge man's strength. Finally breaking free for a moment, he lunged to his feet and reached for his dagger, only to find the points of a dozen Malbolian swords thrust before him.

A boot was suddenly slammed into Eradrin's back, driving him to the stone floor again.

Thomar had drawn his sword and he and the twenty Ravenite Court Guards rushed to the steps preparing to join the fray. However, they were met by the Malbolians, who were five times their numbers.

"Desist!" Shabael shouted, having risen, and regained his composure. "I command you. Stop now!" The soldiers on both sides paused and looked at the king, his robe bloody from the gash to his body. The Queen Highest Mateah went to Shabael and placed a hand on her son's shoulder. Her neck seemed lowered and shoulders hunched higher. Her face was angled downward but her eyes were looking straight ahead, making the bottom half of her pink pupils visible with wedges of white beneath. It was a wicked look from one whom many deemed the cruelest person ever to exist in Skyeden. After an attack on her son, every person in the room expected a quick death sentence to be forthcoming.

Mateah stood at Shabael's side and handed him a cloth to press against the wound in his body. Shabael took the cloth and coolly wiped the blood from his abdomen, then gave it back to his mother. She folded the cloth and gave it to one of the soldiers. There was dead silence in the court as she raised her head and silently let her eyes touch on every person in the court.

Shabael realized she was waiting for him to speak first. Appreciative of that, he pointed to Eradrin. "Bring him before me."

"No!" Thomar burst out, and the flat of a sword struck his head. He dropped to his knees and fell forward. His mother, Juliana rushed to him, holding him upright.

Two Malbolian guards seized Eradrin by the arms, lifting him up and toward the Emperor.

"Kneel," Shabael commanded.

A collective gasp was heard from the crowd. None suspected this would have been Shabael's first words or that he still intended to carry out the ceremony after Eradrin had attempted to kill him. Their eyes were on the king, but the presence they felt most was that of the Queen Highest. She was visually seething with anger, not toward her son, but for the audacity of these pathetic conquered people making such a feeble attempt to kill her son, the El Qui King. This was her moment spoiled by an idiot who would be king.

"No, I will not kneel to you!" a defiant Eradrin rasped.

"Bring me his mother." The whispered words came from the Queen Highest, prompting another collective gasp came from the assembled people.

Juliana Donachie had been the reigning queen of the Ravenites for a millennium. She was infamous for her compassion, forever loyal to the King, and mother to the tribe, grieving with them at the loss of loved ones, celebrating with the birth of new babes.

It had been hard on her watching the young grow old and die because they could not partake in Ascension. For a thousand years, they had been rulers of the north. They shared the land with the

Hicool, Highlanders, and the Nahbra; and, they had made a tolerable peace without war due to the natural boundaries of the land. To lose everything now would ensure another thousand years of accepting fully that they served rather than ruled. Many felt that the Creator had abandoned them because of weaknesses in their resolve. The Queen had understood and felt their pain. She had been the heart of the kingdom, all the while grooming Dayanna to succeed her. Now, with Dayanna gone and the King slain, she had become mother to them all.

"No!" Eradrin shouted a second time as the soldiers stood preparing to bring his mother to the Queen Highest.

"It's all right, my King," his mother said. She kissed the stunned Thomar on the forehead and squeezed his hand. "Don't worry; it's all right." Turning to face the throne, Queen Juliana lifted her gown several inches off the floor and walked toward the throne steps, the hard heels of her shoes echoing upon the stone floor. The footsteps sounding were those of a self-assured walker. She did not misstep nor waver.

As Eradrin watched through the circle of guards, he had never felt so proud of her or his heritage. Juliana wore a purple gown, woven in gold, and her hair was coifed into an intricate weave with rubies and gems. Upon her head was the Queen's crown, a raven with spread wings that linked to the back. The raven was layered in diamonds, collected the first year after the exodus of Eden, the land at the heart of Skyeden where once had stood the Tree of Light and Tree of Dark.

The two queens faced each other on the stage, their contrasts most evident. There was a grace and inner glow to Queen Juliana as she stood straight and held her shoulders back and head high. The Red Dragon, Queen Highest Mateah, was in direct contrast, exuding an aura of evil power.

Still, Mateah had an awesome presence with not an ounce of extra flesh; a classic hourglass figure with a generous bosom and flattering clothing to enhance seductiveness. She enjoyed using her beauty as power to literally melt a man with desire or turn him to stone with a scornful glare. She held her head high and walked down the steps to meet Juliana at the bottom.

She turned slightly so she could see Eradrin, and then looked at the bloodstained sword Shabael was holding again.

"Queen Donachie, please stand beside me," Queen Mateah said, smiling sweetly. She placed her hand around Juliana's elbow and assisted her to the top level. Eradrin was now standing on the ninth step.

Queen Highest moved to the left of her son, looked at Eradrin, then back at her son and the sword he was holding before the court.

"Perhaps it is the blood on your sword, my son, which offends the Prince."

"Ah, I am sure you are right, Mother," Shabael agreed. He examined the blade for a moment and ran a hand along the steel. "Yes, you are right, Queen Highest. Bring the Prince before me. "

Eradrin offered no resistance and stood before Shabael.

The king held the sword over Eradrin's shoulder, turning it over several times, deciding which side of the blade was stained the most. Slowly, he dragged the blade over Eradrin's shoulder as if wiping it clean on his robe. Turning the sword over, he did the same on the other shoulder, then examined the blade, turning it to catch the light.

"There now. That is better is it not?"

Eradrin remained motionless and silent. Guards on each side held his arms in a firm grip.

Exaggerating a puzzled look, Shabael asked, "Mother, what will happen if I must ask a third time for Lord Donachie to kneel before me?"

"He will become a motherless prince," Queen Highest answered without hesitation.

She drew her dagger, the same one that had slit the throat of Dayanna's brother, and then looked at Eradrin with a smile that could have seemed to ask: Want a cookie?

Eradrin noticeably blanched, but descended upon one knee.

"With the greatest of pleasures, I the Grace and Supreme Ruler of Skyeden anoint you, King of Ravenland," Shabael said while tapping both of Eradrin's shoulders with the sword. I pronounce to the world, King Donachie of Ravenland."

High Priest Calibri passed the crown to Priest Belthine, who presented it to the Emperor. The crown was made of white gold with the head of a raven at the center with its wings completing a circle.

The moment that Eradrin had always dreamed of, the moment to feel the weight of the crown placed upon his head, had arrived. However, he was not feeling joy. Had he dreamed the man who killed his father and humiliated him before his own people would bestow the crown, he would have orphaned himself as a child and wandered the northlands the whole of his life.

Shabael smiled and pointed his sword to the court, then sheathed it. "I stand aside. Take the throne, King Donachie; it is rightfully yours." He gestured for the guards to release the reluctant king.

Eradrin stood for a moment, staring at the throne made of the skeletons of the Draven and the arms of the chair made of raven skulls. His father had sat on this throne all of his life. Taking a deep breath — closing then opening his eyes — the new king approached his throne. He turned to face the court; his face flushed with raging emotions prepared to sit.

"My King, may you please forgive my intervention at this momentous time," Queen Juliana interrupted.

The Malbolian guards reached to draw their swords but Queen Highest waved a hand for them to relax.

Eradrin, only inches from sitting, froze and stood upright in front of the throne. He straightened, looked curiously at Juliana and his mind raced as he pondered what she might be about to say. "Yes, Queen Mother?"

"I ask the Emperor Shabael and Queen Highest if it might be possible to include in this ceremony a ritual that has been traditional for every Ravenite King of the past who has taken the crown. The presentation of the Sword of the Ravens."

"You jest?" Queen Highest broke in, her pink eyes flashing. "Your son only moments ago attempted to kill our Emperor!" The request had obviously caught Mateah off guard and she was replying emotionally. Catching herself, her cheeks reddened.

Unfazed, Shabael nodded and said, "I understand. You may bring the sword forth."

"Thank you, Emperor El Qui," Eradrin's mother said. She turned toward the back of the court. "Please have our armorer bring the Sword of Ravens."

A long moment passed, before the court chamber doors opened. The armorer, dressed in ceremonial black robe and pants, approached Juliana, bowed to one knee and presented the sword in a silver box with a bed of red silk.

The Ravenite Queen Mother lifted the blade from the box and turned toward the throne.

"You may approach and present the sword to your new king," Shabael said.

Queen Juliana held the sword delicately in her hands and turned her gaze upon Queen Mateah, keeping constant eye contact as she passed. There was not a man on the face of Skyeden who would have walked between those two at that moment for all the riches of the world.

Familiar with the platform, Queen Juliana stopped directly before her son and turned her eyes away from Queen Highest.

Eradrin watched his mother, a lump in his throat and pride in his heart, in awe of her courage and dignity in representing the Ravenite Kingship.

"As Queen Mother of the Ravenites, I bequeath to you, the sacred Sword of Raven that has continued an unbroken chain of possession from the first Ravenite King, to your father, and now to you, my son, my King. Bow, please."

The pride and emotions swelled within Eradrin. Bowing before his mother had removed the taint of the Malbolians. It was a feeling much like a rape victim wanting to make love with her true mate to wash away whatever shame or disgrace she might have felt from the despicable act.

"Do you, Eradrin Donachie, King of the Ravenites, vow to abide by the codes of honor and justice to serve and protect the people of your realm?"

"I do."

"Do you give oath to accept the Sword of Raven as symbolic of your virtue, that your wit be as sharp as its blade, its balance be your fair justice, its unbending strength to stand for the rights of your peoples? Do you vow to raise this sword in the name of your people and the Light you serve against those that threaten life, liberty, and freedom?"

Eradrin knew the weight of those words and had wondered if that part of the oath would be left unsaid.

"I will," he answered while looking directly at his mother but remaining alert to any El Qui reaction.

"Then, as honor of my station, as your Queen and Mother, I give the Sword of Raven to the new king," she kissed the blade and presented it.

"I accept," Eradrin said.

Under all the drama, the threat of violence and the loss of her husband, Queen Juliana stood proud and smiled. She took a step backward, gathered her gown, and descended the throne steps, returning to her place in the court. The smile was still on her face but was not returned by Queen Highest as she walked past.

"King Eradrin, you may assume your throne," Shabael said.

Everyone in the court apart from the royal family of El Qui knelt on their knees in homage to the new king.

It was at this moment that Eradrin realized the capacity of hate for the El Qui had become fathomless. The Sword of Raven's weight, the feel of its hasp in his hand, restored confidence within him. He closed his eyes and silently vowed that he would avenge the death of his father and Dayanna with the blade that had crowned him.

Shabael stood before Eradrin as his bodyguards inched closer and watched the new king's hands as he held The Sword of Raven on his lap. Priest Amila Belthine approached, ready to present the crown to Shabael. The crown had been created during the year the Ravenites had begun building Skye Castle on the side of the mountain. Amila was one hundred and twenty-five years old, his hair snow white. His assistant, John Daren, a rising star in the priesthood, carried the crown for Amila, giving it to him before he approached Shabael.

The crown was made of white gold with the top rim consisting of small ravens linked in a circle by their widespread wings. Beneath each raven was a horizontal quarter-inch of wood with fingernail-sized jewels of shifting iridescent colors. Beneath this ran a complete line of diamonds.

"As comes with the crowning, the Ravenite Crown," Shabael said, a smile on his face. Only Eradrin was able to see beneath Shabael's facade of pageantry a tension drawn as taut as a bowstring, reminding him of the arrow whizzing toward Dayanna. He forced the memory from his mind and tried to concentrate on the moment.

As the weight of the crown settled upon his head, a tingling sensation spread across the top of his skull and continued to move downward, along his throat, into his chest, to the tip of his fingers, his legs, and to the ends of his toes. It was an electric sensation, mindful of being too close to a lightning strike. He closed his eyes when the crown rested upon his head and in that darkness a small light, carried like a torch in the night, was moving through eons of time, growing larger and larger as it approached him. A raven carried the Orb of

Light. Suddenly the whole of the blackness was consumed in blinding light as though he floated miles above the surface of the sun, the kind of light he had not seen in a thousand years.

Faith, my son. The Light. It shall shine again. Through ring of fire, three shall come on raven wings. The spoken word shall be key. Be King. The War of Light is coming.

The consuming light blazed, and then vanished abruptly; Eradrin's body spasmed and he opened his eyes.

The expression on the new king's face was as if he had just communicated with the Divine. He was vividly aware that all were looking at him. Until that moment, he had questioned why he was to be made king to a defeated people, a people of Light that lived in the dark. Suddenly, in a flash of revelation, he knew why he was fated for the throne. The countless hours of warrior training, studying battle strategies, learning logistics of army movement and supplies all made sense.

I am king now. The Creator has given me this power for a divine reason.

His father's voice had said the Light was to be brought by three upon the ravens' wings. Was this merely dream wishing? *I am a "fated" one placed here to prepare for the coming of the Light? Is it real? My heart says yes. The Malbolians have suppressed our dreams only achievable with freedom. We are their subservient zombies. Freedom! The Light! The Light will bring us balance and merging and union with the Divine through Ascensions and immortality so that no longer must we watch our children die.*

It is now time to act as King.

"My first command as King is to proceed with the funeral services of our departed great king, my father, my Queen Dayanna, and all those that lost their lives yesterday. To direct these orders, I appoint my brother, Thomar Donachie, as Viceroy to the King."

Thomar removed a bloodied hand from his wounded head and stood rigidly at attention. "As so commanded, with honor, My King, I accept."

"Your Majesty?" Queen Highest Mateah said, "May I approach?"

Eradrin nodded assent, the hairs on the nape of his neck stiffening in apprehension.

Queen Mateah positioned herself between the court and Eradrin, standing so that only he could understand the words she whispered. She put her lips against his ear as she spoke.

"If you ever attempt to kill my son again," she murmured, her voice as deadly as a snake's venom, I will personally inflict the most unimaginable horrors to all that carry the Donachie blood. Do you understand?" She clenched her teeth on Eradrin's earlobe and increased the pressure. No one in the court could hear or see what she was doing, but Eradrin flinched and his face reddened. To the side, Shabael lips curled in a smile.

"I hear you." Eradrin said in a voice so low that only Queen Highest could hear.

She released her grip and stepped back, gracefully removing a drop of blood from her lips with her forefinger.

Shabael marveled, *Oh, Mother, you are so bad."*

Mateah turned to face the court and spoke loudly and clearly. "Let the Ravenites learn today that Malbolians can be merciful. In that vein, we rescind the blinding of a child each day."

Sighs of relief sounded throughout the throne room.

Shabael waited, knowing there was yet more to come. *What are you up to, Mother?*

Mateah answered that silent query with her sweetest smile and approached Shabael, walking between Eradrin and the court. This time it was Shabael's ear into which she whispered. "Do not worry, my son. These peasants fear us still. But what better way for these weak minds to feel our power and respect us than to suggest the cruelest of deeds and then recant them out of a sense of fairness and humanity?"

Queen Highest then turned to the throne and said, "Forgive me, King Donachie, for the interruption. Please continue."

Eradrin rose and sheathed the Sword of Raven. "This court is dismissed. Let the funeral ceremonies begin two hours after the Moon of Night rises."

CHAPTER 29

EMERGENCY AT SILVERTON MEMORIAL

Tap. Tap. Tap.
Tap Tap. Tap.
The crack in the windowpane ran like a jagged line of lightning.
Tap. Tap.
Pieces of glass fell from the window, breaking into smaller pieces as they struck the floor. The white raven flapped its wings and moved away from the window. It rose into the air and hovered over the edge of the roof of the building, then descended again.

For a moment, the full moon blinked out as a flock of black ravens descended upon the old oak tree. The birds found their perches, but remained silent. Their heads were cocked to one side as they stared toward the hospital window, poised to take flight.

The white raven, which had broken the glass, dropped to the hospital windowsill and cranked its head from side to side to look inward.

"Caw!" Rearing its head back to the full length of its neck, the raven struck the window — one, two, three, four — times in rapid succession, causing the crack to run from one end of the pane to the other. It had reared its head back for another strike when the ravens exploded from the oak tree like a black fury chorused in "caws" and

hurled themselves toward the white raven with their wings pinned back and talons extended.

The white raven reacted by swooping its wings in a powerful downward thrust to heave itself up and over the ledge of the roof as the attacking ravens approached. It made a screaming "errookkkk!" From above the roof dozens of white ravens descended, accompanied by several Darklings. Trails of light began to stream from the streetlamps and the lights flickered crazily.

As the black ravens converged on the white bird, they were unaware of the white ravens and Darklings' attack. Deadly talons tore into the shoulders of their wings and sharp beaks tore at the flesh of their throats. Where the skin was pierced, little streamers of light emitted. A Darkling pinned a black raven to the wall, where two of the white ones attacked it. The escaping rays light spilling out of the black raven were sucked in by the Darkling. The doomed bird made one last caw of death before its inner light was deleted. The Darkling released its corpse to fall lifeless to the ground, and then leapt into the air to snag another black raven.

Within moments, the ground was littered with the black ravens. The white ravens, their feathers stained with red, gathered into a group. They rose in unison and flew at the hospital window, shattering the glass that broke into little glints among the dead ravens strewn on the ground. The parking lot lights flickered on and off, graying as their streamers of light followed the Darklings.

As the Darklings entered the room, they rose to the ceiling. Then they began to merge within one another, forming into a plasma cloud that began to solidify and descend to the floor. The shifting black mist exposed physical parts that melted within themselves and began to divide into dark spider web like threads. These threads merged into a wet plastic gloss, which then changed to a texture of flesh-like material, its dark color began fading into a tanned skin hue. The shape of a head and shoulders, waist, and legs, began forming into human shape, rising in height. Globs of the material began to lengthen and divide into arms, hands, and fingers; and toes began to develop from the feet. Facial features began to take shape. Long strands grew from the head and began to form into hair.

Moments later the transformation from Darklings to human was complete. Mansi remained still for a long moment with her eyes closed, giving her body time to orientate itself, get the feel of the gravity, give her muscles time to regain their functions and be able to breath, feel air drawn into her nostrils, spreading into her lungs. She opened her eyes, surveyed the room, and moved across to stand in front of the mirror on the bathroom door. She raised her hands and gingerly touched her cheeks with her fingertips, then stroked the hair that fell to her waist. She opened and closed her hands, assuring herself that everything was in order. Then she turned slowly in front of mirror, eyes roaming over her twenty-three year-old body that was actually almost one hundred and sixty-three. She was nude and she allowed her eyes to linger on perfectly shaped breasts and curvaceous hips. Though her temporary body was made entirely from the Darklings, Mansi felt feline and slinky and on the prowl. The transformations always gave her a sense of renewal and healing, although at times leaving her feeling somehow fragmented. After past events such as this, she had suffered nightmares of walking down a street and having various body parts drop off onto the ground, reforming into leathered wings and talons and sending passersby into an attack of panicked screams.

The tile floor was chilly to her bare feet as she turned and looked at the young man lying in the bed. Half of his face was wrapped in white gauze, as was the rest of his body. Both arms were in slings and his left leg was elevated. The monitor by the bed issued a steady beat with a running line of his heartbeat and breathing.

She had watched him for many hours through the eyes of the Darklings or by using mind-meld with a raven prior to the accident on the mountain. His hopes, his dreams, his fears; she knew them all. He was a close friend with the One in which the Malbolians were interested. As she stood over him, intuition told her that this young man named Freddie would also play a huge role in the future.

Several weeks earlier, Mansi had been awakened by a voice in a dream. *"The Ravens are coming."* The earth magic was stirring. She could smell it in the wind; hear it in the distant thunder; in the constant running of stream water where she lived at the Dark Tree. Since she was six years old, she had been in communication with the other side, but now it seemed there was a sense of urgency.

In the beginning, she had thought the dark creature and the white raven that came to visit her at night were the ones who spoke to her through telepathy. Then she eventually began to realize it wasn't the bird or the strange creature that drew light into itself, for they were

273

mere carriers, like living radios or SKYPE without the video. The "voice" told her it was a man who lived far away in a world much like her own. He told her to do things, things she hurried to accomplish as she sought his favor and he never left her. Through the telepathy, he taught her how to create magic with the ravens, the Darklings, and the tree. He taught her a religion of Dark and Light, and taught her the ritual of Descension after she had dedicated her soul to the Dark Light.

He was a great Emperor and King — Shabael was his name — her Dark Guardian Angel. She dreamed of the day when a passageway would be made available so that she might cross over and be with him. He had given her the title as Queen Highest of Earth. If she was Queen, then he was her King. She kept her body pure and virginal, her thoughts only of him. As a healthy young woman, she had desires. However, she feared that if she gave her body to another, she would be deprived of the magic. Many nights she lay in her bed and pleasured herself to fantasies that she created of him. She visualized his eyes, his strong jaw and passionate kisses, and the ecstasy swelled within her.

Mansi moved to the foot of Freddie's bed and placed her hands on the cool metal frame. She knew the importance of her mission, knew the black ravens were reaching out to him, trying to protect him. However, their power was not great enough to shield him. This was her most urgent mission and she would not fail. It was a matter of life and death for millions and most important to King Shabael that this tree be found. Although she was not sure yet as to exactly what role she was to play, it was obvious that Freddie and his friend Dylan were important factors in finding the tree's location. Had not one of the ravens brought a branch from the Tree of Light to Dylan? Were they attempting to have him locate the Tree of Light? Why? What role could a teenage boy play in this struggle of possessing the Light?

I will find out.

Through her conversations with her Dark Angel, Mansi had come to realize she had abilities in Dark Magic that none before her had possessed. With these abilities, her gifts and powers were great enough that men would sell their souls to achieve them. Now, with this accident, Freddie had been literally delivered to her on a chromed stretcher. These events, with causes and effects happening as through some divine intervention, created paths for those less suspecting to follow, like pieces of driftwood carried down a stream to a desired location. Yes, there were forces at play, a battle of Light and Dark that would affect not only this world but also others. The Dark and Light forces were like chess players and the events were like the board pieces, each seeking to destroy the other, sometimes making moves to force the other into a desired move. It was happening all around her.

Freddie. Freddie … I know you can hear me. I am Mansi. I come bearing gifts, my love. Gifts of love and happiness. You are hurt and lost and I have found you. I will heal you. I will love you, Freddie. See me through your mind's eye. I am your beautiful angel, Freddie, and I have come to save you.

Mansi stared at the broken figure in the hospital bed and knew this was the epitome of loneliness and sense of low self-esteem that a teen-aged boy could attain. Freddie, even before the accident, had been a pathetic figure in her view. She dreamed of a muscular man with long hair and burning eyes. Freddie was a slumping, thick-eyeglasses, skinny, pimple-faced kid who looked one hundred percent the computer nerd. Although he was a mechanical wizard, one had to question how he could hold a wrench without falling over. True, he wielded a special kind of magic. She had been watching him since he was a first-grader playing with tinker toys and Legos. Unscrewing things, dismantling clocks, lamps, stereos, PCs, motors and cars. There was a reason he was in Dylan's life, of course, and that was why she had been assigned to watch him. Now she was so close to learning how he was to be used in finding the Light.

Mansi had studied everything about Freddie and knew his life story as well as her own. He loved western movies, especially the old black and white ones that played on the Turner Classic Movie Channel. That was a time when technology was just beginning to walk on its own legs and a man had to figure things out; a time before electricity had been discovered and steam power was vogue.

Freddie had been too young to feel the full impact when his mother had abandoned him for the driver of the semi. But it still contributed to his nerd-like existence. Women leaving their husbands was a common occurrence, but a majority of them took the kids when they went. His mother had left him behind, just another piece of dirty laundry for someone else to pick up. When he was old enough to wonder about it, Freddie just added another piece of luggage to his burdened life, reasoning that she had simply not wanted him.

There had never been much hope of another woman coming into the Sanders home. Mike Sanders had felt much the way Freddie did when his wife took off with the trucker. His first reaction was to inhale. Inhale the whole damn rotisserie chicken, eat the whole damn box of black walnut ice cream, and finish it off with a six-pack of pint-sized Falstaff. Then he ordered two large meat-lover's pizzas for him and the boy and ate them while flipping between commercials of four baseball games and finishing off the night with a pay-for-view flick titled "Bad Blonde Blows Buffalo".

Mike Sanders was just a lonely and depressed good ol' boy who thought his life was solid with his own garage, a wife he loved, and a little boy he adored. The desertion by his wife left him depressed for weeks, but he slowly pulled himself out of the dumps and began rebuilding his life. Little Freddie found the same solace by working with his dad after school. Father and son reveled in cogs and crankshafts. Happiness was a purring engine.

Freddie had never experienced the attention of a woman, especially not a beautiful woman such as Mansi, and she was intrigued by the possibilities. If by a miracle he should survive, and there was no certainty in that as his body was virtually destroyed, he would be wracked with pain and wheelchair bound. He would virtually be a vegetable in human form. However, with his connections to the Chosen One, Freddie could be her spy. If her theory was right, she would have something to offer him that no logical man in his situation could refuse. The love and desire of a beautiful temptress who could promise and deliver anything he desired. Mansi licked a speck of dried raven blood off her forefinger, drew a deep breath, spread her legs, wiggled her toes on the tile floor, and began the seduction of Freddie's soul.

Freddie.
Freddie.
I come to you.
Freddie.
I see you standing alone in the field. Do you see me? Open your eyes. Yes...
Hello, Freddie. I am your dream. I am with you in this field of wheat.
Reach out and touch me, Freddie. Feel that I am real. Yes, let your fingertips touch my face. Do you feel me, Freddie? Am I not real?

I see you looking at me. I know you can hear me. You are hurt, shocked, and withdrawn from the world that is filled with pain and hurt and ugliness, but I am real.

Oh, Freddie, I am your love. I have been with you all your life as your guardian angel. I am your true love. Do you find me beautiful? I see in your eyes that you do and all that you see is yours.

I know you are so hurt and broken. I know you will never walk again. Half of your face is destroyed; your arms and legs have multiple breaks. Even your kneecaps are missing. You mind is injured, too, Freddie. You may not be able to think as you once did or put things together.

But you need have no fear, my love. I am your angel. I can give you life again. The doctors will place you on life support and your father will be asked to donate your organs. He will have to say yes, and you'll die Freddie, die in a place without dreams or me.

But I will show you how I love you, Freddie. I will give you immortality and you will have me as your lover. We can make love, and you can be the man you are supposed to be.

I can take you to another world where you will be a genius. It is a world without electricity and light. The genius that's in you, the inventions you will create, will have you to be known as the greatest mind of our world. You will be as strong as a warrior and you will make love to me.

So close your eyes now. Soon you will be at the crossroads, my love. The choice is yours. You can awaken with powers you never dreamed of attaining … and you shall have me, Freddie. All you have to do is say yes. Let me hear you say yes, and it shall be done and we will be together forever.

You will be able to run again, my love. Run through the fields. Feel the wind against your face. And when you look at me Freddie, you will find love in my eyes for you, lips that you can kiss, and a body desiring your love.

I love you, Freddie. Say yes with a simple kiss.

Yes. That's it. Yes.

The door to the ICU unit abruptly opened. The nurse was looking down at her chart when she entered, checking on the dosage she was to inject in Freddie Sanders' IV. Without warning everything went dark. She heard clacking. Just as quickly as she was able to look up from the chart, the light was returning.

The nurse dropped the chart and screamed. For a moment, she almost thought she had seen a woman explode like a burst bag of black cotton balls with leathered wings and then escape through the window. The silent scream died in her throat as suddenly as it had started. She clutched a hand to her throat and watched a single curl of black smoke hanging in the air for a moment longer until dispersing.

Then the impossible happened. The unconscious patient, swathed in bandages from head to toe, sat upright in the bed, raised a multiple-fractured arm, and pointed in the direction of the nurse. "I love you, too," he said, then collapsed.

The nurse was no longer a logical thinking, calm veteran with ten years of ICU experience, but was reduced to the animal emotion of survival instinct. She bolted from the ICU, screaming, breaking the sound level record of the unit that had received its first patient fifteen years earlier. She threw the exit stairway door open and lost her footing, bang-bang-banging down the twenty-five steps on her back and finally crashing onto the landing, her left leg crumpled underneath her bruised body.

The first responder to reach the nurse was a co-worker in the unit. The nurse grabbed the responder's jacket, and babbled, "Bird girl go boom! He loves me?" Then she screamed again.

CHAPTER 30

THE SECRET REMAINS SECRET

Dylan hit the print button, watched the sheet of paper roll out of the printer, and placed the photo of the 1986 Chevy truck on the stack beside his computer. The grill was wrong. Okay, so he would begin checking out the older model Ford pickups.

"I'm getting nowhere," he said to himself, kicking his rolling desk chair against the side of the bed. "This is nuts." He was restless and worried and the bizarre scene on the mountain road kept playing repeatedly in his mind's eye. The prized Indian motorcycle sailing over the embankment and the pale green truck roaring behind him; the roaring pickup engine, the blurred image of the grill and bumper that he couldn't quite get in focus; three jerks wearing pillow cases over their heads with eyeholes cut in them; plaid shirts and jeans. Yeah that narrowed it down to just about every guy in the county. Pale green was an unusual color for a pickup, though. Obviously a repaint. A lot of power under the hood, though, because it sure had hauled ass leaving the scene. That had to be a custom motor in that chassis. A truck that old had to have someone servicing it pretty often. Maybe check some of the local mechanics, but that wouldn't be easy either. All these good ol' boys had a block and tackle hanging from a backyard tree. Or maybe even a front yard tree. Maybe Mike Sanders would know something. Yeah, Freddie's dad was probably sitting at home alone downing a few beers and feeling the hurt of his son. Or, more likely, he was at the hospital hoping for an encouraging word from the doctors.

Dylan turned his computer off and went downstairs to find his mother sewing a button on one of Robert's shirts. "Mom, we're alone?"

"Yes. Spencer and Robbie decided to go into the office for awhile." Sally raised her eyes and peered over the reading glasses. "Are you okay? Are you hurting anywhere?"

"No., I'm fine. I'm just worried about Freddie and wishing I knew who owned that truck." He zipped up his jacket.

"You're not going out are you? It's ten o'clock, son."

"Yeah, I know. But I'm too worked up to sleep. I was thinking of taking my bike out for a ride around the block and try to clear my head,"

"Well, when you get back, I'll give you a couple of Bufferin. They'll help you relax. Don't be too long, your dad will be home soon."

"It's all right, Mom. I'm not afraid to face him. What's he going to do, yell some more? I'm doing nothing but riding around the block. I'll be fine."

"Okay. I'll wait on you. And be careful, we've had enough excitement for one birthday."

Dylan turned and looked at his mother

"Is something wrong?" she peered over her glasses again.

"You aren't going to tell me?" Dylan asked.

"Tell you what?"

"Mom, last night you said you had something to tell me but I had to wait until tomorrow. Well, today is tomorrow."

She looked at him questionably, took the glasses off her nose, and folded the arms like an ironed Sunday school dress. "I'm sorry, dear. I don't remember."

"Huh? Come on, Mom? Really? Last night you said you had waited eighteen years to tell me. And now all of a sudden you can't remember what it was. Mom? What is it?"

"I don't know," she said, her voice a low mumble.

Dylan had seen this look a hundred times when his father was threatening to hit her for some reason. It was a kind of "Sorry I deceived you" look, or "Are you gonna hit me now?" She seemed to shrink within herself.

Dylan sat down on footrest of her chair and placed a hand on her arm. "Mom, is something going on I don't know about? Has Dad threatened or hurt you?"

Sally raised her head and he saw the tears in her eyes. The upper parts of her nostrils were coloring, lifting and falling because she was breathing quicker, not in panic mode yet but in the vicinity. She reached out to push his hair back from his forehead and he could feel her trembling.

"I'm so sorry that I've put you in this ... this horrible situation," she said and tears began flowing down her cheeks.

"Mom, what? What are you talking about?"

"I know he hates you, and he's made Robbie hate you, too. If only I had been strong enough, had the courage that a mother who loves her child should have, I would have stood up to him. I should have been able to keep him from hating you."

"Come on, Mom. I know Dad doesn't love me the way he does Robbie, but I'm used to that. I can live with it. He's the sheriff and the people in this county think he's some kind of god. They don't see the same person that we do. No one can blame you for being scared. I sure don't."

"Yes, but there's so much more that you aren't aware of, Dylan. I've never told anyone. It's just ... every time it's your birthday it really hits home. It tears me up inside and makes me think how horrible and guilty I am ... not just for the abuse you've taken over the years, but because I've done nothing about it."

"But, that's okay, Mom. I don't feel that I'm damaged. Hey, we're still breathing." Dylan smiled, trying to soften the mood.

Sally seized her son's shoulder and her eyes seemed to be piercing through his and directly into his brain. "Son, listen to me! You do not know what this man is capable of."

"Mom, what are you talking about?"

"I can't tell you. I can't. I've already said too much. Listen! Don't you confront him with any of this. I can't bear the thought of something happening to you. I can't chance that!"

"You can't chance what, Sally?" Sheriff Morgan asked. He was standing in the doorway. "Just what the hell are you talking about?"

"I ... I ..." Sally stammered, an immediate give away she had just been busted and didn't have an alibi.

"What have you told him?" Morgan asked. His hands dropped to his sides and curled into huge fists.

Dylan rose to his feet and stepped between his mother and father. "Dad …"

"No. I want to hear this. What has my loyal and devoted wife been telling you, Dylan? Get out of my way, boy!"

Robert stepped through the doorway, a malicious grin on his face. He was carrying a nightstick and slapped it against the palm of his hand.

Dylan was too angry to hold anything back. He was eighteen years old today, a man in many ways, and he wasn't about to listen to abuse being heaped upon his mother. "All she said was that she was sorry for all the years you've treated me like crap and I think she was going to tell me about a college loan she could get for me," he said, his eyes locked on his father's in an effort to make his words ring true. He knew the sheriff was expert in reading telltale signs of suspects being questioned.

"What school? What loan?" Morgan needled. He settled back on his heels and some of the anger seemed to drain from him. Robert sensed the mood change and silently replaced the nightstick in its holster. There was a look of disappointment on his face.

"UNC-Chapel Hill," Dylan said in a low voice.

"Chapel Fucking Hill? Jesus H Christ! And you're going to get a loan? Well, I'm pretty damn sure you couldn't get a scholarship. But how the hell did you get accepted in Chapel Hill?"

"I wanna know what for?" Robert chirped in.

"Know for what, you idiot! Shut up!" Morgan snapped, suddenly rising onto his toes in order to obtain that "I'm superior to you" stance, the God to the common people look that he used in any confrontation. "Damn it, what was I … Oh, yeah, what makes you think you can get in UNC? They start a School for Morons?"

"Stop it! I can't stand this!" Sally screamed and began stamping her feet, Robbie's shirt falling to the floor and the table lamp toppling.

Robbie moved quickly and caught the lamp in mid-air.

Sally dashed around her irate husband to the doorway, stopped, whirled around, and screamed. She ran down the hallway and knocked off the wall a large picture of Morgan that had been taken during his inaugural swearing in as sheriff. The glass shattered across the floor.

"Jesus, is everyone here insane?!" The sheriff roared, his face red with rage, the scar on his face converting into a 2.

"Like coo-coo for Cocoa Pops." Robert said, recoiling in case of an exasperated round house.

"Well, this has been fun," Dylan said sarcastically. "I'm going out for awhile, just a ride around the block. Please don't sit up for me."

"Why don't you do us all a favor and go for a blindfold ride on the interstate?" his father said.

"Good one, Dad," Robert aped.

Dylan walked out and purposely left the front door open. He hopped on his Schwinn, thinking wishfully that it had been the only bike he had ridden that day

CHAPTER 31

APPEARANCES ARE DECEIVING

"Aribon, you still here?" Eradrin asked.

"Yes. I'm here. I only closed my eyes while you repeated the story of your crowning. I relived it through your words. It was as clear as if it were yesterday. I remember the guards rushing up, one of them striking my father on the back of the head. That was the most exciting day of my life and I've always wondered what you were thinking that day. Thank you for sharing this with me."

"Sometimes it's good to remember even the bad things. It renews my passions. Tell me Aribon, are you afraid of death?"

"No. When you are mortal and get to my age, living takes quite an effort. It's like having been awake for two days straight and you get a strong yearning just to ..."

"Lay your head against a tree and close your eyes?"

"Yes, that's the feeling." Aribon reached over and patted Eradrin's hand. "This feels right, Uncle. Although I must admit I have never grown accustomed to looking a hundred and fifty-six with you in your thirties." He gave a little chuckle that ended in a wheeze. "Look at us. I should be the uncle and you the nephew."

"The appearance doesn't matter. In my mind's eye, you'll always be my little nephew. It's true that Ascenders don't age physically, but the emotions of our hearts do. Appearances are deceiving. Feelings are real."

"It's nice being here with you, Uncle. I am so tired; so weary."

284

"I love you, Aribon. You have been my close friend for many decades and I will sorely miss you."

"Will you watch over my wife, Uncle? I know she'll have our sons and daughters and their children to care for her, but my greatest sadness is leaving her husbandless." Aribon's body was wracked by a chest-rattling cough.

"Ease your mind, Nephew. If ever any of your bloodline needs aid or assistance in anyway, I will be there."

Aribon sighed and rested his head on King Eradrin's shoulder. "I guess I'll never see a day of light, my King. You know, that has always been my dream." He placed his hand over Eradrin's hand. "When I pass, take my father's ring and give to my son, Nathan."

"I will." Eradrin said, his voice low and sad.

"No need for sadness. I know where I'm going and I can already see it in my mind's eye. There is daylight there. Ah, but to see Lake Waccamola in the daylight. I've been told that the surface glimmers like diamonds. I look out over the lake now and I see a boat bearing our fathers. Look, they see me now and are waving to us." A long silence grew between them and Aribon's breathing slowed. "Tell me about my father and the funeral," Aribon said dreamily.

"After the crowning I had never seen your father so passionate," Eradrin began "We were in my chambers …"

CHAPTER 32

AFTER THE CROWNING

"Just think! Two more inches and you would have killed him! Two more inches and that pig would have been butchered." Thomar was pacing back and forth. "You were so close to killing him. Well, if nothing else he'll bear the scar for the rest of his life."

"Had I come close to that," Eradrin said, "a healer would have saved him, or most likely he would have cast the wound back into me. Remember, his sword was forged by fire within the vibrational sphere of the Dark Tree. To kill Shabael would take an instant death strike. Only weapons of Light Tree vibration can create a non-healing wound."

"Maybe you should have swung for his head and decapitated him."

"Good point. Wish that I had. I was proud of Mother tonight. Weren't you? She stood up to the Queen Highest in subtle ways, and some that were not too subtle. The looks they gave each other were the purest hellfire of hatred."

"Mother best beware not to tangle with the Red Dragon, though," Thomar said. "That woman is a she-bitch. I know that one day she shall have her reckoning. Oh, how I wish it could be by my blade!"

"Not so loud, Brother. These walls have ears. In addition, beware of the shadows. Chances are a shadow is a Darkling. There is no place that we can call a sanctuary while the Malbolians remain here."

Eradrin gripped Thomar by the elbow and they moved to the railing of the balcony. The wind was swirling at this height, but it would make their conversation less likely to be overheard.

"Before I was crowned, you said we could fight back in small ways," Eradrin said, his voice low and conspiratorial "We know that if we continue to live under this darkness, we are doomed. If the Creator fates me King, it is my obligation to see the Ravenites live under Light once again. When we bleed, do we not leak blood and Light?"

Eradrin pulled Thomar closer and whispered in his ear. "I had a vision when I was crowned. A raven brought the Light and our father spoke to me. He said three would come on raven wings and for us not to give up our faith. He promised we will have the Light again."

"What do you mean? Father spoke to you? Is this real or a dream?"

"I wasn't dreaming. I was awake and had but closed my eyes as the crown was placed on my head when it happened. I believe this to be true."

Thomar gripped Eradrin's forearm. "This is great news. It will inspire our people. We spoke of small raids on the Malbolians and I was thinking that if we made swift and decisive strikes — quick in and out — they would be kept on edge. At least it would be something to show that our people are not the docile dogs they seem to think we are. And, perhaps if we left evidence that suggested we came from the White Sands, they would not even suspect us. They think we are a crushed and desolate people right now."

"You mean make it look like raids by Nomadic tribes?"

"Yes, why not? Several years ago, a Malbolian unit ran across a wandering tribe of them. They encountered each other at a watering hole and the Malbolians killed the desert hunters and took their supplies but left the horses."

"Yes, I remember that incident. The horses were small but fast and they were well cared for. I remember them well when they wandered through our kingdom. We were amazed that the riders milked the mares when water was scarce."

"Aye, I remember we dared each other to take a sip. You threw up, and I joined you moments later."

"I do recall that, rather vividly."

"Well, you know that we still have some of those horses. I have cared for them, and the young ones are purebreds. We have at least twenty that we can use during the raids. Yes, we dress as Nomads and ride those horses; and, the Malbolians will think it's a revenge strike."

"Are you forgetting there are guards at our gates who will become very interested in your party?" Eradrin asked.

"Not if we do this right now, during the funerals. Is it not customary to cover the horses?"

"It is."

"There you go, my King. I'll have the horses pull wagons with flowers and go out the northeast gate. We'll tell the sentinels we are laying flowers on the Mount of the Tree of Life. Instead, we take the secret passage tunneled through the mountain that comes out on a level with Lake Waccamola. Then we'll ride up the shore and keep going until we reach the River of Great Divide. There, we will ambush them, then cross back over the river. We'll double back at nightfall and re-enter the northeast gate seeming to have returned from the ceremonies."

"It sounds like a workable idea," Eradrin said, "but there are Darkling eyes throughout the kingdom. They will see you. Maybe you could create a campsite away from Skye Castle."

"Yes. That could work. Then, after each attack we'll leave a trail crossing the river, but double back."

"Do you still have some of the nomads' weapons?" Eradrin asked.

"I do. There are at least a dozen blades of varying designs hidden in my home," Thomar said.

"Why am I not surprised by that," Eradrin said, grinning widely.

"I'll need men because I can't use any of the Raven Knights, only some of our staunchest citizens. Good men should not be hard to find because the blood is boiling within us all after the treatment by the Malbolians. We need at least a dozen swordsmen who share our hatred for them."

"Very well. Select your men and warn them that this is of utmost secrecy. Not even wives may be told of the mission. The El Qui must never be able to link these attacks to us, do you understand?"

"I do, my King. But I must tell you, I've not felt this excited for something since a sun rose over our land."

"I understand, my brother. I, too, hear the songs of freedom in the treetops and in the cries of the ravens." Eradrin lifted his head to feel the wind moving across the terrace against his face. The people below were scurrying through the streets in preparation for funeral ceremonies that would soon commence.

"Three shall come on raven wings," Thomar mused. "Three? Three what? Three Lights? What else did he say?"

"That was it, and for us to keep the faith. I miss our father, although without him I feel there's been a weight removed from our hearts now that we can proceed with a plan of action."

"Aye. I feel that, too. I'm burning for vengeance, Eradrin. I will start gathering my men now. As soon as we're together, we'll proceed."

"What's your immediate action?" Eradrin asked.

"I'll attend father's service then slip away. I wish you were riding with me, Brother. We'd be fighting side by side."

"That I would love," Eradrin said. "But we both know that I must remain here."

"It is our time now, Brother. What we begin today, we must never give up," Thomar said.

"We keep the faith till the ring of fire and coming of the three on raven wings," Eradrin said. "Be safe my brother. Come home soon as possible. You'll need to assume your role as Viceroy."

"Yes, my King. Brothers of War!" Thomar stopped at the doorway to the chambers and embraced Eradrin. "Promise me one thing."

"What could that be?"

"If something should happen to me, would you watch over Aribon as though he were your son?"

"You don't have to ask. Yes. I will be honored. You know that what we do from this moment forward will be the cause and effect that will not only affect the kingdoms, but the spiritual realm of the Light and Dark. We lose ourselves in the petty egocentric immediate circles of our little worlds and forget the war between the Light and Dark. All that exists will break if there is not a balance. Remember, our mortal lives are here, but an eternity awaits where there may exist a larger battle."

Thomar embraced Eradrin a second time and then walked away wordlessly. All that was needed to be said had been spoken.

Eradrin looked over the balcony to his people. Outside the gate, by the bridge of Lake Waccamola, where the lowering platforms placed boats on the landing upon the lake's shore was where the ceremony would be held. He could not see the landing from his point of view, but could see across the lake to the other shore.

What he did not see was the shadowy object on the other side of the balcony railing descend the wall.

Giving the railing a double tap with his hand, he entered his chambers and saw his personal staff dashing about, amassing his formal armor and deep purple robe.

"Alfie, is the Queen preparing?"

"Yes, my Prince. Oh … I'm sorry, please forgive," she bowed profusely. "My King, she will be joining you shortly."

CHAPTER 33

QUICK STOP AT THE QUICK STOP

Dylan hopped on his Schwinn and peddled down the street, headed for Freddie's house. If Mr. Sanders was home, he most certainly wouldn't be in bed yet. Not with everything that had to be going through his mind. After a few hundred yards, he stopped pedaling and coasted to a stop. *Something isn't right.* That seemed to be a familiar feeling of late. So many times he had sensed some presence, something looking at him with malice. As a kid, there had been the closet and under-the-bed fears, but this was different. More ominous. Still, he wasn't a toddler anymore. He was a man and he would handle those sudden feelings of fear with rationale.

Still, it was eerie. In recent weeks, for example, he would be deep into studying when he suddenly became aware that something was looking at him. First, of course, his reaction was to check for a sneak attack by the devious Robbie That dimwit was always coming up behind him, always looking for some way to get under his skin. But these feelings hadn't been caused by the bad brother. The door would be closed and he'd turn back around to find a branch moving ... or something else ... like shadows shifting at places where there should be no shadows. Still, he could hear Robert, *"Ha, afraid of your own shadow, Dipshit?"*

Several times at night recently he would sit up and swear something was staring at him through the window pane. He could even envision a pair of red eyes glowing in the dark. And again he rationalized it by reasoning that it was probably Robbie pulling another prank with the lasers he loved to use as an annoyance. It had been only a few weeks ago that Robbie purchased — or shoplifted — a couple of laser lights at a nearby Family Dollar Store. On that night, while doing his homework, Dylan heard a dispatch on the radio he always kept turned on that someone was red dotting people going to the teller machine at the Bank of America. One guy, a veteran recently returned from a third tour in the Middle East had been targeted and when the red dots appeared on his chest, he dove to the ground, belly-crawled to his car, retrieved his assault rifle, and called 911. There was no doubt in Dylan's mind who had pointed the beams. Big little brother.

But now, here on a lighted street only a few hundred yards from his home, he was experiencing the feeling again. *Jesus, I'm a man. I'm not afraid of the night.* He shrugged, looked around, saw nothing, and resumed pedaling. *There it is again!* He hit the brakes and turned to look to his left toward a long stretch of woods. *Could have just been a dog.* He listened carefully for snapping twigs. But all he heard was the wind rustling the fallen leaves. He suddenly thought of his dream of flying and when out of nowhere he had been attacked by some dark thing and a white raven. He raised his eyes and peered up into the branches of the nearby trees

The moon was almost full. Huge fat clouds moved quickly to the pace of a strong wind high above. Autumn was beginning to settle in and some of the trees were losing their leaves. There were still a few clinging to the branches, though, and there was a lot of mistletoe among them. He thought of the last autumn when he had shinnied up a tree and gathered some of the parasite plant for his mother. Always the entrepreneur, she had tied a ribbon around each of the pieces and sold them at her shop. Maybe he would do that again. One of the trees — it looked like a red maple — still had most of its leaves. It was funny how moonlight turned the red almost black. *Wait a minute. What was that?* Rays of moonlight danced along the trees, illuminating snatches of branches and trunks and moving them from light to shadow. He followed a patch of moonlight moving through the trees like a ghost until it reached the red maple. It disappeared momentarily only to emerge on the other side. When he returned his gaze to the tree, something was different. *Wasn't that top branch on the right filled with leaves a moment ago?* He was pretty sure it had been because the limb made this nice upward arch like an S leaning backward. Suddenly the streetlight behind him began to flicker. *Jeez!* What a haunting night this was with the moving clouds, the rattling of leaves, the little electric hum coming from the power lines overhead.

Okay, so this scene would make a cool photo or maybe inspire a painting someday. He pulled his Droid phone from his front pocket, tapped the screen, and turned on the camera. He pointed the phone toward the tree and snapped a photo, producing a blinding flash that revealed a thousand red eyes.

"Caw!" A raven's cry sounded from the direction of Dylan's home. The bird swooped down from the sky almost touching Dylan's head and emitting another *"Caw!"* as it passed. A sound almost like the roar of an ocean wave exploding from its crest engulfed Dylan.

Hundreds, maybe thousands, of bat-sized winged things spewed from the red maple, *clicking* and *clacking* like a rattler's tail times a thousand. Those sounds, Dylan was pretty sure, were the sound of teeth and claws; and, without even realizing he was doing it, he was suddenly pedaling furiously down the street.

"Caw!" The raven cried from ahead; and, not even thinking why, Dylan peddled in that direction with the swarm of dark things in hot pursuit. The clicking and clacking grew louder and more furious. The sounds were so loud that Dylan could not hear his own scream as he barreled down the street.

"Clunk. Thud. Splat. Scrrrreeeekkk," sounded around him; and, he realized the dark things were crashing into mailboxes and parked cars. The sounds of nails on metal made a screeching sound effect. From somewhere in his mind, he pictured Freddie having a climatic geek moment: *"Kewl, Dude! 3D sound effects!"*

Dylan suddenly realized that he was screaming, but with all the surrounding chaos, the screaming was like blowing a dog whistle at the top of your lungs. No matter how hard you blew, the sound could not be heard by humans.

"Caw! Caw! Caw!" The raven was at the street intersection to the right, seeming to be directing him to go that way. Then Dylan realized why. There was a Quick Stop that was well lit with several cars in the parking lot.

Something sharp snagged the shoulder of Dylan's jacket and then fell loose as the material tore

Ten yards to the store.

Thud! Clang! Splat! A car alarm began blaring. For the first time, Dylan dared to look over his shoulder and saw one by one the streetlights blinking out, smothered in this rolling, airborne mass of blackness. The "things" seemed to sense him looking at them. A black mass of wings and teeth and claws surged toward him, surrounding him.

The back tire of the speeding bike suddenly popped, sending it into a spin where it struck a curb. Dylan hit the ground and went rolling into the parking lot.

"Ahhhhhhhh!" Dylan yelled as the momentum sent him crashing into a young Afro-American woman carrying a bag of groceries. Two Almond Joy candy bars were the first to fall out of the bag, joined by a pack of M and M's and two pint bottles of Miller High Life. The bottles shattered, sending a spray of beer over 65-year-old Harold Robertson, who had innocently been filling the tank on his Ford Escape, and who twenty minutes later would end his eight years of sobriety.

"What the hell is wrong with you, white boy?" The girl pulled herself up and angrily aimed a bright red sneaker in Dylan's direction, barely missing. "What the fuck, man? What? What?!"

Dylan jumped to his feet and looked back at the street that he had so hastily exited. Empty. Quiet. No dark shadows. Streetlights glowing. Normalcy. A routine ten-thirty at night scene. Pastoral. Except for one bruised 18-year-old, a banged-up Schwinn with a flat tire, one very angry Afro-American girl, and a bewildered old man who was just trying to get home with a half-gallon of Edys butter pecan slow-churned ice cream.

"I'm sorry; I hit the curb," Dylan mumbled. "Let me pay for the beer."

"You damn right you gonna pay for the beer, sucker! You gonna pay for my hose. You gonna pay for my nails. You scuffed up my new Nikes. You ruined my hair. My blouse is ripped. Oh, you paying, white boy. That's at least a hundred bucks, not counting the emotional damage."

"You seen it, Mister," she tuned to the still speechless Mr. Robertson. "You a witness?"

"Me?" Harold wiped the beer off his pants and sniffed his fingers. His eyes rolled and then refocused. "I don't think it was intentional, miss."

"Intentional? What does that mean? The sucker knocked me down, stomped on me, and ruined what was going to be a big night for me and Jerome. Yeah, you just wait here, white boy. I'll send Jerome over here to collect!"

Dylan was trying to regain his senses from the horror he had faced moments earlier. Now he wasn't sure that this wasn't an even more threatening dilemma. The woman was frenetic, doing this left, right bobbing movement with her neck as though with each word she spoke she was dodging a punch. "I could be dead right now," she howled. "I could have hit my head on this parking lot and I could be *dead!*"

The movement reminded Dylan of a chicken. Plus he sensed she wasn't going to end her cackling until some kind of settlement had been reached. It didn't help matters that a gawking circle of customers had gathered to see what the fuss was about.

"Here, ma'am," Dylan handed her a card with his address and phone number printed on it. "Bill me, Lady. I'll pay what I can. I'm really sorry that this happened."

"Don't ma'am me, white boy! You damn right you sorry. Smoking weed. Yeah, folks, smell that? Smoking him some Mary Jane. Yeah, you one of them crazies that dream of shooting kids in high school, ain't ya? All you white boys do. Yeah, you be sorry, all right! Give me a ten right now, so I get me some more Miller. Honkie! Cracker! Probably a gay honkie cracker, too."

Dylan fished a ten-dollar bill from his wallet and gave it to her. She hitched her skirt, pulled at her hose and stomped back into the store.

"Woman like that could drive you to drink," Harold Robertson said, adjusting his red baseball cap that read "Don't Forget My Senior Discount" on the front. He sniffed the beer on his fingers again, then slowly raised a hand and licked at the finger. He placed the gas nozzle back in the gas pump and walked into the store, heading straight for the beer cooler. Eight years. Shot in one crazy night at the Quick Stop.

Outside, Dylan scanned the deserted street. No traffic. No dark things. No blazing red eyes. No clicking and clacking. No 18-year-old "manboy" about to wet his jeans. There were some signs that something had happened here, though. Several mailboxes were teetering to the side as though some teenagers had ridden past and whopped them with a baseball bat. A few trashcans were turned over. A stray cat was already rummaging through one of them.

Dylan reached over his shoulder and felt the tear in his jacket. That was real. He examined the flat rear tire of his bike and found a half-inch needle-like thing protruding. *Jesus! Is that a tooth?*

It was only a short distance to Freddie's house, so Dylan decided to complete the mission he had begun. He rolled the crippled bike along the pavement, periodically peeking back to make sure the crazy woman from the Quick Stop wasn't coming after him. *Jesus! A gay honkie cracker! Wait until I tell Freddie about this.*

CHAPTER 34

SHABAEL TO EARTH WITCH

The parking lot lights flickered and streams of wavering-ghostlike light drifted toward the center of the huge oak tree. The white raven Masora alit on a branch a foot above where Mansi was crouched. Darklings nestled around the trunk of the tree. Settling in and giving its wings a final shake, Masora bobbed its head then turned to one side so that its right eye was facing her. Mansi knew that when Shabael was within the consciousness of the Masora, he would always turn to the side.

Mansi's heart raced with so much anticipation that she had to consciously control her breathing. On most occasions when Shabael spoke to her through Masora the voice was barely audible in her head. She had learned that she had better perception of the words if she kept her eyes closed while he was speaking. Their talks could last several minutes at a time before the telepathic connection began to fade. Minutes, sometimes an hour later, the conversation could be resumed. To detect messages one had to be silent within and without conscious thought . It always sexually aroused her knowing that the Emperor was with her alone.

"My Emperor, may I speak with you?" Mansi asked.

"Always," the white raven croaked. The word sounded harsh coming from the bird but it was sweet music to Mansi. Most of their communication was telepathy except for the occasional one-word response. Always ... always is a good word. *Oh, to win your heart, to*

somehow reach you through the stars. My heart, my soul, my love I give to you.
Mansi had a sudden surge of panic, praying that the thought had gone undetected through the telepathy.

Mansi opened her eyes and watched the raven for a moment as it seemed to be waiting for her to speak. If only she was in the presence of her king and able to see his face. "The friend of the Chosen One is in peril of losing his life," she said. "He remains unconscious, but I have contacted him through telepathy and felt his acceptance. He is injured to the extent that he will never walk again. My offer to heal him will be accepted, I think. I believe I can command the Darklings to integrate him and make him whole again as it was done with me. If so, he would belong to us. He would be the perfect spy to help us learn the location of the tree."

Why do you have the power to command this?

"I'm not sure, my King, but I've thought long and hard on this. I can only speculate, but I believe this power is limited to the Darklings and the ravens that entered the portal when Dayanna was taken from the tree. These beings perhaps share a vibrational state with humans."

How many of these portaled Darklings do you have left?

"By my count I believe there are enough for two integrations. I thought I would reserve the last for you, My Exalted One. You have said you are immortal to death from natural causes. However, if you are integrated you can form and disperse at your will. You can fly with your consciousness in one of the ravens. If you are ever mortally wounded, My King, if you have access to the Darklings or white ravens, you can be integrated and restored."

If I am integrated and then injured while in human form, will I heal when I split into the ravens and then return to human form?

"No, My Emperor, you will still bear the injury, but a healer can assume your injury and pass it on to another living thing. The Darklings are your backup."

Masora the raven suddenly reared back, then leaned forward, *When a wound is inflicted, how much time passes before the ravens come to integrate? What if you die before they reach you?*

Mansi smiled ruefully, "If you have a healer, or if I should be at your side you wouldn't need integrating. It would depend upon the distance you are from the Dark Tree where the Ravens will be roosting. Ah," her eyes lit up, "unless you commanded them to always

298

be near. I have not seen the ravens fly beyond sight of the Dark Tree, but when commanded they will obey me."

All that is well and good, but how would that help me when I am here and you are there?

"This is why I asked to speak to you, my King. The Lighted ones have a great interest in this Dylan person. The white branch that the black raven brought to him was an attempt to bring him to the White Tree, but he as of yet has no understanding of this. If we can mortally wound him, it is my belief, my Emperor, that his guardian raven will summon the ravens from the Tree of Light. Then I can have his raven followed back to the Tree of Light. Moreover, if you allow me to integrate this Dylan's friend, we will have a spy."

"I have developed a special relationship with the Darklings in my care; and, they will integrate him upon my request. In fact, it is being arranged as we speak. We are only awaiting word from you, my King. I have dispatched a Darkling to the Dark Tree to bring the others." Her nose suddenly twitched from a prickle of pain. "This is only a speculation, but I think when the Darklings and ravens entered the portal they shared a human vibration; and, that's why only those have the power to integrate."

This is intriguing, Shabael communicated telepathically thru his raven.

"Wait …" Mansi touched her nose to ease the pain. "I just realized something. You said the ravens consumed Dayanna before they flew into the portal. This means the ravens from your world already had this power. In addition, you say this had never happened before? Never even with your Darklings?"

No. That is interesting.

"So that raises the question — what caused them to do what they did? Maybe the Darklings never had that power until they went through the portal with the ravens. Sire, this means that the ravens where you are could have this ability."

Never in our history has this been observed by Malbolian or Ravenite. It seems there is this intensifying of things. Magic is growing; portals are appearing. Are these things accidental events?

"They are like pushings, my King. Events are pushing us to predestination."

But who? Or what? Shabael asked.

"This I do not know. Perhaps there are two forces at play, Milord, those of the Dark and of the Light. I am not sure at this time, but I do know that someone in the mountain tribe has a great interest in this Dylan. You said that you were about to destroy the Orb of Light when the ravens began circling and then a portal was created. I think they did this to save the orb. That portal opened to my side. I'm wondering if we created the same circumstances if a portal would be opened. If one did open, there is no guarantee that it will go to your world. It could be a void. It will be a risk of life because wherever the light goes we must follow. But who knows what wonders and other worlds could await us? Or, as is my greatest hope, if I am able to place the Orb of Light into your hands then we can meet at last?

"We know that a force of some nature draws Dylan to the Indian tribe. It was not by chance he visited. And, although they did not speak, he saw Raven." As Mansi spoke, she remembered how her heart had quickened when she realized Dylan had seen her from the window.

"We have to be cautious because there is a barrier we cannot cross sacred ground where the tribal ravens live. It is their safety zone but also serves as their prison. My Darklings are posted all around; and, they can detect when Light magic is used. The boy, Dylan, was contacted through a dream state last night. He merged with his raven to follow his escort to the tribe until we intercepted. We know why he's being drawn there."

"Yes," the voice from the raven croaked as the connection began to weaken. *I am very much aware of the interception. I have a new scar as evidence.*

A wave of dizziness suddenly swept over Mansi. She tightened her hand around a branch to steady herself. "We are fading, my King. I must go. If I can turn his friend into one of us, through him we can gain access and possibly learn of their plans and the location of the tree."

"One other thing: If we are unsuccessful in this, allow me to mortally wound Dylan, for I believe his guardian raven will seek the Tree of Light to save him and there the Orb of Light may be. I will possess it and do with it what you will. My hope is the ravens will feel the threat of our approach and will create a portal between our worlds."

Once she had spoken those telepathic words, she was physically exhausted and breathless. Mansi rested her head against the tree. The communication had sapped her of energy and strength. From past experience, she knew that going beyond a certain point would cause blood to gush from her nose and a headache so intense that it seemed to shatter her brain like glass, making her incapable even of thought.

What if we fail? What if this Dylan should die? Shabael asked with urgency in his communication.

"Ohhh," Mansi moaned. Every word she received was like a knife stab through skull and brain tissue. The pain was excruciating. "Don't fear. We'll learn what we need through his friend."

You realize what actions you take will have immeasurable effects on events of worlds? Yes, there are greater forces than our own that flow the streams of time drawing chaos to conflict. It is up to us to hack pathways for what course they run. If — no, not if — when the Orb of Light is in our possession, we will conceal its shine for eternity. You are invaluable to our cause, Mansi. Your ideas speak of great wisdom, reasoning, and truth. Turn the Chosen One's ally to our cause and we will seize the Orb of Light. Have intent of destruction blazed in your mind and perhaps a portal will be created. Mansi? There was no response. Shabael willed his white raven to Mansi's shoulder and it pecked at the hand that was covering her nose. Her eyes were open, filled with panic. The telepathic conversation had gone on for too long. She felt the pecking of Masora's beak and removed the hand from her nose. A spray of blood spurted, covering the raven's chest. Blackness consumed her.

"Caw!"

The bird's cry cut through her consciousness and Mansi tightened her grip on the branch that was slipping from her blood-wet fingers.

Down below there was movement in the hospital parking lot and a woman's laughter caught Mansi's attention. A couple who appeared to be in their sixties were walking arm in arm to their car. Mansi was hunched over, still in agony, placing her hand along her nose and forehead. With her mind's eye, she attempted to seize the ruptured veins, but the energy to summon the dark magic only ripped and burst more veins. It was as if trying to catch tiny dancing water hoses after their spigots had been fully opened. "Away!" she cried, sending a vision of a clenched fistful of ruined veins out of her body and into the man walking with the woman.

"Did you see her children? Weren't they a disgrace?" the wife was saying when her husband suddenly yanked his arm free of her and clamped his hands to his head. He muttered an unintelligible spew of words and died before his knees hit the pavement.

As his body dropped to the pavement, a quarter fell from his hand and began an eerie, teetering, roll. He had gotten the coin from a vending machine a short time earlier and proudly informed his wife that it was a North Carolina quarter. The wife — unaware that her husband was a dead man — fixated on the quarter. She watched it roll and then begin spinning on edge, finally coming to rest head's up. That's when the wife realized something was terribly wrong with her husband and began screaming for help.

Mansi clung to the trunk of the tree, unbelieving that she had not fallen. She knew that she had been close to death. She found herself implausibly thinking that telepathic injury must have been in the small print of the healing immortals of natural causes clause. Her breasts, arms, and strands of her hair were covered in blood. It reminded her of the first horror movie she had seen many years ago called "Carrie", where the girl gets covered in pigs' blood at her high school prom.

Mansi remained in the tree, still trying to recover from her brush with death, as hospital personnel removed the dead man's body from the parking lot. Some thirty minutes later, she had successfully healed herself through transference and was ready to resume her mission. She turned her eyes to Freddie's hospital window and waited for the Darklings.

The window was being replaced and no doubt, Freddie had been moved to another room, perhaps even one with a security guard posted at the door. Several guards were outside searching the grounds of the building for any evidence of what might have happened. One guard was even posted on the roof where she had been earlier. As Mansi watched the hospital, the nurse who had entered the room and left screaming down the hallway, exited the building and went to her car in the employees' parking lot. Obviously still unsettled, she was dabbing at her eyes with a tissue.

Mansi was still unsettled, too. She tried desperately to focus on what she had to do next, but her mind was still not quite sharp. *Kind of fuzzy around the edges.* Telepathy would have to be used with the boy and the Darklings. Therefore, she had to regain her resources before that could happen. The pain had been gone for almost an hour but the memory of it gave Mansi a feeling of dread. She had obviously burst a blood vessel in her head. That could have meant instant death if the circumstance had been different and there had not had a chance for transference of the injury. Even if she had a few moments to perform the healing, it would necessitate logical thought. Pain, such as she had experienced earlier, whitewashed any kind of involuntary commands. A great sadness and feeling of foreboding enveloped her.

For all of her life Mansi had felt that she been alone. From the moment Raven had appeared that night on the mountainside, everything had seemed to change for her. She was consumed in a constant state of jealously and envy which caused her to begin to hate everyone. When she saw someone receive affection or sympathy, she wanted to roll her eyes and spit. Her grandmother was a healer and although she was only a child, some of the village people came to her for the same. The difference was that when Mansi laid on the hands and chanted, it was not with prayers of healing but for spells of destruction. Eventually, the people learned that this child was not a healer but the bearer of pain and death; and, they avoided her.

Then the white raven had appeared. At first, it spoke to her through dreams and the bird could obviously read her mind. Gradually she began to understand that it was King Shabael using the bird as a transmitter. Then one night she realized that she was talking to Shabael while she was still awake. Acting on impulse, she made an opening under one edge of her hut and concealed it by placing a box against it. From that time onward, when the raven visited he would peck on the box, she would move it to reveal the opening, and the bird would crawl through and perch on top of the box. When she leaned over and propped up on her elbows, she was eye to eye with the bird.

Mansi had just turned eight when she was instructed in how to create the Dark Tree. When she was eighteen, she saw an opportunity of payback to the village she despised, which in return, despised her. She went about her mission without remorse or regret. At least she wouldn't have to see Raven and listen to that annoying soft voice always so filled with kindness. Her new family members were the Darklings and the white raven. The Darklings hunted food for her and at night the white raven filled her head with dreams. At first, the Darklings brought her rats and opossums left over from their foraging. However, eventually she taught them that her tastes ran more to rabbits and deer.

It was a quiet life as living things tended to shy away from the Dark Tree along with the things that lived in and under it. While the world developed around her, she remained ageless after being integrated with the Darklings on her eighteenth birthday. She lived with the Earth, not on it. Her years in the village had taught her everything she needed to survive. And if there was anything she lacked, she had only to make the Darklings aware of that need.

It was amazing to her that for thousands of years Indians lived on the land and there was hardly any evidence remaining of how sacred they had thought the Earth. In less than two hundred years, America had literally been paved, sectioned, and hot-wired. The land, once so pure, had become an animal den. Moreover, these disgusting human animals didn't have enough common sense to poop elsewhere and to take care of the Earth. Mansi, now evermore eighteen, remembered as a child when there were no roads. She could stand on the mountain and not see a house or a road. There were no streetlights to diminish the stars of the skies or pavement to numb the feel of the Earth. There were so many people now who had never touched the soil, never run barefoot or drank from a stream that once had been pure.

The thoughts saddened Mansi. If she should become mortally wounded, there was no one to heal her. There was no one to aid her in anything other than the Darklings.

As she rested, her thoughts strayed and she felt herself becoming sexually aroused. She was a healthy eighteen-year-old and her hormones were sometimes alarmingly active. She had never experienced sex, other than from self-gratification. However, she often watched television from her home beneath the tree roots and sometimes got caught up in the intimate scenes of passion. Still, she longed for only one man, King Shabael. She would wait for all eternity to share her passion with her king. Only one person really knew her and cared. Only one person had been with her since childhood. And only one person would ever make love to her.

Earlier, when she had stood naked at the foot of the young man's bed, she had willed her naked image into his mind. As she had spoken seductively, she had felt her own body reacting. Mansi wondered what it would be like to really have sexual relations. Now she sat in a tree, hanging on for dear life as her strength returned, and pondered her past and future.

She had learned many years ago that she could will people into doing things.

She first became aware of this talent while waiting in a checkout line at a Food Lion grocery store to purchase a bag of potatoes. A woman with a piled-high grocery cart and a snotty-nosed kid was behind her in the line. The kid was intent on a new game, trying to see how long he could stretch the string of snot from his nose with his fingers. The mother's back was turned as she was checking out the various chewing gums and antacid items aligning the counter. The kid was sitting in the foldout part of the cart, his legs dangling from the holes, his arm stretched out full-length with a long string of snot from each finger attached to his nose. He gave a toothless grin to Mansi and proudly showed his new Guinness Book of Records talent, offering her some if she wanted to try.

Mansi grimaced and her brow knotted as she gave the snotty kid a little telepathic push. The kid jerked upright, made an ugly hog-snorting sound as he snarked in mucus like shotgun plugs, and loaded his double-barreled nostrils. He turned halfway around in the cart, reached out, lifted his mother's loose hair from her neck, and let loose with a full double-nostril blast. The result was like shooting two baby jellyfish with slingshots as the glob struck the mother's neck. Tiny tentacles of snot dangled and seemed to wave like happy children after completing a daredevil stunt. *Hey! We're okay, you wanna try?* The mother sounded an inhuman cry of surprise, jumped forward, and whirled around as she instinctively put her hand to the back of her neck. She was mortified when she pulled her hand back and discovered long, gooey strings of snot that continued to stretch with the movement.

The baby slapped its hands on the metal tray and gurgled what might have been a laugh. The distraught mother ran past the cashier, leaving her son in the cart as she searched for a restroom.

Mansi smirked at the kid and with her index fingers extended, she shoved the cart to the side and paid for the bag of potatoes.

It was a talent that Mansi came to appreciate more and more over the years as she practiced it on humans, animals, and even insects. She learned that anything that possessed a functioning brain, she could *push*. The Darklings were the easiest to control. They were too easy sometimes. She had to be careful of her thoughts because the Darklings would act on them instantly, which would then cause

305

something or someone to have a really bad day. She tried to avoid situations that tested her patience. That time at the park had been particularly gruesome.

It was a beautiful Sunday morning around eleven-o-clock when many of the residents of Silverton were in church or still asleep. That morning she decided to visit the municipal park in Silverton. Despite the perfect weather, there wasn't a kid on the playground. Walking alone, Mansi exulted in the warm sun. She felt wonderful and decided to rest on one of the benches. Mansi had closed her eyes to enjoy a moment of bliss when she was startled by the wailing of a child at a nearby bench. The young Puerto Rican woman was yapping away on her cell phone, oblivious to her child in the stroller.

"Waaaaa! Waaaaa! Waaaaa!" The child, who appeared to be about three years old, screeched and shrieked and hit that high note that twangs along the spinal cord and holds one hostage for several seconds. Mansi turned toward the mother and tried glaring at her. The woman was chatting away with hardly a detectable break between words, oblivious to anyone or anything but the cell phone. Apparently, she had given the child a bag of Lance peanuts that had been torn open. The nuts were scattered on the ground where a gray squirrel was grabbing them and stuffing them into an already packed jaw.

"Waaaaa! Waaaa! Wa…WAAAAAA!"

SOMEBODY SHUT THAT BABY UP! Mansi shouted in her mind. Before the sentence was completed, she saw something move in the shadow of the pine tree that was hanging over the baby carriage. On the nearby sidewalk, a young man suddenly stopped and gave his mp3 player a shake and a questioning look. Even the mother was shaking her cell phone and saying, "Hola? Este usted?"

Mansi's eyes widened. She grimaced and waited to see what was to happen next. The baby carriage suddenly began shaking violently. The baby's legs kicked up and it screamed, "AAAAAAAyyyyyyyEEEEE!" The torn bag of Lance's peanuts flew into the air. A bright splash of red began to spread along the inside of the carriage.

"Que pasa? Si, Maria"

"Waaaa!" The carriage shook again, threatening to fall over. Mansi couldn't believe the mother still hadn't noticed.

"Salí de la casa. Mi madre es una locura."

The baby made one last desperate cry as a line of blood shot across the grass and the stroller fell over on its side.

"What the mierdae?" The woman dropped the phone. She saw the squirrel bounding across the grass and heading into the trees. However, she did not notice the fist-sized shadow dart out from under the stroller's blanket and into the shadows of the pine tree.

"About time, Jeez, girl," Mansi said to herself and quickly left the park.

That incident was reported on the local television news show that night at six. A young female reporter explained that the park had temporarily closed while the county's animal control unit searched the area for an unidentified animal that had maimed a child in its stroller while its vigilant mother had been distracted for a moment.

Therefore, Mansi reasoned, she would have to be very careful what she thought when her Darklings were around.

She learned that too many *pushings* in a short space of time could result in a pain much like ice-cream brain freeze. It was as though an ice pick was being jabbed behind her left eye. Sometimes it lasted for as long as three days. She had learned to restrain her thoughts when she was involved in a tight situation such as this one. *Just be careful.* She was beginning to feel normal again and the blood had dried on her skin. She wanted her clothes but they were on the roof where the security guard was standing, probably hoping a nude girl would show up to claim them. Normally, she would have *pushed* the Darklings to retrieve the clothing when the guy turned away, but she was still afraid to try. Then she saw the movement of a shadow as one of the Darklings took flight toward the roof. She smiled. They read her thoughts even without her *pushing.*

She stared at the guard silhouetted on the roof a few hundred yards away and decided to risk a gentle *push.*

Aren't those Golden Arches pretty? I can just look at them forever.

The security guard was wondering what the woman, who had been wearing the jeans and leather-laced jacket, looked like. Hell, he was really wondering what she had looked like after she had taken them off. He hoped she would come to the roof to get them. *I'm hungry,* he suddenly thought, pulling at the waistline of his pants, and turning northward. There was a McDonald's there, the neon lights bright yellow in the night. *Yeah, love them arches,* he thought, admiring how they made a perfect M, *and yeah, they're yellow like mustard and the cheese.* His stomach suddenly rumbled. *Jeez, what's this about? I just ate a full dinner a couple of hours ago.*

The Darkling crept over the edge of the building, reaching out with thin shadowy tentacles and pulled the clothing away.

A few minutes later, Mansi was clothed. However, after watching the guard on the roof run from side to side and talking into his radio, she decided to wait another hour before she went into action. Besides, her system could use the rest. She wasn't sure how much energy she was going to need for the next *pushing.*

CHAPTER 35

PANDORAS NIGHT

Lightning ripped through the dark blue night. The cragged peaks of the Malbolian coastline cut through the inland-moving storm clouds. Ragged lines of lightning raced westward.

After his encouraging talk with Mansi, Shabael was jubilant that at last they were doing something with the Orb of Light. If only he could create a portal to Earth. Things were moving now. It was true just as his priests had detected; there was a sense of spiritual building. Possibly, tonight, one of his life's dream would be accomplished. If he were struck by lightning, it would be a sign that he was a true appointed one.

"Yes! Strike me!" an excited Shabael shouted while flinging the double doors open and rushing onto the balcony. A gust of wind blew papers from desks and toppled over candles in the rom. The draped veil over his bed billowed in the wind.

Four Red Gold guards rushed into the room with swords drawn and Shabael whirled around to face them. "No, no, I am fine. Leave me and lock the doors. No one may enter! *No one!* Can you not hear the voice in the winds?" He ran to the long display box beneath his father's portrait and withdrew the old sword. Queen Shawndeli ran up to the guards, who blocked her entrance, moving her backward into the chambers and closing the doors.

"Shabael?" Shawndeli called out as the doors closed.

"Lightning runs through my blood. Anoint me!" Shabael cried out to the storm. "Father! I feel your spirit within." Shabael thrust his father's sword into the air. "My enemies attack! Strike me with lightning so that I may blaze black with darkness. Purge my soul! Make me worthy, as my grandfather and father before me! I am King, now blaze me!"

Lightning shot from the low-lying clouds, zigzagging northward. Thunder roared. The wind cutting around the parapets created a wavering but unending howl.

"Why do you deny me? Am I not worthy? I am El Qui! Deny me no more! I command it!"

Shawndeli pressed her ear against the closed chamber doors, and then turned to the stoic guards. "I can't hear anything with the wind and the thunder. One of you go and fetch Calibri! Oh, the storm is too severe. Wait. Open up the adjoining balcony now!" Shawndeli had changed from her royal clothes and was wearing a simple gown. She ran through the adjoining bedroom and through the opening balcony doors. The rain immediately drenched her and made the gown cling to her body.

"Shabael!" Shawndeli cried from the neighboring balcony. "You do not have to do this!" Her words were snatched by the howling wind and flung soundlessly into the raging storm.

"Blaze me with Light!" Shabael cried to the stiletto of lightning. "What must I do? What must I swear upon?"

Lightning broke overhead as the storm raced westward. Shabael thrust his sword upward. Thunder rumbled, shaking the foundations of the castle.

CHAPTER 36

IN THE LAND OF GENESIS POPCORN IS SERVED

It had all begun so simply. Before the Trees of Light and Dark were separated, there were no separate tribes. No war had ever been fought nor iron forged into blade to strike another. The land had never tasted the letting of blood from violence. The people were immortal and none knew death or illness. They did not know how their kind was created but saw themselves as a herd of animals that lived off the land of their world of Skyeden. No one knew who had given their world its name, but they existed in harmony. Animals did not fear men; and, as they did not feel threatened, men walked among the animals without trepidation. While lions preyed on other animals, they did not attack man for man respected the wild beasts and never showed malice. Animals were not slain for food; man grew and harvested his sustenance. The sun and a moon rose in the day. At night, a larger moon rose.

Every summer there was a great harvest of the corn. Men, wives, and children gathered for the gala occasion. The fields were vast, spreading over the foothills like a great sea of green. After the collection of the corn, the men and women gathered to celebrate around the Tree of Light and Tree of Dark.

A woman using a thin slate of volcanic rock to heat her food was shucking corn. Some of the kernels fell onto the hot slab. She felt something lightly strike the side of her face, looked down, and found a curious white puff of something. A little popping sound drew her attention to the hot slate and she watched as a miracle happened before her eyes.

"Look!" she grabbed a fistful of kernels that she had shucked and scattered them on the volcanic slate. Several curious women gathered and watched as the kernels begin to tremble and move on the slate. One of them popped, hurling a white piece toward them. They cried out and watched with fascination as the first woman picked up the white morsel and placed it on her tongue, then drew it in and started chewing.

"Hmm! Good!"

Several more pops sounded, each sending a white puff of corn into the air. A little girl squealed with excitement as she attempted to catch it. Another small girl shouted, "Pop, pop, pop, corn!"

"Popcorn," the first woman said, smiling. "Popcorn!" She picked up another piece. "Hmm. A little seasoning might be good."

The gathering women tossed fistfuls of kernels onto the hot plate and minutes later were laughing and jumping as they added kernels and attempted to catch the popcorn. Soon the plate was inches thick in kernels and they eventually figured out that less worked better.

The mother of Simone El Qui gave him a fistful of the popped corn. Not wanting to share his bounty with anyone, he picked his way through the crowd, went to the Dark Tree, and found a comfortable spot among the myriad of gnarled roots. The old roots were very thick, some of them extending a few feet above the ground. Simone sat down and leaned back against a root, staring at the popcorn in the palm of his hand. He was examining a piece of it when a white raven landed on a root beside of him, cocked its head to one side and stared curiously at his hand.

The children were still excited, gathered around the fire, snatching at the popcorn pellets as they exploded off the hot slate. A twelve-year-old girl caught a kernel and gave it her brother. The six-year-old raced through the crowd and found a spot to sit upon the roots of the Tree of Light. The flock of black ravens already there were undisturbed by his arrival, simply shuffling a couple of feet to one side in order to clear a spot for him to sit. One of the birds hopped up onto the boy's knee. Neither Simone El Qui under the Tree of Dark, nor the young boy sitting under the Tree of Light could know that at that moment, not only their lives, but also their worlds, would be forever altered.

The midday sun was surrounded by a clear blue sky, with the exception of one large dark cloud. When the cloud moved into the path of the sun, it created a sudden darkening, causing some of the people to look up.

The storm was sudden. Lightning flashed. Thunder rolled through the hills. Within milliseconds, an eye-scorching jagged white line shot downward and was met by a line of lightning from each tree. Those who witnessed it swore that the bolts leaving the trees and clashing with the one from the sky burned an image of an upside down Y into their retinas. People screamed and cowered to the ground, covering their heads with up-thrown arms.

As suddenly as it had appeared, the cloud passed and light returned. There were a few moments of eerie silence before the terrified children began their wailing. Parents thankfully clutched children in their arms.

Then a single ragged scream hushed even the babbling children. All eyes turned to see Simone's mother collapse to her knees under the Tree of Dark and lift her smoldering son from among the huge roots. The boy's clothes were shredded. The odor of burning hair mingled with that of the popcorn. A red V was burned on his left ankle and a ragged scar ran from his elbow to his palm where the lightning had exited his body.

One scream had barely died before another was in the air from the opposite direction. The mother of Aremis Donachie fell to her knees by her son's body at the roots of the Tree of Light and began wailing.

It was at that moment that the separation of the people began. Without conscious thought or decisions, people simply went to one tree or the other to learn what had happened. The giant trees became illuminated. The Dark Tree had a bluish neon tint that made the branches appear as see-through tubes. The Tree of Light's branches turned pure white. In addition, in the crown of each tree, there was an Orb of Light emitting the same color of its branches. The trees emitted a humming sound and their vibrations could be felt on the ground surrounding them.

The two boys struck by lightning survived and were deemed anointed by the Gods and the two Trees. Each would grow into Kings, ruling over tribes. The event also caused the first of the "mergings." And, eventually the kings discovered that they had telepathic links to their ravens.

Several mornings after the lightning incident, Simone was within the consciousness of a white raven that came upon a dead rabbit and began feasting. This image created a great stirring of hunger within Simone. His mother found him a few hours later with a knife in one hand, a butchered rabbit in the other, and bloodstains on his lips. Within a month, all of those that had lingered by the Tree of Dark had begun eating meat.

Slowly, this new delicacy on the menu was adopted by some people with the Tree of Light, although most felt an unease with killing and eating animals and remained on vegetarian diets. As time passed, however, even they began eating meat on special occasions.

As the populations grew, groups began splintering off, hoarding their food and dwelling among themselves. Secret signs to one another became different languages. Hunting became too tedious for many so the people raised crops and built pens to hold animals that would be used for food. With free time to think about more than foraging for food, the people turned to religion. Differences between tribes grew. Fights broke out between individuals, tribe members and the different tribal groups. A man was killed, the first person to die at the hands of another. This event had never happened before. Therefore, serious religious thought ensued.

During this period, the boys who had been struck by lightning had grown into young men and were deemed Messiahs. Before the lightning struck, the people had sung songs and read poetry together. However, as time passed the songs and poems became specific to each tribe and were no longer shared. Tensions built as the differences between the tribes grew. The Malbolians were industrious and raised animals for food. The Ravenites kept animals only for pets. They hunted their food as they needed it, and worked tirelessly in the fields to raise corn, wheat, and vegetables. It seemed with each encounter between tribes, there were escalating problems. Arguments, once sporadic, began to happen more frequently. It was obvious that serious trouble was brewing. Soon, if something did not stop the escalating problems, violence would ensue.

Eventually it was decided that there would have to be a separation before the people began slaughtering each other.

A meeting of the tribes and their splinter groups was called for the tribes to discuss the solution. Naturally, each tribe wanted to make its home around one of the trees. During this time, the first rites of Ascension were made with Aremis Donachie. During the ceremony of dedicating himself to the God of Light, he rose in the air and black wings appeared upon his back. From that day forward, he could will his wings to appear and fly short distances. He gradually became aware, however, that when the Moon of Night rose the energy was drained from him.

Simone, learning the news of Donachie's Ascension, held his own rites, dedicating his soul to the Tree of Dark.

The Malbolians and Ravenites were by far the largest of the twenty tribes represented. So it was decided that they would each claim a tree and separate their peoples. Drawing upon the history of the trees, it was agreed that the Malbolians should claim the Tree of Dark. Each tribe constructed huge carts with large wooden wheels, dug up as much of the trees as they could, loaded them on the carts, and departed in opposite directions. Thus were the kingdoms of Malbolia and Ravenland formed on opposite sides of the great country of Skyeden.

When King Shabael took the Malbolian throne, he commissioned scholars to write the El Qui Bible in which were recorded times, events, visions and prophesies. The years passed and there was no aging of those who had been given the rites of Descension. However, the great king had become bored and put into operation his plan to steal the Orb of Light from the complacent and unwary Ravenites.

That had been successful and exciting, but the centuries flowed past and except for the occasional flash battles with the Ravenites or members of one of the nomadic tribes, the energetic Shabael found himself dreaming of great battles. He had welcomed the invasion of the Ravenites after they had stolen the Orb of Light back, and now he found the futile assassination attempts rejuvenating. He needed a war. Bullying those you had already defeated was pathetic.

That was why he stood on his balcony in the midst of a raging thunderstorm and cursed the gods for not allowing a bolt to strike him.

"*I am El Qui!*" He shouted to the sky. "Why give me lands and power? Why make me a great warrior when you give me no good use.

Why have you not anointed me as one of your sons? Strike me! Give me a sign! Give me *something!*"

The wind howled, blowing dust and sand from the shore inland. Streams of the sand raced between the parapets and towers. The crystalline particles turned bluish when snatches of moonlight filtered through.

Grabbing the railing with one hand, Shabael lifted himself upward, the wind constantly at his back, his white hair blown straight back. He thrust his sword toward the sky, holding on with one hand and his knees braced against the top railing.

The howling wind made it impossible to hear Shawndeli's pleading for him to come back inside.

"Lightning is the fundamental source of the universe! It is the voice of God; it is ether; God's spirit! I am your son!"

CHAPTER 37

RAGING STORMS AND PASSIONS

High Priest Calibri was on his knees amid a circle of other priests in his study in the Black Tower. They were offering prayers, for the belief was that during storms God was present and more willing to hear the supplications from his servants. Calibri suddenly gasped and paused in mid-sentence, clutching another priest's shoulder to assist in lifting himself up.

"What's happening? Something is happening! I can feel it!" He hurried to the large window that faced the Dark Tree and placed his hands on the glass so that he might feel the vibration of the tree. The vibration was frenzied. Something bizarre was about to happen. Never had the Priest Highest experienced a foreboding of this power. *The king is dead?* No, no, no. Something else. This must be divine intervention coming. "Do you feel it," he asked the others as they gathered around him, all fixating on the Tree of Dark, which was emitting a powerful humming sound as its electric neon hue brightened against the dark sky.

Meanwhile, in the Emperor's Tower in the chambers of the Queen Highest, Mateah rode her lover, sitting astride the huge man and grasping the bed veils on each side with her hands to give her thrusts added power. She threw her head back and uttered a half moan, half scream as the orgasm ripped through her body. She gave a glorious climatic cry and collapsed on the man's chest.

Moments later she rose, stood nude beside the bed with her perfect body glowing in the aftermath, her thousand-year-old breasts firm and proud, and said, "Now get out of my sight, you pig!"

Lightning crackled, splintering the night and striking the Tree of Dark. A zigzag flash arched from the tree and struck the Emperor's tower.

Calibri almost put his face through the pane of glass. The Tree of Dark had been struck! Fire was blazing in three branches. The spheres of light were blinding and the neon blue in the branches grew in sight-defying intensity. The priest felt a wave of vibration strike his forehead and then race out the back of his skull. The other priests were on their feet, crying out in fear as they gathered around Calibri and watched the three burning branches as the flames defied the strong winds and urged straight upward to the sky.

"Get me proper clothing and guards," Calibri ordered. "I must see the Emperor now." Several of the priests hurried from the room.

Queen Mateah watched her confused lover gather his clothes as she covered herself with a robe and went to the window. She had never seen the Tree of Dark blaze so brightly. Her eyes widened as she realized that flaming branches midway up the old trunk were causing the brightness. A high-pitched sound caught her attention. She swung the door open and quickly stepped out onto the balcony. Even above the rushing wind, she was able to hear Shabael's name being called. She looked across to the king's balcony and saw Shawndeli rushing out and dropping to her knees.

"My Queen, what is happening, the chagrined lover said as he struggled to get dressed.

"I'm not sure. Something has happened in my son's chambers. I must go." She stopped and faced the man still busily lacing his jerkin. "Zo, are you absolutely certain all the evidence concerning the assassins has been destroyed?"

"I am, Queen Highest. I met with them behind the incinerators, where I told them what a great job they had done, and in payment, I killed them. I burned their snaky bodies, My Queen. As for their weapons there is nothing left but charred melted globs."

"Good job, indeed! Those incompetent worms! The queen still lives and my granddaughter has no tongue. Zo, I spoke too sharply to you before. You were magnificent, as usual. You are my favorite by far. Stay close, my stallion. I may need you soon."

CHAPTER 38

A DAY FOR FUNERALS

"It's amazing how clearly I remember those days, Aribon. Here, let me put this rolled blanket between your head and the tree trunk."

"Thank you. Thank you for telling me all this," Aribon said. "I always wanted to know what happened with my father and you. I always wanted to ask but felt it would be best for you to tell me when you were ready."

"I will tell you all of it," Eradrin said sadly. "But for you to understand my actions over the past one hundred and fifty years, I must tell you what I learned after your father's death. I will describe what I have learned in sequence so that you may better understand it all. Moreover, I must say that by telling this to someone I will finally receive validation that my actions were prudent. So hang on my friend. Let me take you back over what has befallen me. Then I would like your assessment.

"I will try to follow as best as I am able," Aribon said. He coughed. "I wish I were Ascended that I might serve you longer."

"I, too, my nephew. Now make yourself comfortable." Eradrin rose to his feet, turned and looked at the huge oak tree. Gently touching the trunk, he began his story.

"Three weeks before the raven brought us the Orb of Light, the Priest High Council were in session to name the new leader. Amril was the first to announce resignation from his post rather than die holding his position. Thus, it was looked at as an opportunity to bring new ideas into the council. There were many elder priests deserving of assuming the role and many viewpoints were argued. After eight hours of deliberation, one hundred ravens were released from the cathedral tower tagged with the name of the new High Priest, John Daren. Daren was young, only forty years old, and of course had not been Ascended. Never had a man so young taken the post, but the priests in their wisdom deemed new blood was needed.

"When a new High Priest is appointed, he must partake in a vision quest that is said to define his path and also foretell the future of the Ravenites. This vision was privy only to the High Priests for various reasons and I was told of the visions the day your Father died. On the day of the funeral …."

Eradrin headed the funeral procession as it moved toward the front entrance of Skye Castle. From the corner of his eye, he saw his brother, Thomar, leading the wagons of flowers. The smaller nomad horses concealed in the funeral ceremonial dress attracted no attention from the watching Malbolian soldiers. The shrouds showed only the horses eyes and draped within a foot of the ground.

In the courtyard was a large wheeled wagon that contained one of the Malbolians' orbs of seeing. An ominous "dong" continually sounded from within as a hanging metallic disc was rhythmically struck in order to create the proper vibration for a seer to receive reception of the Darklings observances from strategic locations. It was an ability that the ravens did not possess; and, the absence of that power made Eradrin even more aware of his peoples' vulnerability.

As he led the procession, King Eradrin was achingly reminded of the absence of his father and Dayanna. Normally, he would have been walking on his father's right. However, today, he was king and he walked in the center of the street. How many times had he walked this path with Dayanna? Then he simply had to hold his hand out and it would have been taken by his beautiful future queen. Now there was no one to his left. His mother walked beside him on the right, her hand resting above his elbow.

A sudden commotion ahead and to the left of the procession caught Eradrin's attention. Several people were swarming through the gate, obviously excited about something. He recognized his sister, Saydee, astride her horse, accompanied by a small escort of guards. Saydee had been in the southeast portion of Skyeden, studying earth magic with the Hicool, a highly intelligent class of people, known for their grace and love of nature. As she neared the head of the procession, Eradrin's heart swelled with pride and love. She was dressed in an iridescent black and blue-green gown, woven in silk and topped with a hood, fashioned in the Hicool spiritual and flowing style.

Saydee's fair skin, framed by her black hair, presented an ethereal beauty. But it was the gift of unlimited sympathy that showed in her blue-green eyes when she listened to another that made her so beloved. She had shared that trait with Dayanna; and, that was another reason there was such concern for her. With Dayanna gone, Saydee had made herself even more accessible to the people. Her unexpected arrival now had lifted their spirits on this terrible day. Eradrin was overjoyed to see her too, but her presence also brought some dread. The Malbolians were still here and this concerned him. He was especially worried about Queen Mateah's reaction.

Eradrin's own reaction was to go to his sister and welcome her with open arms. He desperately wanted to ease the feelings of pain and helplessness that he knew she was feeling. He resisted the impulse, not because he was King, but because his enemies' eyes were upon him, as he was sure any emotion shown toward his sister would be to her detriment.

Saydee dismounted and embraced Eradrin as he felt the hair on the nape of his neck begin to rise. The Malbolians were watching. He whispered, "I love you, sister, but cannot show it. If they discover how much you really mean to me, they will use it against me. I truly wish you had not come."

"No," she insisted. "I missed your crowning but I will not miss my father's funeral. Father is gone … the Viceroy is dead. Your love, Dayanna, and her brother. All gone. How can you bear all this?"

"Because I have to. Because I am King. Weep for the both of us, Sister. But be wary. The wolves are circling." There it was, the reason why he loved her so much, why she was so precious his heart. Even in the midst of personal tragedy, her thought was "What else are *you* going to have to bear?" Eradrin smiled and whispered, "I love you, sister."

He reluctantly turned away from her and resumed walking. The six-year old Aribon walked behind with his mother, holding her hand, not as much for him as for her. That's what the Donachies did better than anyone; console one another during tragedies. With the experience of a thousand years of heartbreak and tragedy, they were masters of sharing grief.

Eradrin marched on, his mind racing with his new duties and responsibilities. He felt as though a great weight had descended upon him. His knees felt weak and he worried that they might buckle with any step. His party reached the gate and moved left to the descending stairs on the side of the mountain wall. It was one hundred steps from there to reach the landing on Lake Waccamola and a line had formed waiting for the lift. On a normal day he, too, would have taken the lift to the elevated landing, but today, he wanted to feel every step, savor every melancholy moment of grief. He would not deprive himself of one step or one ounce of the emotion he was feeling over the loss of his father and Dayanna and all the others who had died in the hope that the Orb of Light could return one day and restore the balance.

Meanwhile, Thomar and his men along with the half dozen wagons had reached the Tree of Light. He motioned for the men to pull out the large scroll of yellowed paper and preserved bamboo.

"Hurry, we haven't much time. Bring the thread here. Get the basin and the oil," Thomar ordered. "Stay alert. Make sure no one comes from the castle and keep an eye out for Darklings."

Thomar hoped his archer hidden on the castle tower was prepared to play his role in the drama that was about to be played out.

Emotion rose within Eradrin. Taking this first step down to the shore was acknowledging the reality of it all. He reached out for the mountain wall to steady himself and somehow found comfort in the coolness of the stone.

"God bless our fallen king!" a cry came from above. Eradrin looked up and saw that the castle wall was lined with people seeking a vantage point.

"Great Creator save us!" another cried out, the anguish in the voice touching Eradrin's heart. It was the voice of a lost soul, searching for hope. Did all his people feel this way too? *My people. A thousand years we have endured. We only live to suffer, to know no joy or freedom.* No longer was he the dutiful son in the background, he was the King. He closed his eyes, pressing his palm against the cool stone of the mountain, as if to suppress the pain and suffering of the land and people. Yes, the land suffers as much as the people do. Had they been under submission so long that his father, his mother, and everyone had grown numb and dehumanized. Had it taken the death of his father and Dayanna and this endless funeral ceremony to awaken them, the harsh reality cutting through the anesthetics of a thousand years of hopelessness.

"May the new king bring us light!" a woman cried out.

Eradrin caught his breath. It was as though the woman was in his mind reading his thoughts.

"Save us!" another cried.

"We are all dead. Save us, new king!"

Eradrin's heart raced with bridled emotion. He saw tears streaming down his mother's cheeks and she was biting down on her bottom lip to control her emotions.

Another cry rang out. "Creator, save us! The Light is forever gone!"

Anger, sadness and the torment of helplessness raged inside Eradrin. He glanced at Saydee and her eyes urged him to stay calm. Keep control, she seemed to be saying. She leaned her head to the side and looked into his eyes, feeling his turmoil and understanding the emotions that were boiling beneath the surface. He drew a deep breath, nodded to his sister, and gathered himself. If he lingered longer, it might encourage the people to shout more and act out their emotions against the Malbolian soldiers standing at every corner. That would be disastrous. A slaughter. He withdrew his hand from the wall, his fingertips touching the grit in the palm of his hand. It was going to be lonely as King and he realized he had no idea of the weight of it all. *Move. Step down before they riot. Oh, Father ... Dayanna ... how I miss you.*

"God save us, King Eradrin! Can you not hear our souls?"

"I do!" Eradrin answered. "I hear you all!"

Queen Juliana raised a cautioning finger to her lips and whispered, "*Shhhh. Shhhh.*"

"*Caw! Caw! Caw!*" A dozen caws suddenly sounded from above and a small flock of ravens began descending. As Eradrin's eyes followed them down, he saw King Shabael with his hand poised in the air as a dozen archers stood near him with bows drawn taut.

As the ravens descended, they separated. One bird approached Eradrin and perched on his shoulder. A second raven alit on his mother's shoulder and a third attached itself to Saydee's wrist. A smaller bird came to rest on the boy Aribon's shoulder.

It took a moment before recognition came for Eradrin. His personal raven, Ravenstorm, had a higher blue sheen than most. Its head was a little thicker and when it opened its beak, it appeared to be smiling. It was the kind of smile a warrior would make when he was about to deliver a deathblow to his opponent, or perhaps a raven, knowing the mouse he was about to devour was his for the taking. *Oh, yes! This is Ravenstorm!* "Do my eyes deceive me? Ravenstorm, is it you? You are alive?"

"Caw!" Ravenstorm bobbed its head up and down. The blue sheen of his feathers glimmered in the torch light. The little smile was in place.

"Sapphire!" Saydee said a low excited voice as she recognized her raven, then turned to Queen Juliana. "Mother, is that Ralflin?"

"It is! Sweet Creator, it is. He has returned."

Eradrin looked up at the terrace and saw King Shabael whispering in his mother's ear. Queen Mateah motioned for someone to come to her.

A long, piercing caw sounded from above; and, the perched ravens seemed to lower their heads as though they were offering mini-bows.

A huge raven appeared above the castle walls, spreading its large wings to their full span and settling on a parapet by a large torch atop the castle wall.

"Oh Holy Creator, it's red!" someone shouted, and the cry reverberated through the street. "Look! It is our dead king's raven!"

Eradrin looked on in amazement. It was indeed Red Raven. Just as mighty and majestic as he had ever been.

Red Raven spread his wings, lifted magnificently into the air and slowly descended. Eradrin raised his right arm to present his wrist and the raven perched on his arm, its claws firm around his right wrist. Leaning forward, Red Raven turned its head so that its left side faced Eradrin and edged a little closer. There was hardly an inch from eye to eye. The brown iris was huge in the half-light; the flicker of a torch from the terrace reflected in its eye.

There was intelligence in that eye. It moved to and fro and seemed to stare deep into Eradrin's soul. Then Red Raven rose on the tip of its claws and spread its wings. *"Caw!"*

The other ravens immediately answered with their caws and shivers of excitement raced through Eradrin. He knew that the caws were some kind of acknowledgment, but wasn't sure exactly what was happening. Were the ravens simply paying respect to his slain father? Movement on the balcony caught Eradrin's eye and he saw King Shabael leaning so far over the railing that he appeared in danger of falling. His hands were clenched on the railing and there was a look of astonishment and disbelief on his face.

"Look!" a Malbolian guard suddenly shouted from the atop the castle wall. All heads turned and looked skyward to where he was pointing.

There was a collective gasp from the crowd.

"Eradrin?" Saydee grabbed his arm. Even the perched ravens turned their heads and looked.

Rising from the face of the mountain where it curved away from sight, arose a large orb of yellow light. It was rising higher and moving across the lake toward the landing.

"The sun!" a woman suddenly shouted.

"Light!" a child said, pointing.

All around the landing people were falling to their knees. The glowing object was larger than the Moon of Night. It was a bright white yellow moving higher and toward the front of the castle.

"It is an omen!"

"The dead King's Red Raven gives his blessing and the Gods bless our new King!" a man shouted.

"Praise the creator!"

"Give it to me!" Shabael's shouted command rang above the clamor. He snatched the bow and arrow from the soldier, quickly took aim, and released the arrow. Unwavering, the arrow arched toward the approaching yellow orb. A hole appeared in the center of the light where the arrow struck and the mysterious orb flickered and wobbled.

A woman screamed. A flock of ravens flew toward the faltering orb. Red Raven issued a loud caw that sounded more like a squawk.

The orb burst into flames and began to disintegrate as it descended to the lake's surface. The flock of ravens scattered into the dark horizon. Pieces of the material that had been used to build the kite-like orb scattered over the lake's surface, drifting down like fist-sized fireflies. The people on the lake's shore could hear a hiss as the burning pieces struck the water. During the distraction, no one saw the ball of fire tossed from the tower terrace that landed atop the Orb of Seer wagon.

Shabael handed the bow back to his soldier and nodded toward Eradrin. "You may proceed, new King."

Eradrin remained still, staring hatred and disgust at Shabael, who appeared oblivious to his action. The Queen Highest was staring out toward the area from which the air float had appeared. She quietly motioned for a guard and pointed at the face of the mountain where it turned away, obscuring the area in which the Tree of Light stood. Eradrin's heart sank a little. *Move, brother. Keep moving.* The soldier listened to Mateah's instructions and quickly left the terrace.

There is nothing I can do now, Eradrin thought. Shabael's shooting of the float during the funeral ceremony was an offense that made his soul burn. Couldn't the bastard have shown at least a shred of respect by allowing one gesture of hope in the symbolic passing of King Aremis' soul leaving his body and ascending to the heavens? Or had he seen through the attempt at a brief distraction?

"Brother, we should continue," Saydee said quietly, bringing him back to the reality of the moment.

"Yes." Eradrin said and began moving down the stairs when the bell to the observation tower began to ring. It was struck four times, then stopped and repeated; the pattern for a fire alarm.

Eradrin again suppressed a small smile. He paused and saw mass confusion on the street. Part of the crowd was backing away from the area, while others crowded in to see what was happening. Eradrin motioned to one of his honor guards to check on what was happening. The remaining guards formed a tight circle around the royal family.

Eradrin looked back at the terrace and saw Queen Highest Mateah rush back outside and lean over the balcony to get a view of what was causing the commotion. She turned suddenly and stared directly at King Eradrin.

Shouts to make way came from the courtyard as a number of Malbolian soldiers rushed to the flaming Seer wagon with buckets of water. Black smoke billowed from the flickering flames. The guard that Eradrin had dispatched returned, breathless and eyes wide with excitement.

"My King, it appears falling debris from the float caught the Malbolian's Orb of Seer wagon on fire."

"Really? That's too bad. I trust we are doing whatever we can to help douse the flames."

The guard tried to mask a smile. "Yes, Sire, our best. However, the contents of the wagon must have been highly flammable. It is engulfed in flames and it doesn't appear that anything can be saved." The suppressed smile broke through. "In the excitement, horses pulling a wagon loaded with stone became startled and 'accidently' struck the Seer wagon. The rocks shattered the orbs in the wagon and the black waters spewed onto the ground. That certainly scattered the onlookers. Who knows what evil lurks in that foul brew?" The guard snickered.

"Thank you. Now return to your post," Eradrin said, trying hard to keep his own smile from showing. *Oh, what have you done, my brother Thomar? What can we expect from you next?*

"Are we under attack?" Queen Juliana asked.

"No, Mother. There's nothing to fear. Just an accident." Eradrin placed a calming hand on her arm. He raised his eyes to the terrace and saw that Queen Mateah was still watching him. He couldn't see well enough in the dim light to interpret the expression on her face, but had an idea what it might be. *That's right, witch bitch. Yes, we caused it. What are you going to do about it?*

The Queen Mother stepped away from the railing and spoke to another guard, who immediately departed from the balcony. Shabael didn't notice. He was issuing orders to a group of soldiers on the ground below. He barked a command and six men with horns sounded a piercing note, cutting through all the commotion and chaos. Shabael yelled, "Enough! Silence! Mourn your dead king and be done with this! Now!" Then he turned to Queen Highest, took her by the arm and they left the terrace.

Saydee touched Eradrin's arm, having caught his glance to the terrace. "I warn you now, Brother. Do not toy with the Red Dragon Queen. The only way you can best her is if she chokes on the marrow she sucks from your bones."

Eradrin blinked and proceeded to descend from the face of the mountain. The Moon of Dark was still below the top of Skye Castle, casting eerie shadows.

"I move in shadows now," he said, his voice low.

"Be brave. We have learned there is no one, no God, that will reach down from the heavens and flick King Shabby Tail to the side," Juliana said.

"Mother?" Eradrin was surprised by her words and hopeful that she would restrain herself when they reached the landing.

"I hate the El Qui," Queen Juliana continued, ignoring her son's warning. "Every wrong thing, every bad thing in my life, has been because of them!"

"Mind your steps, Mother, a fall from here would be fatal," Saydee said, hoping to break through the mood of the moment.

"It's time to grieve for our Father, Dayanna, and our Viceroy," Eradrin said, "and we must control our emotions. Everyone is watching us, our own people as well as the Malbolians."

It was impossible to see across the lake because of the perpetual darkness, but Eradrin knew from memory that the trees on the far shore would have appeared no larger than his thumbnail. He had been so young then, but the playfulness of life had been wrung from that long ago boy like water from a wet rag. The memories now were of grief, the sense of loss, the sun never rising, and the populace seeing their children die of old age without the possibility of Ascension. It was no wonder that the suicide rate was so high. The Ravenite population was continuously shrinking, no more from death than from defecting to the Malbolians. Who could blame them? They were immigrating from darkness and gloom to possible immortality and a healthy economy.

Perhaps we could merge with the Darklings. Or would the emperor allow me to merge with a white raven as I am of royal blood? Go ask him. Heretic!

What am I king of? A sorrowful state with only a dark future. Power to you, Thomar. Stay free and set up your ambush. Give the El Qui a taste of what fear is.

"We are the conquered. It is our place," his mother suddenly said, the anger and belligerence gone from her voice.

"No, Mother. To accept this station in life is to deny the Illuminator. We cannot do that. We are the guardians of the Light; and, it is we who have failed it. We must not give up hope."

"Hope does not spring eternal," she said. "We have fought longer and lost more than our people can bear. You say the Light has not abandoned us? *Really?* Where is the Light now? Where is my beloved husband?"

"I am sure the Illuminator has a greater understanding in the scheme of things, Mother."

"Perhaps it is we who are foolish, giving the Illuminator human qualities when it is but a natural phenomenon. It's akin to calling cold the God of Ice. There is no mind, no heart, no sympathy, no love. We could as well have chosen a stone to be our God!"

"Mother! Why do you speak of this?"

"Because I am angry. I am hurting inside. I am lost without my husband," a sob wracked her body. "I hate the El Qui. I hate *God!*"

"Oh, mother, mother, please!" Saydee patted Queen Juliana's arm, attempting to console her.

"Come," Eradrin said gently. "We must continue the procession. It's almost over." He understood his mother's grief. Still, it was surprising and depressing to hear her speak in this manner.

"Eradrin, listen to your sister's warnings of the Red Dragon," his mother began again. "The she dragon is God to our world now. If our God is truly the Illuminator, perhaps he has deserted us and taken the Light to another world."

His mother's continued rant alarmed Eradrin. She had a low tolerance toward injustice. However, after a thousand years she had learned to hold her tongue when a Malbolian blade was figuratively at her throat. Now, with the death of Father, Dayanna and all the others, the public humiliation, the degradation, her pain was too fresh and deep to think of concealing the emotions. Surely, she did not mean this. The raging storm of emotions would pass. These statements were the hiss of steam escaping the boiling kettle. She needed to scream.

"Say no more," Eradrin whispered to her. "When we are on the landing, we will talk. Right now, the entire kingdom and the El Qui have their eyes upon us. Our behavior will determine much of our people's interactions with us."

"I know that. Don't worry, I'm fine."

Saydee reached a hand to her mother's hair. "Let me fix this; it's beginning to fall loose."

Juliana slapped her daughter's hand away. "This isn't a beauty pageant. It is a funeral. Right, son? Leave me alone; I'll control myself."

When they reached the landing, guards cleared the area so they could walk down the shore. At that moment, Eradrin saw the squad of Malbolian horsemen riding north toward the hidden passage that

Thomar was taking. A low moan escaped from his lips and again Saydee noticed his distress.

"Where is Thomar?" she whispered.

The guards formed a half circle around them and cleared the area for their passage. Eradrin's heart raced as the squad of Malbolians passed the area where his Father laid and then they disappeared in the gloom. He had no doubt about their destination.

"Our God is here," Eradrin whispered into his mother's ear. "You understand that even though you are angry and hurt."

The boat designated for Dayanna was aligned with moon glories and purple night blooms with sheets of satin trimmed in gold. Her ceremonial purple gown lay atop the satin sheets representing her body.

The boat bearing King Aremis was decorated with gems mined from Skye Mountain. Red and blue stones glowed warmly in the light from the torches placed on the beach. The royal family banner waved in the wind.

The old priest Amila was helped to rise and his white hair, yellowing with age, resembled a small cloud floating in a night sky. The newly appointed priest Daren was present by his side.

Eradrin reached out a hand to steady the frail Amila. The boy Aribon stepped from behind the king, appearing mature and older in his mourning robe and jacket, and took the old priest's arm. Eradrin nodded and smiled approval.

Amila's hands trembled in Eradrin's grasp. "My new King." He reached up to cup Eradrin's cheek and looked into his eyes. "I was there the day you were born. I saw the excitement and wonder in your father's eyes as you, his new son, came into this world. I remember the love he displayed for you and his Queen. Do you remember, Juliana?"

Juliana smiled and nodded. Saydee handed her a small linen cloth and the queen dabbed at her eyes.

"The world has grown dark since the Light has gone," Amila continued. "There are no flowers of sun to marvel at or shadows to follow us. There is no rite of Ascension or great powers of healing. There is only suppression. No sunsets, nor sunrises. For a moment, the Orb of Light was returned to us and it gave us hope. It roused the warrior within our hearts and gave us courage to fight for its possession; for the one chance ... the one hope ... that the ancient

331

myth and prophecies be true; that it's Light could ignite the Sun and Moon of Day again. That we, as followers of the God of Light must have faith, the Light shall return again. Many of us died for that dream this week. Our sons and daughters, our husband and wives, our King and Father, his Viceroy and daughter, our future queen. They are no more among us. They gave their lives that our dream may still shine on. And as I commence with the ceremony, we will ignite the passage of life to forever blaze in our memories. So bright shall our king's spirit shine in all this darkness that our Creator will see us again. We must understand that it has not been God who has been lost to us, but we who have been lost to him. With the light of our beloved departed king, we show the Great Creator that we believe again! We see you! The light is our faith! I share with you now what the Creator said to me this morning, 'If ye shall light your faith; then I shall light the world.'"

Amila's inspiring words surprised Eradrin as they rose in strength and volume. This wizened, fragile man spoke words that might move a universe and perhaps even a God into action. The message brought an excited murmur from the crowd and pushed Malcolm into action, moving past the Malbolian soldiers as he approached Amila. "That was an inspiring eulogy, Priest. Now come with us and sit and rest your weary body and mind."

Eradrin's mind was racing. Amila's words had acted as the removal of a blinding veil from his eyes. Even in the forever gloom, Amila's words blazed like stars in a sky void of them. This old man on the verge of death had spoken words of past and coming glories that could inspire warriors. This man, who had literally given his life to the service of his people, had never taken the rite of Ascension, and lived only to serve and love others.

Eradrin tensed as Malcolm took Amila by the arm. *How dare this man interrupt the Priest?* He fought the impulse to intercede.

"I will assist him," offered John Daren. "Step aside Aribon; stand by your new king." Aribon nodded and assumed a position by Eradrin's side. Malcolm and the soldiers stepped back.

A sudden collective gasp came from the onlookers and Eradrin glanced over his shoulder to see that King Shabael, his wife and his mother had moved to the ceremonial site. Eradrin tore his gaze away as emotions boiled within him. When the buzz among the spectators had subsided, Eradrin released himself from his sister and mother's holds on his arms and stepped forward. It was his turn now. *By the Light, Amila, the world will hear the echoes of your words for generations. I pray that I can be as inspiring. Father, can you hear me?*

All eyes were upon the new king and the moment weighed heavily upon him. He had looked into the eyes of his family members and his people and understood their dependence on him. He was king. His father was dead. No more. No more as with the sun that had once shone. Not a sound came from the throng of onlookers, only the gentle lapping of waves upon the lakeshore, the flapping of banners in the breeze, and the occasional nickering of a horse. These people were his responsibility now and that weighed heavily. Scanning the crowd, he recognized the hope, the fear, and the anxiety in the eyes. The people were seemingly as hopeless as abandoned children were. They looked to him as freshly hatched birds with their necks stretched out, their beaks opening, and closing as they fought the pangs of starvation. *However, they do not starve for food. They starve for Divine Light. Their souls are starving for answers and for action. Blessed Illuminator, I am here! I am your servant. Help me to serve you in a way that will bring hope and Light to us again.*

Saydee reached inside her robe and removed a pendant, placing it around Eradrin's neck and letting it fall to his chest. It was a pendant King Aremis had often worn, a circle with three rays of light emitting. *Oh, my sister.* Saydee seemed to always know just what to do. He reached up, cupped her hand, and kissed it. It was time to be king. He glanced down at the pendant. A circle. A ring. *Three shall come on raven wings.*

"I shall hear Amila's words in the back of my mind until the day I die," Eradrin began. "For what seems but a brief moment we were blessed by the Orb of Light. And this has cost us our King, a future queen, and all the other citizens who have sacrificed their lives to remind us that all is not lost. We, as Ravenites, must hold our faith.

"Today, we mourn the passing of our longest reigning Ravenite king — my father. He was appointed King by the Great Illuminator when the Trees of Light and Dark grew side by side. My father and King Shabael's ancestor were designated as kings by a bolt of lightning that struck at the Light Trees." *And damn you for killing my father! Damn you, who killed an innocent boy.*

A moment passed as Eradrin gathered himself and focused on regaining his path of thought. "For a thousand years Emperor Shabael has sat on the Malbolian throne. And now I sit in my father's place. My father's greatest dream was that one day the light shall shine again and we shall return to our formal glory."

Malcolm took a step forward. Priest Amila struggled to rise to his feet. Juliana and Saydee were captivated, their faces rapt with attention.

"Our world will one day have balance again. There will be peace among the tribes. That is my father's dream and we must keep it alive. Allow the hope to shine in your heart that one day — one glorious day — the sun shall rise again. I never once knew my father to act unjustly. We often referred to him as 'The Mountain' because of his deliberate actions. Yet, his decisions carried the weight of the mountain, as was his will. It took me many centuries to understand how to move like a mountain. However, due to the good advice and wisdom of Priest Amila, who explained we were not to literally move as a mountain, but to feel its weight, and majestic height when making decisions."

A dark cloud of sadness suddenly enveloped Eradrin. The king was dead. There would be no new memories to be formed.

"As my father departs us, so does his knowledge, his experience as King, the history of our people. *The experience of having your throat cut.* Such a mighty loss we have suffered. Oh, Illuminator, so did the Ravenites love your chosen one. He led us through the darkness and it is now my time to lead us to your Light."

Eradrin made a quick motion with his hands; and, the soldiers surrounding the shrouded boat gently pushed it into the lake water as its sail billowed. "May your Light shine forever, Father, Great First King of the Ravenites." Turning to the archer, Eradrin gestured, "May I have the honor?" The archer nodded and gave the bow to his new king.

Eradrin tested the bow, pulling the string back, gauging the tension. The archer ignited the arrow and handed it to Eradrin. "In birth you lighted my life and, as your son, I ignite the departure of your soul into the hands of the Illuminator. Good bye, my ..."

A sudden urgent cawing interrupted Eradrin's words.

"Look," someone shouted. Eradrin raised his eyes to see a brilliant red raven swoop down and perch on the mast of the ship.

"The King's Raven." The murmur swept through the crowd.

Eradrin inhaled deeply. "Forever shine, Father!" He released the arrow and it flew high, and then arched in descent toward the boat. Red Raven cawed loudly, spreading his wings and rising quickly. The arrow struck Red Raven squarely in the breast and he fell into the boat. Eradrin remained motionless, the bow still pointing to its target. He lowered his head and felt tears running down his cheeks.

Surely, Red Raven's act of devotion was testimony that the birds had not forgotten their ties or loyalty. Even the Malbolians would have to acknowledge this.

A large flock of black ravens appeared and alit on the beach to the north. Their frenetic actions were proof that they were aware of the proceedings. They understood that the King had died and, for whatever reason, had come to the scene of the services. Red Raven had consciously maneuvered himself into the path of the arrow in such a way that when struck he would fall into the boat. Eradrin felt a chill on his skin and sensed goose pimples rising. He experienced a sudden spark of emotion. Was it hope? He darted a glance at Queen Mateah and noticed that she was again issuing orders to one of the Red Gold guards. The guard nodded and gave his horse a little kick in the side to get it moving.

With the boat carrying King Aremis to a blazing finale in the lake, it was time to bid farewell to Dayanna. A fresh surge of pain and loss rose within Eradrin and he closed his eyes. From the moment she had been torn apart by the ravens until now, he had kept the hope that somehow she was still alive. He had dreamt of the ring of fire and of her return. Now he must face reality. Shabael had killed her with an arrow, and the ravens had somehow made her disappear.

Why? Why did you do that? You took my love. You took the light. I do not understand.

For the first time in Eradrin's life, he doubted the intentions of the ravens. Had they offended them somehow? No. That wasn't it. Of all people, the ravens seemed to adore Dayanna. How many times had he come into the courtyard to hear the sound of her laughter and find her sitting among a group of ravens? One day they were doing aerial stunts for her attention. *Oh, they loved you as much as I.* Eradrin staggered and placed a hand on the burial boat to steady himself. Suddenly he found it hard to breathe and dropped to his knees on the sandy shore. He had never cried for her loss or for his father, but he was devoid of emotion. Seeing his father's blood on the blade of the sword when he was being crowned had roused him. Even talking of war and vengeance with Thomar had stirred him deeply. With Dayanna gone and his father slain before him, he had become aware that he was teetering on a threshold of no return. Nothing roused his passion or even angered him. There were no real plans against the Malbolians. Even Thomar was attempting to carry out a plan of vengeance that he had boldly designed. A king must not only have a strong mind, but a heart. It frightened Eradrin that as king he could understand that he could never be touched by emotion. If that happened, you would be considered a King with a Malbolian heart. His father had told him that.

"Eradrin! Oh, you break my heart. Are you ill?" Saydee asked, her voice concerned. She lifted on her toes to look into his eyes.

"Oh, Saydee, I feel again!" He wiped a tear from his cheek with a finger. "Look, I have shed tears."

Eradrin drew a deep breath and gathered himself. *I feel as though I've just awakened.* He rose to his feet and brushed the sand from his robe.

You are your father's son, he heard the voice of King Aremis say. *Hide your pain. Step away from it. As king, you must place your emotions in the no-mind cell. You will grow to hate being king under the Malbolian rule. The only way to survive is to remove passion. Never show affection toward anything, for it shall be used against you.*

"Dayanna was born a princess to the Ravenites," he said, ignoring the voice in his mind and addressing the crowd. "You loved her as much as I. She was to be my wife, our future queen, and mother to my children. We grew up together with her father as acting Viceroy. From the moment our eyes met, we were soul mates. Never have I seen eyes so beautiful and so displaying of emotion. She laughed and loved with those eyes. Her thoughts were always pure and of others instead of herself. Many times, I witnessed our finest citizens weeping with her as they discussed past sins, lost loves and lost fortunes. I often thought I saw the presence of the Illuminator within her.

"She gave her life so that we might continue to possess our dreams. When the raven carrying the Orb of Light had its leg caught in the branch of the tree, she put herself in harm's way to free it. That was her final act."

Eradrin raised his eyes and stared straight at King Shabael. "*Curse you ten thousand fold, demon. My love died from your arrow and I will find you, even if it is in the afterlife, and stab you once for each day I have lived without her.*

336

"We now send sweet Dayanna to the heaven that awaits her. This shall be a day of joy in Heaven as it receives such an angel of Skyeden."

Eradrin motioned for Dayanna's boat to be pushed away from the shore and the soldiers eased it into the water. The sail filled with the breeze and the boat moved silently away. Again, the archer handed him the bow, then the flaming arrow.

As Eradrin raised the bow, a flock of ravens lifted into the air and flew toward the boat. He was poised to fire the arrow, but waited to see what the ravens were doing. They perched on the boat, facing the shore.

Do you want to die with her? Don't you know her body is not there?

"I will love you forever, Dayanna! Farewell!" Eradrin released the arrow and it sailed high into the sky before descending. The ravens remained motionless on the boat until the arrow struck the silk-wrapped bundle that represented Dayanna, and then they lifted into the air. The bird leading the exit carried a burning piece of the cloth in its beak. They soared into the sky in a V formation with the lead raven carrying the flaming cloth. A few hundred feet above the water, the bird released the cloth and the ravens circled to watch its descent. When the cloth hit the surface of the lake, the ravens scattered and disappeared into the darkness.

"The Light of Skyeden," Eradrin whispered and turned to a nearby guard. "My father's sword," he ordered; and, the blade with the two raven heads etched into its hilt was passed to him. Eradrin turned to face the lake and intoned, "Priests Amila and Daren, please come forth. Mother and Saydee please remain by my side." The crowd surged forward. Shabael's wife, Queen Shawndeli, dismounted.

"Take my Father's sword, Priest Amila," Eradrin directed. Daren placed his hands under Amila's to help support the weight of the blade.

"I kneel to make my vow to the Great Illuminator, to my Priests, my family, the Ravenites that I serve, and the Emperor Shabael. I, Eradrin Donachie, do pledge to be a good king. Forever shall the hope of Light burn bright in my heart. I say this before our conqueror, the Malbolian King, that he may at his desire have my life's blood drain into this sand. Our lives can be ended with a slash across the throat but our souls shall never be conquered, for there is the eternal flame that burns and will rejoice on the day of its union with the one true Light. I vow as King that I will bring life and light back to our people. We lost the Orb and in one hundred and fifty years, it will be a thousand years we have lived without it. I vow that if we do not have the Light on the eve of the one-thousandth year, I will remove myself from the throne with a final law enacted that no Ascended king may sit on the throne a day more one hundred years without the recovery of the Light. Mortal kings will be limited to ten years. So be it! This funeral ceremony is completed."

The people reacted with confusion. They had come to grieve their dead king and to celebrate the new ruler. They were expecting to hear words of encouragement from King Eradrin. They were starving for a few crumbs of hope. Instead, he was declaring that he would abdicate the throne if the Light was not regained. They had just attended the funeral of their only King since the beginning of their tribe and now they would surely lose his successor, one of the blood ordained by the Illuminator. Who would take the throne then? Thomar? Aribon? Someone appointed by the Malbolians? Was he so confident in his ability to bring the light back? And taking a wife so quickly … every power-hungry mogul in the kingdom would be presenting their daughters. How was he going to have time to evaluate potential wives while he was searching for the Light?

Eradrin's purpose was not lost to Queen Mateah, however. "Look at them," she said to Shabael. "He's getting them worked up for a revolution. Must we kill them all in order to preserve peace? I say that we should kill him and the rest of the Donachie family right now while we have them gathered here. This is a funeral ceremony, so let's celebrate death. Place Malcolm on the throne."

"No, Mother," King Shabael said, his voice calm. "This could be a turn of fate that we will recall as one of the greatest triumphs of the Malbolians. For when the allotted time does pass and Donachie steps down from the throne, the faith and religious beliefs of the Ravenites will be shattered. The people will be leaderless and rudderless and will voice their vows to us, giving up their religion and beliefs to become Malbolians and descend into the Dark Essence. I am delighted by this turn of events, Mother. I could never have devised a scheme of this magnitude. A hundred years is but a blink of an eye for us immortals. When that century is past, the hope of the Light returning will be in ashes. Our new king is already destroyed. He has just presented us with his kingdom and doesn't realize it."

"He is motivated, though, and will spend those hundred years searching for the Light," Queen Mateah said. "I promise you, my son, that my eyes will never leave him."

Mateah turned toward the lake and peered into the perpetual darkness. "My scouts have not yet returned with word on the launching of that aerial float. It was a brazen act of revolt to inspire hope in these people. They must accept that the Light will not return to this world." Irritated, she pointed at a Red Gold Guard. "Go! Learn what is happening with my scouts and report back to me."

"Yes, Your Highness!" The guard bowed. "Out of the way! Move!" He jerked the reins and the horse reared on its hind legs, scattering the nearby onlookers.

The crowd was beginning to thin as people returned to their homes or visited nearby establishments to share drinks and observations of the myriad of happenings during the day. King Eradrin and the royal family remained on the shore, staring out across the lake water.

Queen Mateah surveyed the surroundings, thrust her arms outward, and shouted, "Malatee!" Malatee was the only Darkling to have ever merged with royalty. He wore the honor like a badge and the other Darklings were wary, giving him a wide berth.

Malatee's response was immediate. It launched itself from the parapet, evoking a few screams from citizens who happened to be looking in that direction. Nearby torches flickered as their flames were attracted toward the Darkling's movement. A moment later, Malatee was perched on the queen's arm, its form ever shifting in its darkness. A black eye here, a claw there, leather scales; they appeared and disappeared in the shifting ever-moving dark smoke that made up the phantom figure.

"Send me visions of what you see around the Tree of Light," Queen Mateah ordered. "Find for me those who launched that airborne float. Be gone!"

Malatee gave a shrilling cry as it flung itself down the beach and quickly disappeared up the side of the mountain.

Shabael watched his mother in action and smiled. "Shall we return to our quarters?

"No. Not just yet. I must learn what Malatee has to show me first. I am convinced there was a connection between our Seer wagon being destroyed at the same time this float appeared. In fact, I think all of that was simply a distraction for something else."

As Queen Highest expressed her suspicion, two of the Red Golds returned from the Seer Wagon. "Well, did you learn anything?"

The guard bowed. "Your Highest, one of our soldiers reported seeing a ball of fire fall from the side of the tower and strike the roof of the wagon."

"From the tower?" Queen Highest spurred her horse, causing the protective guard to move with her. She looked up at the tower, and then turned to where she thought the float had been launched. Debris could not have flown that far, could it? The wind was blowing in the direction of the tower, however. Perhaps the breeze could have carried embers. Still, the soldier said the flame had fallen from the tower.

"Mother, what is it?" Shabael asked.

"Suspicions. And these black ravens! Archers!" she suddenly commanded. "Put an arrow through any black raven that you see!" A murmur of protest sounded from citizens who heard the Queen Highest's orders.

Shabael turned in his saddle, observing the distraught people around him. "Stand ready!" he shouted to his Red Golds. The guards unsheathed their swords and tightened their protective circle.

"Akilleh!" Queen Shawndeli suddenly shouted, summoning her elite troop of warrior women Sword Dancers who had gathered perhaps a hundred yards away. She turned to Shabael. "Permission to go on a scouting mission, My Emperor."

"Yes. Go, by all means," Shabael said, feeling a little exasperated by the series of rapid developments. Had he entrusted too much power to the women in his court? He could end it all with a wave of a hand, but decided to let the scenario play out. Besides, he was beginning to experience a slight sense of unease. The majority of his force was still in Skye Castle above them. Most of the Ravenite people were unarmed. Nevertheless, should they stage a mass attack and come at them from all directions, his soldiers could be overrun. "Move these people out of here!" he ordered in a voice that rang along the shore. "Send them up the stairs or the lift. Now!"

Queen Shawndeli exited the protective circle of guards and guided her mount to the front of her Red Death Sword Dancers squad. The women, some of them as muscular as men, wore bright red silk and red leather clothing. Their choice of garb was not solely for aesthetic purposes, but also for mobility. The women were highly trained and could slice the average Malbolian warrior a dozen times before he could swing his heavy blade. They proved themselves annually in a contest was with the Red Golds. The Red Deaths, Queen Shawndeli's personal creation, numbered one hundred, but she was the most expert of the group. Her warrior skills only enhanced Shabael's affection for her. She was beautiful and dangerous, a killer who had been tested on the battlefield.

Shabael sighed and accepted the roles of his wife and his mother. One rode with the Red Death. The other with the Red Dragons. Let them have their desires fulfilled. Yet every time Shawndeli rode off with the Red Death unit, he felt a strong sense of dread, a kind of dark omen of the future. He fretted that one day his queen would not return and he would face eternity without the greatest love of his life. He endured nightmares of leading a search party and finding the women massacred. He could forbid her being a warrior, but that would be an insult to her. She was as well prepared as a warrior could be and she was proud. Denying her that passion would be a cruel slap in the face. She would not abide it. He watched her ride away and prayed for her safe return, that this would not be the day that he led a desperate search party.

"May King Eradrin approach, My Emperor?" Malcolm asked from the outer circle of protective Red Golds.

"He may," Shabael said.

"Emperor El Qui, may I inquire what is happening?" Eradrin asked. He was on foot and resented the Emperor's higher position mounted on the horse. If there was anyone to truly understand the respect to be given to a King or Emperor, it was Eradrin. But with this Emperor, who had killed his father, his love, a future brother-in-law, and countless other Ravenites, he felt no respect. Only the bitter taste of loathing in his throat. It took all the self-discipline and restraint he could muster to keep himself from slashing the emperor's horse's legs and bringing him to eye level before driving a dagger into his chest.

"We have dispatched squads to investigate these distracting occurrences during the ceremony," Shabael answered. "If you will kindly assist us in removing your people from this area, perhaps we can get through this without casualties." Shabael brought his horse two steps back and waved his men to form a circle with Eradrin on the outside.

Eradrin reluctantly issued instructions for his guards to have the citizens clear the area. Shabael heard a slight moan from his mother and turned toward Mateah, who had her head thrown back, her eyes wide, quickly recognizing that she was receiving a vision from Malatee.

"It's all right my love," she said in a voice that was only slightly above a whisper. "Do not look directly into the tree. Where are they?" She drew a deep breath and began to rub her temples. "Yes, follow the hoof prints."

"You must go around," Queen Highest said, responding to the Darkling's vision playing in her mind. "Do not be fearful. The tree will not harm you. Hurry."

The Darkling's telepathic vision showed ruts from wagon wheels and strange hoof impressions. Not as deep a depression as might be expected from the heavy Ravenite horses. Blood on the ground. A discarded knife. A dented Red Gold helmet.

Queen Highest began massaging her temples. Her eyelids flickered. Shabael moved his horse closer and placed his hand on his mother's saddle horn to steady her nervous mount.

She spoke in a lowered voice as she commanded Malatee. "Hurry! Go to the other side of the mound!"

She grimaced as the Darkling's visions played out in her mind's eye. A severed hand, leather padding, a fallen horse, a Red Gold with an arrow through his chest. A robed Ravenite squirming in his own blood.

"A little more, Malatee. Who did this? Where is my guard? Show me a little more!"

"Bitch!" A familiar Ravenite face appeared. Thomar, the King's brother. The heel of a boot suddenly blacked out the reception from the Darkling.

"Ahhhhh!" Queen Highest shrieked in pain. Her horse reared, throwing her to the ground. Shabael felt something tear in his arm as his mother's saddle horn was yanked from his hand.

"Mother!" Shabael jumped off his horse and cradled his mother's head.

"Run! Run!" Jump from cliff! The screaming Queen Mateah abruptly sat up and then collapsed in Shabael's arms.

Thomar skidded to a stop at the edge of the cliff beyond the Tree of Light. "*Damn it!* I had her. I know that was *her*. If she recognized me, it's over," he said, frustratingly kicking at the ground with his boot.

"You think it still lives?" One of Thomar's men asked from behind.

"The Darkling is dead, but the queen is too evil to die. By the Gods, another inch and I would have pinned it. Come! We best go. Our ruse has been discovered. Down the passage now. There's no going back now."

Thomar ran back to the battle scene, which was littered with bodies, mostly Malbolians. "Gather up their weapons and armor. Strip the Red Golds. Free the horses from the wagons and bring them with what you can carry. Hurry to the passage!" Thomar scanned the dark horizon but could see nothing. No one was coming yet. Not yet. "Hurry! If they catch up with us before we've had time to regroup we're dead."

Kneeling on the lakeshore, Shabael lifted his mother in his arms. A shout rang out from the onlookers. "The Queen Highest is dead! Red Dragon is dead!"

"Help me on my horse and give her to me! No! Wait." Shabael braced his footing and clutched his mother in his arms. "Wings!" He almost buckled as he felt energy course through his back, an agonizing tightness that made him want to scream. Then he felt huge surging relief and heard the *"whoosh"* of wings expanding. He bent his knees and lifted into the air with great effort because of the additional weight of his mother. The other Red Golds extended their wings and rose with him. The faithful Rageton appeared alongside and grasped Shabael's elbows to help propel him upward. They rose over the castle walls and came to rest on the balcony adjoining Shabael's quarters.

Shabael placed his mother on the balcony floor. "Mother?" He slid his hands underneath her body and lifted her head upward. "Mother." Queen Mateah's forehead was turning a dark purple from the blunt blow Malatee must have received. "Send for healers! Dispatch fifty men now to the Tree of Light. Find out who did this and bring them before me!"

Two female healers rushed onto the balcony and one of them dropped to a knee and felt for the Queen's pulse. "Very faint. I fear she is dying."

"Heal her. Heal her now!" Shabael commanded.

The healer turned to one of the Red Golds. "Bring me an animal! Any animal, so that I may perform a transference."

"There's no time!" Shabael said. "Use her!" He pointed at the second healer.

"Me?" The healer's face paled in the torch light.

"You! Now, or so help me ...!" Shabael yanked his sword free from its sheath and placed the point of the blade on the kneeling healer's chest.

The healer placed her hands on the Queen Highest's head. "Out!" she commanded, tearing her hands free and grabbing the second Healer. "Take this wound!"

"No!" The second Healer wrenched free, her eyes going wide and wild as she staggered backwards, striking the balcony railing and falling over, hitting two men who were walking past. Wheeling around, Shabael saw the healer supine in the courtyard and then returned to his mother. He glared at the healer, who continued administering to the queen.

"Look," the healer said suddenly, pointing at the forehead of the Queen Highest. The purple bruise on her forehead was beginning to fade.

Suddenly the Queen Highest sat up and clutched Shabael's shoulders. "The king's brother," she gasped. "It was the king's brother." She collapsed in Shabael's arms.

"She still lives, My Emperor," the healer said, immense relief showing on her face.

"You are fortunate," Shabael growled, and in one graceful movement, jumped to his feet and sprouted wings again. He spun around and dived off the balcony, the Red Golds following his lead as their wings extended.

From below, Eradrin watched Shabael and his guards fly in the direction of the Tree of Light. *Something has happened. If only I had wings!* "Mother, I want you and Saydee to return to your quarters. I am going to the Tree of Light and learn what has happened there. I'm afraid Thomar is in trouble. Guard! Escort Mother and my sister to their quarters. Also, arrange for twenty horsemen to accompany me to the Tree of Light."

"May I go with you?" Priest Daren asked.

"Yes. Come walk with me. You may very well be needed." Eradrin said, noticing that the despised Malcolm was lurking nearby. "You, Sir, can give me some personal space. Our talk is for my spiritual needs, not for your traitorous ears."

Malcolm's head twitched, but he retreated a few steps under Eradrin's angry glare. The new king and his new priests walked briskly up the steps. "Do you know what has happened? Daren queried."

"No, not for certain. However, from what I have observed, I think the Queen was receiving images from one of her Darklings. Apparently the darkling was injured and being in the state of converse, the queen received its injuries."

"Do the human and the merged animal receive the same injuries?" Daren asked.

"Yes. At least, I hope so." Eradrin glanced over his shoulder to ensure that Malcolm was beyond earshot. "Our problem is, if the Queen Highest lives she may have seen who or what struck her. "

"Then I will pray for the poor Ravenite's soul if he is found," Daren said.

"I join you in that prayer, Priest. Did you notice the actions of our ravens? Our personal ravens came to us, just as my father's Red Raven went to him. Did you observe how it flew directly into the path of my arrow?"

"I did, my King. I believe the ravens are very aware of us. With the Light magic gone it has prevented our direct communications, but I believe they are still with us. They know our hearts. It is a sign there still is hope. All is within our grasp, if only we can find the Orb of Light before it is destroyed."

"If it is destroyed, then all is lost," Eradrin murmured. "I honestly don't think we can endure the Malbolian rule for much longer. "Surely, there is a solution. Our Great Creator would not desert us."

Daren squeezed Eradrin's arm and leaned closer. "There is something I must tell you, my King."

"What?" Eradrin asked, looking over his shoulder at Malcolm, who was covertly watching their every move.

"I cannot speak of it here. Until I can, however, make no rash decisions. I am breaking protocol by this, but if true, Milord, I can assure you that our moment will come." Daren turned away from Eradrin and rejoined Amila

Realizing what he just said to the King, Daren was desperately fighting the emotions raging within him. He felt he had just made a great mistake. Suppose his vision was not true or had been misinterpreted? The Creator had paved his way to be the High Priest appointed by the priests' council and now his swollen ego had led him to tell the king of the vision. Perhaps it had not even been a vision, but merely a dream. *No, my faith is strong.*

When he rejoined Amila, the old priest wrapped his long, bony fingers around Daren's wrist, and whispered in his ear. "Be careful what you do and say. The vote appointing you was not unanimous. You cannot be viewed as having caused a King's failure. If that should happen, you will most certainly be hung and God's relationship with man will be damaged. "

"I understand," Daren replied, his heart racing. *Fool!* When a new High Priest was appointed, it was dictated that he must partake in a three-day vision quest. On the second night as Daren fasted in quarters where air was thick with incense, a vision came to him. It began with a terrifying image of the great tree burning. When the fire began to subside, Daren lifted his eyes to the sky and a ring of fire appeared. People that he could not identify and whose figures were distorted by heat waves and shadows, tumbled through the circle, one holding a glowing branch. Now he must determine how and when to interpret the vision for His Highness. He mentally chastised himself for having broached the subject.

When they reached the walls of the castle, Eradrin turned to look over the wall at the lake below. The last glimmers of fire on the boats of his father and Dayanna were being doused by the water as they slowly sank beneath the surface. The embers blinked out just as their life force had. All that remained was darkness with the Dark Moon reflected dully on the lake's surface. Eradrin motioned for his guards to remain on the ground, ignoring the posted Malbolian soldiers. The Red Gold elite were using their wings to maintain surveillance with approximately thirty of them airborne, circling the grounds. They lingered in position for twenty minutes, the near maximum of their flight potential and then were replaced. A shadow shifted, probably a Darkling. These shadowy devils seemed to be lurking everywhere.

Eradrin paused and raised his face toward the dark sky. "Great Illuminator, I beseech you to protect my brother. He has served you well and is risking his life for your Light. What can I give you in return for his safety? I have lost my father and my future queen. I do not understand why you would let your people suffer and die by those of the Dark. Why do you allow your people that worship you to be so punished?"

CHAPTER 39

AN ARROW TOO WIDE

Thomar spurred his horse, leading the Ravenite soldiers along the shore. A few more miles and they would turn north into the woods. He looked skyward over his shoulder, searching for a shifting shadow that would be a Darkling. If only he had struck that Darkling harder with his boot! He was sure that the resourceful Malbolians could tap into the Darkling's mind and recover its final images. "Saymayo! Saymayo!" a rider appeared to Thomar's left, riding parallel to him on the beach. The horseman was dressed in nomadic garb and rode the same breed of small horse.

Thomar reined in his horse and threw out his hand to signal his men to stop.

"Who are you? Thomar shouted.

"Saymayo! Saymayo!" The nomad looked like one of his soldiers but Thomar was not familiar with the language.

"Come closer, I can't understand …"

"They're coming!" One of the soldiers shouted, pointing. A group of horsemen bearing torches and riding fast were approaching.

"Dismount on the edge of the woods," Thomar ordered. "Let's keep the lake behind them."

Thomar turned back to the mysterious rider but found that the man had moved up the beach to the line of trees.

"Hurry! God, they are flying. Hurry!" Thomar shouted, gesturing with his arms. "Dismount, drop to one knee and place your swords beside you. Arm your bows."

Thomar could see the riders, riders dressed in red uniforms and being led by a woman. *The emperor's wife?* "It's the Red Deaths!"

"Hold your arrows until my command!" Thomar shouted to his kneeling soldiers.

The hundred Red Death warriors galloped onto the scene. Darklings mingled with them like patches of darkness. Streamers of light from the torches revealed their positions as they moved across the sand with amazing speed.

"Ready your aim," Thomar said, and raised his bow. He aimed for the leader whom he had no doubt was Queen Shawndeli. How bold these Malbolians were. How easy it would be to lure them into a trap.

"Hold," he commanded as the Red Death squad thundered toward them, the horses' hooves kicking up sand and the clamor of sheaths and weapons loud on the quiet beach

"Hold! Thomar ordered."

"Ahhhhhh!" One of the younger men cried out, threw his bow to the ground, and fled. Two others broke rank and followed him.

"Stay, damn it!" Thomar shouted. The break of the line also broke the focus of the soldiers. When in a state of terror concerning what was likely a hopeless situation, the slightest distraction could be catastrophic. And in that lost second of turning to see their ranks breaking, the Darklings had leapt a hundred yards in advance of the Red Deaths.

"Now!" Thomar cried, and fired his arrow toward the queen. He didn't wait to see if the arrow struck its target, but grabbed his sword and rose to his feet. Bedlam ruled as the Ravenite soldiers confronted the attacking Darklings, which attacked with bared fangs and slashing claws. Teeth and talons clanged against the weapons.

Of the three arrows fired at Queen Shawndeli, the first missed cleanly, whizzing past and beyond her. The second struck the front quarter of her horse, making the galloping animal lurch forward and dip. This movement saved Shawndeli's life, causing the third arrow fired by Thomar to miss by inches rather than strike her in the throat where it had been aimed.

Thomar swung his blade high as an airborne Darkling dived at his head. The blade slashed through it, but the Darkling reformed in midair and came at him again. There was no substance to the body, just a yawning black hole. *How does one fight these creatures?* He summoned all his energy, focusing his inner Light on the Darkling. It worked! The Darkling began to dissipate and its murky remains fell to the ground where it disappeared in a dark swirl.

Hooves thundered and the earth trembled as the Red Deaths roared into the fray. Thomar stood, bravely confronting the leading chargers, but they swept past him and just as suddenly, Queen Shawndeli was upon him. The nostrils of her wounded steed blared. Her sword was raised in striking position. Thomar stood firm, his own sword ready to strike. The queen pulled hard on the reins, causing her stallion to rear on its hind legs. It was a beautifully awesome, terrifying moment in time.

Thomar threw caution to the winds and ran at the rearing horse. Someone was about to die. He summoned all his strength and energy and prepared to slash the woman before her horse's feet returned to the ground. However, as he prepared to bring the blade forward for the strike, his life energy drained from his body and left him unable to complete the killing move. He was so struck by the aesthetics of Shawndeli's beauty that he suddenly found himself in a vacuum. He stood frozen, the deadly sword held above his head poised for the strike. And he could not do it. He knew at that moment that he was a dead man. Nothing could save him as he watched the magnificent rearing steed settle to all fours, the queen's sword poised for the kill. She created a glorious, mind-numbing picture of death. Her silky-white hair and blazing ruby eyes were going to be the image he took with him into eternity.

A crushing blow from behind suddenly sent Thomar crashing to the ground as one of the Red Deaths rammed him with her horse. Hands flipped him over onto his back and the points of two swords made indentations in his throat.

"Spare him," Queen Shawndeli ordered. "He is King Eradrin's brother."

CHAPTER 40

KILL THEM ALL

"Lord Malcolm, My King," one of the guards announced. Malcolm was climbing the stairs to the balcony, the hood of his robe covering his head. Bowing, he held his hands at his waist.

"A very sad and stressful day, Your Majesty," Malcolm said, his face obscured in the shadow of the hood.

"Yes, indeed it is," Eradrin replied. "What is the latest on the condition of the Queen Highest?"

"She lives but is in a restful state. Apparently one of the healers took her injury, which was so severe it killed her."

"It's always a tragedy to lose a healer. Send my regards to the Queen Highest with word that I hope she recovers quickly," Eradrin said.

"Yes, for the sooner that she may leave Skye Castle. I must say, King Eradrin, I am surprised after all this time and domination that there still remain hopes for the return of the Light."

Eradrin sighed, tired of the word play and only wishing that the oaf would go away. *A shove over the balcony would do it. Send the fat, blubbering fool to the rocks below. Go away!*

There were no signs of troop movement on the western shore. *Suppose Queen Shawndeli has been killed? What if she and her elite guard never return?* That thought made his blood curdle. He had no doubt the Queen Highest would know the identity of the one who had caused her injury. *Please, Illuminator, protect my brother, Thomar.*

351

"I have no doubt the Emperor will be inquiring about the ravens," Malcolm continued prattling. "You know he has ordered any black ravens seen within the castle grounds to be killed."

"We cannot allow that," Eradrin protested. "Our people have hundreds of pet ravens and the Ascenders still maintain their merging abilities. Killing the birds would be devastating to them."

"Yes, but you cannot deny their behavior earlier. It appears that there have been new mergings. Is this so?"

"No, Malcolm, you know that cannot happen without the proper illuminations and vibrations. We have not had that ability in a thousand years."

"Yet, even so," Malcolm raised his hand gesturing to a great Divine above, "your personal merged raven perches on your arm, then your late father's makes a dramatic appearance. Think of the odds for that to happen and at the time it did. I must admit I was touched by the gallant gesture of your father's Red Raven. Oh, how noble a gesture to proclaim its love of your father by throwing himself in the path of the burning arrow. Oh, how dramatic! The very conception of that plan strains credibility. What a great proclamation that was that relationships continue between Ravenites and ravens."

"What is your point, Malcolm?" Eradrin didn't try to veil his impatience.

Malcolm cocked his head to one side and his eyes brightened. "Your Highness, I fear such behavior will warrant the Emperor to issue a law of death to all black ravens."

"To even speak of this idea is for no other purpose than for cruelty," Eradrin said, scowling. "Why don't you just eradicate us all? Order all that will not renounce the Light as their God to be executed." He stretched his arms out and extended his chest toward Malcolm. His voice lost its calm and the volume raised several octaves. "Come on, Malcolm, kill a king. Kill all the ravens. Kill the mothers, the wives, the girls, the boys, the rabbits and squirrels, kill them all!" Eradrin made a sudden move and snatched the small dagger wedged beneath the rope belt Malcolm wore with his robe. He placed the dagger in Malcolm's hand and lifted until the point was against his throat.

"Do it! Start the flowing of blood with mine!"

"My King!" A Ravenite guard attracted by the commotion stood at the door, his sword drawn.

"No. Stand down!" Eradrin ordered. "Everything is under control. Well, do you have the heart black enough to start the cleansing, Malcolm? Do you?"

Malcolm smiled as if he had been offered a flower by a child. He relaxed his grip, then suddenly grabbed Eradrin's shoulder and shoved, attempting to thrust the blade into his neck.

But the muscular and younger Eradrin banged Malcolm's hand against the rough stonewall and the dagger fell free. Eradrin sprang upward from his knees, thrusting a shoulder into Malcolm's midsection. The momentum of Eradrin's attack sent the two men sprawling across the narrow stone walk.

"*Gaah!*" Malcolm moaned as the air was knocked from him. Eradrin rose to his knees pinning the man to the ground. Malcolm's hood was partially ripped. He struggled for a moment, and then began wheezing.

"Really? You tried to kill me, you insolent toad? Listen carefully to me now!" Eradrin lowered his head and whispered the threat in Malcolm's ear. "This I swear to you, traitor! If ever you raise a hand against me or if I so much as hear a negative report of your actions against our kingdom, I will cut you to pieces and eat you myself. Moreover, if that does not kill me, it will at least make me a God among men. Fear me, Toad, for you witness the birth of a darkness that when compared to the Queen Highest will make her seen as bright as the Sun of Day. I will eat you, then piss you, then shit you off this very wall. Do you understand?"

"Yes, Your Highness" Malcolm said, near panic.

"Do you really?" Eradrin seized Malcolm's ear lobe with his teeth and bit down. Malcolm howled. A nearby Darkling lurking beneath the balcony screeched. Eradrin grabbed Malcolm's dagger and hurled it toward the Darkling, whose scream hit such a high note that it white-blitzed Eradrin's brain. Eradrin bit down harder, feeling his teeth meeting and his mouth filling with blood.

"Yes!" Malcolm wailed.

Eradrin released the cowering, moaning Malcolm and rose to his feet. "Get up before you are seen in such a state, you human excrement! Rise!"

Malcolm stood, gasping and clutching his ear as blood dripped between his fingers.

"I think we are through with counseling this evening, don't you think?" Eradrin asked, wiping blood from his lips. Malcolm's gaze fixed on Eradrin's bloodied fingertips and, for the first time, Eradrin saw fear in the man's eyes. Malcolm slowly retreated from the menacing glare, reaching behind with his free hand while the other still clutched his ear. He found the ladder and fled so quickly down the rungs that the palace guard was barely able to evade him.

CHAPTER 41

RETURN OF THE SWORD DANCERS

"Look!" one of the gate guards said, pointing to the westward shore of Lake Waccamola. Torchlights borne by riders were moving toward them.

"Look!" Someone else shouted from the ground level. It was King Shabael returning with his guard. They alit atop the castle gate, their wings folding inward. Shabael glanced curiously toward Eradrin and then turned his gaze to the shore. Seeing the approaching torches, he dove off the gate and sped downward, extending his wings slightly and pinning them back to gain velocity. His guards followed.

Eradrin leaned over the balcony, watching the scenario unfold below. The blazing torches revealed the Red Deaths squad, but he did not see either Queen Shawndeli or Thomar.

King Shabael and his guards landed on the shore several yards ahead of the advancing group. He cupped a hand over his eyes to peer intently, but could not locate Shawndeli. She wasn't among the front riders where she normally rode. Shabael's breath caught in his throat, but then he saw her riding another horse, coming up quickly beside the unit. She reined her mount to the front of her guards and raised her hand to halt the Red Deaths.

"My Emperor," she said, a sense of pride on her countenance and in her voice. "We intercepted an armed force of Ravenites. We have prevailed and I bring you the brother of King Eradrin as proof of their involvement."

355

Shabael sighed, smiled, and made no attempt to disguise the immense sense of relief he felt to learn of her safety. The king opened his arms and Shawndeli dismounted, paid homage by dropping to one knee in the sand, and rose to be embraced.

"I can't explain to you the love and pride I feel at this moment," Shabael said, pulling his wife close. "I should have known that my concern was useless because you always bring glory to the Malbolians." He suddenly noticed a stain of blood on her sleeve and what appeared to beads of blood dangling on a loose braid of her white hair. "Pray that this blood is from our enemy, my love, for if ever a drop of your blood is spilled, woe to the man who causes it."

"No, I am not injured, My King. However, I can report that seventeen of the Ravenites are no longer breathing our precious air. And as a memento of our excursion, I present to you King Eradrin's brother." She motioned to a bound figure on a horse flanked by two of the Red Deaths.

"Oh yes, that one. He struck Mother's Darkling with his boot and almost killed her. Had it not been for the sacrifice of one of our healers in granting transference, the Queen Highest would be dead."

Shabael approached Thomar, whose wrists were bound upon the horn of the saddle, the reins held by one of the Red Deaths.

"Oh, Thomar, what shall the Queen Mother have in store for you? She is so inventive, you know, always amazing me. We shall learn soon, because if there's one thing you depend on, it is the swiftness of her judgment. I promise you, your state of pondering your fate will be brief. If I were you, I would use these final moments for the repenting of transgressions. Surely you do not desire to be denied the Light." Shabael paused, looked up, and then glanced around. "Oh, but what Light is that? I cannot imagine what is in store for you in the afterlife, you rebellious bastard. But I promise that the only light you will see there will be from the fires! It would almost be worth my own journey to Hell just to witness your arrival."

Shabael turned to Queen Shawndeli and helped her back onto her mount. "Take time to compose yourself and wash this unholy blood from you, my love, and return to me. The Queen Mother and I have a reception we would like you to attend this evening."

"I will not be long, my husband."

Shabael kissed her forehead, summoned the wings, and soared to his quarters in Skye Castle.

CHAPTER 42

WARM BUDWEISER AND COLD LOGIC

Knock. Knock. Knock. Dylan rapped his knuckles on the door again.

"Give me a minute. Hold on." Mike Sanders opened the door, still wearing the clothing he had worn at the hospital. There were Budweiser cans strewn around his recliner like Indians circling a big bear. His shirt was half out of his pants and his hands were covered in black grease. Several smears of grease ran along his forehead and under his eyes where he had rubbed his face.

"Sorry to come barging in, sir," Dylan said, wondering if he should leave. "I just wanted to talk with you about what happened on the mountain. See if we could make some kind of sense out of it. But something really scary happened on the way here, too. Something was chasing me; like a bunch of crazy birds or something. They were swooping down at me and one of them poked a hole in my back tire."

"Come on in," Mr. Sanders said, waiting until Dylan was inside, then sticking his head out and peering around before closing the door. "I'm too wired to sleep. I can't stop thinking about Freddie. I should be at the hospital now, but the doctors insisted on me coming home and trying to get some rest. I mean, he's in a coma. He doesn't know if I'm there or not. Been having a little private conversation here with my friend, Bud."

Dylan nodded. "I understand, Mr. Sanders. I wish I could have given the deputies a better description of the truck. But all I can remember is that it was old and some kind of weird light green or

357

bluish color and I'm pretty sure it was a Ford. There were a bunch of guys standing in the back, but they were wearing some kind of masks over their heads. Looked like pillowcases. That's all I could see, then I heard the crash. I can't believe what Freddie's bike looked like. I didn't know a frame could bend like that. I've never seen anything like that before, have you?"

"Ain't like nothing I've ever seen," Sanders answered. "And, I've been in this business all my life. Hope your Dad catches those sons of bitches. Murdering bunch of red necks." He slumped in his recliner and grabbed another Bud out of a cooler beside the chair. There was no ice left, just water. There were a couple of pies sitting on the kitchen table along with two vases of flowers. The neighbors were being thoughtful.

"Want me to put those in the refrigerator?"

"I guess. There's a box of chicken in there if you're hungry. Lot of women been stopping by. They mean well but they're about as bad as the lawyers. Bet you I've got a dozen texts from lawyers. Ambulance chasers. For the next month, my mailbox will be stuffed with letters telling me how many millions of dollars I can make from lawsuits.

"Tell you the truth, I'm worried about what your daddy may do, son. You know, he has a point. I never should have turned you two kids loose on those cycles. Just never dawned on me that you'd really play hooky and head for the mountains. Never too old for a good case of stupid, are you?"

Dylan decided to keep silent and stared at the photos on the wall. All of them were of Freddie and his dad, from his birth until two days ago when they were high-fiving with a beautifully restored Indian motorcycle standing behind them.

"Mr. Sanders," Dylan began, his voice breaking with grief, "if there's blame, I deserve it. It was my idea to ride up the mountain. Just a crazy idea. But I was so excited I couldn't stand the thought of spending the day in school. Please don't blame Freddie. I was just dumb.

"And I want you to know, sir, that whatever happens now, you and Freddie have enjoyed more life together than any fifty fathers and sons I know. Freddie's the best guy I've ever known and you know he's my best friend."

"Yeah, I do know that, son. I'm praying that he'll pull though this. Even if he never walks again, he'll still be the light of my life. He's the only good thing that ever happened to me. I watched him tinkering with cars and bikes and I saw myself twenty years ago. He was so proud of those Indian bikes. They weren't just bikes to him, you know. He said they were like ladders that were going to take you two to the stratospheres of babes and wild adventures."

Dylan laughed. "Yeah, that's Freddie all right. Oh, you should have seen him when we stopped for a Mountain Dew. He actually flirted with a girl. I'd never seen him walk so tall. He really was on top of the world. And you're the one who helped him have that feeling. You know, he was still conscious when they pulled him from that bike. He kept asking for his glasses, saying, 'I have to fix this.' I found the glasses and they were broken, but when I set them on his nose, he seemed to calm down … like in his mind, he was fixing himself."

"Well, I can't sleep," Mike said. "I've got the phone in my shirt pocket and every time it rings I think it's going to be that bad call. I had the bikes towed to the house, then sat down, had a beer or three." He chuckled, a rasping sound that was far from being a laugh. "The longer I sat, the more I worried about Freddie, so I went to the garage and tried to work on the bikes. I tell you, son, I'm as much of a wreck as Freddie's bike. Come on. Let's go to the garage. I want to show you something."

They stepped outside. Dylan looked down the street for any signs of what had pursued him earlier. *Two wrecks in one day.* His Schwinn was propped against the steps. As they walked to the garage, he flashed back to the morning, when he had first seen the Indian cycles. It seemed only a moment ago that Freddie had been sliding the bay door open and wishing him a happy birthday.

Yeah. Happy birthday, Dylan. You caused this by talking Freddie into riding up the mountain. Some best friend. Stupid!

Mike opened the garage door. "I've been doing some work on yours. That's where all this grease came from. Hard to believe, but it can be repaired as good as new. The fender was dented, the mirror knocked off, the foot stand bent, the clutch handle broke, and the rear light gone. But it's nothing that can't be fixed. Good thing you had safety bars or the bike would have been destroyed."

"Wow," I didn't really get a chance to look at it after the accident. Sounds like it was totaled." Dylan said, as the image of him and the bike being hurled over the mountain returned. He remembered free falling on his back, seeing the ledge above and then seeing the bike

359

only a few feet away, falling with him. Then everything had gone black. He reached up and touched his cheek, remembering things brushing against his body. Claws, eyes as black as the feathers. He felt a dizziness come over him.

"Whoa, Buddy, you all right? You need to sit?" Mike asked.

"I don't know what happened," Dylan sat down on the floor and grimaced. He had skinned his left leg and slightly burned his right ankle when it had touched the hot exhaust of the bike before he was thrown free. He stood up and ran his palm across the leather seat of the Indian, feeling the softness against his palm. "I - - I don't know how to say this, Mr. Sanders, but something really strange happened up there on that mountain."

Sanders drained the last of the beer and crumpled the can in his hand. "What kinda strange you talking about, son?" He picked up a wrench and looked around for something to tighten ... or loosen. Something. Anything.

"I remember laying the bike down because I was going too fast. The bike slid across the pavement, went over the curb, and struck a rock, but we went around the rock and over the side."

"Over the side?" Sanders tossed the crushed can at a basketball hoop nailed above the fireplace. "You went over the side of the mountain? What? Son, the patrolman said it was a thousand foot drop off that overhang."

"I know. I don't know what happened. I was free falling with the bike. All I know is I went over the ledge. I remember my bike and me falling at the same rate of speed and thinking, 'Wow, it's heavier but we're staying side by side. I know it was weird that I was thinking that, but I remember it really clear. That's when I realized I was going to die. Then there was this crazy black blur of cloud that seemed to gather and lowered me down to one of the ledges."

"You want a Bud? Think I need one more." Sanders grabbed a warm beer from a six-pack sitting on a shelf that held a case of metric sockets and an Angelina Jolie Tomb Raider movie poster.

"Sure," Dylan said. Why not? It's a crazy night. He pulled the tab and turned the can up, the warm beer almost making him gag. He swiped an arm across his mouth, trying to hide the grimace, but Sanders wasn't noticing. "Do you believe in angels?" Dylan asked. "I never have, but it's the only explanation I can come up with. I mean, both the bike and I should have been splattered on the rocks. But look at me; the only injuries I have or the damage to the bike came from us skidding on the pavement, not from the fall."

Sanders took another drink of the warm beer studied his young friend's face. "No idea how you just stopped flying out into space and came to rest on that ledge, huh?

"No. I remember my arm hitting the rock. And I remember sliding toward it and thinking my head was going to be cracked open like an egg, but I only brushed it with my arm. I remember reaching out for the rock as I fell backwards. After that, everything's a blur."

"Sometimes your head does crazy things. Don't worry about it. All that matters is that you're standing in my garage drinking a Bud."

"Yeah, I guess you're right. It's a miracle I'm even alive. I feel kinda guilty, really, seeing Freddie laying there all bandaged up and unconscious and I'm walking around as if nothing even happened. God, I've never seen a bike so mangled as his. Looked like it was in a junk yard compactor with Freddie on it."

"Freddie's gonna make it. You gave him his glasses. He'll fix himself."

"You're right. He may be in a coma, but I'm pretty certain he's got that mind working overtime mending all the broken parts."

"Here," Mike tossed Dylan the keys to the semi-repaired Indian cycle. "Take her out. See if she's okay."

"I can't. Not after what's happened," Dylan protested, feeling goose pimples on his arms.

"Oh come on. I can't get in any more trouble than I'm already in with your daddy. You know what they say: If you fall off a horse, you gotta get right back on it. Go on. I know Freddie would want you to. It'll do the both of us good."

"All right, Mr. Sanders."

"Uh, call me, Mike. Mr. makes me feel old."

"Alright, Mike. My Schwinn is shot. If you think so." Dylan took the keys, threw his leg over the bike, and sat on it, slowly placing his hands on the handlebar controls. It was inconceivable that he was even alive much less sitting on the bike that he had ridden off a thousand-foot drop. This couldn't be happening, not at almost midnight on a school night. He had been having a lot of weird dreams recently. Maybe this was just another.

"Come on," Sanders said, placing a reassuring hand on Dylan's shoulder. "Do it for Freddie."

"All right. For Freddie."

Dylan reached over, retrieved his scratched up helmet and tightened the chinstraps. "If it's OK, I'll just leave my bike in your yard and pick it up tomorrow." He kick-started the Indian and the roar of the engine was magnified in the garage.

"Yeah, boy! Sweet!" Sanders raised a clenched fist. "You on it, you bone it."

Dylan laughed and bumped fists, then rolled the bike down the drive and out onto the street. He looked both ways and scanned the treetops before moving onto the road. His nerves were shaken. He reached the intersection where the convenience store was located and saw the woman with the spilled groceries was still in the parking lot, talking to a police officer. *Jesus! Am I going to be arrested?* He thought about turning around and going back to the Sanders' house. But then he shrugged, pulled his helmeted head down close to his chest, and rode past the store without attracting a glance.

It was only a few blocks back to his home. He really wasn't in the mood for speed, so he cruised along at about twenty-five miles-per-hour. Dylan loved the feel on the Indian and thought the clutch actually seemed smoother. He drew in a deep breath and felt the tension ease from his shoulders. The air was cool and refreshing. He could almost feel tensions, worries, and thoughts of craziness draining from his body and soul. Maybe everything would be all right after all. Freddie would survive and they would still be together. *I will be there for you, buddy. Whatever you need. If you're paralyzed, I'll roll you around and scoop the bedpan underneath you. Remember all those times you said you wish you could be another Stephen Hawkins? Be careful what you wish for, huh? But just think, Winkie; you've got your mind and you can accomplish so many things ... Oh, shut up, you dumbass! That's all just so much lame bullshit! Oh, God! I'm so sorry, Freddie. I'm so sorry.*

"Cawwww!" The black object sped past his head. Dylan braked the cycle and placed both feet on the ground. What was that?

Dylan, help me. Help me! OH MY GOD!!!!

"Freddie? Where are you?" He was alone, standing in the middle of a neighborhood intersection and he was hearing Freddie's voice? *Freddie, I heard you. I heard you loud and clear.* Icy fingers of fear played up Dylan's spine like a piper's hand. His breathing quickened. Something was here. Something was really close. The awareness terrified Dylan to the point that he couldn't find the will to move. He tried controlling the involuntary trembling, afraid to glance around. Afraid of what he might see.

A streetlight lamp about a hundred yards ahead suddenly exploded. Dylan held his breath. There was a streetlight between him and the one that had just popped, but the street was basically dark. He could see light from windows in some of the nearby houses and wondered if he should knock on a door. None of this stuff seemed to happen when other people were around. *Am I going insane?* The remaining street lamp suddenly flickered and a long wavering stream of light snaked its way through the darkness. *Run. Run now. Get this bike started and get the hell out of here.*

The street light suddenly blazed again and then popped with sparks flying. The thing was moving now. Whatever it was, he could sense it getting closer. The thing suddenly leapt at him from some thirty yards away. Dylan raised his hands for protection while allowing the cycle to fall to the ground. He couldn't really see his attacker, but smelled it and felt the dark energy that sucked at his life and pulled at his very soul.

Fighting panic, Dylan struck out and grabbed at his attacker, but his hands couldn't find anything to grasp. *This is it. This is how I die, on a dark street in the middle of the night. Happy eighteenth birthday!*

The ravens slammed into the dark demon, a being that was like a starless night, shifting, and rolling into itself, with a glint of leathered skin, claws, razor teeth, and sounds of churning and gnashing. The birds attacked viciously, but the dark thing was too quick, too elusive. It tore into the ravens. Claws, feet, wings, and feathers were flung into the air as it ripped the birds apart. Still, the ravens persisted. The black demon cloud drifted a few yards away, hanging in the air. Waiting. Menacing.

Dylan kicked the Indian cycle into gear and sped down the road. Several of the ravens flew ahead of him. They were directing him. Leading him. But where? Dylan wanted nothing more than to go home. He wanted this insane night to end. However, the ravens made it clear that they expected him to follow them. When he slowed near the driveway to his home, the birds circled and cawed. What was he supposed to do? They had just saved his life. He rode past the driveway and followed the ravens. He understood now where the ravens wanted him to go. Freddie. They were telling him that Freddie was in trouble.

CHAPTER 43

THE EYES HAVE IT

"Well, that's it then, Dr. Atzez said, wiping the sweat from his brow. The ICU room was crowded with nurses and techs gathered around the bed. "Someone contact the father and have him meet me here. I'll have to ask him about organ donation. It is not marked on his license. Well, we did all we could, but he's no longer breathing," the doctor said. "Keep him hooked up to the respirator. We need to keep him alive as long as possible in order to keep the organs from deteriorating."

The medical staff departed from the ICU and gathered around the desk down the hallway. Nurse Lindsay Talbot remained in the unit, cleaning up discarded packages and used tissues. A movement at the window attracted her attention and she looked up to see a dark mist gathered outside. The nurse was captivated, causing her to drop the articles she was holding. *Amazing!* The mist, or whatever it was, had the most beautiful brown eyes. The eyes were huge; so loving and pleading. *What?* Oh, the eyes were asking her to open the window. *No problem. Happy to be of help.* Nurse Talbot stared into those beautiful eyes; feminine eyes that made her grow moist between the legs because they reminded her of an experience with her first cousin, Nancy. Nancy knew of her lesbian tendencies as all her family did, and she had smiled at her knowingly with eyes widened to suggest there was a mutual yearning. Although it had been years ago, Lindsay had never forgotten that moment. She had often thought of that look, of those beautiful brown eyes, so big and so hard to turn away from because they touched the depths of her sexual ecstasy. She had spent many joyous moments in her bed alone late at night as she stared into those haunting eyes. Now the eyes were back, unblinking, intense, and reaching into her soul. Nurse Talbot moved to the window, raising one hand to reach for the window latch while her other hand raised the white skirt and eased toward her inner thigh.

Yes. I want you too, baby. I want to touch you deeper than any man could. Open the window. Open to me the warm wetness of your tongue and kisses.

Nurse Talbot issued an audible gasp. She glanced over her shoulder and saw that the door was almost closed. No one would see them. It would have to be quick, though. Her fingers gripped the window latch and slid it back. "For you," she whispered. She opened the window and took a half step back, closing her eyes. She could feel the warm dark mist flowing around her; feel its light touch and warmth move beneath and over her shoelaces, around her footie socks. It moved as gently and sweet as a lover's fingertips around her calf and behind her knees, causing a deep ache between her thighs. She felt herself tense, hoping and pleading that the fingers would continue to rise up her legs when she suddenly felt a drain of energy. She opened her eyes and tried to cry out but didn't have enough energy to do even that as she watched the dark mist pull away from her and begin consolidating into a solid mass, taking on a human form. It was a female shape that appeared. The long streams of smoke evolved into strands of hair as the neck, shoulders and arms formed.

Mansi smiled and leaned forward as if to kiss the young nurse as a swarm of Darklings came through the window and covered her. Talbot wanted desperately to scream but one of the Darklings slithered through her open lips and into her throat. She desperately clawed at her throat and back-pedaled toward the door. The Darklings seized her, a half-dozen of them, and moved to the open window. They flew through the opening as Nurse Lindsay Talbot desperately continued to try to scream, her legs kicking and arms thrashing hopelessly.

One of the attendants at the nursing station thought she heard something and lifted her eyes from the medical chart she was reading. When she heard nothing else, she resumed her work at the same moment that Nurse Talbot's lifeless body was deposited in the branches of the old oak tree in the parking lot.

CHAPTER 44

THE PASSING OF FREDDIE

Dylan brought the bruised Indian motorcycle to a skidding stop in the back parking lot of Silverton Memorial Hospital. It was dark as the lamplights were off. *Why am I not surprised?* He scanned the area carefully, taking a special note of the huge oak tree and the dark foliage toward the top that must be a large cluster of mistletoe or an opossum nesting. Then a flickering light from one of the hospital windows caught his attention. It was the only window open on the floor — the fourth floor, the Intensive Care Unit floor. *Freddie's floor!* As he watched, cold fingers of fear gripped his insides. He thought he saw something no larger than a bird's shadow sweep through the window. Fear galvanized Dylan into action. His best friend's life was at stake and he was two hundred yards of pavement and four floors away.

Throwing caution to the winds, Dylan spurred the Indian with a twist of the accelerator and tore through the parking lot, jumping the curb and sliding to an abrupt halt at the glass admittance doors. The receptionist saw the flash from the beam of the cycle's headlight and rose from her chair. *The idiot was going to crash through the glass doors.* She stood with her back pressed against the wall of the booth, still holding a copy of a magazine with the cover featuring a movie promo for "rTr — Coming Dec. 31, 2014 — Because the World As We Know It Ends in 2015. Pictured on the cover was a long highway aligned with trees with a red light at the end of it. Only this wasn't a red light the receptionist was staring at, it was a young man in a black leather jacket with shoulder length black hair and wild eyes, running through her lobby with a look on his face that suggested something really bad was about to happen. She watched as Dylan yanked off his helmet as he ran past her to the elevator, pounded frantically at the floor button and squeezed through the opening doors. When the floor light popped on at four, the nurse punched the digits on the desk phone for security and hoped that the idiot security guard was awake in his cozy little office at the front entrance of the hospital.

Mansi stood at Freddie's bedside as the last of the Darklings merged with her body. Her head was lolled back, arms outstretched, feeling herself solidify like a sewn together doll whose stitches were melting away into wholeness. The procedure always created a ferocious sense of itching as her consciousness merged into her body, the million nerves messaging her brain of things coming together. At times she wanted to scream in agony. But as her consciousness settled in and the intense itching faded, a rush of relief swept through her. She was Mansi again. Queen Mansi, performing a duty for her beloved king. She smiled and stepped to the window, motioned with her hand, and the Darklings that had accompanied her from the Tree of Dark swept into the room. She watched the shadowy figures gather in the room, then reached over to the monitors hooked up to Freddie and began unplugging them.

"Take him!" Mansi commanded and stepped back against the wall, keeping an eye on the slightly ajar door. Freddie's eyes suddenly opened wide. His hands flailed against the bed railing, yanking at the tubes and cords, causing the IV stand to teeter and almost fall. The alert Mansi caught it in time and steadied it. She appeared entranced as she watched the shadows move up Freddie's arms and legs. It was like watching a fist-sized smoke-black Pac-Man gobbling its way along. How fascinating and yet horrifying to watch the munching of the flesh, seeing the fingers disappear, the meat of the palm, the wrist, now the radial bone. She marveled at how quickly the Darklings consumed Freddie. The white bed sheet was leaving a bloody impression of what the Darklings had just consumed. Oh, they were horrid creatures, these Darklings, but they were *her* creatures; her children that she had watched breed, flourish, and give birth beneath the shadow of the Dark Tree. In addition, she was part of them, for they had consumed her once just as they were now doing with Freddie.

"Hurry!" Mansi commanded, her voice impatient. She looked into Freddie's lifeless eyes, as the sheet over his waist lay flat and reddened. "Soon, Freddie, soon," she in a soothing voice." She reached up to push his hair from his brow, as his head angled down with his chin touching the mattress.

A flung motorcycle helmet hit the floor, bounced off the wall and slid across the waxed tile floor. A young man burst through the doors with a wild look on his face, his eyes wide, and his mouth open. He ran to the last room on the right, threw the door open and cried, "No!" as he disappeared inside.

A final chunk of Freddie's hair was being sucked into a small churning shadow, which then fled through the window.

"You!" Mansi hissed and lunged toward Dylan. Dylan braced for the attack. However, the woman burst into a dozen black pieces of nothing that were flying around him, running across the walls toward the door, and then following the walls back to the window and finally leaping out into the night air.

Dylan lowered his fists and ran to the window. He caught a glimpse of the dark shadows that were joined by what looked like dozens more coming from the oak tree. The dark shadows continued moving skyward, momentarily blocking out the half-moon as they sped away.

"Hold it! Don't move!" The security guard entered the room and came up behind Dylan, his hand on the still holstered pistol.

Dylan moved quickly, feinted a move to the left, then to the right, cut around the guard, and slammed into a second one who was just entering the room. The impact sent both Dylan and the guard sprawling on the floor. Dylan jumped to his feet. With his sneakers screeching on the tile, he tried to run as the downed guard grabbed his ankle. Dylan twisted free and headed for the door, his mind racing with crazy thoughts. *Did you see that, Coach? No tripping, man. Breaking tackles. Touchdown a comin'.* He eyed the door as if it were a goal line and straight-armed the door, slamming it open, creating a scream from the desk nurse that spread to the other three nurses on the ward. Sprinting down the hallway toward the elevator, he heard the ICU door thrown behind open him. He spotted the video camera over the elevator doors and veered left to the stairway. Four flights of stairs but he should be able make it faster than anyone taking that slow elevator. And if they came down the stairs after him, well, he was a lot younger and in much better shape. Odds were he could be on the Indian and long gone before those wheezing windbags could get outside.

Dylan took the stairs four steps at a time, seizing the handrails on each side, and swinging his feet outward and down to catch the next set of steps. He made it to the last flight, but then lost his balance as the toe of his sneaker caught the edge of the bottom step. That caused his knees to bend forward, and he slammed his head against the exit door, throwing him backward. The back of his head hit one of the steps and for a crazy moment the world went into a wild spin and turned black and white, making Dylan think he was somehow sitting on his head and looking up at the ceiling. But the world righted itself quickly and he scrambled to his feet. *No problem, man. No worse than getting hit by a linebacker. Move!*

The feet tried to obey the command, but the knees and upper part of his legs were still somewhere at sea. He wobbled out the exit door into the main lobby and saw the receptionist duck behind the desk. Finally his legs caught up with the rest of his body and he made a beeline for the exit doors.

Mike Sanders was just entering the lobby.

"Don't let them out!" Dylan yelled as he raced past Freddie's startled father.

"What the …?" He watched Dylan run outside and jump on the motorcycle, then turned back to see what the commotion in the lobby was all about as two security guards rushed out the stairway door into the lobby and ran his way.

Dylan urged the cycle over the curb and headed for the highway. Without thinking, he was heading west, in the direction that the shadows had gone. Then his mind began messing with him. This was the first time he'd had time to think and now he wasn't sure thinking was a good idea. The woman with the long black hair and no clothes had exploded into those dark things. Freddie's bed was soaked in blood and there was no sign of him. These dark things, or woman, or whatever the hell it was, had flown out the window and he had no earthly idea what they were or where they were going. And where the heck was Freddie? In addition, why the heck was he racing down a highway in the middle of the night with no idea where he was going

369

And… oh shit! On top of that, he was going to be in big trouble with his dad. *Jesus! Nobody is going to believe any of this stuff. Christ, I don't even believe it!*

He closed his eyes, imagining his father and other law enforcement officers watching the security camera of him running through the hospital. The six o'clock news blurb on the local TV station: "High school student feared dead as Sheriff Spencer Morgan's son is sought for questioning."

The scream of a patrol siren suddenly sounded in the night air. *Great. Hi, Dad. Bye, Dad!* He turned right at the next intersection and had ridden perhaps a half mile when he spotted a flock of ravens silhouetted by the moon. They appeared headed west toward the mountain and he thought, "Okay, why not? It's no crazier than anything else that's happened lately. "Okay. I'm coming!" *Only two ways out of Silverton, east or west, the ravens know best. Yeah, and guess what two roads the deputies will be watching for a guy on a bike? Yeah, a guy on a bike without a helmet. I'm screwed. Well, what difference does it make? Can I dig this hole any deeper? Go for it. Just go for it.*

CHAPTER 45

FREDDIE IS BACK

Mansi and her devoted Darklings watched the flock of ravens and the speeding motorcycle head past them going west. He had come back to the hospital and seen her close up. And now, he was heading west, following the ravens. *Following the ravens where? To the Tree of Light?*

She sat down and leaned against the trunk of the tree. The Darklings, appearing as puffs of black dust, surrounded her, awaiting her command, eager to go after something. "Hmmm." Mansi relaxed and smiled. This was the moment. Finally, at last, there would be another like her. Her will would be his. She began to chant:

"Darklings, Darklings dark in mist
About to give your mother bliss
For within you each there is the piece
A soul and flesh to make a whole
Form you now so I may behold!
Blood and bone a being made
Forever bound to obey
For whence my will denied
Will be the day he truly dies!"

The Darklings that had consumed Freddie began to swirl in a circle just above the ground. The fallen leaves on the ground rose and were caught up in the swirl. Mansi stood, lifting her arms upward as

371

she observed the Darklings. The shadowy shapes began to merge into one another like black tar being poured into a pothole. Mansi could smell the searing adhesion of flesh. This was what had happened to her so long ago. Now she had willed the Darklings to consume and then reconstruct a human. The body became more recognizable with each piece of him melding into the whole of the shape.

The remerging was thrilling and electrifying for Mansi. She could not wait to report this occurrence to the Emperor. And yet, despite the feeling of pure ecstasy that gripped her body, she felt the sense of urgency. She and the Darklings needed to be pursuing the ravens, especially if they might be taking the boy to the Tree of Light.

The wind grew still. The immediate area looked like one of those sci-fi crop circles with the blades of grass, weeds, and bramble all bent clockwise. Standing in the center of the vortex was the figure of a young man, appearing as a doll taken freshly out of the mold. Gradually the black began to fade into flesh color and the nude Freddie Sanders stood before them, his body whole and unbroken.

The new Freddie opened his eyes. Awareness of his surroundings and the beautiful young woman standing before him became reality. This was the girl from his dream; the one who had made him promises of love and sexual gratification. Then his eyes suddenly crinkled and he shuddered as the memory of the pickup truck barreling toward his motorcycle flashed through his mind. He was suddenly overtaken by fear and began trembling.

"It's okay," the black-haired beauty whispered just loud enough for him to hear. "You're safe now, Freddie. As I promised, you are whole again. Can you talk?" She stepped toward him and placed gentle fingertips to his lips. The confusion was obvious on his face. He was dead and broken and needed fixing. Yet, here he was.

"Do you remember your name?" the girl asked, smiling. When he did not answer, she continued. "You are Freddie Sanders and you serve me"

CHAPTER 46

'HE'S COMING'

The first raven alit in front of the hut and quickly moved through the opening flap that formed the entrance. Once inside, it hopped onto a large clay jug and issued a muted caw.

Raven stirred on her pallet and saw the raven, recognizing it immediately. She rose, crossed the room to a bowl, and took a kernel of corn, which she gave to the bird. After sliding on her moccasins, she again crossed the dwelling and pulled back a flap, revealing a sleeping older woman.

"He's coming," Raven said quietly, and exited the dwelling, walking swiftly along a path through the woods that led to the tourist village. She ran to the entrance and stood in the middle of the road, waiting, as streaks of orange began showing on the eastern horizon.

CHAPTER 47

THE EXECUTION

King Eradrin Donachie and his family were being escorted to the Tree of Light, where his captured brother, Thomar, was being held. The king and his family had been locked in their chambers shortly after the return of Queen Shawndeli's Red Deaths so he had stood outside on the balcony hoping to learn what was happening.

Several hours later, the royal family was summoned and brought outside to begin the trek to the shrine. Eradrin, his mother Juliana and sister Saydee were placed in a topless carriage.

As the procession to the tree began, an excited murmur was heard from the crowd following the entourage. A steady influx of ravens filled the sky, heading toward the Tree of Light.

When the carriage rolled over the crest of the final hill before reaching the tree, they saw several hundred Malbolian soldiers and many of the Skye Castle populace who had arrived earlier. In addition, perched in the tree were hundreds of ravens, creating a black shroud among the branches.

When they reached the tree, the soldiers parted the crowd to reveal Shabael, the Queen Highest, and Queen Shawndeli standing on a makeshift platform. Eradrin turned his eyes to the Tree of Light and saw Thomar attached to the trunk of the tree with spikes nailed through his hands and feet. A huge pile of brush and logs were stacked beneath him along the roots and trunk of the tree. Standing to one side was a mammoth Malbolian soldier wearing a black hood and holding a flaming torch.

Eradrin's initial reaction was to leap from the carriage and rush to Thomar. However, the sharp tips of the spears pressing against his body by the escorting guards dissuaded him.

"The Emperor," Malcolm announced to Eradrin and the gathered people, "has given you the privilege to watch the execution of Vicar Thomar Donachie and destruction of the Tree of Light."

An astounded roar rose from the citizens as comprehension of Malcolm's words sank in. There was a surge forward as some in the crowd tried to break rank but the Malbolian guards reacted swiftly, slashing with their swords, stabbing with their spears and clubbing others. Blood spilled in the circle around the tree.

Eradrin reacted angrily. "This is a travesty! You cannot do this! This is a tree of the Divine! Destroy this tree and you destroy the world!" Eradrin attempted to dismount from the carriage and an eager spear drew blood from his left arm. "You can't do this!" he shouted again, but knew his words were futile and mostly unheard among the clamor from the distraught crowd.

As Shabael gazed at the chaotic scene around him from his view on top of the platform, his lips twisted in a cruel smile.

"Son, are you certain of this?" Queen Highest asked. She was standing by his left arm and Shawndeli on the right. The High Priest Calibri was standing next to Queen Highest. "My Emperor, perhaps you should reconsider this," Calibri said, raising his voice to be heard above the protesting of the people.

"I have never been so sure!" Shabael groused. "They tried to kill you, Mother. And, but for the grace of the Great Creator, they would surely have killed Shawndeli."

Shabael moved to the highest level of the platform and shouted to the crowd, which slowly grew silent but for an occasional mumble. The wounded and dead drew a red line between the citizens and the guards stationed around the tree.

"I want you to remember this moment. This is what happens when you strike at the Queen Highest or any member of our royalty. Your Light is dead, your God is dead, and your hope is dead. Nevertheless, you have desired that this tree give Light, and in that, your prayers are to be answered. If you seek to place blame for your misfortunes, look no further than this miserable piece of human garbage nailed to the tree. Blame this on your brother, King Eradrin!"

"It's the end of the world!" someone shouted.

"Kill the man that said that," Shabael ordered; and, a Malbolian soldier decapitated the protestor. The crowd grew silent with only an occasional murmur being heard. The circle of spears guarding the tree was unthreatened; and, the soldiers knelt on one knee, their weapons poised.

Queen Mateah was still smiling, but she was becoming concerned. She glanced at Shabael, red-faced with anger and emotion. *His behavior has become erratic.* His immediate reaction in calling for the execution had pleased her. However, burning the Tree of Light was going too far. The tree had been here as long as man could remember. It had been the holder of the Orb of Light. Angering the Gods was suicidal and she was afraid Shabael was about to cross that line. Did he love her that much? Did she mean that much to him? *No, it's something else.* She looked skyward to the ever-unchanging dark bluish-hued sky. For a thousand years, Malbolians had ruled Skyeden and held the Orb of Light in a dark chamber. They had terrorized and enslaved the kingdoms of the world. These were the people who had proclaimed their souls to belong to the Illuminator. So, where was their God?

"Look around you," King Shabael addressed the throng. "There is no Light. Your God is dead. We have the power. We have immortality. Why do you still insist on resisting us? Instead, come and join us. I am going to prove to you today, for once and all, that your God is dead. Your Light is forever gone. It has abandoned you. Yet, we have not. We are here, asking you to join with us. Come join us and Descend with us!"

"Never!" someone shouted.

Shabael raised his arms in an encompassing gesture. "Listen to me! I am your Emperor! I am the lineage of God's appointed El Qui. Yes, I took the Orb of Light! My father and I smote the Sun and Day Moon from the world! We broke your Illuminator's back. He is as dead as your King Aremis Donachie. I, Shabael El Qui, King of the Malbolians, will also be your king." He extended his right hand and motioned for the flaming arrow. I will prove authority by burning the Tree of Light. "Let history remember this. Am I not worthy now, Lord of the Dark? Thus I anoint myself by this act to be truly accepted as your favorite son."

"No!" The people screamed and several threw themselves into the spears in fatal attempts to reach Shabael.

Eradrin was exasperated, helpless against the guards who still held spears and swords poised and ready to kill him at the slightest provocation. His eyes left the suffering figure of his brother and went to the sacred tree. The tree that had existed since recorded history. It was the connector between the spiritual and the physical world. If the Tree of Light were lost, so would be the link between the Illuminator and mankind.

Shabael turned and looked down on Eradrin. "It is you, new king, who has brought this to fruition. It is time now for Your Highness to bid goodbye not only to your treacherous brother, but also to your precious tree. For I hereby declare Vicar Thomar Donachie guilty of treason and the attempt of assassination upon the Queen Highest. I, as sole judge and jury, find him guilty as charged. I condemn him to death, and with him the Tree of Light."

Shabael lifted the bow and seated the burning arrow. The people grew silent and it seemed the entire world stilled. Shabael drew on the string of the bow until it was fully extended, his muscular arms showing a slight tremor from the tension. Eyes widened with the awesomeness of the deed, Shabael released the taut bowstring, and the flaming arrow sped through the air. As it began its approach into the center of the tree, one of the ravens flew into and was impaled. The bird fell to the ground, its feathers smoldering.

"Another," Shabael ordered, his voice rasping with emotion. The soldier gave him another fiery arrow, and he again fired it directly at the tree. Again, a raven flew into the arrow's path and dropped to the ground with it protruding from its breast.

"Another!" Shabael demanded, his voice growing louder. He loaded and fired and another raven sprang from the tree and took the arrow.

"Another!" Shabael commanded. This time he aimed for the trunk of the tree, drawing the bowstring as far as he possibly could. His arms trembled. Beads of sweat appeared on his brow. He released the arrow that sped so quickly the human eye could not follow it, but a raven again stopped the arrow with its body. The force took the raven back and landed at the base of the tree, where the arrow continued to burn. Two ravens dropped from the lower branches and covered the flame with their bodies.

"Sire?" the bowman asked, holding up another burning arrow.

"No." Shabael looked around him. "Archers, surround the tree and light your arrows."

Eradrin closed his eyes and lifted his face skyward, praying for a miracle. Most of the onlookers were on their knees; many held one another for comfort.

When the archers had encircled the tree Shabael gave the command, "Ready!" The archers loaded the burning arrows and drew their bows.

"Fire!" Shabael shouted.

As the archers loosed their bows, hundreds of ravens erupted from the tree, intercepting most of the arrows. The few that got through and embedded in the trunk were quickly smothered by birds sacrificing themselves.

"Enough!" Shabael paced the length of the podium and stopped facing the tree. "Come," he motioned a nearby guard and whispered into his ear. The guard left the podium, mounted a horse, and rode toward the castle.

"There will be no more attempts to fire arrows at the tree," Shabael said, staring out over the crowd. "It is apparent that the ravens are willing to die to prevent it happening. We will wait until my guard returns and then proceed with the execution of the rebel."

Eradrin managed to get the attention of the Ravenites' Captain of the Guard Winslow Athane. "I wish to speak to my brother during this time of waiting. Will you please make sure that King Shabael hears my request?" Athane nodded and headed to the platform where Shabael stood. He returned within a couple of minutes. "The Emperor grants you permission, as long as his guards are in attendance."

"That's fine," Eradrin said.

"It makes me nervous that you will be so near the pyre, brother," Saydee said. "May I join you?"

"Aye, come if you wish." Eradrin stepped from the carriage. "Mother, is there anything you wish to say to Thomar?"

"Tell him I love him; that we'll be together soon. Tell him to give a hug to his father when they meet. No! Wait! Please I must go to my son."

The captain of the Malbolian guards escorting them nodded his okay and Eradrin helped Saydee and his mother down from the carriage. They began a slow approach to the tree surrounded by armed Malbolians.

The pyre was built so high that Eradrin could not touch Thomar from the ground. So he and the women climbed the steps to the platform where Thomar was spiked to the tree.

Eradrin hugged Thomar's legs and then stepped back. "I am so sorry, brother. Trust me that I remember our promises and will keep them. Neither your life nor your death will be forgotten."

"Thomar," Saydee whispered. "I love you! I pray that soon you will be reunited with Father in the Heaven Sky." She reached out a hand and touched one of his legs.

Juliana had not yet climbed the steps. She tore a strip of cloth from her gown and dipped it in a barrel of water standing nearby, climbed the steps until she was within reach of Thomar's bloodied feet and began to bathe them.

"That feels good, Mother," Thomar said through parched lips. He lifted his head and opened his swollen eyes. His face was bruised and dried blood had stiffened his hair. "I don't want to die, Mother. I want to be with you," he said in a raspy voice.

"Oh, Thomar, My son!" Queen Juliana wailed. "God awaits you. Oh…." She tried to speak but raw emotion stole her words. She placed her cheek against his feet.

"You are a hero to our people, Thomar," Eradrin said. "I will miss you, brother. But you must trust that we will be reunited."

"Your Majesty, you should return to your place now," a Malbolian guard said to Eradrin, who then came down the steps and took his mother by the elbow. The queen wrapped the wet cloth around Thomar's feet and rose to follow her son and daughter back to the carriage.

Meanwhile, new High Priest Daren went to the pyre of wood around the oak tree. He carried a leather pouch of water and a small cup. When he had climbed high enough to reach Thomar, he said. "God awaits, Thomar. Your death will not be in vain. Here, my Prince, drink this." Daren placed the cup against Thomar's lips.

"This is bitter, Priest, could you not have gotten me something sweet in these last moments?" Unbelievably, the tortured Thomar's lips curled in a small smile.

"I know it tastes foul," the priest said, "but drink it. It contains a drug to help you withstand the pain. And I am giving you this." Daren placed a cord around Thomar's neck with a small pouch attached. "In this bag is a powder that when it heats will explode. It will save you much pain."

Thomar blinked and nodded. "Father, tell me. Is there truly a God?"

"There is, Prince Donachie. There is a God and Heaven Sky awaiting you. You will join your father there."

"I plead that you make sure my son and wife are cared for," Thomar said. "May I pray with you now, Father?"

"First, my Prince, I would like to share a recent vision with you. In it, I saw a great fire, which I could not understand until these past few hours. In the vision, following the fire, many, many moons do pass, and then a ring of fire appears in the sky. In addition, I saw beings pass through the ring and fall to the ground. And in the hand of one of these beings I saw a glowing branch."

"A glowing branch?" Thomar asked, his voice weak and trembling. "Do you think this was a true vision?"

"I believe it to be."

"Hope?" Thomar asked a second time.

"Yes, hope. A glowing branch."

"Thank you, Father for sharing this," Thomar said. "This gives me a peace that I sorely needed."

"That is good, my Prince. You will leave us knowing that there is hope. Not all or our struggles and pains are in vain."

Almost an hour had passed when the Emperor's guard returned, carrying a small bundle. He dismounted and went straight to Shabael. After several words, he gave Shabael the bundle and quickly disappeared into the crowd.

Shabael exchanged a few words with Queen Mateah and they stepped down from their platform and walked to the tree, stopping before the pyre. They shared another quiet, brief conversation and moved up to stand on the platform with two masked guards. One of them held an axe while the other held a torch. Obviously one of them was the designated executioner. The guard with the axe placed a basket at Thomar's feet. Queen Highest, standing at the front of the platform, lifted her arm. The executioner moved alongside Thomar.

King Shabael suddenly approached the executioner and asked for the axe. He then turned to address the people. "I, Shabael El Qui, find Thomar Donachie guilty of high treason and sentenced to be executed." He stepped up on a small stool that brought him to shoulder level with the doomed prisoner. Shabael looked to his mother. "May God strike now if our judgment is false," she said and several eyes turned skyward.

The Queen Highest dropped her hand.

Shabael dropped the axe, picked up the bundle the other executioner had brought to the pyre, and allowed the burlap material to fall away. He pulled free a plug to the leather pouch and sprayed the contents on Thomar. Then the great King Shabael snatched a torch from one of the attending guards on the platform and lit Thomar on fire.

People screamed. The ravens reacted by dropping from the tree and flying in a circle around the trunk. They appeared on the verge of attacking Shabael

Thomar screamed in pain as the flames consumed him. A small explosion followed by a bright flash ended Thomar's screaming. The flames spread from his body to the trunk of the tree and began climbing up into the branches.

Shabael and Queen Mateah climbed from the platform and were escorted back their horses.

Meanwhile, the ravens were giving their lives in an effort to save the Tree of Light, their feathers catching on fire as they flew through the flames, trying to smother them. Some of the flaming birds began dive-bombing the Malbolian soldiers, who swung their lances wildly, stomping the ravens that fell to the ground.

The Ravenite citizens panicked, fleeing the mad scene and crying out in terror. For the true believers among them, destruction of the Tree of Light meant the end of the world was coming.

Queen Juliana and Princess Saydee averted their eyes from the flaming pyre and clung desperately to Eradrin. The three of them dropped to their knees and began praying.

"My King!" High Priest Daren joined them, falling to his knees and placing his hand on Eradrin's shoulders so they saw eye to eye.

"This was in my vision that I relayed to you. I saw this great fire, but was not aware that it was the tree. However, remember, I also saw that years from now a ring of ravens and fire will appear here. That someone will come bearing a white branch. It means hope, Milord! It means life continues. Despite all that has happened, you must maintain faith."

"Our Tree of Light is being destroyed! There will never be light again," Eradrin anguished, seeming not to hear the priest. "All is lost." He raised his head and saw the whole of the tree blazing. "What have they done? Great Illuminator, where are you?"

"The Light will never die," Priest Daren insisted. "It is within all of us and I believe the vision to be true. It is my belief that a day of redemption will come."

"When the crown was placed on my head, I heard my father's voice say, 'Three shall come on ravens' wings. Perhaps that is of what he was speaking. Let us pray our world survives this"

Saydee and Juliana exchanged concerned looks and Saydee said, "The time shall come, Eradrin."

Eradrin looked at the burning tree, then at Shabael and the Queen Highest, his eyes glistening with hatred. "Yes. I will wait for the sign. And when it comes, there will be the final war."

CHAPTER 48

UNDER THE OLD OAK TREE

King Eradrin opened his eyes and blinked. It had seemed only yesterday that the Tree of Light had burned. He had endured many nightmares of Thomar burning. Yet a hundred and fifty years had passed and no sign from the Great Illuminator. The El Qui were still in the Neverlands, but so much time had passed without incident that the armies were not on high alert. Peace prevailed. Only the suffering without light continued.

"My King," Aribon said, speaking softly. "Thank you for telling me this. I can now…" he drew a deep breath, "lay my weary soul to rest. I bid you farewell, second father."

'No, Aribon! No! I need you now more than ever. Every year we come here on the day of the burning. We planted this young oak together. You are to live and witness the sign for our return to action. We are going to avenge your father. Please."

"I'm, sorry, My Liege." Aribon's head fell back slightly. His eyes were almost closed and his hands were relaxed.

"Oh, Aribon. Don't leave me!" Eradrin hugged his nephew's limp body tightly in his arms.

Aribon gasped, drawing in a deep breath, and looked up at Eradrin.

"Father? Father is that you?" Aribon lifted an arm and reached upward. "I see you. I *SEE* you! Yes, Father, he is with me now." He

383

paused for a moment as if listening to something. In a strange low voice he said, "*Soon a ring of fire. She comes with three on raven wings.*"

Aribon gasped, his voice low and rasping. "Where there is Light, shall Darkness come and you shall be the King of the Dead!" And with those words, Aribon fell back into Eradrin's arms. His hands were rigid and contorted like claws.

"Aribon, my dearest friend, my nephew, my brother's child," Eradrin began rocking Aribon in his arms. "What did you mean? She comes with three on ravens' wings? I have heard this now for many years. Is it Dayanna? Who? *King of the Dead?*"

"*Cawwww!*" The raven's call came from the cliff side and Eradrin could see the silhouette of the bird with the Moon of Night behind it. The raven was coming in his direction and cawed again as it swooped down to the treetop, then rose higher. It cawed a third time and flew in a circle.

"*Caw!*"

Eradrin rose to his feet and watched the raven continue circling. It made three more orbits, and then began its descent to the ground. It perched on the dead Aribon's shoulder and stared inquisitively at Eradrin.

"*Caw!*"

"Are they coming?"

"*Caw! Coming.*"

CHAPTER 49

BEAUTY ON THE CENTERLINE

Dylan came to the scene of the killer pickup truck incident and slowed the cycle. The skid marks of his bike were still visible in the rising sun. He shivered in the morning chill. Or did something else cause it? He looked down at fuel gauge and realized he might not have enough to get back down the mountain. Oh, well, it was downhill, maybe he could coast most of the way. Why was he even up here? *Because the ravens told me so. Oh, man, I have really lost it now.*

The scene from the hospital played back in his mind with the young woman leaping toward him and how he had ducked, expecting impact and none came. Then his mind replayed all those dark puffs of smoke or clouds, or whatever they were, spilling through the window. *What the heck was that? Oh, I'm so screwed up. Freddie's gone. What am I doing?"*

He shook his body as if to rid it of the memories and moved back onto the road, heading toward the village. *I should just turn around and head for home. It's the morning of another school day and I'm screwing around on the mountain again. And I have to try to learn what's going on with Freddie.*

He had just made the decision to head back down the mountain when he saw her standing in the middle of the road. At first, he thought it was some kind of apparition. The road was misty and the figure was dressed in white. Then he saw the black hair ... and those wonderful eyes.

It was the girl that he had followed yesterday. She had lost him by somehow crossing a deep ravine that was a hundred yards wide. *It's her.* He stopped the bike, straddling it in the middle of the road, expecting her to start the hide and seek game again. However, she was not running away this time. His mouth worked as he tried to say something, but found he was speechless. A surreal feeling came over him.

"Follow me," she said.

"We've been waiting for you."

THE BEGINNING

CHARACTER LIST AND GLOSSARY

RAVENITES
(Special Note: A is for Ascended)
Kingdom of Ravenland
Skye Castle – capital
Stephen Donachie – A First king of Ravenites. Struck by lightning beneath the Tree of Light.
Eradrin Donachie – King, 30 A
Ravenstorm - a raven (merged with Eradrin)
Juliana Donachie – Mother, 28 A
Aribon - nephew to Eradrin age 156
Thomar - brother to Eradrin King Advisor 29 A
Aremis - Eradrin's father 25 A
Dayanna Gatoria – 21 A
William Gatoria - Dayanna's father, Viceroy to King 30 A
John Daren - Newly Elected High Priest
Amila Belthine - Resigned High Priest
Astar Cambel - Healer
Capt. of Guard Winslow Athane

MALBOLIANS
Kingdom Of Neverlands
Pandoras - capital
Shabael El Qui – emperor, King Highest, 34
Mateah El Qui - mother of Shabael, Queen Mother, Queen Highest, 34 A
Malatee - Queen Highest Mateah's merged Darkling.
Alfie – 14. Chambermaid A
Rageton – 30. King's knight and Captain of the Guard. A
Alie – Shabael's daughter, 18 A
Blanca –Shabael's younger daughter, 21 A
Janessa - healer/witch 30 A
Simone - Struck by the Lightning. Great grandfather to Shabael. Dies during War of Kingdoms.
Sastorm – Shabael's father A
Calibri - High Priest A Advisor to the king
Destone - Brother of Shabael A
Malcolm – advisor A

Red Golds – elite guard for royal family.

EARTH
Dylan Morgan
Ravenous - A raven who is Dylan's guardian
Sheriff Spencer Morgan - father
Sally Morgan - mother
Robert Morgan - brother
Freddie Sanders -Dylan's best friend
Mike Sanders - Freddie's father

NATIVE AMERICANS
Raven - aka Dayanna A
Thunder A
Silent Bear A
Kawanda - Medicine woman / Mother's Love
Mansi – 21. Earth witch working with Shabael A

Dreamanity - Only the men of the priesthood and royal family could wear the white robes of their faith, Dreamanity. God Dreamer, one name of their God.

Dravens – Large half dragon/ravens used by the Ravenites before the loss of the Light.

Darklings – creatures born from the Tree of Dark that absorb light and are a contradiction to physics by having physical/non-physical qualities. Light is harmful to them.

Hicool (Highly intelligent, graceful, and tall people that live south of Ravenland along the eastern coast. Saydee is receiving her education through them.

Desert people - Nahbra, nomad tribe that lives east of the Great Mountains.

Ascension – dedicated to the Light

Descension – dedicated to Dark Light.

When a person passes through the rite of Ascension or Descension, they become naturally immortal, gain a special healing ability, and can merge with the totem animal of their tribe. If their merged animal is injured so does the human that it is merged with. In addition, the animal becomes injured when its paired human is injured.

HISTORY
The Sacred Book of Leaves a bible written by Ravenite Tribe.
El Qui Bible written by El Qui Tribe.

Timeline based on the kingdom of Skyeden's calendar

Light Year - Time recorded starting from day lightning strikes the Tree of Light and Dark.

L.Y. – Light Years from beginning of recorded time until 2300 when the Sun and Moon of Day disappear.

A.L. – begins the moment the Sun and Day of Moon disappear.

Tribunal Dynasty 1 L.Y. 1000 years.

Battle of Kingdoms in Ravenland. El Qui army attacks Ravenites and slays first Ravenite King Stephen. Simone El Qui, first king dies. Replaced by Shabael's father, Aremis.

Battle of Blood River 2299 A.L. 600 Malbolians defeated 10,000 Ravenites. First King of Ravenite dies.

Donachie Dynasty 100 L.Y. – 2300 A.L.

El Qui Dynasty 100 L.Y. – 2300 A.L. –

El Qui Dynasty A.L. (After Light)

Present time Skyeden

2300 light taken 3300 A.L. will be 1000 years Malbolians ruled

3150 present time

ACKNOWLEDGEMENTS

Wow, I think it would be impossible to acknowledge all the contributing factors that lead to the creation of RAVEN'S LIGHT. I guess first would be the Great Spirit. The concept of a raven stealing light and bringing to this world from a Native American Tale was the seed. Although RAVEN'S LIGHT isn't a Native American tale but one that includes peoples of many cultures in a fantasy world.

I have to acknowledge the ravens. The day RAVEN'S LIGHT was officially turned over to be published, a flock of ten ravens circled our home eight times. The day I did a little ceremony by Angel Oak Tree to make it our official Second Nations totem tribe, two ravens perched over my head, cawing and squawking for five minutes. The Raven is our official tribe's Totem animal also.

I think of the great fantasy epic genre writers who set the trail such as the Godfather Tolken of LORD OF THE RINGS and George R. Martin for GAME OF THRONES (Special thanks to HBO for a production that I think has changed TV forever). I loved the Stephen Donaldson's Covenant saga. I LOVED the ELRIC series. There are dozens of other fantasy sagas worthy of note, just trying to keep the acknowledgement from being a novel in itself.

As an artist dedicated to bringing more Light into the world, I know through my novels they can get a little dramatic, at times terrifying, some horror, etc. But each of them is about the constant every battle of Light and Dark just on the personal level and/or the nations wide. Though the book is fantasy, it is about the human condition. I want to also acknowledge SECOND NATIONS for their mission is to preserve the sacred knowledge, to learn it, to live it, and to teach it for generations of Native Americans to come. Most of the characters in RAVEN'S LIGHT have a deep connection with the SPIRIT of the land. There's a little mixture of the Kabala idea with the Trees. But mostly, it is about our relationship to the Great Spirit of the Land. In Skyeden, the Spiritual workings are more apparent with straight cause and effect. Although the Ravenites, the Malbolians, the Hicool, and Nahbra cultures have their specific totems, it all comes from the same source. As we gain the sacred knowledge developed naturally with man and nature with Second Nations, we hope through the old Native American Tales lessons can be taught, as I seek to do through Raven's Light.

Stefan Duncan
Oct. 1, 2013

ABOUT THE AUTHOR

Stefan Duncan is a full time artist and author. He was born in Fayetteville, NC and now lives in Charlotte, NC. He spent his childhood summers at Lake Waccamaw, N.C. As the recipient of an Associate Press Award, Stefan's dream has always been to become a successful published author.

While working a variety of jobs for novel research, Stefan became the editor of two weekly small town newspapers. Stefan completed Basic Law Enforcement Training. He became an investigative reporter for the Washington Daily News and rode several nights a week with the k-9 unit sergeant on the 11-7 shift. He covered murder trials plus participated with drug raids, and the apprehension of wanted criminals. He won an Associate Press Award for best investigative reporting and taught creative writing at community colleges. In addition, he had signed a six book/movie contract with a casting agency in Wilmington. Unfortunately, Stefan was forced off the road while driving to Wilmington. He was in a coma for weeks. His parents were asked to donate his organs when it appeared he was dying. During that last minute of life, Stefan woke from his coma. With a dozen broken bones, head injury, and seemingly permanent nerve damage to his legs, writing became a great challenge. As a result, Stefan's dream was side tracked.

Stefan's path to becoming an artist is an interesting story. He discovered from a talking goose (that's another story for another day) that he was destined to become an artist as his means of expression. Gradually feelings returned to his legs as he made his transition from writer to artist. It was discovered that what he lost in concentration with writing, it seemed to have doubled on his art side. Weeks after joining a local art guild, he started getting attention over a "glory tree" that he had done. He thought that the tree was like him and that he had just discovered what he was destined to do. He was meant to do "works of art that would give the world more Light." He made a pact with the Creator, that he would continue creating works of Light if the "manna" kept coming to allow him to do so. For over a decade Stefan has continued this with his art.

Stefan Duncan has been dubbed as the "American Van Gogh" by vangoghgallery.com. He created the impressionistic styles of 'Squiggleism' and 'Illuminism'. He is an internationally known artist who has sold around 1000 original paintings. His mission is to give the world more Light through his paintings. With Light brings hope for the human condition. Stefan is in galleries and establishments around North Carolina and the nation. He works out of his studio at the Charlotte Art League in Charlotte, N.C. and his home. Stefan was featured as one of America's rising artists in Art Business News Magazine. He has appeared on Fox News and Papers, Crafts, Paints TV show on PBC. Mr. Duncan supports various charitable organizations by donating original paintings to their fund raising efforts. Local listings and events are on his website at. http://www.stefanduncan.com He has illustrated for several books. He has been featured in articles in Art Business News, The Charlotte Observer, Charlotte Fashion Magazine, the Fayetteville Observer, and other printed media. His work has shown on the electronic billboard in Times Square and used in movies. Stefan paints live and donates paintings to charities. The Actress Patty Duke has a Duncan painting. He has worked with Adrian Paul, creating paintings with the TV show "Highlander" theme, auctioning them for fundraisers. He does several exhibits a year across America and is always seeking new places to exhibit his work.

One day while driving from an art event in Florida and listening to dramatic music, a movie idea came to Stefan's mind. A week later, a movie director comes into Stefan's studio in Charlotte. Stefan pitched the idea. It was well received so he began writing the movie script. "I can see this as a series, a trilogy of movies or TV series," his director friend said. Stefan went home and started writing and "The Raven's Light" emerged. After many years of being unable to express his creativity through his keyboard, Stefan suddenly rediscovered his ability to paint a picture with words. Stefan Duncan was writing once again. A doctor told him that sometimes a brain injury could heal itself years later. Stefan suddenly could read much longer. He had an over a decade of literature to catch up to and study the fantasy genre. Therefore, if Stefan isn't sleeping or teaching, he is listening to an audio book or reading. He paints and writes every day. He hopes this sudden surge will not fade into darkness. It's been over a year and half now that he started writing "The Raven's Light." This saga will be a lifelong dream comes true. It is written with heart and soul. It touches upon the questions we ask in our daily life. If nothing else, the stories teach us to live in the moment, to value what love you have, and to fight for what you believe to be right.

Now Mr. Duncan is also a novelist in the fantasy genre. He has published short stories and poetry; and, he will have several books published in 2013. His debut novel "Swordslinger - For The Glory Of Love" reached #1 on Kindle's E-book Contemporary Epic Fantasy. This first novel is now available at Amazon, Barnes and Nobles, Books-A Million and other retailers. "Raven's Light" is his next epic fantasy novel to be published. In the near future, "rTr- Red Tide Revelations" will be published. Overall, he calls his work a 'Living Spirit Art.' which includes his books and paintings. The writing has just begun. And the painting continues! There is much more to come from this artist with the brush and keyboard.

Please visit Stefan's website to view his paintings and to learn about new books and other creations. Did someone say movies?....

Karen Troutman, Editor

Stefan Duncan

author and artist

STEFAN DUNCAN BOOKS

<u>2013</u>
SWORDSLINGER
RAVEN'S LIGHT
SKELELTAL SONGS
<u>2014</u>
CREMATORY
RED TIDE REVELATIONS
RAVEN'S LIGHT 2
SWORDSLINGER 2
RAVENOUS
<u>2015</u>
TALE OF WACCAMAW LAKE
DAY OF THE MALEFACTOR
RAVEN'S LIGHT 3
13 TILL MIDNIGHT
<u>2016</u>
TREES
VAMPIRIC
CAROLINA MOON OF THE WEREWOLF
RAVEN'S LIGHT 4
<u>2017</u>
EYES
LITTLE EDEN
REQUIEM ETERNAL
<u>2018</u>
RAVEN'S LIGHT 5

RAVEN'S LIGHT ART & MERCHANDISE AVAILABLE

Raven's Light was the inspiration for a collection of original paintings by Stefan Duncan. These beautiful paintings depicting scenes and characters of this epic fantasy may be viewed online. The original paintings and reprints are available for purchase. The website for Stefan's online gallery is

http://stefan-duncan.artistwebsites.com/art/all/ravens+light/all

We are excited to announce that Raven's Light merchandise is also available from online stores. The art is reproduced on various types of items including t-shirts, caps, I-phone and cell phone covers, coffee mugs, pillows, ties, and many more products. Please visit the stores to see the wide range of item that are available.

http://www.zazzle.com/ravenslight

http://www.cafepress.com/RavensLightStore

http://www.stefanduncan.com/